CW00863792

Chapter 1

His car was parked in the road, the curtains were open and a light was on in the living room. James was back.

His behaviour was inexcusable and yet it was relief at his return that made me stall the car on the drive and cowardice that made me waver, beyond time officially allowed for wavering, before adequately composing myself. This wasn't the first time I'd been abandoned at the weekend, and I didn't know how to the tackle the problem, how to stop the rot. Our marriage was a joke, a thing of raised eyebrows and shakes of disbelieving heads. I saw it, he ignored it. Trembling legs carried me into the house.

He was reclining on the sofa and appeared to be asleep, his head propped up by a cushion, hands arranged gracefully over his chest, a marble effigy to wayward husbands. I went and stood in front of him, heart pounding.

'Where've you been?' I couldn't help it but my voice seemed to whine.

No reply.

'I said, where've you been?'

His shoulder hinted at a shrug.

'Please talk to me, James.' I became aware of the six o'clock news quietly unfolding on the TV in one corner of the room as the silence between us dragged on.

'Tell me where you've been?' This wasn't normal. By now I should be hearing an apology or an excuse for his non-participation in my weekend, which would allow me to gloss over my unhappiness and pretend that this was just a sticky patch that all marriages went through. I couldn't bear to think what his silence meant. Sudden panic threatened to rob me of oxygen and I had to fight hard to breathe. His handsome face, passive in seeming slumber, was hiding away from our problems.

'Is that it? You find it normal to leave here Friday, come home on Monday and not have an explanation? You've not phoned, you've not answered my calls, you've not been at the shop, and you haven't even got the decency to open your eyes and look at me. Look at me!' I shouted, kicking at his foot.

The grey eyes that opened were empty, and in that moment I saw our marriage finally die.

'Is there someone else?'

'Don't be stupid.'

'Oh, will you look at that, at last, it speaks. Where've you been?'

'Out.'

'Out? Out where?'

He turned his head away and folded his arms across his body in what appeared to be a protective rather than defensive gesture.

'Well, I'm glad that clears that up then. Where do we go from here?' My hands were twitching, my heart pulsing blood straight to my brain, making me light-headed. The longer I stood there waiting for him to respond the more tense each moment became until it became embarrassing for both of us.

'Right, that's it,' I broke the silence, 'I'm leaving you. This time it's for real. I mean it, James, solicitors, divorce … solicitors … things, the lot. Satisfied? Happy now?' Still nothing. I left the room bewildered and frightened and climbed the stairs to our bedroom.

Not for the first time, but for the last time, I dragged the faux-leather suitcase out from under the bed. By now James should be following me, persuading me to stay. Why wasn't he?

My head knew we were finished but my stunned heart still refused to accept defeat. In disbelief I shoved clothing into the case and considering the magnitude of the situation, found enough presence of mind to detach garments deemed too offensive and lob them aggressively into a corner. Over the years I'd managed to gather, and keep, an inordinate amount of off-white nylon knickers, shrinking T-shirts, stretched jumpers, shapeless dresses and ... where did those vile navy blue trousers come from? I was such a catch.

A creaking stair forewarned of James' approach. Finally he was coming to save our marriage. Expectancy made me anxious. I dropped the smelly pumps I was holding.

'I'm going out,' James muttered to the doorframe, his eyes not reaching any part of me.

I stared at him in shock for a second before retaliating. 'I won't be here when you get back then.'

A clap of thunder would have been fitting at this point but was not forthcoming. Close to sobbing out loud, desperate for him to come and sit next to me, tell me he loved me, kiss me, stop me from leaving, I nearly reached out to him but didn't and, without another word, he turned and walked down the stairs, picked up his car keys and left. His departure left me shaking and weak, what had I done?

Tears started to fall freely, and packing became blurred and non-selective as plastic carrier bags took on the load the suitcase couldn't hold. I carted it all downstairs and threw the bags into my crappy, two-door shed of a car parked at the side of the non-descript, semi-detached house I'd called home for the last thirteen years.

The January evening was dark and blustery and the rusting car door squashed me repeatedly during my efforts to find more space on the back seat in the shadows cast by the dim light of the house. There was a brief struggle to get the keyboard to fit, I nearly came to blows with the head rest in the process, then I went back to gather some of 'our' things, depositing them on top of a bag of compost, affectionately known as Pete, fermenting in the boot of the car. Finally, I lovingly installed my beloved clarinet in its beautiful black case on the front seat and patted it for comfort; it wobbled precariously on top of two small, battered cases stuffed with plastic bags full of sheet music. There was no more room.

I was all over the place emotionally, veering wildly from elation to crushed defeat and, not deciding where to settle, I dithered over what to do next. I went back inside, sat on the settee and tapped nervous fingers on its arm for a minute before rummaging in my handbag for a cigarette. James detested smoking. I hadn't smoked in years but I'd bought ten earlier as a warped mark of rebellion (ha, that would teach him) and had just managed to prise the first cigarette out of the packet when the phone rang. As I reached to answer the call, it stopped.

Last number recall gave me James' mobile number.

I stood up, I sat down. I stood up, I sat down. I pulled wildly at the cigarette then lit it. My throat tightened. This was terrible. There wasn't a manual I could reach for which could advise me what to do next. Pick up my coat and leave, call him straight back or linger like an insidious smell to battle on? Being a bad smell wasn't an option; I couldn't muster the strength to handle the finality of walking out, so I phoned him back.

As I went to stub the cigarette out in the soil of an ailing yucca plant, I coughed and scattered ash over the table on which it sat. I picked up the phone, waiting anxiously as it rang. It suddenly clicked and I heard sounds that resembled a busy public house and a voice very close said, 'Oh shit, that's the wife.' There was laughter, and then the phone went dead. I looked at the receiver in disbelief.

'How dare you, how bloody *dare* you?' I shouted, grabbed the living-room door and flung it shut in anger then had to grab it and fling it open to get out. The kitchen door received much the same treatment, as did kitchen cupboards and the cutlery drawer.

The phone started to ring again and this time I pounced on it like a crocodile hunter, snarling and breathless.

'Grace, its James.'

'Yeah, so what?'

'I'm just phoning to see if you're still there. I don't know what to say.'

I remained silent, afraid of what was coming next.

'I'm in the gents toilets because I don't want the whole pub to hear what I'm saying. Are you still there, Grace? I don't know what to say other than sorry.'

'Well, that's great, that's just great, I feel so much better now that we've talked things through properly,' I replied, sarcasm threatening overkill. 'I take it you'll be out now till I've gone?'

There was a long pause. 'I think so.'

'Right then, I'll see you around.' I put the phone down before he could respond. That was my one defiant up-yours, grossly falling short of what was appropriate. Never one for drama, I'd shied away from screaming at him down the phone, opting instead for the less aggressive and more subtle use of wounded pride, passion weak from protracted apathy. I'd even been denied the satisfaction of slamming the front door in his face as I left, post immortal words, 'You walk out of that door, don't ever bother coming back.'

I hated him and I hated myself. With neither of us able to deal with failure, we'd come to this – what a pair of cowards. The inevitability of our current situation had been hampered by well-meaning promises of change from both of us in the past. I tried to recall the last time we'd shared any kind of intimacy, or a time when we'd felt comfortable in each other's company and got lost in a haze of isolation.

Without really thinking I walked out to the kitchen, disposed of the cigarette, found a duster and went back into the lounge, wiping the table and spraying perfume to get rid of any smell of smoke. The things you do when your world is falling apart. I took a last look around the room, picked up my handbag and left. Something akin to a singular guttural sob escaped my lips as I closed the front door quietly behind me.

I headed for my parents' house which was about six miles away in the town of Deanhead. Salvation came in the form of Mum and Dad, Ted and Brenda to everyone else. Mum, a retired secretary, was practical and pragmatic with the odd daft moment thrown in to keep people on their toes. Dad, a retired electrician, was still working but at his own pace, fixing washing machines, usually for old ladies, often settling for a piece of cake and a cup of tea in payment.

As I drove, I thought back to the laughter on the telephone and assumed that James and his cronies were there in the pub laughing at me or, worse still, that they were now talking motor racing or whether big tits were better than tight bums, as dispensable and inane as man talk can get. The urge to go and pour a pint of lager over his head then walk coolly out of his life was strong but wasn't up to fighting the even stronger urge to just leg it. Let's face it; I'd struggled to leave the house.

'How the hell am I ever going to get over this?' I asked myself. 'I'm thirty-eight, childless and useless. I don't know any men; I don't want to know any and even if I did who would want me? I'm a total bloody failure. I'm fat. I'm so boring. I'm poor. My arse is huge. I've got no boobs; that's why nobody likes me. I don't fancy anyone. I'm asexual. I can't do this.' Thoughts of this nature bumped into one another in turmoil, dragging me lower to the point where I nearly turned round and went back home and, but for the laughter on the phone earlier, I would have done.

I turned into my parent's driveway. The wind gasped, coldly rushing through nearby trees, rattling the fence panels in their concrete posts at the side of the gravel path, which crunched under my dragging footsteps going backwards and forwards as I unloaded the car.

After ringing the doorbell I shrank like the returning prodigal child waiting for redemption. Dad pulled me into the warmth and gave me a big hug of understanding. He patted my back, allowing me to bury my head into his shoulder, finding protection and strength in his arms. After blubbing incoherently that I'd left James and having covered his shirt with tears and mascara, I eventually regained enough self-control to help him lug the plastic bags into the hallway which started to take on the look of a jumble sale.

'On the bright side of things, you couldn't fit the wardrobe or the bed into the car,' Dad said, standing back and taking stock of the chaos.

By now Mum had appeared followed by Roger, the family canine of disputed parentage, indistinguishable age, unorthodox eyebrows and, in his youth, a propensity to climb aboard cushions and give them a good seeing to, hence the name.

I looked to my parents for support and received it without any questions asked. Dad's arm led me into the sitting room where the living-flame fire hissed, and minutes later he handed me a large scotch and lemonade.

I hesitated before speaking. 'I've left James. Can I stay here a while?'

'Oh love, you can stay as long as you like, you know that,' Dad said.

'Do you feel up to talking about it?' Mum asked, picking up a ball of purple wool and her knitting needles.

'It's over.' I faltered and put my head in my hands, finding it hard to accept what I was saying. 'You know he's been out all weekend, again.' I'd spent the majority of the two days taking it out on my family. 'Well, he was back when I arrived home from work tonight. God knows where he's been, I've no idea; he wouldn't tell me. Just wouldn't speak to me. He walked out, left me packing and went to the pub. I can't believe it's over, that that's it after thirteen years. What am I going to do?'

'Get on with your life without him,' Dad said.

'That's basically what I've been doing, living life without him. I haven't *been* with him since I don't know when and what *really* makes me angry is that I gave up everything to be with him. I could have been a bloody good musician … it's too late now but, d'you know what I mean? Instead, I helped him with his shop and have ended up working in a bank, in a job I hate, to try and keep us afloat financially and this is the thanks I get, bloody well more or less pushed out of the house with a phone call from a bog.' I was swerving all over the place emotionally, from anger to self-pity it was all out there on show. 'God, I'm such a loser.'

'Bloody hell fire love, we've both been worried sick about you. This isn't unexpected. James is a decent enough bloke, but he really is bad husband material and it's taken you a long time to realise it,' Dad said.

'All I want is to be like Mary and Ray, Rebecca and Stephen, Natalie and Mick, even Harry and his mad girlfriend Julia. All I see around me is everyone sharing their lives happily, starting families and I'm wandering around doing a shit ... sorry Dad,' (he hated bad language) '... poo job, and coming home to an empty house every night.' Mary, Rebecca, Natalie and Harry were my sisters and brother, all of whom, I felt, possessed capabilities lost to me.

'They just have a different set of problems. As far as Mary is concerned, Ray is drinking too much. Rebecca is trying to cope with teenage children throwing parties the minute she and Stephen leave the house, and Natalie told me on the phone earlier that she threw a packet of frozen sausages at Mick in the middle of a row yesterday and nearly knocked him out. Harry, well he hardly ever sees Julia because she travels so much with her work. It would be lovely to see a smile on your face again, instead of that pained expression you've been wearing every time I see you,' Mum said. She picked up her knitting again, having said her piece, and clacked away at a fair old pace. 'Put the kettle on, will you, Ted.'

'I can't, it won't fit me.' Dad's standard response amused purely because he never failed to miss the opportunity to tell it.

It was incredibly easy to put a rosy tint on everyone else's lives when my own was in shadows and alarming to think that while I was hiding in them I was so transparent.

Dad came back from the kitchen with a cup of tea and more scotch. 'He's been ... how can I say it?' He searched the ceiling for the right word, 'dire, with respect to looking after your welfare. Far be it from me to judge, but who is nowhere to be seen when that car of yours breaks down? Who went to play football when you miscarried? I'm afraid he really went down in my estimation after that.'

The miscarriage was something that had happened a number of years previously on a Sunday morning, the pregnancy discovered only two weeks before I lost what I'd conceived and, to save me from sinking into depression, I'd looked upon it as nature's way of telling me that something was wrong. Of course I'd cried; I'd ached with longing for the speck of life extinguished before it had barely mutated from a cell, but not knowing what the future had in store, and thinking there would be more opportunities to have children, I clung to the fact I'd been able to at least become pregnant. James had been so unconcerned about the whole thing he'd gone to play football.

'I'm not being funny but are you sure it's a miscarriage?' he'd said, hopping on one leg, trying to get his other into a football sock. 'It may just be a heavy period, or something.'

'James, how can you say that? I took a pregnancy test.' I'd actually taken five.

'I'm just saying that you always go on about how bad your time of the month is…' A beep from a car horn outside had interrupted him. 'Look, I'll have to go, if you need a lift from Out of Hours ring me and I'll drop everything and come and get you, okay?'

I'd let him go and had cried from the depths of my hormones. Maybe that had been the start of our problems. Then again, maybe not, considering I couldn't actually remember having had the sex in the first place to conceive. If I wished to be flippant, I could suggest Immaculate Conception but I think, in reality, it had been a full moon and we'd actually spent an evening together in the same room with alcohol.

'Not all men are like that, Grace. Somewhere out there is Mr Right,' Dad continued.

I choked as the scotch went down the wrong way.

'You can laugh, but somewhere out there is an Evertonian waiting to sweep you off your feet.'

'Now I know you're not serious.'

'Oh, talking of Evertonians, Bren,' Dad said, changing the subject, 'Jeff Pilkton said he has a nearly new wash basin and pedestal in aquamarine if we want it, free.'

'What's wrong with the one we've got?'

'Nothing, I just thought you might like a change. It could come in handy.'

'With all the other handy cast-offs you mean?'

'He's offered the bath and the panel to go with it,' Dad said as if dangling a carrot, slowly revealing the full extent of Jeff Pilkton's generosity by using the drip-feed method.

'No.'

'I'll tell him no, then.'

'That will make a change,' Mum said tartly.

'Okay then, I'll tell him no.'

Even with Dad's assurance, there remained an element of uncertainty as to which way this discussion would go. I looked lazily across at my parents on the settee. Dad's bright, blue eyes looked tired behind his glasses, his comb-over a little more straggly than I remembered. Mum looked incredibly young for her seventy years, no grey hairs or blue rinse, a pretty white blouse and jeans, more youthful than my own clothes.

'Nice top, Mum,' I murmured.

'One pound fifty. Help the Aged, it's a Jaeger shirt you know, very expensive,' she lowered her voice to hushed tones at 'very expensive' to exaggerate the point or to make sure next door didn't hear she'd bought it in a charity shop, 'and it's not even been worn, the label was still in it for £59.99. I got a cashmere jumper for 50p but your dad doesn't like it much, he says its hearing-aid beige. I'll just wear it when he's out.'

Dad was all in favour of bargains and could appreciate the 50p ethic for clothing when a tin of pears cost nearly double that in the local store up the road. 'They've no sense of humour in that shop, you know. I bought a few things the other day and the girl on the till asked if I'd like a bag. I said "Don't you think I've got enough to carry?" and she said really snottily back "Pardon me I was only trying to help".'

We laughed immoderately, the drink aiding and abetting his story.

I put my head back and allowed Mum and Dad's conversation to drift by and take me on a weird, hallucinogenic journey. Apparently, someone called Doreen lived in an oil refinery down the road, sold the cheapest petrol around, had ninety carpets to giveaway, a colostomy bag fitted in her attic, and a budgie doing road-works on the M53 who liked bacon butties for breakfast.

'...Grace.'

'Sorry?'

'Would you like a bacon butty for breakfast?' Dad repeated.

'Love one.'

'Just don't burn the bacon, Ted, it takes ages to get rid of the smell. He hasn't changed, Grace, he still sets the kitchen on fire when he's cooking. I don't know why you have to have it so burnt.'

'I don't know why you like it straight out of the packet.'

Mum tutted, but refrained from further comment, not wishing to have a bacon debate at ten o'clock in the evening.

Drained and slightly inebriated, my eyes were struggling to focus. 'Would you mind if I went to bed?'

Dad helped me cart my stuff upstairs. As I threw the last bag beside the bed I knocked an ornamental rabbit off the dresser, Dad caught it before it hit the floor.

'See that? Like a coiled spring, that's what I am,' he joked and placed the rabbit in its rightful place. 'Get a good night's sleep, love. Try not to worry, everything will be fine, just wait and see. If it helps, I think you've done the right thing.'

'Thanks for everything, Dad. By the way, I know Mum goes mad when you bring other people's cast-offs home but I've got some compost in the car if you want it, been there about a year. Does it go off?'

'Great, don't tell your mum.' He wiggled his glasses up and down from behind his ear and left.

The room I'd shared years earlier with my sister Natalie had changed dramatically but it didn't stop the memories from flooding back. There was the same old airing cupboard in the corner where I used to think the potato man (a childhood creation of mine) lived, waiting to come and get me if the door was left open, walls that were once covered with posters of The Bay City Rollers, Kenny Dalglish and ponies now sported a picture of a lady feeding a goat.

I could almost hear the hysterical giggling under the covers of our bunk beds when either I or Natalie farted loudly, laughing even more when we stank the room out, and it made me smile when I remembered the threats of sleeping in the shed with the spiders if we didn't pipe down. Whispered secrets of our latest crushes, squabbles over toys and books and sighed dreams of how wonderful our futures were going to be all took place here. The scary thing was that I hadn't changed much. I was the dreamer who had waltzed through school then college, a geek with glasses and a clarinet, waiting for things to happen that never did. I'd just as easily dreamt my way through my marriage, still a geek but now with contact lenses, waiting for things to get better, waiting for nice things to happen. I was not progressive; I liked Cliff Richard for Christ's sake.

I stared back at myself from the mirror on the dressing table. Evidence of life having a nibble at the features before me only encouraged them to become more pronounced. Lines, furrows, creases – it wasn't pretty. Unlike my mother, there would be a need to hide the onset of grey hair in the near future. Of course, that would depend on my ability to retain hair of any colour because, on closer inspection, there appeared to be a distinct lack of it at the sides of my head. I took my contacts out, ridding my reflection of imperfection and opened the suitcase to find some pyjamas.

My hand swished about pulling everything up in a heap to find the right ones and, at the same time, closed over what felt like a large circular bangle. Curiosity had me tugging at the jacket in which the object was hiding, I did a double take. Grandma's 1920's gold arm bangle, my heirloom following her death, shone at me when I slipped it out of the pocket. I thought I'd lost it years ago. I'd had the house upside down and had even shed tears when I couldn't find it and finally gave up looking. And here it was. Was it a sign? Grandma's approval? I pulled it on and admired it, thrilled at its appearance before it started to cut off the blood supply to my arm so quickly removed it and slid it on the bedside table and stepped into bed.

Staring at it absently I thought of James – husband of mystery. He'd threatened to buy a replacement and I'd told him not to bother, so he hadn't. Had I ever really known him? Had we ever really tried to discover what made us both tick? Was he missing me or glad I'd gone? Was he sad? I had no idea. We'd obviously relied too heavily on our instant attraction for each other when we first met, mistakenly under the impression that, without any further input, it would be enough to see us through any bad times. I switched the light off.

Mum and Dad readied themselves for bed. Taps gushed, voices murmured, the toilet flushed and, once the old immersion heater had finished gurgling, silence descended.

Looking up at the darkened ceiling I cobbled together a potted version of me in my early twenties, working part-time in a post office, cautiously planning a musical future, auditioning, unsuccessfully, for any clarinettist post available.

As clear as if it was yesterday I saw James' hand holding mine, pretending to read my palm in the middle of a dance floor, his eyes not leaving mine. It was only a short matter of time before my ambitions to be a musician became secondary to wedding plans and working with him at his pine furniture shop. At first it was magical, a shared of labour of love engulfed our days, then when fire destroyed half of his uninsured stock (what had he been thinking?) it nearly brought the business to an end, I was lucky enough to find employment in a bank to help pay the mortgage. And there I'd been ever since. A retired friend of his father's helped out in the shop and I'd slowly lost my identity in both marriage and job, and had done nothing to stop the decline. Why? He most certainly had a hold over me and could turn me into putty with the slightest hint of affection. His ever-increasing late nights out went unchallenged and, to be honest, even tonight I'd have stayed had he said sorry and come up with any form of excuse.

None of my friends or family had gone through this; I knew people did all the time, but I didn't know any. I envied my friends with their children, and with that envy came a new wave of tears which slid like wet candle wax into my ears and hair and my nose clogged up, rasping loudly when I sniffed.

Not being a couple any longer, would our friends still be interested in me or would they keep their distance out of awkwardness, sensing unhealthy, contagious behaviour? What about his family? His brother, his mum and dad and all the aunties and uncles, whom I'd come to love as part of my own family, would they now keep away out of respect for James?

James. I knew I'd let him walk all over me to try and get him to love me but all I'd managed to do in the long run was confuse him into thinking I was a doormat. At the age of twenty-five, he had been my first real boyfriend. The one who'd pursued me into submission and bed. What had he seen in me then that he didn't see now? He'd moved on, I hadn't. I was the one who'd briefly contemplated suicide - wine and pills while listening to Rachmaninov, while he lived life. Thirteen years ended with a rush, the time it took to load up a car and drive off, a few words changing lives forever. I ached with longing to be held and cherished but lay awake all night, stiff, cold, alone and utterly defeated.

Chapter 2

Max Bergin, my team leader in the bank, wasn't very happy when my mobile rang whilst I was serving a customer. It was so cold I'd put my old reliable cardigan on, it had pockets placed low enough to challenge a monkey, and had forgotten I'd plopped my phone into one of them. The fact that the ring tone was a homemade one with a confusion of loud bleeps (I had no idea how to change it back to something more normal) only seemed to enrage him further.

'Can we remember to switch our mobiles off during working hours,' he said loudly enough for the customer to hear, who in turn gave me a kindly look of sympathy. I ground my teeth together, lips rigid, and hoped that no message had been left, otherwise it would be calling me again, causing me no end of anxiety.

Max was extremely good-looking, camp, usually very funny and kind-hearted, but not today. He'd just been denied a promotion. Inevitably, the phone started to ring again and, after dropping it on the floor, spilling the components and effectively dealing with the bleeping problem, I turned my attention to my amused customer and the duty-bound offer of a further loan, credit card or new, improved savings plan.

It wasn't until lunchtime, in the solitude of the ladies toilets, that I was able to call voicemail.

'Hi babe, its James, phone me when you get this message, speak soon.'

James never called me 'babe'. Very suspicious. And since when had he ever said 'speak soon'? Had he just become a complete prat, or had I never noticed before? My initial threats of solicitors and divorce had been acute and well-meant but subsequent inaction had led to a period of inertia as I waited to see what would happen next before I progressed any further. I don't know if you would call it laziness, uncertainty or stupidity. I returned his call.

'Scott, James Scott.'

'It's me, you rang and left a message,' I said expressionlessly and wondered when he would drop the stupid James Bond format from his repertoire.

'Oh hi, Grace, how are you?' He was chirpy.

'Fine, what do you want?' I wasn't.

'Well I just wanted to make sure you're alright first and foremost. I mean, I'd been hoping you might've called me to find out how I was at some point?'

I stopped myself from apologising just in time. My brain hastily tried to launch an intelligent response, to fling the ball back in his court but I'd never been good at sport.

'How are you coping?' I asked, contritely.

'Okay, I'm not sleeping well. Not sure if you'd noticed but I had to close the shop for a couple of days because I was so stressed but I think we've made the right decision.'

My insides seemed to fall out of my bottom and I could only be glad I was in the empty toilets at work when my world finally collapsed. He wasn't going to fight for me any longer, no more promises of change; he'd called it a day.

'Are you still there, Grace?'

'Um.'

Through lack of practise our emotional communication skills were, for want of a better word, shit, fear biting at us both, stunting conversation. After a strained, defensive pause that seemed to be heading for the dreaded all out silence, we both spoke over each other.

'What do you think?' James. 'It's the right decision.' Me.

'I agree.' Me. 'Okay.' James.

Pregnant pause.

'Yeah, yeah, you're right.' I became gushing. 'I've not sought legal advice yet, I needed time to adjust.'

'Do you really think that solicitors will be necessary? We're both adults and we can still be friends.'

Now I felt over-dramatic having mentioned seeking advice. Altogether, the conversation I'd mulled over in my head, the one we would be having, was not going according to plan. The emancipated woman, forging ahead on her own, enforcing equality, was nowhere to be seen as I saw myself in the mirror opposite, cowering in the corner by the paper-towel bin.

'We need to talk,' I said, mechanically.

'I don't think we should discuss this over the phone, do you? Can we meet?'

We, or rather he, made plans to meet at the weekend to sort things out before my phone battery went, cutting any further contact. I was a diluted mess and promptly made use of my surroundings by puking in the nearest loo, just as the bank manager walked in. She was younger than I was in age but twenty years older in the head, with more bounce and vitality than Tigger. She grasped my situation in a few seconds and concluded that I should go home to sort myself out. I started to cry in appreciation and something approaching hysteria. Max, full of concern, helped me gather my belongings.

'I think if you stayed you'd frighten the customers, love,' he said, trying to perk me up. 'We'll implement a new range of colours for compassionate leave on the time sheets, especially for you. Puce would be a good colour for divorce; it'll match the colour of your face.'

It was a very wet journey home with tears and rain mingling to make visibility negligible. I'd left James two weeks earlier but, with the way our conversation had just gone, it made me feel that the final decision had been his and not mine. What was it he'd said on the phone? 'We've made the right decision.' There was no 'we' involved. I'd left him. We? Bastard.

I burst into tears again when I walked through the door and saw Mum and Natalie, my younger sister, having lunch. It wasn't the blurred sight of them eating or the smell of the Cornish pasties they were having for lunch that I found upsetting, it was the thought of being alone, the thought of never seeing James again, the thought of my house missing me. All I wanted to do was go to bed and hide away forever.

Natalie was a PE teacher and the owner of a very lively two-year-old, who was with her mother-in-law for the day. She was also very pregnant. She brushed crumbs off her chest. 'Oh Grace, I told you at the weekend to change the locks and put up more of a fight. Why didn't you? Why's he still at the house and you're here? Can't you see that he's walking all over you? It makes me so mad I could go round and punch the bastard.' Taking her anger out on the pasty she continued with her mouth full. 'And another thing, if you think that you're going to sit here and mope all afternoon, think again, so there.' She swallowed. 'How about doing something really positive, come on, let's go house hunting.'

Mum was always up for shopping no matter the intended purchase, and before I knew it I was splashing water on my face and removing the lines of smeared mascara in the new, nearly-new aquamarine basin in the bathroom.

There was a fight for the toilet and a manic moment when all three of us were trying to cross each other on the stairs. I escaped to the car and waited, staring morosely out of the steamy, rain-studded windscreen.

'You don't mind me eating this in the car do you?' Natalie waved another pasty in front of me once she'd squeezed herself into the front passenger seat. 'It's only my second one. I always say fight a negative with a positive.'

'Since when?'

'Always. It's my motto. D'you ever listen to a word I say?'

'Never.'

'That's all right then.'

Mum was taking her time changing from the blouse she had on, another charity shop bargain, into something that actually fitted her properly.

'I have to bear in mind that my wage is cack so I don't know if I'm going to be able to afford anything. I might not be able to get a mortgage on what I earn,' I said. The thrill of such positive action vied with long ingrained despondency.

'Don't forget you'll have the equity of the house too, and you work in a bank,' Natalie said. 'Just think you'll be able to please yourself, and be as hairy as you fancy.'

She was referring to Mick, her husband, who apparently had a hair issue. He liked it long on top but nicely trimmed, if not removed, from elsewhere.

'When things were really bad and I was all alone in the house, I'd imagine packing a bag and getting on a plane to help in war-torn countries or famine areas or saving an animal species from extinction, just like that, dead easy. Well, that's not going to happen is it? I can't leave the bank, what about job security and my pension?'

Natalie looked at me as if she'd never seen me before. 'What are you talking about? I mean job security would be an issue if you had kids to feed and a mortgage to pay. You're free, so right now's your chance to do what you want to do. Why do you want to run so far away? Go and get a tattoo, dye your hair pink and, I don't know, go busking in Chester. Why don't you try auditioning again?'

'I'm too old and I've left it too late. It's so pigging demoralising, and it didn't get me very far last time I tried, did it?' My foot rammed on the accelerator, revving the engine loudly. 'What the bloody hell is Mum doing?'

At long last she emerged from the house, only to scurry back inside again. Both of us groaned. The windscreen wipers squeaked and jerked into action as I switched them on, allowing us to clearly witness her three further attempts at leaving. Finally, she made it to the car.

'Sorry, but I forgot my purse then I realised my glasses weren't in my handbag, then Roger cocked his leg on the banister as I was leaving. Honestly, his bladder control is worse than mine.'

Rainwater gathered at roadsides waiting to play with cars and pedestrians alike, and much as I wanted to speed up and swoosh through huge puddles I didn't. The aforementioned cantankerous, temperamental old car putting paid to any childish whims.

'I really think I'm going mad,' I said. 'I can't stop counting my blessings that, amongst other things; I haven't got a moustache, how ludicrous is that?'

Natalie laughed and there was a small grunt from the back seat.

'I don't mean a proper man's moustache Mum, I'm not that bonkers, I mean, you know, a hairy upper lip. I can't stop worrying about it and wondering what I'd do if I had to dye the hairs on my face. I'm so lucky that, although my eyebrows would possibly meet in the middle if I allowed them, I don't have to shave.'

'I really think you should go to the doctors,' Mum said loudly above the sound of the rain and windscreen wipers.

Involuntarily, the forefinger on my free hand had started to fondle the nearly-invisible fair hairs above my lip.

'Stop it, you nearly knocked that woman over and you're making me nervous.' Natalie slapped my hand and changed the subject. 'James may have been good-looking once but not now. I hate to say it but he's getting a double chin, not attractive, and I thought he smelt a bit like boiled ham last time I saw him, and he's losing his hair. I hope he ends up on his own, living in the hut behind his shop, regretting he ever let you go.'

'I'm losing my hair and I'll be in the hut next to him at this rate,' I sighed. 'Why didn't he say years ago that he wanted to get rid of me? Why did I stay so long? I'm starting to wonder if one of us is gay, only because I feel so butch around him.'

'I hope you're not referring to moustaches again,' Mum piped up from the back seat.

We pulled up in the supermarket car park and clustered under one umbrella, splashing our way to the estate agents, discreetly shaking excess water onto an inadequate rug on entry. The three of us then meandered round the very expensive properties for sale, complaining quietly amongst ourselves if swimming pools weren't included or if there were only two en-suites and one downstairs toilet. I didn't dare look at the cheaper end of the market, frightened to think that a cardboard box with an en-suite blanket would be my upper limit. A mature-looking lady with thick, grey hair, wearing a navy blue suit and a blouse with a bow rippling about her neck, asked if she could be of assistance.

I left fifteen minutes later with eight sheets of unlikely looking properties ranging from flats to small terraced houses. The rain had stopped but angry clouds threatened to unleash more with only the slightest provocation. Glancing at the first sheet that boasted a very basic first-floor flat with views overlooking a shabby, derelict boatyard, I'm embarrassed to say that I pictured myself in the window with a pot-pourri in one hand and a glass of wine in the other, laughing with mad friends I didn't have now but would have by then.

We piled back in the car and drove home, my excitement growing as Natalie read through the details of each property out loud. It was impossible to avoid the puddles as the school-run traffic mounted, and I tensed when we almost wallowed in something not dissimilar in depth to a bath full of water. Slowing down on the approach to a roundabout that led either to the motorway or up onto the road into our village, the car gave up and ground to a halt. I frantically turned the ignition but to no effect. Other drivers crept past me so as not to hit the bollard segregating the traffic coming from the other direction.

'This is all I need,' I moaned.

'Call your father.'

'Put your hazards on.'

Advice came from all sides. By the time I'd found my mobile to phone 'Superdad' and remembered its battery was flat I was afflicted with a badly twitching eye. Natalie found her phone and handed it to me.

'Hello ... Dad? He's at home thank God. Hi ... er ... I've broken down and am holding your wife and daughter hostage, we're by the motorway roundabout ... yeah, that one ... okey dokey.' I tried to make light of the situation although, by now, I was so pissed off I wanted to launch the phone through the window and walk off down the motorway.

'He'll be here in five minutes.' We sat in silence, all three of us eager to get home with the weather growing colder by the minute. Every now and then a gust of wind shuddered through the car and made it creak.

'I hope I don't go into labour now, I've got some really minging knickers on,' Natalie said.

'What happened to the two pairs I got you from Oxfam?' Mum enquired.

'Oh I used them as dusters, Mum. Sorry, but I don't think even Barbie would have fitted into them,' Natalie replied, her lower lip protruding downwards, her nostrils flaring and her eyes darting sideways to catch mine. She started to giggle, I followed suit and by the time Dad turned up all three of us were in hysterics.

I hate being towed. I always panic and try to brake, not used to being so close to the car in front. My options were pretty limited though, so with a sinking heart I helped Dad attach the rope, well actually I stood and watched him as he struggled to tie a knot.

'Now don't brake suddenly, I'll go as slowly as possible just don't use your handbrake,' Dad advised, standing up with two large wet circles on his trousers, one on each knee. 'If anything should happen, just wave your arm out of the window to let me know and I'll pull up. Oh, and also keep the car in neutral.'

'I know, it's not like it's the first time is it? Listen, Dad, thanks. I'll get you a malt whisky for this.' I smiled the damsel-in-distress smile and got back into the car.

We moved forward but instead of following in Dad's tyre treads, up the road into the village, we headed for the bushes separating the road from the motorway. I tried desperately to turn the steering wheel but it wouldn't budge. There was a loud bang, the rope went taut, we shot forward, he lurched back; collision was somehow avoided and we were yanked to a halt alongside each other. I raised my hand and waved sheepishly across to Dad and noted as I did so that Natalie was frozen to her seat and Mum's head was between us.

'You are a doze!' Dad bellowed. 'The steering lock is still on. Turn the ignition on. Not fully!' he roared as the car tried a valiant effort to find life, bobbed forward before groaning down to silence.

'My waters have broken!' Natalie cried.

I don't really remember the moments after that, other than the words of disbelief expressed from all concerned.

'Don't panic.' 'Shit!' 'You'll be fine.' 'Your contractions can't be every two minutes.' 'Oh my God!'

Dad took control, managed to get my car round the corner out of harm's way and transferred Natalie into his car. Not wanting to be left behind with a large dollop of guilt surrounding me, I ended up being whisked off to the hospital as well, feeling like a spare part and thinking that all we needed was the dog to complete the family outing.

I blamed James. It was his fault. If he hadn't rung I would have been at work and out of harm's way. I'd have been sat doing what I'd done for the last seven years of my working life while Natalie would have been happily shovelling pasties down her, sat in comfort at Mum's.

Instead I sat in disgrace in the corridor at the hospital as Mick arrived too late to be there at the birth of his second child. He was present, though, when a young Spanish male doctor stitched Natalie back together again. A midwife came out of the room sniggering and I could only wonder at the sudden raucous screams of laughter coming from the nurses' bay seconds later.

It was only as I was handed the tiny bundle of human wonder, born on a day I would remember clearly as the end of an era that I was told what had caused such hilarity. The doctor had been swinging on a stool repairing any tearing, chatting away as if sewing a patchwork quilt, when the stool went from under him and he fell, face first between Natalie's legs. Mick's astonishment gave way to humour as he tried to save the doctor any further embarrassment by saying, 'You know, she won't even allow me to do that.' Natalie was too knackered to be horrified.

An ache clutched at my insides when I looked down at the perfect translucent skin, the small scrunched up features, tiny fingers and fair, downy hair belonging to the baby boy that I held in my arms. So dependent, so vulnerable. I desperately wanted to have the baby, the marriage, the loving husband; it was what I'd clung on to way beyond injury time with James. Tears formed but didn't fall.

I had a melodramatic moment. A premonition that this would never happen to me hovered within touching distance, my miscarriage disturbing the present and thwarting hope. What was to become of me? I was so frightened I cuddled baby Matthew too closely, squeezing a loud squeal out of him that quickly brought me back to my senses.

'Watch out, love.' Dad took the baby from me and gave him a last cuddle before handing him over to Natalie. 'We'll leave you in peace and see you tomorrow. Come on, Grace, we'd better get that car of yours sorted.' He put his arm round and guided me out of the ward.

Chapter 3

Five weeks passed, during which time I tried to sort out the minutiae of divorce settlement without making much headway. James, though buoyant on the phone, appeared to be drowning in sorrow whenever we met. I continued to wear my wedding ring for safety and continuity, possibly harbouring delusions of a romantic reconciliation. The pair of us found conversation broaching anything but the weather a minefield of reproach and recrimination.

The whole process wore on my tattered nerves, shredding any last vestige of self-respect I'd cherished. With lagging spirits, I wandered around like the ghost of Jacob Marley until I saw an advertisement in the paper calling all budding musicians to join an exciting local orchestra. At first, I glanced at the advert on page ten then turned to the property section, but I was drawn back to page ten again and again. It said, 'no previous experience necessary', and 'friendly atmosphere'.

Even though I had nothing to lose, it took every ounce of effort to get me to the local scout hut the following Monday evening, clarinet under one arm and a bag of apprehension under the other. The only thing I hadn't been stripped of, other than my clothes, was my ability to play and read music; taking my frustrations out on the keyboard, playing discordant electric beats and dodgy made-up tunes, helped shift the misery to bearable levels. In the last year of my marriage, I'd shared more of my evenings playing the clarinet with the great Monty Sunshine blaring from speakers than I had with my husband.

Prior to that, about three years after getting married, I'd taken clarinet tuition, with batty Elsie Flanders, a former and now 'very old' college tutor. Once a larger than life, iron-grey dinosaur prowling the corridors of Deanhead College of Music, terrifying me into practising scales and techniques at times when others would be practising their alcohol or drug tolerance levels, it had shocked and saddened me to meet her again a number of years later – a withered, rather forgetful shadow of her former self. She had been so overwhelmed to see me, so adamant she wished to further my prospects, that I'd been seduced into taking tuition twice a week. I never called her Elsie to her face; Miss Flanders from Deanhead College of Music remained Miss Flanders in retirement.

Her tuition was taken more out of a sense of duty, as most things were in my life, rather than because she brought anything new to my advancement. As her lessons became more laboured her other students fell away, understandably daunted by the long trances she'd go into or by her sudden reluctance to give any musical advice, preferring to discuss Mrs Beeton's pudding recipes instead. James had recommended I stop going and offered to pay for horse-riding lessons as an alternative pastime. My strong sense of loyalty forbade such betrayal, and besides which, I was good at playing the clarinet, something James had never seemed to fully grasp. Horse-riding? I could only assume that my confession to him years ago that, when I was ten, I'd left a number of notes in mum's underwear drawer asking for a pony, had resulted in his offer.

So 'lessons' continued with Elsie. In her more lucid moments, when I lost concentration, she'd snap the order to try again and raise her eyebrows, much as she had in college, with that ability to make me want to run for cover. In her more deranged moments she would clasp my hands in a shaky grip and whisper, 'I discovered you,' gazing up at me with a look of wonder.

It wasn't until she fell down the stairs on a midnight trip to the toilet, breaking her hip and shoulder that I finally acknowledged that my tuition had come to an end. She was consigned to a nursing home and a wheelchair. I took Elsie out shopping on two occasions after that but, with the best will in the world, I found it impossible not to bash her feet on passers-by, shopping trolleys and clothes stands, eliciting feeble yelps from my passenger.

Having been informed of my ability to play the clarinet the nurses in the home encouraged me to perform in the communal lounge for the elderly residents until a complaint concerning noise levels brought that to halt. Each time, before I left her, she'd pat my knee and say, 'I hope you take better care of your talented fingers than you do of my feet.' She passed away in her sleep, six months after entering the nursing home.

Mum came with me to the sparsely attended funeral where I cried tears for Elsie, for me and for the end of an era. I still missed her, I missed being called Reg (her sixty year old nephew) when she was confused. I even missed the half-chewed Rennie tablets which she'd had a tendency to catapult from her mouth like a hailstorm while cooing, 'Poco a poco, pianissimo, poco piu allegro,' or yelling, 'Fortissimo or mezzo forte!' over my studious endeavours. She managed to use f and p words frequently for projectile purposes.

She crossed my mind as I hesitated in the car park of the church hall where the orchestra practiced, nerves almost getting the better of me. 'I'm doing this for you, Elsie,' I murmured, and heaved myself dramatically out of the car, ignoring the calls in my head to drive home.

Everyone at the orchestra seemed pleasant enough, I wasn't eaten which was a bonus, and even managed to chat with the organiser, Joan Sarney, without sounding too much like an idiot. Frankly, this would have been nigh on impossible with Joan. She reminded me of an old fairy, her voice was light and fluffy, and she seemed to float rather than walk, imaginary wings keeping her off the ground. Maybe it was the cold evening, glimpsed through the broken venetian blinds at the windows, which inspired everyone involved to play at a rate twice the speed of the frantic conductor, an aged man with sweaty armpits.

During the tea break, protocol dictated that I audition. The aged conductor and Joan Sarney hastily arranged a quintet and produced Holst Opus 14 in A Flat for a small audition piece. The whole experience made me want to continue forever lost in music, alive to every note, every chord, with vitality rushing into veins and the joy of life pumping into every part of me. If I was music I could rule the world. I felt like I was radiating light by the end of the evening, and packed my clarinet into its case, a timid sliver of independence finally breaking out of its self-imposed confinement.

'Anyone going to the pub?' the percussionist asked, slapping a glockenspiel stick on his thigh with the same exuberance he'd used in rehearsal. He was a huge, hairy bulk of a man reminiscent of a pony-tailed Grizzly Adams. I'd found out, during the course of the evening, that his name was Fergal Watson. He had introduced himself to me then had laughed at my name, 'Grace Scott! Grace Scott, you play the clarinet well.' Then he'd laughed and joked during rehearsal, and laughed and joked when his cymbals smashed to the floor interrupting a peaceful solo, upsetting the cellist.

He walked over to me and handed me a tulip he had just swiped from the flower arrangement on a side table. Joan had told me earlier that she bought flowers to rehearsal each week to create an ambience and improve the quality of sound. I dreaded to think what the orchestra sounded like without her input.

'This is a welcome to the society present.' He smiled at me, his eyes full of friendship, before he sauntered back to his drum kit. 'Hey, what's better than having flowers on your piano?' he asked.

'Don't know,' I replied when no one committed a response.

'Tulips on your organ.'

I sniggered and so did one of the violinists, an attractive blonde, who was busy texting a message on her mobile; it seemed that everyone else had suddenly gone deaf or had found something interesting to talk about with their neighbour.

'Anna, are you going to the pub?' Fergal asked the violinist.

Anna said she wasn't sure. He grumbled to himself as he put his gear away. Joan Sarney sailed past, humming and spraying large mists of lavender air-freshener around her to settle, like dew-drops, on her back-combed and set hair. I said something that sounded very much like, 'I'll go for one.' It just plopped out of my mouth without asking my head permission first.

Anna looked up from her phone and said, 'Alright, I'll go for one too.'

'Great, get me a pint, I won't be long. What about you, Joan, fancy a drink?' Fergal asked as she drifted past in the opposite direction, this time with yellow rubber gloves on.

'No, no, I need to relax in a hot bath with essential oils and minerals. I have promised myself a facial and I am going to put some cucumber on my eyes. I thought to myself earlier, I must give myself a cucumber job when I get home.'

'Dear God, what a thought.' After Fergal had managed to restore his eyesight, he tapped his head and added. 'A triangle short of a full orchestra that one.'

By now I was in the grip of dread, Joan's predilection for cucumber and its many uses not having the impact on me it deserved. Going to the pub with strangers? What the hell had possessed me? Impulse wasn't a natural reaction in the land I inhabited, it only led to disaster.

The violinist came over to me and smiled. 'Can I cadge a lift? I'm Anna, by the way.'

'Hi, I'm Grace.'

We stepped outside into the freezing night air, which had already started to lay a slippery sheen on the ground, our footsteps the only sound in the quiet car park. It was hard not to be embarrassed when, arriving at my battered heap, I slid on the ice and for the briefest moment ended up on all fours before springing up to find Anna trying not to laugh. I, on the other hand, started to laugh out loud through nerves and was still laughing when I reversed into an unseen wheelie bin with enough force to send it bowling along into sparkling sporty car, bringing my laughter to an abrupt halt.

'Shit.'

I was about to get out and go and look at the damage when Anna said, 'Let's just go.'

'I can't, I think I bloody hit the thing.'

She suddenly became so animated she startled me. 'No-one saw us, just go. Go, go, go!'

'But...' was all I could manage before she yelled, 'You didn't hit it. Go, go, go!'

For the second time that evening, I found myself behaving out of character. We made our escape, bunny hopping out of the car park with Anna jerkily laughing as we pounced erratically off down the road.

I couldn't believe what I'd just done. I'd left the scene of a crime that could land me in a large dollop of trouble; I felt sick.

Once parked up outside the pub I had a good look at the back of my car to see if there was much damage and the fact that there didn't appear to be any only fuelled further misgivings about running away. I followed Anna inside and while she ordered drinks, I chose a table near the window.

'Thanks for the lift. I'm sorry; I don't know what got into me back there. You must think I'm awful. I suppose I was bored and needed a little excitement but I honestly don't think you managed to hit the car.' Anna said, 'If it makes you feel any better, I'll say I drove.

'No, it was my fault. I don't know why I didn't stop, I mean, I've got a mind of my own but for some reason I think it's buggered off somewhere else tonight.'

'No, I'm sorry. I am a bossy cow sometimes.'

I apologised for hitting the bin. She apologised for laughing then said, 'Let's not apologise anymore. It's done now. Don't worry, trust me.' Anna had a confidence that invaded mine and sought to boost what little was left; a bit like having tall friends at school when you're small and ripe for being picked on. Her voice at times took on deep intellect in its playfulness, allowing nothing to get past her without comment.

She was, in my eyes, a beautiful woman of the world. The one I would grow up to be. I felt myself cringe with the thought. I was grown-up; I was thirty-eight. She was married with two children below the age of nine. Her first love, after her children, was politics and, being a paid-up member of the Green Party, she had aspirations of becoming a local candidate in the future.

Although I voted in general elections, I didn't have a clue who the local MP was. Anna, on the other hand, had danced the Lambeth Walk with him at a charity fund-raiser and was on first name terms.

'A nice man, for a Conservative, but if I'm honest he's about as useful as set of handcuffs to a nun. It makes me mad that this planet is being so badly abused and not one of the main parties seems to care. We should be ploughing money into alternative greener energy sources right now, reducing our carbon footprint for future generations. We need to ban all animal experiments and stop live animal exports. GM foods; don't get me started. And what's our government doing at the moment? Planning on invading Iraq, that's what. Did you know that as many as one in four pensioners live in poverty? Men still earn over thirty per cent more than women in the workplace, it's a disgrace. House prices are out of control, the *banks* are out of control. Trust me when I say things are going to change and it's not going to be for the better. I'd be pushing for free prescription charges, eye tests and dental treatment if I was in power. At the moment those on minimum wage struggle to afford the charges but when the shit hits the fan, well, there'll be a million blind people wandering round the streets on death's door with no teeth for want of affordable medical attention.'

Her enthusiasm for her subject soon had me analysing safe seats – previously imagined as a row of sturdy chairs, the cabinet – a pine bedroom wardrobe, a spin-doctor – my GP twirling insanely on a swivel chair. Her husband, Peter, had his own views on councillors and politicians and they seemed to be far from complimentary.

We'd just started to chat about where I worked, when Fergal turned up with a woman I recognised from my audition as the

38

flautist. He came over to us, his giant body making the pub look small, and threw himself in front of his pint while she went to the bar.

'Sandra's gunning for the person who put the bin in front of her car. I don't suppose you saw anything when you left?' he asked.

'Oh no, was there any damage?' Anna voiced in poised innocence. I couldn't raise my eyes from the table.

'No, but she thinks it may have been her ex because the word 'you' was spelt out in chips on her bonnet.'

'You? What's that supposed to mean?' Anna enquired. She raised her eyebrow at me and I gave her a look of heartfelt relief.

'I've no idea,' Fergal smirked. 'I had a look and I couldn't see any word. Just looked like a couple of chips had tipped out of the bin, but she was adamant.'

Sandra came and joined us, delicately brushing the stool before parking her bottom on it. She seemed to have a permanent smile fixed on her face, deceiving few for long, as I was to find out. She placed her bag, Gucci label showing, carefully beside her drink then said, 'Anna, did either you or, I'm sorry what's your name?' she didn't wait for an answer, 'see anything unusual in the car park when you left?'

Again, I took great interest in the table-top while Anna did the talking.

'But why would someone spell the word you? Isn't it possible that it was a freakish accident? It's not exactly threatening is it?'

'You, could mean I'm going to get you, or you as in, you,' Sandra insisted, pointing her finger menacingly at Anna on the last 'you'.

'I'm losing the will to live, Sandra. How many chips were there?'

'Five.'

'How can you possibly spell 'you' with five chips? You're the solicitor, this is very poor evidence.' A discussion on chip spelling then took place while I ached to either laugh or scream 'Guilty!' at the top of my voice. To get away from any more talk of chips I went to the toilet and when I came back, the conversation had changed, happily, to the practice session. Anna purposefully looked sideways at Sandra to make sure she had her full attention and then asked me what I was doing playing in an amateur orchestra when she and others, she claimed, thought I was well above its standard and wanted to know how long I'd been playing, and if I'd played in any other bands. I glowed with pleasure and said, modestly, 'I'm not really any good, I was a bit nervous to be honest and my fingering was all over the place.'

'I'll give you a lesson on fingering if you like,' Fergal leered, snorting and sending a suspicious green-looking object sailing from his nose into his pint. I saw Sandra pull a horrified face and move her bag to a safe distance. Fergal fished about in his pint then continued to slurp regardless. I honestly thought Sandra was going to be sick. He must have changed his mind because he sauntered off to the bar for a new pint. Sandra told us off for laughing and encouraging him then changed the subject to how she had been chosen to represent the North West for amateur orchestral player of the year.

She turned her smiling focus onto me. 'Actually, in your audition you went totally wrong and came in too soon, I think bar 43 or 44, and you really need to watch your end phrases. I play the clarinet as well you see, but the orchestra has too many clarinettists so I play the flute instead. I wasn't going to say anything but it might be to your advantage that I have.'

'Right, yeah okay. Thanks.' Rather than tell her I was classically trained and had a degree in music from a college of no repute, I deferred to her professed greater knowledge, unable to forget the honours degree in compliance I'd gained with James, in a marriage of no regard. There I went again.

'It's the one thing you would be good at hey, Sandra? Wind instruments, you produce enough of your own. How the hell can you say that with the cacophony of sound going on around you? No doubt if the right note had been played it would have been out of tune with everyone else,' Fergal said, having come back from the bar.

'You are far too keen to bring this orchestra down. If I were to be given chairwomanship there would be a few changes I can tell you, Fergal Watson.'

Fergal and Anna put their hands to their mouths in mock fear. Sandra shook her head, smiling at them playfully, hiding her outburst as a joke.

With so few local inhabitants venturing out on a cold Monday evening, we had the pub more or less to ourselves, apart from three men at the bar who exploded into laughter after anything they said and a couple who seemed quite at ease not talking at all. Fergal resumed, chatting about the orchestra and its committee. From what I could grasp, the committee thought it was a good idea to perform to the public shortly, the same committee that spent large portions of their time eating cakes and discussing how to raise funds by having bring-and-buy sales and other very dull enterprises.

Anna decided it was time the committee reviewed its fundraising and suggested a sponsored pole dance would raise far more. Fergal thought that running naked down the high street and seeing how far he could get before being arrested was a rather good way of raising funds. Sandra suggested that he would raise more by keeping his clothes on, and I couldn't think of anything other than threatening to play unless we received £452.86 to keep quiet. It all seemed to be going well until Fergal changed the subject matter.

'So, Grace, what made you decide to join us here this evening?'

'I fancied a drink.'

'I meant the orchestra,' he corrected.

'I was bored at home.'

'Bored housewife? Doesn't your husband mind or is he away a lot?'

'He's away all the time now, I left him recently.'

'Sorry, I always put my foot in it, but you're wearing a wedding ring. Tell me, was there someone else?'

'Fergal, leave the poor girl alone,' Anna said, then by way of explanation, 'He's in sales.'

'It's okay, I don't think there was anyone else,' I said in answer to his question, my heart starting to beat a little faster.

'I meant for you, not with him, who in their right minds would dump you?'

Smoothie.

'It's a bit like me and my ex,' Sandra said. I could see Anna and Fergal roll their eyes. 'I started an affair that has shattered him to the point of throwing cold chips over my brand new car.'

'James and I just fell out of love; he seemed to prefer his pine furniture shop and nights out,' I explained, trying to get the conversation away from the bloody chips.

'Not James Scott the pine dealer?' Fergal asked.

'Yes, why?'

'Oh nothing, I just, erm, know him through business.' I'd only known Fergal a short space of time but to be me he suddenly looked rather shifty.

'Am I missing something, Fergal? He's not to my knowledge a dodgy businessman or anything, just a dodgy husband,' I said.

Fergal laughingly referred to a money problem that he'd had in the past but which had been sorted since and then changed the subject. The rest of the evening passed discussing favourite overtures, least-favourite eighties hits and remembered types of sweets from our childhood. Fergal wanted to make sure I was coming back to play next week and so did Anna, both of whom I considered as friends after one evening spent in their company.

Sandra really wasn't my cup of tea. Too much time spent up her own backside made one try to steer clear from too much contact. She played the flute so she could head up the woodwind section to boost her importance. Had I met her whilst in James' company I'd have accepted that there was something wrong with me for not particularly liking her but, with my new-found courage, I saw her as a selfish, self-centred bighead who could remain that way as long as I didn't have to have much to do with her. I slugged down the last bit of shandy and decided to go. Fergal said he'd drive Anna home so I left them to it and trundled carefully home along freezing roads singing, at the top of my voice, to Frank Sinatra's version of 'That's Life'.

'But if there's nothing shaking come this here July (ba, ba, da) I'm gonna roll myself up in a big ball and die, my, my.'

I didn't really want to roll myself up in a big ball and die, because by July I was determined to be a success, at something, or other, somehow. That gave me four months. Proof in itself that singing about change was going to be infinitely easier than planning or implementing it.

Chapter 4

I lay on the bed reading an article in a magazine under the bold heading 'Confessions of Sex Sessions', which momentarily had me looking up to check that the bedroom door was shut. It was quite obvious from the content were I'd been going wrong all these years. I'd never taken the initiative and dragged James into a high-street shop changing room to have hot, erotic, vertically challenging sex whilst demonstrating a variety of gasps and moans, keeping life outside the cubicle oblivious to the deed. I'd never hung from the lampshade trailing empty toilet rolls, string and sticky back plastic, singing Elvis. Blue Peter's guide to erotic sex. The mind boggled. Early Saturday evening, and I was already dressed for bed in ugly, washed-out, brushed-cotton pyjamas with a women's mag for company while everyone else in the whole world partied.

The article brought to mind James' face when I'd attempted a sexy strip for him, managing to get down to black bra and itchy camisole knickers before his look of disgust or was it fear, had me grasping for the dropped clothing and running upstairs to hide. I'd cried in bed and we'd blushed at each other the next day, my display unmentioned and buried beneath a heavy weight of embarrassment. It was alright for him to sneakily watch porn (I'd found his secret stash of DVDs) but it wasn't alright for his wife to try and emulate his underground viewing material. Hanging from the lampshade? He'd have had me certified. Honestly, where did these people find the nerve?

A beautiful, sultry young girl with long, brown, cellulite-free legs and a pout to put fish out of business glowered at me from the next page. Maybe if I looked like that I would have the courage to reveal more flesh and flirt till I was sick. Deep in troubled thoughts, I didn't hear the phone ring until Dad knocked on the bedroom door. I hastily closed the magazine.

'It's Anna for you,' he said, handing me the phone.

'Hi, Grace, it's Anna here, I wondered if you were doing anything this evening?'

'I don't think so,' I answered cagily, wondering if I was going to be asked to baby-sit.

'I'm going to The Fox to sing karaoke with some friends and wondered if you were interested in coming along; it's a laugh if nothing else.'

'Erm, I'm er, um, not really a singer and feel a bit off really, Anna, but thanks anyway.'

'Oh well, give me a ring if you change your mind, I'll be going out about half-eight if you're interested, if not I'll see you at rehearsal Monday.'

'Okay then, thanks.'

I chucked the magazine on the bedroom floor, wandered downstairs and threw myself on the chair opposite Mum, who was trying to thread a needle without much success. Music accompanied Dad in the kitchen while he drummed on a pan waiting its turn to be dried. On the telly a blonde girl was enthusiastically insulting her blind date, an audience and Cilla Black laughing at her vicious attack. I watched it for a minute or two, fairly certain I was missing something.

Dad came in to the lounge, chopsticks in hand, followed by the sound of Bert Kampfert and his Orchestra.

'They don't make music like this nowadays,' Dad said, sitting on the arm of the settee. He was right there. For a minute Bert and Cilla vied for audio ascendency and it decided my evening. Were Mum and Dad deaf?

'I'm going out.'

'Want a lift?' Dad said, drumming the chopsticks on his knees, body moving in time with the beat.

'Thanks.'

'Where to?'

'The Fox, its karaoke night.'

'Not 'thee karaoke' at 'Thee Fox'?' He stopped drumming.

'Yes why? Is it bad? Have you heard of it?'

'No.' He carried on drumming.

'I think I've changed my mind. I'll stay in.' All of a sudden Bert and Cilla weren't so annoying.

'Oh go for God's sake, get yourself out and don't be so bloody miserable,' he said.

With a bit more urging and sound advice from Mum regarding washing my hair before leaving the house, I rang Anna back, rushed about trying to find something tenuously associated with the word trendy to wear and rapidly applied false tan to give me some colour.

I walked into the pub like an apology, hoping Anna was already there; otherwise, I would have to turn round, walk out and watch the end of the Lottery with the parents. The Fox wasn't the most salubrious of venues, its dirty carpet sucked at its patrons' shoes. The seventies décor made me wish I'd stuck to black and not decided on a pretty but over-the-top white blouse and cream, out-of-date trousers. Unfamiliar faces jostled at the bar while out of the speakers, and above the sound of Shakira, the DJ swore, asking whoever had stolen his fucking pint to bring it back immediately.

'Over here!' Anna called, waving from a corner not far from the DJ. She looked fantastic in a pair of jeans and black T-shirt with 'Horny Devil' on it. Her short, spiky, blonde hair was freshly streaked, her high cheekbones cherry blossom pink, her eyes alive with excitement.

Drinks sorted, I managed to find a stool and sat on the edge of it nervously tapping my foot to the music playing.

'I've put us down to sing, only because if you don't put your name down early then you don't get a chance later,' Anna said to me.

'But I've never, ever sung karaoke before and I'll be a load of rubbish and get tomatoes or cabbages thrown at us,' I replied. There was absolutely no way I was going to sing in public.

'You'll be fine, just follow me. I haven't a clue what I'm doing but it's good fun and a laugh, especially when you sing like that,' Anna whispered and pointed at a woman, whose bum cheeks were literally hanging out of a pair of gold lurex shorts, murdering 'The Power of Love'.

'Oh, Grace this is Roy, he's the karaoke king round here. Roy this is Grace.' Anna introduced me to the man sitting to her left. 'Grace doesn't realise it yet but she'll be up there singing in a bit.' She laughed, and turned away to chat to a couple behind her.

'Hi there, Grace, friends call me Roy.' Roy, a very tall, bony man, looked up from rolling a fag and licked the paper with a flourish before shaking my hand in a strong grip, his long wispy, fair hair and threadbare leather wrist-bands giving me the illusion of an ageing prog-rock musician. I raised my eyebrows, wondering what else people called him.

'Friends call me Grace,' I replied, wincing as 'The Power of Love' reached excruciating level.

'Hey, good isn't she? Roy said, putting the cigarette behind his ear.

My nostrils flared and my lip curled slightly as if there was a bad smell under my nose but I turned it quickly to a smile when it suddenly struck me that the singer might be his mother, sister or wife.

'So, wow, you fancy having your tonsils tickled tonight do you? Ha, ha, ha.' A fair description of his comment would be to say that he actually chortled.

I responded with a nervous 'Ha, ha,' which tailed off quickly. Was he waiting for me to say something? My eyes seemed to go into the back of my head, searching for appropriate material. Nope, nothing there. I stared at him then at the bottom of my empty glass and wished I'd stayed at home. This wasn't my scene at all. I didn't want to bother making idle conversation with people I didn't know, I didn't want to sing a song in front of a pub full of pissed people and I didn't want to drink myself stupid and get a taxi home later, spending money I didn't have. Although horribly mortified when Roy gave up and turned to someone else for conversation, I didn't really blame him. I tried to think of an excuse to leave, bad stomach pains, headache, evil stepmother and plumped for the bad stomach pain scenario.

'Another double whisky and lemonade?' Anna turned to me.

'Love one.' What was wrong with me?

'Next up is Roy Ditty, Christ; it's gonna be a long night, singing "Born Free".' The DJ had recovered his drink but seemed to be struggling in his effort to find the jester within.

Roy dispelled the ageing hippy image with his song choice. I watched people around me letting their hair down. If I'd had the nerve to tell Anna I was feeling ill I would have been on my way home now to the safety of routine and my room, dreaming of a time when I would be popular, full of confidence and fancied by lots of men. I was sure this would happen it was just a matter of time. Just because at this present moment I was unable to string a sentence together without stuttering or blushing didn't mean I was boring, unintelligent, characterless, it just meant I was shy? Was I missing James? For all he was worth, he was someone I could hide behind, someone I could rely on, someone I could turn to and chat with uncomfortably ... someone who was normally the other side of the pub if not a different one altogether.

Roy, to his friends, was coming to a crescendo ending amidst cheering and clapping.

'Wow, go Roy!' Anna shouted as they both made their way back to the table from different directions. She placed the drinks down and told me that a man with what looked like half his dinner in his beard had just propositioned her at the bar. With style and flair she'd told him that she'd already eaten but had thanked him anyway, which made me smile.

'Now, what are we going to sing?' she asked, after telling me a bit about her family and a recent trip to the RSPCA to buy a cat. They'd managed to choose one that refused to sully the litter tray, preferring to foul the kitchen floor instead.

'Er, no we, I'll watch.'

'Oh please,' Anna begged. 'I don't want to sing on my own, we'll be great, if you don't like it I promise I won't ever ask you again and will buy your drinks the rest of the evening. Look, it's not as if this is the London Palladium we're talking about, this is The Fox in the high street. Go on. '

Anna was very persuasive. My only vision was of us both stood before the masses, one looking and sounding like Carly Simon, the other bright red with sweat, looking and sounding like Simple Simon. Part of me wanted to burst out into joyous song but a larger part wanted to run away and hide.

Anna must have taken pity on me because she said, 'You don't have to if you don't want to.'

'We'll see,' I said, almost longing to grab a microphone and start singing immediately now I'd been told I didn't have to.

'A friend called Glen who's in the choir I joined earlier this year is meeting us here in a bit. You'll like him. My Mum's got the children as Peter's away this weekend on business. I've told you what a knob he is sometimes, haven't I? He's not interested in the choir and hasn't come to see one performance. I think as long as I don't join the committee, he doesn't care.' The hint of derision in her voice left no doubts as to what she thought of this. Up until the age of twenty-five she'd been working for the Crown Prosecution Service and had just finished a law degree when, trying to start a family, she'd suffered a number of miscarriages, her womb unable to carry full term. It had been a case of remain practically horizontal for nine months or don't bother trying. She'd packed her job and ambitions in and had concentrated on starting a family. Peter refused to consider her going back to work, she was to stay at home and nurture the family, which only resulted in her need for secrecy upon deciding to study politics with the Open University.

'I'm involved with 'Care in the Community' and work on Monday and Thursday mornings in the local charity shop.'

'You've probably met my mother.'

Peter had no idea Anna offered her services there. She thrived on it, restoring order and common sense each time she arrived, knowing full-well things fell apart when she left. She loved dissecting every sentence in 'EastEnders' or 'Coronation Street' with her ageing colleagues, debating at length how to make the latest influx of paperback novels sell (buy one, get twenty free), and parading up and down in some of the more dubious offerings in the clothing line while drinking Red Bull to the point of hyperventilation. It was a separate life for her. Peter didn't agree to her having a job until the children were old enough.

'Every so often I'll ask, "How old?" and he'll say, "Older than now," so I'll say, "Okay next week, they'll be older then won't they?" It never fails to really upset him. He's been married before, God, years ago. His ex-wife left him for her boss who happened to be his best friend at the time and I've probably given him more leeway than I should really over his archaic views because of it. I play the violin so badly and I'm a bit past it now for making it big as a singer so – oh, there's Glen. Glen, Glen, over here!' Glen came over and plonked himself next to her, giving her a kiss on the cheek. We were introduced. His aftershave charged at the smell of a burning cigarette stump in an ashtray close-by and cleared my nasal passages.

'Are you a singer too?' he asked.

'Oh no, I'm pretty certain I'm tone deaf and I hate people seeing my teeth.' Oh no, I thought, what am I saying? Where did the teeth comment come from?

'I'm the same but I hate people seeing my Adam's apple wobble when I sing. Mad isn't it?'

I felt better. Two drinks later the three of us were getting on like a house on fire, so much so that other people were now joining the conversation and my opinions, usually reserved and unheard, were free-flowing on any subject to anyone who cared to listen. Glen was happily married to Paula, the local choral musical director, and had been given a pass out for the evening because she was having a few friends round. He'd promised he'd be back home at 11 o'clock, by which time the friends would have gone and she would be lying in bed waiting for him to do the business and make a baby.

'Its hard work you know. At the end of the day, I didn't think having sex morning, noon and night would be so difficult. I'm knackered. Oh well, her temperature is on the up and rather me than anyone else,' he sighed.

'Tell her to lay off a bit, Glen. You're probably producing very tired sperm that can't be arsed with the journey ahead. You should leave it a couple of days and replenish stocks,' Anna said.

'Easier said than done, anyway that's you being called,' he said as the DJ called Anna's name.

'Come on girl, swing your pants,' Anna said and, without offering much opposition, I found myself taking hold of the mike like an old pro and winking at the wolf whistles coming from our table.

By the end of 'It's Raining Men', the microphone was more or less glued to my mouth.

'See, you can do it, I knew you could,' Anna laughed.

'I have to go to the loo, I think I'm going to wet myself,' I replied, lurching slightly.

I glanced at my face in the mirror whilst washing my hands. Amazing what a bit of confidence could do to bring out one's better points, or was it just alcohol? Whatever, it made me feel good.

It was when I started to push my way back that I felt a tap on my shoulder and heard a familiar voice say, 'I thought I recognised those dulcet tones. I didn't know you were trying to break into pop.'

I turned in horror. 'What the hell are you doing here, James?'

'Charming, I could ask the same thing of you.' He smelt of expensive aftershave, not boiled ham, and looked very slim in a tight-fitting Armani T-shirt and jeans, his hair close-cut, a five o'clock shadow staining his cheeks and jaw. No double chin – bastard.

'I'm out with friends,' I said defensively, forgetting that I'd asked the question first. My recently found confidence and beauty dispersed like a puff of flour landing in a mess on the floor.

'Anyone I know?' he asked.

'No.'

'Are you wearing false tan?'

'What?' I stepped back, consciously moving my hands behind my back.

James just looked amused and simply said. 'I thought so.'

How could someone make me feel so cheap with just a couple of words?

'I'll leave so you can carry on enjoying yourself.' He turned to go.

'I will.' Too busy exploring the definition of outrage I had nothing further to add and, with a heart sinking quicker than a sieve in a bowl of washing up, I returned to the table cowed and shaking with resentment.

Just in case he was still there in the pub and watching, I made a big show of smiling and chatting animatedly to my new-found friends who'd lost their importance, making everything I did feel inferior to what was going on in his life. Glen left not long after, grimly determined to impregnate his wife.

'Are you ok?' Anna asked, butting into some old rubbish that had been coming from my mouth for around five minutes.

'What? No – not really.'

'Can I help?'

'Any good at marriage counselling?' I hesitated before elaborating further. 'I met my estranged husband over there a bit earlier. He asked if I was wearing false tan. Why would he do that? Why does he always make me feel so inadequate? I don't know, it's like I've got to check my nose for bogeys or I stink or my hair is a mess and my clothes are totally crap, which they are, look at me.'

'What? Look at what? You look fabulous and I defy him not to go away and wonder at what he's let go. And you don't smell. Do you still love him?'

I smiled a false, totally for the benefit of others smile, and thought for a minute before replying. 'I think so, well, actually, no I don't, oh, I don't know. I know it's over but somehow I can't seem to make my head believe it. I want to find a new man, a new life, a new job, new haircut, new nose, new face, anything that will make me feel better, but I'd only be doing it so that I could show him that I can get by without him. If I couldn't show him and parade it in front of him, I don't know if I would want it. It'd lose its significance. But if I do that then it means that it's all over and we'll never get back together which really frightens me.' The stream of waffle was in full flow. 'I just think that if I'd been better looking, had a better job, was less needy and more fun none of this would have happened, instead I'm left to feel like a big pile of boring crap.'

'You need revenge,' Anna said. 'I know, let's Dr Dick him like they do on 'Cybil', let's set him up with a bloke dressed as a woman, or send his name to the Round Table as a recommendation for next year's Santa.' It all came so easily to Anna as she turned her mind to cheering me up, yet again.

'No I couldn't, I'm too chicken and besides there's this awful feeling inside of still wanting him to think well of me, which is madness but there you go. God knows what he thinks now after me prancing about as if I own the place, wailing like a tone-deaf banshee. Oh God!'

'Okay, it was just an idea,' Anna said. 'What you need to do is get out more and meet other men.'

'Unfortunately, all the friends I know have all got young families and just not into clubbing. Besides, I let them fall by the wayside years ago, which hasn't helped. That's the reason I've joined the orchestra.'

'It's a start. It's really hard isn't it? All my friends are in Newcastle where I lived for five years and they very rarely get over to see me. I learnt the violin at school and took it up again twenty years later to join the orchestra to meet people, but with the likes of Sandra Howard as drinking pals, you can understand why I'm not keen on going to the pub on a Monday. Do you not fancy speed dating? I think it would be hilarious. I'd love a go.'

'What about your husband?'

'What about him? I may as well be a mannequin rather than a human where he's concerned. I used to be the perfect wife, making bread, cakes, even bedspreads. I even used to make myself beautiful for his return from work and would have the children calm and ready for bed so he could relax after a hard day. Can you believe that? It's not like that now. Take yesterday for instance; his arrival home was greeted by me playing the violin and skewing notes, the children fighting and arguing and a bloody huge pool of cat pee on the kitchen tiles, which sent him skating across the floor to his burnt cheese and broccoli lattice pie and chips in the oven. Everything he does annoys me down to the way he reads the paper, he dog-ears the corners with his index finger while he scrutinises every article, even the adverts. Eeyew, it makes my toes curl.'

She pursed her lips and inhaled sharply. 'I missed the orchestra practice last week because I felt so guilty about the way I feel, so I had sex with him instead. I hope I'm not being too indiscreet but I had to shower immediately afterwards to get rid of any trace of his bodily fluids. He wouldn't know because, by then, what a surprise, he was fast asleep and snoring.'

'Don't you like sex then?' I couldn't believe I'd asked such a personal question to a person I hadn't known all my life.

'If I asked him for foreplay I'm sure he'd think I was after a game of tennis. I shouldn't complain, I've got what I wanted, but now I think I resent him. He has people jumping through hoops at work and he expects the same at home, dinner ready, exemplary children, house tidy, sex on tap, all easily forgotten and compartmentalised when he leaves the house in the morning. The children are growing up so quickly, they're not babies anymore and sex over the years has become so mechanical I could draw you a diagram of his moves – uh-uh-uh-uh.' Her hands slapped parts of her body. 'And that's probably exaggerating the length of time he spends on them. I'd rather just play with my pink sparkly thing, which is in need of new batteries come to think of it.' She sighed. 'It's really upsetting but I get more enjoyment from a lump of pulsating plastic than my husband.' She suddenly seemed to see me properly since beginning the summary of her sex life. 'You're the first person I've admitted that to. You must think I'm awful.'

'No,' I said, never having spoken so freely about sex to anyone before. I'd been to an Ann Summers party once and bought a red furry bra that had never seen the light of candles, along with some hideous, too-long, grey fishnet stockings – big wow. Everyone there had screamed and shrieked at the sex aids like a bunch of teenagers but if anyone there had bought a vibrator they'd kept it secret.

Anna seemed to read my thoughts. 'You *do* think I'm awful. Is it because I think my better half is repulsive at the moment or is it because I like my vibrator? Have you ever used one?'

I shook my head, ashamed of admitting either way.

'Did you never sit on the washing machine on spin or offer to vacuum, using the head for areas other than the carpet when you were younger?'

My eyes bulged. For one, it had never entered my head that other people indulged themselves in such a way. For two, our washing machine had been placed under the work surface dulling any vibration, and the vacuum had been an upright one and very hard to manoeuvre at the best of times.

The conversation had taken over; three girls screaming 'Yellow Submarine' and burping loudly down the microphones just an unpleasant cacophony of background noise.

'Nope, I think maybe I'm an alien, or you are.' We smirked at each other. 'I've always been a geek, at school, college, work, boys, marriage. I just don't get it.'

'What?'

'Life. Men. Sex. I mean, it seems I can only learn from my mistakes. I can't quite see what's going on around me till things go wrong, by then it's too late. Like when I was eighteen and was nearly raped on holiday. I'm afraid Eduardo got the wrong idea. First willy experience was up close and personal. Why are blow jobs called blow jobs? If you blow down a penis wouldn't it fill with air and explode? Anyway, I'll never forget fighting to keep my head from being forced onto it. I was terrified; there was stuff everywhere, on my face, in my hair. I was called prick teaser, the rest, when all I'd wanted was a bit more booze and a bop.'

'My God, that's terrible. Maybe you should seek some counselling.'

'I'm just glad it wasn't a lot worse. I've been two-timed, three-timed, ignored and dumped by the few boyfriends I had before meeting James. I played hard to get and lost. James was different. I know it sounds mad but he wooed me, and I couldn't, or wouldn't, see when he'd lost interest, although everyone else could. Oh well, I'll probably end up living alone because I don't want to make the same mistake again.'

Anna thought for a moment. 'I think that learning from your mistakes is what life is about, otherwise how do you stop yourself from becoming a victim? I had to be kept away from boys when I was younger. I nearly got caught in the broom cupboard at school screwing one of the male cleaners. Had to pretend I'd taken a wrong turn then walk into geography class with no knickers on.'

There she was, doing those 'things' I'd been reading about earlier on.

Anna said, 'I don't really know what I learnt from that, other than to carry a spare pair of pants at all times in case of emergencies. You see?' She produced a thong from her handbag and hung it from her index finger in front of her eyes, which in turn crossed trying to keep her clean briefs in focus. 'I know, we should go dancing one night. Come and join the choir. You'll love it, no sex just singing and it will show your ex that you've got a life without him and he's the one missing out.' She was by now, a tad pissed, chasing the straw in her glass around with her mouth only to poke it up her nose instead.

'The only way I'd prove that would to be to climb Everest naked on a donkey with a forty-piece brass band following and a personal good luck card from the Queen slapped on my forehead.'

We both laughed. 'We've got the band, we'll get a donkey and you have a birthday suit so all we need now is for the Queen to write you a message and you'll be flying out to Nepal next week. No, honestly, join the choir,' Anna said as the bar staff started clearing up around us.

'Come on ladies, please, your time is up. Finish your drinks now please; I want to go home tonight.'

A tired looking barman repeated himself as he collected the remaining glasses off the table.

'The alternative is for me to find a wet kipper and slap you with it, Grace. The choice is yours. Think about the choir. It could be the start of a new you, and me.'

Chapter 5

That night had been an eye-opener for me. It made me realise how insular and boring I truly had become. Half of me wanted to remain that way, terrified of rebuke or ridicule, and the other half of me threatened change but wasn't fully committed to the cause. Being overlooked seemed preferable to sustaining my dreams of success.

The more I tried to shut the confusing thoughts out of my head the more they seemed to want to be heard. In my misery just one tiny thing during the day had to go wrong to make me turn into a frustrated, tearful, self-pitying wretch, either in my favourite toilet cubicle of the two in work or in the sanctuary of my bedroom.

James seemed to be struggling too; when we spoke, it only managed to make matters worse. He finally admitted that his doctor had prescribed anti-depressants and he was finding it hard to pay me off with equity from our house, where he was still living and was getting bogged down with worry, creating a no-go area around money matters.

Mum and Dad stood by me and never once suggested I should move out, never once said I should be fending for myself. Dad had found a whisky-drinking partner, someone he could have discussions with about football and the state of the country. Over the last two years a number of his close friends had passed away and his grieving soul missed their company; a solitary male amidst women drooling over Mr Darcy, Aragorn and James Bond.

I would often catch him talking to inanimate objects such as his freshly laundered socks for instance. 'Hello son, are you on your own? We can't have that, can we? Shall we have a look for your partner upstairs? Come on then.'

He talked to the dog in the same manner but got less sense back.

I realised this was where I got the idea that all my clothes chatted to each other once I'd left the room; I wasn't mad, it was hereditary.

'Oh you're new, real cotton, hey? Nice to meet you. Oh yes, I'm one of her favourites, been here years, she can't live without me, in fact most of us here are ancient in wardrobe terms. What, you too? Lying in a plastic bag for the last year? At least I made it to the wardrobe.'

I can't, and won't, discuss the cutlery drawer and what went on in there once I'd finished putting knives, forks and spoons away after drying-up.

Getting back to relative sanity, I think Dad enjoyed the extra company around the house. Mum had heard all of his views before on numerous occasions and so wasn't as easy to bait. Dad's favourite saying, 'man is the hunter' and forecasting Mr Right's appearance would make me laugh. He could be a prude, and on one particular occasion, he told Mum to sew up a slit in a skirt she'd bought because he didn't want other men looking at her legs. There had been a stand-off, neither prepared to give way, one sat in the garden with a big woolly jumper on and the other in the house watching black and white movies on BBC2 while I flapped between the two of them making sure I didn't take sides and remained firmly on the fence. With Dad's creed being never go to bed on an argument it meant that it was slugged out between the two of them that evening. Dad apologised, said she could wear her skirt how she liked and Mum sewed the slit up. He certainly knew how to play the game.

My love of music came from both parents in different ways. As long as Dad had music to keep him company he would happily shut himself in the kitchen after a meal to wash the dishes, lots of trad jazz, sixties, James Last and 'Matchstalk Men and Matchstalk Cats and Dogs'. My love of classical music came from Mum, who loved nothing better than popping some music on and watching the telly with the sound down while doing the ironing.

There was always something going on in the house, even if it was only Roger pinching food out of the fridge and shutting the door behind him to hide his tracks. None of us knew until Mum discovered a piece of string in his bed, the only evidence that there had once recently been a beef joint on the empty plate in the fridge. I came in from work one afternoon, tripped over four second-hand carpets rolled up down the length of the hallway to find Dad placing a lock on the fridge door and Mum wearing a, 'we're not keeping the carpets so don't even go there', look.

It was lovely to have the company but, this aside, I was starting to panic. I felt desperate. My life was going nowhere and seemed out of my control. Stress was manifesting itself as shallow breathing, crying, hysteria, sleepless nights, anger and self-loathing. If James could have help with pills then why shouldn't I? His problems weren't any worse than mine! He wasn't the one living back at his parent's home at the age of thirty-eight, but then he had to find the money to pay me off.

There is a point where unselfishness becomes a selfish action in its own right. Leaving others to make all the decisions so as not to upset or affront, only leads to renouncing fault or censure, laying it firmly elsewhere and in the process losing the respect of others. It made me wonder if I'd ever stamped my feet and demanded anything from anyone, ever. As a baby had I not even bothered yelling my guts out for milk? Had I just sat there instead, insipid, waiting for a bottle to be produced no matter how much I wanted to be fed?

I was reminded of a time when I was with a friend from school and a bowl of apples was calling to me from my friend's living-room table. Not wanting to be cheeky, but feeling a desperate need to eat one, I finally came up with the fact that I felt 'eaty drink' as though I wanted something to eat and drink at the same time, while my eyes rested on the apples. I just waited for my friend to offer me one, which she did. Had I come straight out and asked for an apple, what would I have done if she'd said no? Without doubt I'd have died of humiliation. By implying a general desire for something rather than bluntly asking for what I was partial to saved embarrassment all round, but the only problem was it left me at the mercy of others trying to fathom out what it was I wanted of them, and it seemed that, as I was getting older, I was becoming more obscure.

This particular foible wasn't helping my confidence in any way either. I was in awe of newsreaders, singer songwriters, actors, directors, weather forecasters, basically anyone who seemed to be able to cope with doing more than one thing at once. Elton John, how could he perform on a stage in front of thousands, playing the piano and singing at the same time? The attractive newsreader, years younger than me, how could she sit there and read from something in front of her as though she'd memorised the whole news for the day? How could someone my age direct an award winning blockbuster film? I was hardly able to cope with stamping a paying-in book and returning it without shaking, wondering if I'd forgotten something important, wondering if they knew I was a waste of space.

Two weeks later I sat at a desk in work, fiddling with the telephone wire. The night before had seen an upsetting meeting between James and me. I had tried to discuss the matter of taking my name off the mortgage, just in case I wanted to get one on my own. This hadn't been received well.

Unable to deal with confrontation I buried my head in the proverbial sand, waiting for the pain to leave, and while there I read an article about CJD, quickly jumping to the conclusion I'd contracted it, convinced that I had the tell-tale signs; shaking hands, blurred vision, memory loss.

I dithered for a number of minutes before calling the doctor's surgery to make an appointment; the stress incorporated into this one action made my palms slippery with sweat. As usual, the receptionist made me feel awful for ringing and having the nerve to need a GP, and after getting a grudgingly given appointment I booked the next day off, spending the rest of the afternoon in work trying to look busy. Max ignored the vacant expression I chose to wear and overlooked the blatant dereliction of duty towards company targets, he could sense when someone was on the edge and close to causing a dramatic scene.

It was impossible for me not to be uneasy when I walked into the surgery next morning and sat on the edge of a seat in the sunny waiting room. My whole body shook and shallow breaths increased my anxiety encouraging a nervous twitch in my left eye. Mad thoughts ran wildly, from throwing my handbag across the waiting room, screaming and running hysterically out of the door to breaking out into a musical number such as 'You'll never walk alone.' I overcame this by patting my handbag as though it was a pet.

A child in a red coat with candles running from both nostrils and a nasty cough threw a wooden brick in my direction then started to ram a car into the wall. There was a vague attempt from its demoralised mother to stop the anarchy but this was only met with screams and more wooden bricks being hurled in temper. A thin elderly gentleman with a walking stick, white hair and skin to match rattled out an occasional cough from the depths of his inverted chest, while a lady with her shopping trolley parked in front of her kept sighing heavily and staring at her fellow patients waiting for eye contact to start a conversation.

During silent periods, when the child looked for other toys to lob or destroy, my gurgling stomach performed to the waiting room with the virtuosity of an orchestral warm up until I was finally called forth to the doctor's inner sanctum.

Dr Primp (the spin-doctor) swivelled round on his chair with gymnastic dexterity.

'Hello, Mrs Scott, what can we do for you today?'

I thought I was going to cry with fright.

'Well, I think I may have mad cow disease?' To give the doctor his due, apart from raised eyebrows, batting eyelids and the loss of his voice when he opened his mouth, he seemed to take my self-diagnosis seriously. 'I have the shakes, my vision is blurred sometimes, and I have palpitations, oh, and, I almost forgot, my memory is getting worse.'

'I see.' He coughed. 'Excuse me one moment.' He reached for a plastic cup of water, drinking it noisily before turning back to me.

On his instruction I flapped my hand onto the opposite arm and repeated it with the other hand. He looked into my eyes with a light, checked my pulse and took my blood pressure.

'I think we can rule out CJD. Your pulse is rather fast. Have you been taking any exercise?'

'No. I'm going through a separation at the moment so I've not really given it much thought to be honest.'

'Exercise may be an idea,' he suggested, kindly.

'I was thinking that, maybe, I should take some anti-depressants like Prozac or something.'

'I don't like to prescribe it really,' he said, rolling back to his desk on his swivel chair. 'What I would suggest though is that you take up a sport. For instance, I'm running in the New York marathon next month. You can sponsor me if you like.'

I felt sick. I wanted to cry, 'Please give me some pills, please give me some pills, anything to help me,' but instead I just sat there and stared at him with what I supposed was an interested look on my face.

'Oh right.'

'If I prescribe an anti-depressant it will take a while to start to work and once it does take effect it then takes months to wean you off it. Exercise, like running for instance, is the natural equivalent of the drug and is an immediate tonic. It sets your endorphins racing around your body and gives you the lift you need.'

No pills! I've got to start running. Oh my God.

'Take my word for it. Try some exercise, and if you still feel the same in two weeks come back and see me. The sponsor forms are at reception.'

I was dismissed. I was mortified.

The car somehow made its way back home on its own with me gulping and blubbing like a coffee percolator behind the wheel. Why couldn't I have pills to ease my pain? I couldn't go on, not like this, my mind was going crazy. And more to the point, what must the doctor think? I'd actually gone into his surgery and told him I had mad cows disease. Sweet Jesus riding a bicycle!

The house was empty and within seconds I was prostrate on the bed soaking the pillow with tears before falling into an exhausted sleep, sunlight shining warmly through the bedroom window.

When I woke an hour later the sun had gone leaving me cold and reaching for a fleece. Although it was oppressively quiet in the house I could hear the joyful sound of children in a distant school playground, carefree, happy, and, closer to home, the tinny beat of a radio and someone whistling along to the melody. I had to get out. On an impulse I found my car keys, jumped into the car and headed for the beach. The tide was coming in with a brisk sea-wind to help it on its way.

I stepped onto the promenade and lent against a barrier, taking a deep breath of salty sea air. The horizon went on forever. My shoulders relaxed. This was the place I always came to when I was low. There was nowhere else to be when problems seemed too great to surmount. The sea danced, kicking up frothy, white underskirts before collapsing from the effort into exhausted bubbles on the sand. After a while, the rhythmic sound of its mass pushing forwards, dragging back, pushing forwards, dragging back, gave the lulled sensation that I was moving forwards, backwards, forwards, backwards, till I realised I actually was. Mother Nature threw sunbeams out through silver clouds, proudly presenting herself. Seagulls wheeled in and out of the sun's spotlights crying freedom from above. How trivial things seemed when faced with all this beauty.

I had a choice, either turn into a manic-depressive with no desire to fight back and no reason to get up in the morning or count my blessings and get on with things. I was alive, I could see, I could hear, I could run about and do handstands if I so wished, I could appreciate the beauty before me and I had my parents and my family. I wasn't alone and I was loved. How selfish could I get before realising how fortunate I was already? When had I become so self-obsessed? How had I let my problems take over and consume me so massively?

A gust of wind blew down my neck of my fleece making me shiver and an empty Toffee Crisp packet shot past, tripping and scraping over the sand below, chased by invisible assailants. I watched it distractedly until it disappeared from view.

It had seemed such a good idea at the time to get married, everyone else around me was, and although I'd escaped a career of musical uncertainty – God, the agony of failure after each audition, the endless disappointments, the doubts of not being good enough hacking at my self-confidence – it was only to find I'd jumped out of the frying pan into the fire. It served me right for being such a coward. Well, I'd paid for my mistake and now it was time to break free.

New life surged through me, inspired by the sea. So what if I had a rubbish job, at least I had one. So what if I had no money, at least I had an income. So what if the man I thought I had loved and pledged my life to didn't want me, at least I'd found out. So what if I didn't have a place of my own, at least I had a home. So what if I was thirty-eight and never going to have children. I came to a crashing halt. Emptiness threatened. There had to be something. I had my clarinet.

I always considered myself a girl rather than a woman. One day I'd wake up as an old lady and wonder what had happened to my womanhood. I thought of Elsie Flanders' final years, her decline into defeated weakness and a spinster to her last breath, and was galvanised into wanting to fit in as much life as possible before it happened to me. I had to change, even if it was only to put into practice the doctor's advice. My health was the main factor, and although this had been in question a few hours back it was apparent now that it was still intact. One hurdle surmounted. Strauss' 'Sunrise' burst into my head and suddenly I wanted to jump down onto the sand and run with arms outstretched until I fell over at its crescendo.

So, now the decision had been made to get a grip on things, to spearhead this exuberance my first port of call tomorrow would be the local swimming baths. Yes, that would do nicely, even if my bikini bottoms fell off if I dived in. Okay, so, put new bathing cossy on the list of things to buy before said swimming fiasco. I took a last look at the timeless seascape, took my wedding ring off, popped it in my pocket and headed for the shops.

True to my thoughts, the next day I carried out the plan of action. Rather than look on it as an evil thing that might destroy me, I tried to look on it as a remedy that might help me. I couldn't help the brief, sneaking thought of 'attractive man' with a tan and broad shoulders leaping in to save me from drowning but I quelled this immediately. It was just as well because the pool attendant was a girl with pigtails and acne and, apart from a couple of kids dive-bombing into the water, I was relatively safe.

The doctor, much to my amazement, had been fairly accurate with his diagnosis. It left me tired, my limbs aching from unused to activity and that evening, for the first time in a long time, I slept soundly throughout the night.

I had no money for a holiday so prevailed upon my elder sister Mary's good nature and invited myself to her house on the outskirts of Birmingham for a long weekend. With sunshine and shopping, coffee shops and restaurants on the menu I started to unwind. Mary was as barmy as I could ever remember and had taken up playing the piano, much to her husband and children's alarm, but she was learning quickly and set her stall to teach me all she knew on my four-day break. I also spent a long weekend in London taking in a West End show by staying at my brother, Harry's apartment in Battersea. He introduced me to his circle of friends, who, in the main, were nice, apart from just one or two having an annoying, 'yah' syndrome, and that, 'where's your flat cap, northern girl', attitude, guarding handbags in case 'the Scouser' nicked a couple of items for her journey home. Harry had lost his accent at university and, rightly or wrongly, an accent can prove to be a major factor for some when forming opinions; it goes without saying that to think such a thing threw me into the same category.

I would have visited my other sister, Rebecca, in Scotland but she was planning to come and stay for a week at some stage soon. I didn't go; I took out a loan and bought an account-busting, top of the range R13 clarinet instead, falling in love with it immediately it touched my lips.

Slowly but surely, as the weeks passed by, I learned to accept my separation. Mini-catastrophes, the hair dryer exploding, a new white top washed with a leaking black sock, the stereo losing its voice due to old age, were treated with mild to middling irritation rather than tears. The moustache compulsive disorder, given meagre fare to nourish its madness, wasted away.

I continued playing with the orchestra on a weekly basis and hadn't seen Anna since our night out. She'd sent her apologies and didn't turn up to any rehearsals. Fergal explained that she was giving her family more of her time because she felt that, over the last months, she had seriously neglected them. I went to the pub and had a shandy with the stalwarts of the society after rehearsals, and went regularly to The Liverpool Philharmonic Hall to see any concert with anyone willing to go with me.

We also played a few concerts of our own, much to the delight of our dedicated family and friends' audience, who it is only to be supposed couldn't hear us properly to applaud with such gusto when we finished. Mum and Dad religiously turned up to each one. Joan Sarney took over conducting once 'the aged one' retired and, like all good fairies, waved her baton wildly about like a magic wand. Strangely, I was encouraged by Sandra the flautist, who said I should take up lessons to improve.

After grappling with the guilt generated in Elsie's memory, I started tuition with someone Joan recommended, an old friend, a man called Mr Gerrard who constantly drank bottled beer during our hour-long sessions, offering the occasional, ever-declined, swig when my mouth dried up. He had nicotine running up his fingers with a generous amount staining his goatee beard. This would deceive anyone into thinking him incapable of blowing into any instrument other than a breathalyser but not so, his lungs were made of steel, his ability on the clarinet unquestionable. He eradicated bad habits, taught me how to interpret compositions, gave my fingers inspiration, my mind concentration. He galvanised me to study great (and not so great) works at every opportunity. Lessons were inspiring not only because of this, but also because he entertained with stories from his past, playing in orchestras', bands', on the streets, you name it he'd done it, all in the cause of music.

The only time my tranquil state was interrupted was when I had dealings with James. He was still struggling to meet the agreed twenty thousand pounds equity and had only managed to cough up a cheque for one thousand. Our friendship remained intact purely because, as ever, I was putty in his hands, accepted his excuses and couldn't find it within me to embark on bitter rows and recriminations, playing the martyr with fortitude.

Apart from this, I was in a nicely contrived comfort zone, practising on my new clarinet whenever I could, swimming when I could and playing cards on a Sunday night with Mum and Dad and their friends. Not exactly the high life but it was a start. On the odd occasion, Dad would coax me into playing songs before an audience, the neighbours and friends or, on one embarrassing evening, the video man who had come to fix the video recorder. The item in question was so big and ancient we needed permission from the National Grid to switch it on. Mum, not being of gadget mind, unable to embrace DVD, had managed to insert a video back to front and upside down, hence video man's appearance. Dad stood proudly by and drummed lightly on the windowsill as I fumbled 'Hello Dolly' on the keyboard in utter embarrassment. Video man had worn a look of surprise and had left as hastily as he could without appearing rude.

And so my life went until I was approached to audition for a quintet and I found myself joining a choral society.

Chapter 6

I sat in a large church hall watching people enter, scraping chairs loudly on scuffed woodblock flooring when they found a seat, and wondered what I was doing there. It was debatable whether warmth had ever found its way through these hallowed walls where cold had the monopoly and had me pulling my polo neck over my nose to defrost it and block out the smell of mouldy, damp walls.

Anna, very much instrumental to my participating in this chorus-singing lark, was at that moment sat next to me chatting with a very pale looking woman called Diane who had a mop of greying, mousy, brown hair and who, in contradiction to her appearance, had a voice that carried well above the hubbub around us giving me, two seats away, a good insight into her private affairs.

'I came in last week from singing and Tom was waiting for me, asking me what time I thought it was. I said, "Half past nine, do I get a thousand pounds, or something for getting it right?" He said, "Funny aren't you, I always go out on a Wednesday with the boys," and banged the front door as he left. Tom Jenkins is a wanker and that's all there is to it. I nearly threw my boots at the door after him, you know. I mean, I've only been doing this for the last ten years.'

Anna shook her head in mutual disgust. There was a large element of ladies on parade, ranging from a woman with what looked like a tea cosy on her head and pea green woolly socks encasing her cankles, to someone who appeared to have turned up in a mother-of-the-bride wedding outfit. The men for the most part sat together for strength in depth and safety. The high ceiling had a mouldy discolouring at its edges and was graced by large pieces of pealing plaster hanging precariously from it, ready to fall on anyone who might sing out of tune.

Yes, it seemed Anna had a lot to answer for. She had turned up at the orchestra a week ago after a long absence and had played her violin like she was doing heavy duty ironing. It was the same evening that I'd been asked if I'd like to audition for a quintet being set up by a friend of Mike Yorton's, our most competent oboe player. Mike was a quiet unassuming character and I'd been quite flattered that he'd thought to ask me.

'Of course, I'm in only because Beryl's a good friend of mine, brilliant bassoonist,' he'd said, packing his oboe away. 'But she's looking specifically for clarinet at the moment. She's auditioning a week Saturday, I think. Anyway, I'll give you her number and you can call and arrange a time if you're interested.'

Anna had come along to the pub after the rehearsal and had plonked herself next to me.

'My violin needs tuning or I need to practise more,' she said.

'Are you okay?' I asked.

'Yeah fine. No, actually, I'm fed up! Join the choir with me next week.'

'I don't think I'm quite ready to tackle more than the orchestra at the mo.' I chomped on a packet of cheesy Wotsits. 'The clarinet's the only thing I'm alright at.'

'Don't be so ridiculous, you're also really good at doing yourself down.' She made me smile. 'Get yourself out there. You should be playing at the Liverpool Phil not the local scout hut.' She was a great morale booster.

'Actually, I may audition for a quintet.'

'Get you. Fantastic. Don't let Sandra know.'

'She's at the North West Musician of the Year Awards Festival at the moment.'

74

'Oh, and she's kept that quiet I'll bet.'

'She's okay.'

'No she isn't.'

'Yeah, I know.' I conceded and changed the subject. 'How've you been? Fergal mentioned you were sorting out family matters?'

'I was – am, in fact. I mean I am trying, but honestly I don't think Peter is. I had a row with him a few nights after the karaoke evening. I told him about the voluntary work and the degree and he was so angry he nearly left me. Said I was nothing but a liar and that he'd struggle to trust me ever again. I...' She stopped and nibbled at her thumb nail. 'Well, I promised him I'd give up the voluntary work and the orchestra but, whether he liked it or not, I was going to complete the degree. D'you know, I'm actually better educated than he is? His part of the bargain was to be at home more for me and the children. And guess what? We see less of him now than we did before. He's not being fair on the children. Anyway, I've decided to get out at least one night a week. I'm going to drop out of the orchestra but I'm going to continue singing with the choir. Why don't you come with me?'

'Why are you dropping the orchestra?' I didn't want to lose touch with her.

'I don't know. Let's be honest, I'm quite shit at playing the violin really. I think, you should come with me next week and we'll have a laugh. Please? I'll see if Fergal will join too.'

Anna was alight with intent, insisted on picking me up and taking me the following Wednesday and I was easy prey because I liked her. At no time had there been any mention of an audition. This only came to light as we entered the hall.

'An audition?'

'Oh, it's nothing, just think of the Weather Girls.'

There was a sudden large influx of sound as established members piled in. People hugged and exchanged loud fat kisses on cheeks, chattering excitedly about holidays, work, houses and in one instance a yacht. A yacht?

I was suddenly caught up in the midst of things when Glen from the karaoke night waved then bounded over to kiss me on both cheeks.

'Hi, Grace, how are you? Glad you've come, Paula will be here in a minute, hi Anna, hi Di.'

All three of us chorused. 'Hi Glen.'

'How are you?' I asked.

He puffed his cheeks out. 'Still exhausted. Hey, Anna...' Anna stood up to chat with Glen.

'I hear you're going through a divorce.' Diane turned to me.

'I am, it's great, you should try it,' I said, lightly but firmly indicating the conversation as a non-starter.

'I'm sorry, I wasn't being nosey or anything. I think you're very brave.' She stretched her legs in front of her settling in for a long conversation. 'Marriage is overrated. Men are tossers. Tom, that's my husband, doesn't even like being in the same room as me, but then complains when I'm out. I get up really early in the morning to make my daughter, Heather's, breakfast and get her ready for school and he stays in bed till I've left for work. I make mine and my daughter's tea and we eat together, he waltzes in with a take-away most nights. We go shopping, he goes fishing. I don't know why we carry on. I sleep perched on the edge of the bed and he's at the other edge, you know. Thinking about it, I'm sure I was reading the paper the last time we had sex. Being on your own must be very liberating.'

'Heart breaking more like.'

'Absolutely. We'd end up splitting our child in two and I'd be the one out on the street. Not that I'd leave really! Who'd have me?'

'That's exactly what I thought.'

'Really? You've not got bosoms that need hammocks to keep them pointing the right way or padding in unusual places.' In a desperate need to boost her own morale, she raised a combat trouser leg to show off a battered doc martin boot. 'My ankles aren't bad I suppose, and I'm a great singer. You're cute and dainty; you won't have any problems in finding someone new.' Unlike my abortive attempts at seduction, it was quite clear that Diane made no effort with bright plumage to attract her other half.

'Believe me, cellulite doesn't discriminate. It's not easy being Miss Average,' I smiled.

'Absolutely. Got plenty of cellulite over here too.' She prodded her thigh and smiled back.

More chairs scraped as people shuffled along to make room for the late-comers, gossiping loudly until a small, slender woman with long, curly, fiery red hair walked in with folders and bags weighing her arms down, whereupon the noise levels dipped.

'Hello everyone,' she beamed. 'For those who don't remember, I'm Paula your musical director. Now before...'

Everyone stopped their conversations apart from the woman in the wedding outfit who was regaling a glazed looking lady next to her about a trip to New York.

'And then my daughter introduced me to the mayor, imagine, I was in my old jeans and a pullover which is not my favourite.'

Paula shouted. 'Hello there, Irene, we are ready to start.'

'I'm ready when you are,' Irene said and mumbled something to her relieved looking neighbour.

'Now,' Paula resumed. 'Before we broke up for the summer holidays we'd discussed updating some of the songs for the concert in November in aid of... doobree doo, cancer. You all gave me preferences of songs you may like to sing and, well; quite frankly not one of them has made it onto my revised list.' Her gentle Welsh accent tried to soften the blow.

I sat bemused as a murmur of dissatisfaction ran among the rows of chairs. None of the old favourites? Where's Brigadoon? Quite shocking! This young pup changing things without a bye or leave.

Paula waited for the mumbling to stop. 'Also our new pianist, Lawrence Wilding, will be here shortly. He's kindly offered to help out while we find someone more permanent after the sad loss of Beatrice Taupington-Smythe. So things are going to be very different from now on. Your newsletters should have informed you also of the new finishing time of ten o'clock so I hope your vocal chords are up for it. Right, here's Lawrence now so I'll hand out these song sheets and we'll get started.'

Lawrence Wilding sauntered to the piano in army combat pants and a loose check shirt that didn't match but didn't disguise the pert buttocks beneath the pants or the handsome square shoulders beneath the shirt. Good-looking, slim, wiry and taut were all words that summed him up. His light-brown hair was crew-cut; his eyes were crystal clear and looked blue from where I was sitting.

'Ooh, I say,' Diane breathed.

With difficulty I turned my concentration to the vocal warm up; the hall resounded with sopranos, tenors, altos, and basses all shaking the hanging pieces of ceiling with vibrato before, under Paula's direction, we launched into the 'The Chorus of the Hebrew Slaves'; the hairs on the back of my neck rose as the society brought the song to an end. They may look an odd bunch but the sound they managed to achieve as one voice certainly made up for any differences of appearance.

From behind his piano Lawrence appeared pleasantly surprised and had a quirky smile on his face in appreciation, a small gap in his front teeth rendering him utterly lovely. Hello, hormones. Suddenly I wanted to be a member and part of the group and it had nothing to do with the wonderful singing.

After twenty minutes of singing a lady, in a tartan gathered skirt accentuating a wide girth, hovered conspicuously at a far door and cleared her throat, nervously mouthing 'Tea's ready' to Paula.

'Okay, thanks Florence, fifteen minutes everyone and back here again,' Paula shouted. Poor Florence of the tartan skirt had fled in fear of being trampled upon.

Diane kindly offered to get the teas while Anna offered me a cigarette. We went to the entrance of the hall to smoke like outcast lepers.

'Well, what do you think?' Anna asked.

'I think they sound brilliant,' I replied.

'Not the society, I mean Lawrence. You really need to get in there before anyone else does.'

'Well, he's very good looking and everything, but don't buy a big hat just yet. I mean, for a start he may be married or have a girlfriend and for another he may think that I look like the back end of a bus.'

'You're gorgeous, what's your problem? You should go and make him notice you. I know if I was in your shoes I would,' she said. As I've said before, I liked Anna.

'To be honest I'm more concerned with having to audition later, I could end up dying of embarrassment or being arrested by the voice police.'

'You are hopeless.'

'I shouldn't be smoking either, I don't even inhale, what a waste.' I flung my half-smoked cigarette down the steps outside the door then ran after it and put it out properly. We walked back into the bustling room to look for Diane.

Lawrence passed us and stopped next to Anna.

'Do you have to pay for the tea?' he asked her with a melting, musical voice.

Anna's eyes sparkled as she struck up a conversation with him as easily as if she'd known him all her life. I stood apart a little and wondered how it was that some people seemed to attract attention with no effort, like a lamp with moths fluttering about it while others; I for instance, had the effect of a turd bobbing in a public toilet. The thought bought a smile to my face but the reverie was cut short when I realised that Lawrence was smiling back at me. Say something, say something I urged my brain. I overheated and sounded like a mouse from Bagpuss when I said. 'Yes, they sell biscuits too apparently.'

'Oh great, catch you later,' he said and wandered off.

'Didn't you hear a word we were talking about?' Anna asked.

'Oh no, do I need a gun? What a cringer,' I replied.

'What's up?' Diane asked. 'Sorry the tea's a bit cold but got chatting and forgot.'

'Grace has got some serious flirting issues,' Anna laughed. 'We'd moved on from tea and biscuits, you loon, and were talking about where he'd learnt to play the piano. I didn't know the Royal Academy of Music was big on confectionary, I don't think he did either.'

'Drink your tea, love,' Diane comforted.

'How good do you have to be to be a member?' I asked after I'd calmed down.

'I would say as long as you're not tone-deaf you'll be all right. The fact that you're youngish and quite pretty will probably help,' Diane said. 'I've been here about ten years and honestly we need some new blood, although I suppose there's been a difference since Paula has joined as musical director. Phil Simpson, the chairman, has given her his backing so I'm glad we aren't doing any of the old stuff. If I'd had to sing Brigadoon one more time I'd have moved to Scotland in search of it. Don't worry, Grace, Lawrence must be used to women acting strangely around him as I've just stuttered when saying hello to him and Marjorie Price just went pink and fled to the toilet. Hey, Paula, this is Grace who's hoping to join the society and she's a little nervous.'

Paula came and stood with us. 'Oh don't worry; we won't eat you. If you stay behind after the rehearsal we'll just ask you to give us a quick song and that's it, we're not expecting Kiri te Kanawa. We'll let you know there and then and you can come along to the pub with me if you like. Glen can't wait, I'm afraid he only comes here so he can have his pint in the pub after. I think it's time to start rehearsal again, you'll be fine,' she said, then yelled. 'Time everyone.'

The second part of the rehearsal flew by and before I knew it everyone was leaving.

'Are you going to the pub?' I asked Diane.

'I can't, Tom's not happy with the ten o'clock finish as it is and I've got my little girl at home. I'll just veg on the settee with a beer and watch a film with helicopters, guns and people shagging in blue lighting. Good luck, you'll be fine; I'll see you here next week.'

'Are you ready, Grace?' Paula asked as the room cleared. 'What are you going to sing?'

'Erm, don't know.' I felt like a schoolgirl in front of the teacher.

'Here, sing this.' Paula handed me a song sheet from 'Me and My Girl'.

The room was now empty now apart from Lawrence who yawned and stretched his arms above his head and Phil Simpson, the chairman, who sat beside the piano shuffling his Jesus sandals on the floor, eager to be off to the boozer.

'Ready, go,' Paula said as if starting an egg and spoon race.

'Leaning on the lamp post' was not exactly what I had in mind for an audition piece but then I hadn't come up with anything better so, off I started, Lawrence trying to keep up with me. Never had the song been sung with such haste and with so little control. Phil and Paula both nodded to each other.

'Well done,' Phil said, grabbing his jacket.

'You're in,' Paula said, picking the papers up and thanking Lawrence for staying behind. I needed a drink.

'Come on you two I'll take you both to the pub so we can have a doobree do, you know, a celebratory drink. Are you coming with us Phil? Phil?' Paula did a double take, Phil had already gone.

As we headed for Paula's car I apologised to Lawrence. 'Sorry about the biscuit thing earlier, I must have sounded a right berk. I was miles away.'

'What were you smiling at?' he asked.

'Oh, nothing. That was a pretty awful audition. I sounded like Tweety Pie on helium.'

'It was different but not out of tune, you just hurried it a little,' he said kindly. 'I actually thought you were smiling at me.'

My heart lurched with a thrill of excitement I hadn't felt in years. 'I'm not that forward unfortunately, it usually takes me weeks to know someone before such a thing occurs, anything before that would have to be put down to wind.' Eeyuk, how could I have said such a thing?

'I'll bear that in mind and stand up-wind from you in future.'

We stood in amicable silence as Paula made room on the back seat for a passenger.

All three of us ended up humming my audition piece in the car.

The pub, The Buccaneer, was an olde worlde pub with wood beams and several toothless wonders arranged at the bar, one half of its lounge practically empty the other filled with amateur opera singers sitting in friendly groups, few of them averse to being loudest in the 'now hear me' stakes, that euphoric state I only reached after excessive amounts of alcohol.

Anna had a large whisky and lemonade waiting for me and offered to buy Lawrence and Paula a drink. Eventually settled, I couldn't help but feel rather elevated, sat opposite the musical director and next to the good-looking pianist. The other members seemed almost reverent towards Paula while a few of the younger members of the society seemed to speak a little louder to draw Lawrence into conversation. More to the point, Lawrence's right leg was so close to my left leg it would have been difficult to slide a piece of paper between us but I couldn't move away, being dangerously close to edge of a long bench. He didn't seem aware of this and as he leant forward to hear what someone was saying I felt the muscles in his leg tighten, and took a quick gulp of my drink. Anna gave me a knowing look.

'Where do you work, Lawrence?' she asked him.

'Mainly from home,' he replied.

'Interesting. Doing what?'

'Mainly property development. Bit of plumbing today,' he said loudly. 'Had my hand up an old lady's soiled pipes earlier.' He received a few hard stares from a couple of nearby elderly members, which brought on a quick apology that went down well and gained him brownie points for future indiscretions.

'Anyway, what about the weather, very inclement for this time of year, don't you think?' I said to cover the pregnant pause. 'Aren't you going to become the permanent piano player?'

'No, I'm just helping Paula out. I've got my own blues/jazz band together so I can't commit to it full-time,' he explained.

'Grace plays the clarinet so you should ask her to join. There you go, Grace, you can leave your hated job at the bank and become a full-time musician,' Anna said, plunging in and putting order into everyone's lives.

My face bloomed into colour with embarrassment. I opened my mouth to say something and closed it again when nothing came out.

'Yes it is very inclement for this time of year,' Lawrence smiled.

Irene in the wedding outfit had collared Paula and was describing her trip to New York. There was a large beer stain down the front of her garb now and she was not of the same clarity of mind or voice as she had been earlier in the evening. A gentleman called Boris, who looked very snappy in a waistcoat and yellow cravat, decided to give his rendition of 'The Pearl Fishers' egged on by Glen. Phil Simpson was having a heated debate on the merits of Burgundy wine as opposed to Bordeaux with a chap who looked like Margaret Thatcher. The lady with the tea cosy on her head called Bobby, the lady not the tea cosy, started to sway in her seat annoying the girl to her left, who was nose to nose with a man in navy overalls.

'Are they always like this?' Lawrence asked.

'Pretty much,' Anna replied. 'It's worse after a concert. It's your turn for the drinks, Grace, do you want one Lawrence?'

Lawrence was tempted but it transpired he had to get back for his dog Gnasher, a spaniel getting on in life with tendencies to poor bladder control. He went to stand up and, seemingly without thinking, firmly gripped his hand on my leg to heave his body up.

I yelped.

'Bloody hell, sorry,' he apologised, patting my leg in apology.

'Don't worry.' I shooed him off and tried to act as if a good-looking man grabbed my leg then patted it on a regular basis. The last time a man had touched me was New Year's Eve when sloppy drunken kisses were awarded to the nearest person and the local pub pervert had grabbed my bum. James had found it hilarious, I hadn't, and while I'd tried to get my husband to kiss me to bring in the New Year he found ways not to.

When Lawrence had gone I relaxed.

'You two make a lovely couple,' Anna said.

'Ha, ha, very funny. I'm never going out with anyone ever again.'

'Oh, don't be so ridiculous, drama queen, what's wrong with you?' She arched a perfectly shaped eyebrow at me.

'I don't know. I'm not right in the head.'

'Do you seriously want to be an old maid?'

'I need more time.'

'Well, at some stage you're going to have to take the plunge. Do you think your ex is sitting at home pining for you?'

'No.'

'Well then. Just lighten up and give other men a try. Lawrence won't be available for long and you'll miss your chance. You know if you go out with him you don't have to swallow on the first date.'

I choked on my drink.

'You're not practising already are you?' Anna's humour received a defensive frown.

'Are you thinking what I think you're thinking?' Paula interrupted. 'Bit of a dish is our Lawrence, and no he's not taken at the moment so you're free to flirt all you like with him. He'll love it.'

I had a sinking feeling that people would dissect any tiny conversation, glance, look or smile Lawrence and me exchanged in future and surmise I was chasing after him.

'Look, can we talk about something else? I'm really not ready for this. Men and me don't mix. I've got one dangling me on a string as it is at the moment and to be honest it's enough to be going on with.'

'He's very good in his band you know. I've known him for years, sang in a band with him a long time ago, and the only thing I would say is that he doesn't keep his doobree doos, you know, his girlfriends, for very long. I think maybe, because he has women throwing themselves at him, he doesn't have to try. Besides, he's absolutely loaded,' Paula explained. For a second I'd been worried about what Paula was going to say after using her strange fill-in word, doobree doo.

'There's a challenge for you.' Anna nudged me.

'Enough,' I said through gritted teeth.

'I'll stop if we can go dancing on Saturday night. I know, we could ask Diane if she wants to come too, she never goes out and never comes to the pub after rehearsals,' Anna said enthusiastically. It had to be said that Anna liked to keep her thoughts on the go and didn't seem to wallow on one subject for long. 'We could all go dancing, I'll ring her tomorrow. Peter's away working and the children are with their grandparents and I don't fancy being alone.'

I smiled at her. 'You make me laugh with your 'dancing'. I'd love to go 'dancing', if it was left up to me I'd probably never dance again. Saturday it is then.'

Chapter 7

Saturday morning brought sunshine through the open bedroom window along with small sporadic gusts of chilled early September wind that made the poplar trees in the garden shiver. A lawnmower hummed in the distance, its sound bringing with it the smell of cut grass. I lay in bed and looked out on a Simpson's sky, bright blue with cartoon clouds, and stretched languidly, my nose itched – 'Kissed or Vexed?'

Mum and Dad had gone to Mary's in Birmingham for the weekend, primarily for Dad to sort out a problem with their washing machine, so I had the joint to myself until my other sister, Rebecca, arrived around four o'clock Sunday afternoon for a week-long visit.

I rubbed my nose again, put the stereo on high volume and pranced about in my knickers and bra, singing in front of the mirror to George Michael's 'Freedom'. Fed up because I didn't look like Naomi Campbell, I pulled my jeans on and found one of the horrible baggy jumpers given a stay of execution in the mass cull on the night I'd left James. With statically charged hair I padded downstairs, picked up the paper and the post and went into the kitchen, humming 'Freedom', step-ball-changing my way to the kettle.

After letting Roger out, I picked up the phone to call Beryl to enquire about her quintet audition then put the phone down. Say she'd already found someone. Say she didn't like the sound of me. I picked the phone up again and dialled, a furious internal voice screaming at me to put the phone down and leave it till later. Would later ever come? Too late, the phone was answered on the third ring.

'Oh, er, hello, is that Beryl?'

'Speaking.'

'Oh right, good, good. Erm, I'm Grace Scott, and Mike Yorton gave me your number for a quintet audition?'

'Ah yes, he mentioned you might ring. He's rather taken with your ability.' She sounded mid-fifties, the hint of a lisp making me warm to her immediately.

'He's a proper gentleman.'

'That he is. Now, unfortunately I'm out all day today and I've got a busy week ahead. Let me see … can you manage next Saturday, one thirty? Very informal, just bring two pieces of music and of course your clarinet.' She had a breezy laugh. We had a chat about her plans for the quintet and I took her address.

There was a great sense of accomplishment when I came off the phone. What had I been getting so worked up about? Life was moving on and I was participating. Unfortunately Mr Gerrard was away for the next couple of weeks so this audition was going to be done without his input. A little worrying but I was up for the challenge. I poured hot water over a teabag and sat at the kitchen table waiting for it to brew and was about to read the paper when I noticed a letter addressed for my attention. I loved getting mail even if it was a bill as it gave me a strange sense of worth.

My eyes widened as I read the contents. Anger was explosive and instant. I yelled at Roger, threw my trainers on, grabbed the letter and my car keys and slammed out of the house, seething in the car, taking some of my frustration out on the accelerator. Pulling up outside my old home I stormed up the path.

James came to the door looking a little nonplussed until I flung the letter at him through the doorway.

'What the fuck do you call that?' I shouted at him.

James picked up the letter and looked at it before commenting. 'It's for a divorce. I'm doing this so you don't have to pay and we can get divorced before two years of living apart. I thought you'd be grateful.'

'What about the lies, you shitbag?' I was shaking.

'Stop shouting and come inside.' James went to take my arm and pull me inside.

'Don't touch me,' I hissed.

He stepped back. 'Hey, before you start, you've had plenty of opportunity to do this yourself you know. I can't petition for divorce and also say it was my fault, I've sought legal advice and this is what I've been told. If you want to go and see a solicitor then by all means go ahead but this way, I have to pay and you don't, it's called unreasonable behaviour and it seemed to be the easiest way.'

'For you maybe but I have to go about for the rest of my life with the stigma of being the reason for the divorce. You look like bloody Snow White on this, you bastard.' I snatched the letter from him. 'I will speak to a solicitor but in the meantime you had better get the money for the equity to me and fast.'

I saw hurt in James' eyes but for once I ignored it, turned and stalked down the path back to the car, grinding gears as I drove off, not glancing behind.

Screaming and punching the steering wheel didn't really help. Reeling off every swear word I knew, banging the car door, the front door, the living room door and landing on the settee in a heap didn't either. Six points raised on that letter and all of them tearing into my inadequacies as a wife, as a woman, a complete reversal of the truth as I saw it. When had I stopped our sexual relationship? When had I started going out at night without him? When had I forgotten he existed? When had we argued? When had I said I didn't want children? When had I flirted with other men? I couldn't sign it and I wouldn't. In the past eight months I'd skirted the issue of divorce and money, knowing he was struggling with the situation as much as I was. I knew that the breakdown wasn't entirely his fault; I'd handled certain situations very badly, miss-timing my approach, treading on eggshells when I should have been stamping on them or vice versa. With hindsight I would have gone about things differently.

Less than an hour ago I'd been prancing about semi-naked glorying in my freedom. Now it was being handed to me I didn't want it. Divorce was inevitable but could I really take all the blame? Why hadn't he wanted to touch me? Something about me turned him off. Was I too passive, not dirty enough in bed? Was I too podgy, too ugly? Why hadn't he wanted try and make a family with me? He would have made a wonderful father. I put my head in my hands and managed to find more tears, this time calmer, more reflective.

I was still being manipulated but really who was at fault? I was. Hadn't I decided some month's back not to wait for things to happen but to be the instigator instead? Well, so much for such high ideals, as here I was again in much the same situation but with diminished responsibility.

I sat up shakily and went to finish making the cup of tea I'd started earlier. Crying was so exhausting. An idea popped into my head, pack a bag and run away to London, anywhere. Fight or flight. My initial fighting talk now made me want to run as far away as possible from the situation. It was disturbing that no matter how angry I got I always ended up wanting to 'run away, run away' like the knights in Monty Python's Holy Grail. There I was, already creeping towards the fence, looking for a seat from where I could view all sides to James' actions and make excuses for him.

The landline phone rang and I let it, watching it closely as if it was going to jump up and bite me on the neck. It went onto answer machine.

'Get out of bed, lazy. Anna here, give me a ring when you get in, up, back, God I hate talking to these things. Why don't you ever answer your mobile? Tonight, tonight won't be like any night,' Anna sang and put the phone down. My mobile was somewhere around and obviously needed charging again. I stroked my upper lip, suddenly thankful that I was going out tonight. Spending the evening on my own was not an option. I rang Anna back, while waiting for her to answer her phone I looked at my face in the mirror and knew it would need some serious pampering and, as for my hair, well, it was safe to say I'd looked better. What must James have thought of me? Who bloody cares! But look at the state of you. I don't bloody care. Yes you do. You look a mess.

'Who looks a mess? Thanks very much.'

The mirror must have been talking out loud. 'Oh God, sorry Anna, it looks like I've started talking to myself.'

'Who said that?' It shouldn't have made me snigger but it did.

Once we'd agreed to meet at hers at eight I took myself off to Natalie's to have a moan. She was having problems of her own with postnatal depression. The house was spotless. Her current state of mind had her cleaning at two o'clock in the morning. She was bouncing about as if on speed, changing the children's clothing twice while I was there and was never far away from a bottle of bleach to clean away imagined stains. Her face had come out in a crop of spots, which left me feeling positively healthy.

She stood by the sink in the kitchen discussing the matter. 'Just sign the paper and have done with it,' she said, wiping the draining board again.

'But it's all lies,'

'Who cares? Nobody will ever read it and so what if they do? You know the truth and it sets you free.'

'I care.'

'Do you want to be divorced or not? Seriously. Because the way you're behaving seems to me like you are holding on to a marriage that is well and truly finished. Grace, face it, you don't have to sign your name with 'divorcee' after it once it goes through, it's not a label you have to wear warning others off. I don't know how you feel, I can only imagine it, but surely once you get this over and done with you can get on with your life. Excuse me a minute.' She handed me a plate to catch the crumbs from a biscuit I was about to bite into.

'Where was I? Oh yeah. I know it doesn't help, but people get divorced every day and although marriage these days is taken fairly lightly by some, you need to stop taking it so much to heart and try to make the best of things. I think you should speak to a solicitor, get your money and put this whole thing behind you.' Natalie paused. 'I'm sorry, it must be awful for you,' she sympathised. 'At least your face isn't a dot to dot,' she added on an up note.

'Oh Natalie I'm so sorry, here's me going on about a stupid letter and there's you trying to cope with two children and spots. Will you just sit down and put the bloody dishcloth away,' I said.

'I can't, I think I'm going mad,' Natalie said but came and sat down at the table anyway, keeping hold of the dishcloth.

'Have you been to see the doctor?'

'No, he'll only give me anti-depressants and I don't want them,' she said and slowly slid the cloth over the table surface.

'No he won't, I've tried that already, he'll tell you to run a marathon. Maybe that would be a good thing because then you'd be too buggered to clean.'

'I'll be fine. I'm going back to work soon so that should sort me out. The children are fine apart from the baby having a severe case of bumaphobia.'

'What?'

'Oh, you know what Dad's like, came round the other day like a tornado to put a new socket in the kitchen for us, sat down and squashed Matty into the cushion. Can you believe it? Look, I'm sorry if I appeared to shout at you about this divorce. In a way James is doing you a favour but it all boils down to how desperately you feel about the allegations. Don't think too hard about it though because that is half your problem. Your initial response is normally the correct one. The longer you leave it the more inclined you'll be to talk yourself round. I know you, you analyse everything until you haven't got a clue what to think.'

'And I know you and know you'll carry on cleaning once I've left. You'll have to go to D.A. – dishcloths anonymous – if the condition gets much worse. What am I going to wear tonight?'

'I've got a nice pair of manky maternity pants if you're stuck. Saying that, we'd probably get about four of you into them, where are you disappearing to?'

'Oblivion.'

I decided to fight a negative with a positive and went for retail therapy. My age and natural reserve persuading me against anything as frivolous as short skirts, I plumped for tight trousers, a top that gave me a bit of boob structure and some new boots, all exempt from criticism; my interpretation of stylish and James' differed wildly. I conjured up his image in the changing-room mirror and blew a raspberry then stuck two fingers up at him hissing 'ner ner nee ner ner.' I felt a lot better.

Although the days of me keeping new shoes at the side of the bed so I could see them when I woke up in the morning had long passed, I dressed with excitement in the new clobber later that day.

'You did say eight o'clock didn't you?' I asked, a bit put out when Anna answered the door in a dressing gown and a towel wrapped round her head.

'I know, but the children didn't go till six o'clock and then Peter phoned and said he won't be back till Monday evening so we had a big row on the phone. I suppose that at some stage I'll have to ring and apologise, I said some really awful things, then again, so did he. You look fabulous; love the boots. Diane should be here shortly, I won't be long so help yourself to a drink.'

I settled myself in front of the telly with a beer.

Diane turned up but didn't appear to be very relaxed in what she was wearing. The combats and Doc Martins had come off out of necessity, black patent sandals and a long skirt with a split up the side had replaced them. Her overblown, flowery top accentuated her large breasts unfavourably.

'I don't think Tom knows what's hit him, it's the first time in years – probably since Heather was little – I've gone out and just left him in charge. I didn't tell him until he got back from fishing, because if I'd told him earlier he wouldn't have come home till it was too late for me to go out. I'm bound to pay for it tomorrow but it's very hard to say no to Anna.' Diane peered into her blouse and rearranged her tits.

'Sounds like we've all had a day of it,' I said. 'My ex has accused me of all sorts in an effort to get divorced'.

We weighed up the merits of having a man in your life. In our current frame of mind we couldn't find any, so we moved onto the bad points, which we were still discussing when Anna eventually entered the sitting room all shiny and ready for a night on the tiles.

'Wine any...what are they?' Anna stopped, staring at the split in Diane's skirt. 'They look suspiciously like pop socks to me.'

'What's wrong with them?' Diane asked.

'They're pop socks.'

'So?'

'They're revolting, pull your skirt up.'

Diane did. 'What?' she asked. She had long legs only to be sliced in two, the bottom half resembling hanging salami. 'What's your problem?'

'Look, they're pulled and you can see the seam at your toes, and they're starting to ladder and ... what the fuck ... no ... are they aubergine? You need to take them off.'

'My legs are too white and I haven't shaved them because I left it too late and I get a rash. Grace, help me out here.' Diane looked to me for back-up.

I let her down. My silence and face pulling said it all.

'Follow me,' Anna said and we all headed for her bedroom, which welcomed us with decadent opulence. Semi-erotic paintings, nude statuettes, seductive lighting, strategically placed mirrors, a four-poster bed, thick, deep-red drapes at the windows and a carpet that sprang underfoot like moss begging for sinful action, could all have been regarded as tacky but somehow presented itself as tasteful and sophisticated.

Diane looked at herself in the long mirror on the wall, pulled her skirt up again and curled her lip. 'I still don't know what's wrong with them, you know?' she said in a half-hearted manner.

'Here, put these on instead.' Anna unwrapped a new pair of black hold-up stockings and threw them at her. 'And while you're at it try this on, it doesn't suit me. You can have it if you like it.' She tactfully used the 'doesn't-suit-me' excuse rather than the 'it's-too-big-and-doesn't-fit-me' explanation and handed Diane a silky, low-cut top.

'Should I just go home?' She whipped her flowery number off.

'Come here; let me sort your bra out.' Anna yanked at the straps, pulling Diane's boobs a good inch higher to stand loud and proud. 'There.'

'Christ, I can't breathe.' Diane walked into the bedpost, the top floundering over her head.

'But you look fabulous.' Anna pulled it down into place.

'I could close the curtains and live in here,' I said dreamily, lying on the bed.

'You're welcome to, if you take the husband that goes with it,' Anna replied.

'Oh God, pass, never again.' I shuddered.

Diane promptly put her finger through one of the stockings. 'I'm so sorry, that's why my socks laddered; I'm not used to wearing them. Anna, I think my bikini line will stop them from sticking, it's half way down my legs and out of control.'

'Don't even go there,' Anna warned.

I started to laugh and Anna rummaged in her drawers for another pair.

Once Diane had sorted her leg-wear out and marked the difference the changes made both visually and psychologically we descended downstairs again.

Anna uncorked a bottle of champagne, which filled my head with bubbles of nonsense before even leaving the house.

'I just want to say that if a man comes near me tonight I'll smack him in the face,' I said.

'I just want to say that if you do you'll be arrested,' Anna responded.

'I just want to say I like pop socks,' Diane joined in.

'I just want to say that you *should* be arrested,' countered Anna.

'I think in the words of dumped and scorned women around the world that all men are bastards,' I said.

'Not just dumped and scorned ones,' Anna said bitterly.

'I've decided, I'm coming back as a man next time round and I'm going to have a ball,' I continued.

'Two would be better,' Anna said, pouring out the remaining champagne.

'Absolutely. I've often wondered what sex with another woman would be like. Have you? I do like a bit of girl on girl porn. Am I the only perv here?' Diane said, the bubbles obviously having gone to her head as well. She kept lifting her skirt to look at her legs.

'I prefer watching threesomes. I kissed another woman to get Peter going once, and it worked,' Anna said. 'I suppose it gave me a kick seeing Peter's reaction, it really turned him on. Thinking about it, it's probably the last time I had great sex. Can't kiss a woman every time I want decent sex with my husband though, can I? Or can I?'

'It can't be any worse than kissing Tom. From what I can remember it's like putting your smackers onto a freezer door and expecting a response.'

'Call me a boring old cow, but it doesn't do anything for me, the girl thing not the freezer thing, well both actually,' I said, realising that I'd almost indicated a fetish for domestic appliances. The taxi pulled up outside.

'How do you know if you've never tried it, come here and give us a snog,' Anna laughed, grabbing her coat and chasing us both out of the door.

The country-club we arrived at was in the middle of the nowhere and maintained its country air by resembling a large cattle-market. The dance floor was a Saturday Night Fever throw back. Men surrounded its periphery, eyeing up the talent before them. I groaned inwardly and thought, 'I'm too old for this, I want to go and drink more Champagne at Anna's.' Instead I found myself being steered to the bar.

'I think I'll go to the loo,' I shouted above the music and headed for the ladies.

The toilets themselves were of secondary consequence, the mirrors were where it was all happening. In a haze of hairspray I joined in, searching through the crap in my bag to find a lipstick, an out-of-date lip balm and a huge can of deodorant, then went to find the girls.

'We were just talking about body language and how you can tell if a man is interested in you,' Diane said. 'I wouldn't have a clue. Don't all men just want a shag? If one looked at me I'd assume he fancied the person I was with, even if that person was Tom and if a bloke chatted me up I don't think I'd know how to handle it. No-one ever fancies me.'

'I'm right there with you on that one, going by past experience. Although I met James in a club and he didn't try to get into my knickers the first night. He must have liked the frightened rabbit look.'

Diane turned to one side and checked her stockings, briefly flashing bare flesh.

'Yes they're still in place, thank God.'

'That was a bit flirty, lady,' Anna said.

'Really? Should I look again?'

'I'd love to have the nerve to do that,' I said, referring to a stunning, young girl nearby who was feeling her body up and down, wildly shaking long locks of hair while swaying in front of a group of lads loving every minute of her performance. 'Do you think we're too old to do sexy like that?'

'There's a time and a place and if I caught my daughter doing that I'd kill her,' Anna said.

By now all three of us were swaying to some thumping dance, mega-mix, slurping foul orange drinks from bottles.

'I don't think I'd ever have the nerve, I think I'd start to cry or laugh,' Diane said.

'Listen to you both. What do you sound like? How old are you? Ninety? I don't know about you but I'm in my prime and I'm fully aware of my assets and how to use them and so should you be.' Anna said, pointedly looking at Diane's breasts.

'No one's getting their hands on my assets tonight, thank you very much,' Diane replied loudly.

'That's a shame,' a voice said over her shoulder. Diane turned to see the biggest set of white teeth on the planet grinning at her. She immediately put her shoulders back and sent her boobs skywards. So much for not being able to handle the situation.

'Your assets are in multiples surely, little lady,' the teeth said.

'Not so much of the little,' she replied, pushing her chest out a bit more.

We left Diane to it and went for a dance. Before long, two young lads had started to dance with us by just sidling up and shuffling in front of us. I couldn't decide whether I was actually dancing with my partner or not, with his eyes rooted to the floor it was difficult to tell. The age of chivalry no more. I assumed that men had just stopped asking women to dance when the more common response received was 'fuck off'.

Eventually I walked away and wondered if he'd noticed I'd gone. Anna was animatedly laughing and chatting away with his friend. Diane was still at the bar deeply engrossed in conversation with the teeth so I raised my eyebrows, smiled at her, ordered drinks and stood and people watched, avoiding eye contact, pretending this was my preference to socialising. I bobbed my head slightly to the beat of the music and hummed along self-consciously.

Anna came off the dance floor shaking her head at me. 'You look like you're having a really shit time.'

'I'm fine.'

'Well you don't look it. You won't attract any attention with a face like that.'

'I don't want to attract attention thanks.'

'Stop being so bloody boring. Stand your ground, hold your head up high and make men look at you, make eye contact. You're shuffling between people like a bag lady.'

Was I really? There must have been a look of shock on my face. 'The guy I've just been dancing with wasn't exactly entertainer of the year.'

'Oh well, in that case, that's all the men here sorted, we'll have to start on the women,' Anna said sarcastically. 'You and I are going on a stroll and I want you to chat someone up. I mean it. You can do it I know you can, just do it for a laugh. I want you to start talking so I can hit on the mate just for fun. It doesn't mean you have to take them home and get married.'

'I can't.'

'You can.'

'I can't.'

'Look, this one's nice, and just look at his friend.'

Before I knew it I was pushed in the direction of a huge loud-speaker in front of which a young man with floppy blonde hair and an air of university student imprinted on his clothing stood.

'Hi, nice necklace,' I shouted at him, pointing to a rhino horn hanging from a piece of leather around his neck. 'I'm going to kill her,' I thought.

'Thanks, I've not long come back from Kenya, my one bit of memorabilia from a great holiday. Ever been?'

What had I been expecting? A proposal of marriage? A look of alarm? A hasty retreat? In my panic I hadn't expected such a friendly reception.

'No. Do you come here often?' I flustered.

'No it was my first time.'

'What?'

'First time in Kenya. Have you been before?' I think he may have spat in my ear to make himself heard.

'No.'

It was scintillating stuff. We moved away from the speaker greatly enhancing his chances of being heard as he chatted on about his safari holiday, sleeping lions, aggressive baboons, hot-air balloon trips over the Masai Mara, being sick after a shed load of sambuca. He was quite cute.

'Can I get you a drink?' he asked suddenly.

'That would be great, thanks.'

'I'm Ben.' He introduced himself pushing his blonde locks from his forehead.

'Grace.'

Two drinks and a bop on the dance floor later and he'd moved in for a snog. Both Anna and Diane were nowhere to be seen. Although I'd had a fair amount of alcohol by now it hadn't dulled my senses where kissing strangers was concerned. It would have to be over fifteen years ago since my last venture into these waters and Ben did appear to be quite young. I hesitated before I let him move in. My mouth disappeared into a wet and sloppy world of saliva and tongue. I tried to remove it before I was sucked in completely, never to see my friends and family again, but by now young Ben had me like his quarry against a wall and was a determined package of youthful testosterone. In the end, rather than fight it, I tried to make the best of things by kissing him back to see if this did anything to improve matters. No, it was still like putting one's lips into a bowl of un-set jelly. He guided my hands to his six-pack. I broke away for breath.

'Wow,' I said. 'You've certainly had a lot of practice. It must be all that kissing the girls at university.'

'Oh, I'm not at Uni, I'm in the sixth form at high school.'

I gulped. 'I need to go to the ladies.'

'Don't be too long.' He touched my cheek gently with a tenderness that sent an unwelcome shiver down my back. How nice to be touched, how awful that it was by a seventeen-year-old school boy.

As I turned to walk away, I was drawn to a group who had just entered the club; at their head was an exotic looking couple. The girl was beautifully oriental and had a man's arm about her that slowly slid down her back to caress her perfect bottom. The man, who at that moment bent to kiss her, looked familiar. No, it couldn't be. Was it? No. Not James; not twice in one day; not kissing another woman, not with friends, who before the break-up had been my friends too? It was. I continued to stare, failing to fully swallow what I was seeing because a sick feeling was rising up the other way. I knew I would have to leg it to the toilets or puke here in front of everyone. I flew past Anna and Diane coming out of the ladies and made it just in time to throw my head over the loo.

They must have thought I was pissed. I could hear them clucking outside the toilet door and further off someone else retching in sympathy. The safety of the toilet cubicle, however much infested with rampant germs and stank of sick, was preferable to leaving and bumping into James and Miss Saigon,

'Grace, come on out. Are you okay? Grace?'

I pulled myself together and opened the door so suddenly that both Anna and Diane nearly fell into me, and was totally embarrassed when several girls looked over to see who had been responsible for vomiting and making them all want to join in. Anna handed me some toothpaste, now was not the time to go into her bag's contents, and Diane put her arm around me and led me to the basins to clean me up, still under the impression I was drunk and would cannon all over the place without her assistance.

'I need to go home,' I said and quietly explained the reason why. Both of them sympathised and agreed it was best that we should head home, so while I tried to patch myself up they went to get our coats and order a taxi. There was no sign of James when I furtively crept out of the toilets to find Ben hovering about waiting for my return. He gave all the signs of wanting to take up where he'd left off. I told him I was old enough to be his mother.

'I don't care,' he replied.

'Well I do.'

'Chill, babe, and relax.'

'Besides I've just been sick in the toilets and really don't smell very nice.'

'I have no sense of smell,' he persisted.

'I don't feel well.'

'I'll kiss you better.'

'I'll call your mum.'

'Man, just tell me if you don't want to be with me.'

'Okay, I don't want to be with you.' I ran away, following Diane who'd by now obtained our coats. The evening didn't get any better once we got outside into the cool refreshing night air. Anna was sitting inside the taxi arguing with no other than James who was holding the taxi door disputing her right to it.

I very nearly turned to Diane to tell Anna to get out of the taxi and wait for another while I went and hid behind some nearby bushes, but an inner voice forced me to re-evaluate the situation and dump the thought in favour of standing up for my friend and to also let him know I was there.

Anna was holding her own, adamant that she had every right to be seated whilst using her flirtatious wiles to win him over.

'I do hope we're not going to have another fight, twice in one day,' I said, coming up behind him.

James's face paled and he stepped back from the taxi door. 'Scott,' was all he could say as it dawned on him why someone was sat in his taxi.

'Nice evening? I'm sure you have. Where's the lovely girlfriend? I've had a cracking night, me and my friends haven't stopped laughing, it's been hilarious. Anyway, must dash, thanks for the taxi.' I slid past him and as Diane sheepishly went and sat in the front seat with the driver I slammed the door shut. The taxi didn't zoom away in a hurry as I wanted it to, instead leaving a couple of long awkward seconds for us to glare at each other - I looked away first. Adrenaline careered headlong around my body as we slowly moved off. I put my head back and closed my eyes. Anna put her hand briefly my shoulder.

Yellow street lamps sporadically scanned my face creating brighter images behind closed eyelids of my ex attached to another woman. A beautiful, young woman. Why couldn't she have been an ugly, fat old bitch? That would have given me the opportunity to feel superior. Is that all you can manage? I'd think. Is that what separation has given you? Well good luck. I'm better looking. Ha! A pathetic slither of triumph. Instead I saw him undressing her lovely slim body with shaking hands, eyes heavy with longing. Stop it, stop it. My eyes flew open. Bastard. That was it, I hated him. She could have him. He could become her problem; she could deal with the selfish git, deal with his cold, off-hand demeanour, his childish tantrums, his lies, his odd disappearances. I relinquished all responsibility. It actually felt quite liberating.

Diane turned in the front seat with a large grin on her face and said. 'I had a great time tonight, we should do this more often.'

Chapter 8

James is seeing another woman, you kissed a schoolboy, you could be arrested, divorce imminent, you were sick, you told him, huh? James looked good, his girlfriend was a stunner. He was out with the friends you once shared. Divorce imminent, divorce imminent, divorce, divorce.

I rolled over in bed the next morning in an attempt to dispel the manic, stock-market behaviour going on in my head but it was no use and, after a few false starts and some 'f' and 's' words, I got up. I threw myself into the shower where hot, gushing water found signs of life and, capitalising on this, I ate four crumpets, took two paracetamol and played Verdi's 'Requiem' at high volume.

The evening had fizzled out with Diane bouncing happily with flirtatious thoughts, alcohol and stockings through her front door, me refusing Anna's offer of her spare room, preferring to cry in the privacy of my own bed, Anna waving at me from the back of the taxi having urged me to meet her for lunch next day.

Now I felt ready to take on the world. I wanted to find a flat, change my job, dye my hair, get fit, become beautiful, have my teeth whitened, and unearth a boyfriend from somewhere (ooh, Lawrence). Apart from adding Lawrence into the mix, it was pretty much the standard knee-jerk response to James' behaviour with all the staying power of paper underpants. I karate-chopped the armchair and then apologised to it.

The doorbell wouldn't have been heard had it not been for Roger. James looked at me from the other side of the pale-green glass door panel which made him look sick.

'Hi, Grace. Hi, Roger. Can I come in?' God, he was good at using the humbled approach, he actually was pale green.

'Yes, as long as you're not going to tell me how bad things are for you,' I replied, defiantly opening the door further to allow him in.

Roger gave one last bark and led the way to the kitchen, misconstruing where we were going and so missing out on any further involvement.

I led James into Dad's small office from where he undercharged his clients, and pushed papers to one side of the computer desk to park myself on the edge. James rolled a worn swivel chair a safe distance from me and sat down. I waited expectantly for him to wangle his way out of last night's fiasco.

'I've called to try and sort things out once and for all. I just want you to know, first and foremost, that Simone and I have just only started to see each other; in fact I only met her last week so it's not been a long-term thing or anything like that. And she's not the reason why I've sought divorce either, I was thinking of you when I did that so that you could get on with your life.'

'You're a truly saintly man. And there's me thinking you were a self-centred git. James, you really stink of bullshit.'

'No, I don't. It's Hugo Boss.'

'Ha, ha, not from here it isn't. Do I have dickhead written on my forehead?'

'No honestly, it's an aftershave.'

'Be serious.'

'I am. I miss you, Grace.'

'That's nice.'

'No, I really do.'

'Is this you trying to sort things out once and for all? What are you trying to do to me, James? What d'you want me to say?' I couldn't believe what I was hearing.

108

'Sorry?' He looked hopeful.

'What? Am I missing something? You want me to say sorry? Sorry for what? Not being perfect? Not being more independent? Not carrying on the way we were? I'm not the one who's found someone else.'

'I saw you last night.' He made it obvious what he was implying.

'What?' Admit nothing, just look guilty.

'Tonsil hockey on the dance floor with someone half your age.'

'If you mean having a drunken snog I ... Oh, no you don't. Don't try turning this around.'

'I'm just saying, we're both...'

'No, no, we're not both anything. I kissed a teenager at a club, something I regretted while it was happening. You are seeing someone else and have been for God knows how long. In fact, if I'm honest, I don't want to know how or when you met, because if you *did* tell me the truth I think I'd have to set the dog onto you.'

'I meant what I said about missing you, things just aren't the same.' His game-plan would have possibly worked six months ago, but not now.

'Okay, I give up. When will this end, James? I know this sounds mercenary but all I want from you now is the money you owe me from the equity on the house. I've held back because I stupidly thought you weren't coping without me, but seeing you last night ... well...'

'I have the cheque here. It's for the full amount; I've had to take out a loan...'

'Stop. Stop it. I don't want to know! You're doing it again! I won't be made to feel guilty for what I'm entitled to.'

We stared at each other. James eventually looked away and withdrew a cheque from his jacket pocket and handed it over to me. This was it. This was the end.

'That's probably the longest conversation we've had in years. If only you could have been more honest with me sooner I could have moved on by now. Look, I'm finding this very difficult ... but I have to tell you I'm not going to sign the divorce papers. Not because I don't want to, but because of what's on them. If they can be toned down a bit I'll reconsider and make life easy for both of us. You know and I know that what is on them is far from the truth and I just can't sign it.' I'd said my piece. 'And also we need to look into getting my name off the mortgage.'

'Talking of which, you need to change your surname.' He afforded the magnitude of his remark to that of changing a light bulb. His mouth carried on moving; I wasn't listening.

Change my name? I liked being Grace Scott, if for no other reason than it made people smile. Everyone knew me as Grace Scott. I loved my parents dearly but I didn't want to go back to Wentworth, it put me at the bottom of any list. I tuned in again properly on, 'The mortgage bit is harder because I'm self-employed and I've got to prove I can manage it on my own, which is easier said than done. You'll be all right, you work in a bank.' James stood up. 'I'd better go. Are your mum and dad and the rest of the family okay? Is your dad still doing jobs for nothing for waifs and strays? I've got a wiring job for him if he is. Say hello to them for me.'

'I will, and same to your family.'

James made for the front door. 'Bye, Roger,' he called. 'Is he still humping cushions?'

'Not now, he's getting on a bit, libido not quite what it was.' I swallowed heavily dragging tears back. 'Maybe along with changing my name we should change his back to Prince.'

I held the door open for James and watched him walk down the drive. He turned and waved; I waved back and closed the door. Empty, I sat down on the settee and looked out of the patio window onto the sun-dappled, leaf-strewn lawn. A fly had made it into the living room and was buzzing and head-butting the window with mounting confusion.

If I was to make sense of the last thirteen years I would have to make sure I learnt from the mistakes made. Lesson one was never to get involved with a man again. Extreme and boring, nevertheless a worthy rule to set as a bench mark. Lesson two was to never allow anyone close enough to cause damage, this I was sure I would pass with flying colours. Lesson three was to make sure I kept a lid on any expectations, ultimately safeguarding disappointment. Roger came and parked his bony rear on my foot. My eyes drooped. I started quickly and glanced at the clock on the mantelpiece, lunch with Anna! With a great deal of effort, I released the fly to freedom then changed out of the sloppy, comfortable track-suit which had never seen the stresses of a keep-fit class and changed into jeans and a jumper. I rooted around in my bag for any change from the night before and made a mental note that I should be back for half three to greet Rebecca, who, if living by her usual creed of obsessive punctuality, would be at the front door with luggage at four. She was ostensibly coming to see Mum and Dad because she hadn't been home for some time but was hoping to get to see Mary at some stage in Birmingham too. Her two sons and daughter were all at school and wouldn't be seeing the family till Christmas.

I was quite unprepared for the scene that confronted me when I parked in Anna's wide driveway in Carpenters Road. Objects were floating, or plummeting in the case of heavier items, from the upper windows onto the flowerbeds in the front garden. The next-door neighbour stood blatantly watching the show from his front door. There was a moment of dithering once out of the car where I nodded at Anna's neighbour, he nodded back, and waved at Anna from her upstairs window as she launched a suit and a towel with 'his' embroidered on it with a downward trajectory that must have pulled her arm out of its socket.

She disappeared from the bedroom window and reappeared at the front door, her face telling a story without the lips moving, betrayal and vengeance featuring highly along with unbridled anger. I tripped over the doorstep and she slammed the door shut with such ferocity it made the walls tremble. Unsure what to say I asked her if she was all right. She eyed me sardonically then led the way into the kitchen, finding it hard to muster words of any coherent content.

'Fucking bastard, fucking, fucking bastard.' She rammed the lead into the back of the kettle, sending water shooting out of the spout. 'Aargh.' Covering her face with clawed hands, pressing her nails into her forehead she presented a defeated figure.

I went to her and put my arm round her to convey solidarity. The kettle boiled at which point Anna lifted her head and automatically went to sort some coffee out. She slopped milk onto the counter top and lobbed sugar haphazardly into the cups.

'He's having an affair. Not just a one-off mind you, oh no, this has been going on for ages, so while good old wifey here has been sat at home trying to save the marriage, he's been off shagging her in nearly every hotel in Britain.'

I expressed disbelief. She handed me something that resembled soup rather than coffee then went to stand looking out of the kitchen window with shoulders so brittle they might snap if touched.

'He doesn't know I know his computer password. I don't know why I did it but I went into his email account this morning, and it's there for all to see, where he's going to meet her, what he's going to do to her when they do meet, everything apart from the hotel name. I know they're somewhere in York. He hadn't even bothered deleting some of the messages from, and to, her. It's sick reading. I knew something was wrong. I've crucified myself over the fact that I don't want him to touch me or come near me. I've not gone back to work and stayed at home, for what? So he could happily sow his wild oats elsewhere. I'm so fucking angry, I want to rip his head off. He let me try to save the marriage while having an affair. What sort of arsehole does that? I just can't believe it.'

I stared down at my distorted reflection in the cup of coffee in my hands and sipped the revolting concoction without comment. Anna remained staring out of the window. I took in the fact that the opulence that reigned in the bedroom did not transcend to the kitchen. It was as basic as possible and nothing seemed to match, it was as though it had all been thrown together and told to make the most of it. My eyes were drawn to a display of ornamental china plates sitting on a heavy-duty picture rail, and to one in particular of a God-awful painting depicting the head of a mad-eyed cairn terrier.

'When are the children due back?' That plate was seriously disturbing me.

'Tonight, but I'll ring his parents and ask them to keep hold of them a while longer. I've not finished yet, there's more stuff to go out of the window. All of it has to go. Donald next door is nursing a semi with excitement, keeping his wife abreast of the situation.'

'When's Peter due back?'

'Tomorrow.' She couldn't stand still. 'Look, I'm really sorry, I don't want to drag you into this but I need a proper drink. I need to get out of this house, come to the pub for one so I can think straight?'

'Okay.'

She marched out of the kitchen on a mission and a few seconds later I heard her speaking on the phone upstairs but couldn't quite make out what was being said. Life was never dull when Anna was involved; she had an innate ability for causing chaos for good or bad every time we met. There was no way this lady was meekly going to accept her husband's behaviour or let him get away with it. James who, up until I arrived at Anna's, had taken up all my thoughts, was now given little or no room. I stared at the maniacal terrier plate, it stared back at me. I was sure it moved.

Anna came back into the kitchen. 'I still can't get hold of him on the phone. His parents are going to keep the children tonight. Where's my purse?'

I followed her out of the house, observing how the scattered clothing was now attached to bushes further down the garden, fluttering in the light autumn breeze and some of which was heading towards the front gates in a bid to escape. Anna smirked at the chaos around her and greeted her neighbour Donald, who was hovering on his front doorstep, with a friendly hello, preferring to pretend she was off shopping rather than falling to bits. He, in turn, headed quickly back indoors to update his wife.

Anna sat in the passenger seat of my car for the short distance to the pub as if balanced on a clothes line. The pub was scattered with Sunday diners. We collected our respective drinks, one double gin and tonic and a large glass of orange juice, and found a spare table.

Once seated, Anna spoke again. 'I don't want him back in the house. He can go and live with Nina the Hyena instead. Nina the fucking Hyena,' she repeated to herself.

'Nina? Do you know her?'

'Know her? She's a work colleague of his. I've had the bitch and her husband round for dinner. I cooked them braised pork pot-au-feu; in my kitchen! I'm vegetarian.'

'She's married?'

'Jonathon Reece-Cracken.'

Blank look.

'Councillor.'

'Oh.'

'I've left a message on his answering service. The shit is well and truly going to hit the fan when he picks it up and finds out his wife's having an affair. You know, I was going to drive to York to try and catch them. Jesus, I'm glad I didn't because if I'd found them I'd have been arrested for GBH. I would have gone too, after throwing his things out of the window, but you turned up so, thanks for saving me the journey, and thanks for helping me out of jail.' Her glass was almost empty.

The doors to the pub banged open and a keyboard entered, for all the world as if wandering in on its own for a pint, until its owner followed through the interior doors.

'Oh look, it's Lawrence,' Anna observed.

I looked properly and briefly noted the pleasing sight of Lawrence Wilding wearing a Beatles T-shirt and jeans. A man followed with mousy, untidy hair falling over his face making it hard to tell the front from the back, pushing what looked like large speakers and an amp. Fresh, clean air breezed in with them. Two more men entered; one extremely tall and nearly as wide carrying a double bass case the other small and stocky, hauling cables, a small case and a cymbal. After depositing their gear in a cordoned-off part of the pub they all headed straight for the bar. I turned back to Anna who had finished her drink and was stabbing at her mobile.

'One more drink then I'll have to go.'

A loud crash announced the entrance of the drummer laden with cases. I headed for the bar and found a gap at the far end, putting a great distance between myself and Lawrence and his friends. Not enough it seemed though, he waved over at me as I was being served, and shouted. 'Good to see you, Grace.'

'Hi.' I smiled shyly and looked away choosing to remain aloof by wearing a fascinated expression gazing at a crusty old postcard of Blackpool Tower hanging on the bar wall. With heated chest and cheeks I walked back to Anna with the drinks, only too aware that his band mates were all having a good look as I went.

'I still can't get through to him. What is it with telephones? What's the point in having one if you don't use it? I'll have to go in a minute, I can't settle. I'll have to get the locks changed, and I've not finished destroying his stuff yet.'

From the time I'd called at Anna's I'd hardly said a word, I didn't really need to as sounding boards rarely, if ever, give advice. I just wished that she could get through to Peter before she exploded. It seemed that my prayer was to be answered when she dialled his number and finally managed to get a response. Her hand shook but her voice was low and strong.

'You lying, cheating low-life is all I have to say to you. Fuck you and fuck Nina, oh sorry you are. The locks are changed and your belongings will be in the garden if they haven't been stolen by the time you get back from your sordid shag fest. I'll see you in court.' She flung the phone onto the table and took a large mouthful of gin and tonic. 'Don't look round but here's Lawrence,' she added and smiled encouragingly at him as he made his way over. I could only marvel at her composure.

'Are you here for good seats for tonight's performance?' he asked, drawing up a chair and sitting down.

'Could be. Are you any good?' Anna asked.

'You've never heard the Nota Gains play before have you?'

'That doesn't answer my question does it?' she answered.

'Well, we've got a recording contract and hopefully we'll be touring America next year.'

Anna's phone lit up and started buzzing.

'That's if we can get Sangster a work permit and convince Shrubby to leave his kids.'

I was torn between listening to Lawrence and watching Anna, who rose from her seat and walked outside.

'Was it something I said?' he asked.

'It's an important call. What sort of music do you play?'

'Blues/jazz.'

'Jazz? I love Chris Barber and Monty Sunshine. Any of theirs?'

'Not really. The Shrubster may though in his spare time. We write a lot of our own music, and put our own slant on well-known stuff. So, have I tempted you to come tonight?'

'I don't think I'll be able to make it. I've got my sister coming to stay.'

'Bring her along too,' he said. His eyes never wavered from mine. 'Anna's told me you're a bit of a pro on the clarinet and it'd be good to get your verdict, see what you think. We'll dedicate a song to you if you turn up.'

'I'll try, as long as you don't dedicate 'Hey Fatty Bum Bum' or something like that if I do manage to get here.'

'So you *have* seen us play before. Hey, Shrubby, sorry, we can't do the Fatty Bum Bum number tonight,' Lawrence said as the short, stocky man I presumed was Shrubby strolled over.

'What?'

'Grace this is Trevor, commonly known as Shrubby. He plays the clarinet too so you'll have to come and see us now.' Shrubby and I glanced at each other as his logic bypassed us both.

Anna came back into the pub shaken and pale. 'I'll have to go.'

'You okay?' Lawrence asked. His lovely face looked concerned.

'Know a good solicitor?' She finished her gin in one gulp and picked up her bag.

'Oh, err.' He suddenly found his knee very interesting.

'Break a leg tonight and see you in the week.' She was already on her way out.

I quickly said goodbye and Lawrence followed us as we headed for the exit as if seeing us out of his home. He laid his hand lightly on my shoulder as he quietly said in my ear, 'Seven thirty.' Overcome by his interest in me, I was all over the place. Lesson one dumped in a matter of hours. I couldn't resist turning to look in through the window and caught Shrubby looking back with a hesitating smile twitching at the corners of his mouth. I returned a smile without much enthusiasm before he disappeared from view. The lengthening shadows of the

118

afternoon sun lent a chill to the car park and made goose bumps stand to attention on my arms.

'Did you get to speak to him, Anna?'

'He's not owning up to it. He's on his way back to discuss things with me but is saying that Nina isn't with him and maybe one of the kids is playing a prank on us. I put the phone down on him. Can you believe it? Imagine bringing the children into this. You've been brilliant, thanks for the advice and help.'

'Anytime,' I replied, and grinned at her assuming she was being funny. It faded when I realised she wasn't.

'Do you want me to stay with you?' I loathed the idea of leaving her on her own. She shook her head.

'Sure?'

'Yes, my brother's on his way to change the locks and I've a few phone calls to make. I'll be fine.'

I pulled up outside the house. 'Ring me if you need anything.'

'Thanks, Grace. Don't worry, I've a lot to do before Peter gets back from York. Besides, you have a date tonight. I'll ring you tomorrow and you had better be telling me you made it or else.'

Chapter 9

Rebecca and I entered the pub at nine o'clock. It was difficult to get near the bar for bodies, which threw me a little bit because I'd pictured myself languidly sitting in an empty bar, at a table in front of the band with a glass of champagne while they played music for my ears only. Instead I was faced with a free-for-all.

Rebecca was three years older than I was, a lady from her lovely head down to her manicured toenails and insistent on driving and not drinking. She owned and ran a bridal shop on the outskirts of Glasgow, and had that air about her that shouted style. She had embraced the idea of going out wholeheartedly when it was put to her, as had our parents when they arrived back from Birmingham. Dad, aching with the flu and unused to being ill had shuffled off to bed. Mum had overdosed on shopping and wanted a night in with Inspector Morse. It was a wonderful welcome for Rebecca.

Before I'd gone out that evening I'd taken Dad a hot lemon drink up to his bedroom where he lay cocooned by a duvet with his head poking out of the top for air. The strong smell of Fisherman's Friend tablets fought a battle with a lavender air freshener and won.

'How are you feeling, Dad?'

He wasn't too ill to give me a look of derision. 'I've felt better.' His voice croaked two octaves lower than normal.

'You're sounding great. Can I call you Barry White?'

'No.'

'James called today, asked after you and the family.'

'Did he ask you to move back?'

'Not exactly. He gave me a cheque instead, for the full amount.'

'I'm so sorry.' He patted my hand, his was clammy. 'It's for the best, love.'

'I can look for somewhere to live now.'

'I don't know why you want to leave, your mum and I love having you here. Maybe you should stay with us until you find the 'right one'.

I raised eyebrows.

'Go on, bugger off and go and have a nice time.'

'See you in the morning, Dad.'

I couldn't look directly over to where the band was playing even though I wanted to make Lawrence aware that I'd made it. It is impossible to say why my actions were always so perverse and forever in complete opposition to what my heart desired. I can't explain why for instance, instead of confidently parking myself within his view, smile on my face, attracting lingering looks from him, my legs were compelled to take me round the other side of the pub.

We managed to find enough seats for us to both perch on next to two young girls downing shots. Rebecca went to the toilet leaving me to sit quietly, contemplating my inner-turmoil and the jazz music until the conversation next to me drew my attention.

'Fuck me, when he gets a load of what I've got to offer he won't be thinking, like, Indian takeaway I can tell you, more like English take me any way.' Girl One.

'Where are you going to do it?' Girl Two.

'At his of course, as long as the dog's not watching. Did you see the way he looked at my legs? It's in the bag. I might even give him a tit-wank if he's a good boy.' Girl One.

I choked on my drink and pretended to have a cough.

'Listen you, I'm going to have to lie through my arse later and pretend you're too sick to come to the phone when Jeremy rings, so, like, you'd better make it worth it. Say he finds out?' Girl Two, giggling.

'Er, like, how's he going to know unless I take a video and, like, show him when I get home or you tell him.' Girl One.

'How're your piercings?' Girl Two.

'Fine, it makes fellatio better so when I suck his dick it'll heighten his pleasure. You can put your eyes back in their sockets now you nosey old cow, we're going to the bar, see ya!'

Holy Crap, she was talking to me. I don't know if it was because she'd called me old or because I'd been caught listening that ashamed me more. I didn't know where to look or what to say so I snorted and turned my head away as though I hadn't heard properly. Only one other person seemed to have heard her comment and that was a young lad sitting at the next table who hadn't taken his eyes off Girl One's legs throughout.

'Class, not.' He spoke across his mate's back to me.

I shrugged. 'Lucky Fellatio, hey?' At which he snorted into his pint.

'Grace, what are you saying?' Rebecca asked in a hushed tone coming to sit beside me with another drink. She mouthed the word fellatio and gave a quick demo. For some reason I'd gone into the realms of doublet, hose and Shakespeare.

'Oh God.' We both started sniggering. 'Oh, Fellatio, Fellatio, wherefore art thou, Fellatio?'

'"Though this be madness, yet there is method in it", Hamlet.' Rebecca quoted.

I wracked my brains. '"The lady doth protest too much, me thinks", Hamlet?'

122

'Ooh, ooh, I know, "Take you me for a sponge?" Hamlet again. I can't remember any more. Did we both only do Hamlet at school?'

'"Oh, Edmund, can it be true? That I hold here in my mortal hand, a nugget of purest green?" Blackadder.' My wit amused me at least. I told Rebecca what had happened.

'What a pair of slappers.' She sighed. 'Girls grow up so quickly. Trying to keep a grip of what Kirsty's up to is nigh on impossible. She wants a bloody Brazilian now and a boob job when she's sixteen. Why? I've told her no way, she's beautiful as she is. I go on and on about contraception and hope she's sensible. It's not like it was in our day, snogging and love-bites.' Kirsty, my niece, was coming up to fifteen, looked eighteen, behaved twenty-four.

I cast my mind back to when we were younger. 'I'm pretty certain, when you were fifteen you were still prancing around to Les Sylphides wearing a tutu and huge, school regulation navy knickers, with me and Natalie in black leotards behind you. You wanted to be in the Three Degrees, remember, until we forced Dad to break it to you that you were tone deaf.'

'I was devastated, I'd always fancied myself as a pop star till then. Owning your own shop doesn't have the same ring to it as 'pop-princess'. I've had to make do with being a 'shop diva' instead. How's life, living back at home?'

'Great, meals ready for me when I get in from work, company in the evening. The only thing is that at some stage I'm going to have to buy or rent a place because I'm not going to grow up if I don't try to fend for myself. Dad doesn't see it that way but I can't stay there forever.'

'Poor Dad, he looks poorly at the mo. I'd like him to come and re-wire the shop when he's better. We're coming to stay-over Christmas night. The kids love it.'

'Really? Aren't they trying to find reasons not to come, and wangle it to party with friends instead?'

'No, believe it or not, they love Christmas at Mum and Dad's.'

'Oh God, Christmas. It's going to be really odd without James.'

'You're better off alone, I'm sorry. Anyway, how are you coping without him?'

'Better now than at the beginning. I mean, I've had to get out there and find a new life which, when you've got no self-confidence to start with, is difficult. I used to hide behind James and now I can't. Like us sitting here for instance, I should be waving at the band but look where I am. I can't blame him; I think I've always been like this.'

'There's too many can'ts for my liking and you think too much that's your problem,' Rebecca said.

'So I've been told. Shall I get another drink?'

The pub was rocking. I fought my way to the bar and stayed out of sight around the corner; I was a shrinking violet even though I didn't want to register as one. On the contrary, I wanted to get up there with the band and join in with my clarinet but the reality was that I would remain hidden and leave without so much as a ta-tar.

It was as I was pushing my way back to Rebecca that I heard the dedication made by Lawrence.

'This next song is for Grace Scott, who earlier on today asked us to play the great classic 'Hey Fatty Bum Bum'. Now much as we would love to dedicate this to her, we feel we could do much better in finding something more appropriate. We know where you are Grace and this is for you.'

I could hear Rebecca laughing as I walked the walk of an old soak back to the table with a face the colour of Ribena. What the hell must Lawrence think of me? I felt conspicuous in a spotlight only the mortified bask in, but at the same time felt my insides floating from their rightful positions as the band started to play 'I'm in the Mood for Love'.

Rebecca childishly shoved me in the arm with her elbow. Although I squirmed in embarrassment, the grin on my face must have exposed teeth normally only seen by the dentist. We both sat and listened until the song was over.

Rebecca was the first to talk. 'I think someone has an admirer.'

'Oh my God, I can't speak,' I said, speaking. In my head the words to the song floated like an echo. 'I'm in the mood for love, simply because you're near me'. Did I really do that to him or was it just dedicated because it was the next song on their play list?

'There's no point remaining here, come on you, enough of sitting here out of the way. I want to meet the man singing that song to you,' Rebecca said, standing up.

By this time I was away with the fairies, in a land where fluffy clouds replaced flooring and invisible ribbons of love pulled me off the ground. Rebecca remained standing, clutching the drinks and I floated off to the ladies. I breezed through the door to hear first, then see Girls One and Two applying lipstick in front of the mirrors.

'She's probably an old troll so don't worry about it. It's probably his aunty or something, or maybe it's to do with one of the other lads.' Soothing.

'Don't be so stupid. He's never done that for me and my fucking brother is, like, his best friend.' Petulant.

'Maybe that's why.' Appeasing.

'Well she'll have to get past me first to get to him.' Fighting.

A toilet flushed and drowned out any further conversation I may have heard. So, it appeared that Fellatio was Lawrence and I was going to have a scrap on my hands with a gorgeous but foul-mouthed bird tonight if I thought of going anywhere near him. It was like being back at school but nothing could take away the romance that had unexpectedly happened my way. I found Rebecca and let her lead the way nearer to the band, there being no point in pretending I was unaware of what had taken place. We were shoved from all angles, our drinks remaining by default within their confines, but at last I could watch Lawrence amongst all the heads and bodies and appreciate his obvious magnetism. The rest of the band gelled so completely they had the public baying for more. I caught Shrubby's eye and blushed as he stared blatantly back at me, seeming to know the reason I was there, quite used to the fact that his bandleader was the target for the majority of the female population in the pub and quite possibly some of the male population also. His eyes softened before he closed them to belt out a high note. Rebecca and I joined in and whooped for more and laughed and shared in the headiness of being picked out favourably by a group that was obviously going places.

They ended the evening with a blues number written by Lawrence called 'Now you're gone' sung so intensely I heard nothing else but his voice. His passion made love to my head and led it to a dreamy scene of us lying on a fur rug in front of a golden log fire. Liberated, my hormones rampaged with, let's face it, sickly romanticism and I was having a lovely time until applause intruded.

'I take it you fancy the lead singer?' Rebecca said when the noise died down. 'You've not taken your eyes off him.'

'Don't be ridiculous. But, yes, he's a bit of alright.'

'What about the clarinet player.'

'What about him?'

'He kept looking at you.'

'How much have you had to drink?' I was back in the real world, trying desperately not to take a peek to see where Lawrence was.

'Sober.'

'And deluded. The clarinet player's married with kids. Ha, ha, ha, ha.' The moronic laugh was added for the benefit of Lawrence who at that moment was on his way over to us with a pint in his hand, grinning from ear to ear, high on adrenaline.

'You must be Grace's sister you look very alike, it's nice to meet you and I'm really glad you came. We're going for a curry. Fancy joining us? We just have to pile our stuff into the van and then we'll be ready.'

'Okay,' Rebecca said, before I could prevaricate.

'I'll just go and get everything sorted and I'll be back. Don't go anywhere.'

'You hate curry, it makes you sick,' I muttered to Rebecca when he'd gone.

'If I don't go you won't will you, so I don't mind.'

There was no sign of Girl One or Two around. Maybe I'd imagined the dreadful scene from earlier. Rebecca spent the next fifteen minutes putting me off any sensible conversation with meaningful smiles. Eventually it got too much.

'Stop it.'

'Stop what?'

'Smiling.'

'I always smile.'

'Not like that you don't. See, you're doing it now.'

'I'm not doing anything.' She smiled at me.

I pinched her hand. She pinched mine.

'Ow.'

'Are you two going to have a fight? Excellent.' Lawrence came at us side-on, catching us by surprise. 'Right we're ready, Shrubby will drive us there in the van and he may come for a curry or not as the case may be.'

'It's alright I'll drive, I've only had a glass of wine. Want a lift?' Rebecca said.

So it was that Lawrence and I ended up getting out of the car in front of the Indian to hear Rebecca pipe up from behind the wheel that she was tired and had decided to go home after all. As her car disappeared round the corner I turned to see Lawrence already heading for the door, unconcerned that I'd been deserted and tagged behind him like a groupie.

It was only just brighter inside than it was out with a red ambience lending itself to a brothel-like quality. Three members of the band were already in place at a table, throwing down beer as though it was due to be rationed shortly. Lawrence led me over but before he opened his mouth a voice shouted, 'Over here at the bar, Lawrence.'

I knew who it was without looking. Finally I was going to be able to put a name to the little cow from earlier. Lawrence wandered over to her while I stood feeling a bit gormless before I decided to just sit down and order a drink from the passing waiter. Shrubby, the only one I knew, was not of the three now downing chasers. They all nodded at me, raised full pint glasses and raced each other to down in one. I was pretty impressed. Lawrence was still at the bar when Shrubby turned up and sat himself opposite me with his back to the wall.

'Have you been properly introduced? This is Sangster trumpet and percussion, Rich drums, Percy double bass, bass guitar and vocals, this is Grace. Where's his lordship?' he asked looking about for Lawrence.

'Shenaya's here, bloody stupid bastard can't keep his mouth shut, he just can't help being an arse in encouraging her.' It was Percy who answered.

'Great, pint of Guinness please,' Shrubby grabbed the waiter's attention. 'Great.' He didn't elaborate any further.

By now I felt really uncomfortable with a mixture of bitterness at being left like ragtag by my sister and regret for having said I'd bother in the first place. It had seemed like a good idea at the time. Shrubby leant forward with a look of wanting to say something without actually forming any words. I leant forward to try to catch what it was he wasn't saying so by the time he managed to ask if I'd enjoyed their performance we were practically head to head.

'I wanted to get up and join in,' I said.

'Oh, you sing don't you? I forgot.'

'I'm after your job.'

'Play the clarinet?'

'Not nearly as well as you do but if your hands should fall off one day I could fill in for you until you get better.'

'Oh no, look my hands have fallen off, now's your chance.' Shrubby held his arms above the table with his hands up his jumper sleeves.

I was still smiling when Lawrence and the little cow came to sit at the table.

'I bring provisions,' Lawrence said, depositing four bottles of red wine on the table. 'Get stuck in everyone.'

The three boys at the end of the table groaned at the sight of his companion though needed no encouragement attending to the wine and neither did little cow, who was finally introduced formally as Shenaya. We ordered food.

'Hi again.' She smirked at me. Maybe I wasn't so attentive earlier but had there been such an expanse of perfect neck and chest on show in the pub? I stared back at her through narrowed eyes and nodded, my worth not allowing me to be so two-faced as to greet her as a long-lost friend or someone I liked, when my preference would be to smack her in the mouth.

'Stunning as usual tonight, boys,' she said, mindlessly sweeping me aside.

'Yes I thought so,' Lawrence agreed, joking.

'You particularly. I was sat next to someone earlier who was more interested in, like, what I was talking about than listening to you though so I turned round and gave them a piece of my mind in the end.' Shenaya glinted in my direction.

'Surely you shouldn't have been talking in the first place then,' Shrubby said, pouring himself a glass of wine.

'I have to talk at the moment to get used to my pierced tongue, look.'

'Put it away.' Shrubby turned away and looked like he was going to be sick.

'It looks okay; does it make you dribble though?' Lawrence peered into her mouth.

'No but the one in my lip does.' She dripped so much sexual innuendo even I understood what she was implying.

'No point in condoms then, that would only rip it to shreds.'

'Never, like, have sex without a condom. Lawrence, I'm surprised at you.'

The waiter produced starters that were attacked viciously as soon as they landed on the table.

'Sex with a condom? What's that like then?' I chirped.

'Have you never, like, had sex then, are you, like, a virgin or something?' Shenaya asked, her antipathy towards me momentarily forgotten in her disbelief that an old codger like me should have gone through life without at least trying it, even going as far as to show me pity.

'Like I'm, like, old enough to be your, like, mother. When I met my ex-husband I got to know him first before, you know … it … I…' Oh God, I slithered to a halt. 'Great poppadum's.'

'Thank you,' Shrubby replied and caught my eye. Lawrence laughed and my spirits rose. The only trouble was that Shenaya was not to be deflected. As someone who I was hoping would play a very small part in my life she was doing a great job of taking it up at the moment with her incredible lack of tact. Her mission was to get Lawrence into bed or die trying. Quite how the large blob of mango chutney ended up slowly sliding down her cleavage is anyone's guess, but there it was wending its way between her breasts whilst our heroine of the minute created an Oscar-winning performance in drawing attention to her ordeal. And Lawrence? Gentleman or tart, tried to rescue the chutney by using his fingers to stop it being sucked like water down a plug hole, Shenaya squealed and wriggled on her seat in ecstasy. I didn't know whether to be embarrassed or amused at her complete lack of subtlety. If it had been done without design, it would have been highly entertaining but as this was as contrived as a dire sit-com I found myself wanting to reach for a remote control to turn her off. Unfortunately, no such item existed so I was the unwilling witness to Shenaya grabbing his hand, supposedly as a joke, and pushing it further down her top. My estimated time of departure was hastened somewhat. Dreams of a log fire, the amber light glowing through whisky in cut glass, the sheepskin rug keeping our nakedness warm all disappeared as Lawrence encouraged her behaviour. Shrubby was tucking in to the poppadum's while the rest of the band looked on with humour, generating ribald comments.

The arrival of the main meal interrupted any removal of clothing she may have been contemplating. I say this with an acid tongue for I was maybe a little jealous of the attention she was receiving. I dunked naan bread into curry so bright it could be radioactive and wondered how long I should stay before making my excuses. Shenaya pushed her food around on the plate; Lawrence did little better but did manage to gulp three glasses of wine down in quick succession then poured a fourth. Shrubby shovelled his main course down with the same conscientious approach he'd shown the poppadum's. Possibly because he was married he seemed the only man at the table who had found Shenaya's antics a bit of a bore. I found myself warming to him as an ally, a nearly bald, bespectacled comrade, especially when she tried to feed him with some of her own uneaten food and he looked at her as if she was trying to poison him. The three others quickly headed for meltdown with a vindaloo, beer, brandy-chaser recipe making the route to perfect nuclear fallout later. All this time innuendo and clever chat had been parried between all five guys. I knew drinking red wine was not a good thing, it played havoc with my brain, but my hope was that a bit of chicken curry would counteract the effect. Every now and then Shenaya would join in, with her forte being innuendo she outdid them all. I say this ironically, a smile on my face because as the red wine started its hallucinogenic sojourn I could have sworn that I, and many others, saw the majority of her arse as she bent down to adjust the strap of her stiletto before departing for the toilet.

I started to giggle loudly at her barefaced cheek, a continuous battle within promoting feelings of confidence and self-doubt scrapping each other in order to be top banana. Both Lawrence and Shrubby had grins on their faces, though I'm pretty certain their thoughts were not going through the same process as mine. I was scared of her, not scared of her hitting me or starting a fight, but scared of her crudeness because she had all the subtlety of a scud missile. I was feeling my age. Her behaviour threatened me in some way, as if superiority was hers because she had youth, the nerve to flash her bum in public, swear loudly and offer herself shamelessly with all her metal bits along for the ride. If I allowed this to continue I would end up having to consider the amoeba as a close relation and give up on being a woman. My God, I had just classed myself a woman for the first time. Encouraged, I shook my head and, letting my fringe fall in what I hoped was a provocative way, leant forward to speak to Shrubby in a subversive way of letting Lawrence know I wasn't relying on him. My line of conversation fell short of sexy and landed on plain outlandish.

'That was great but if you plugged me into the mains now I'd generate enough power to heat three small houses.'

'I'd heat Anfield,' he replied.

'Do you support Liverpool then? I do too.'

'Arsenal is the only team,' Lawrence said, before Shrubby could reply, and continued to explain why with his customary enthusiasm. I felt a bit awkward for Shrubby who sat back and let him get on with it but I was not opposed to having

Lawrence's full attention, or did he have mine, either way the full moon that had recently made a brief appearance was now forgotten. The other members of the band were now trying to pick an onion *bhaji* up with a straw, gaining uncertain looks from a young Indian waiter at their hilarity.

Lawrence originated from London, forming his first band when he was just sixteen, much to his mother's dismay who wanted him to be a doctor. After a long time, with no success and many arguments, the band split. He tried other permutations while studying music, none of them working until he moved up North after the death of his estranged father to take on the property development company left in the will to him and his brother. Lawrence and the Nota Gains got the name when he informed his mother he was putting another band together. His optimism for the band's future was infectious, engrossing, so much so that when Shenaya came back from the toilet, sitting down heavily to make us aware she was back, we glanced at her and resumed the conversation.

'How long have you been playing with the current set-up?' I asked.

Shrubby sat up and took an avid interest in the conversation.

'We'd had a problem with bloody clarinet and sax players until Shrubby turned up like a godsend. They don't come much better,' Lawrence said.

'And what's wrong with clarinet players?' I asked, pretending to be affronted.

'They keep sodding off to get married. Before Shrubby we had Johnny B, he met an Irish bird at a gig, and was married and living in Ireland before you could whistle an Irish jig. And before JB we had mad-arse Tony the Train who got done for drink driving. He ended up marrying the arresting officer, having two sprogs and moving to Spain.'

'They run some distance to get away from you. What do you do to them?' I asked.

'Okay, so I used to hit them on the head with a wooden spoon and didn't pay them, but that's normal isn't it? Shrubby's been with us a year and he positively encourages it.'

'You can spank me with your wooden spoon anytime.' Shrubby joined in at last.

'And me.' So did Shenaya. 'All covered in melted dark chocolate.'

I groaned. That was it; I'd had enough of her. Much as I liked Lawrence I wasn't prepared to compete with a twenty-year-old self-professed sex goddess for his attention so I dialled for a taxi on my, for once, fully-charged mobile.

'Here you are darlin' I've got a silver spoon and some mango chutney, will that do? Let's see that arse again.' Sangster, the man with no face, just hair shouted across the table. Childish sniggers followed.

'Get lost, dog breath.' Shenaya shouted back. It was one thing for Lawrence to drool but not for a drunk, longhaired hippie to.

I sorted out money to pay the bill, grabbed my jacket and said my goodbyes. I don't know whether it was the drink, the food, Shenaya, the company, but I was starting to feel dizzy and my head hurt. Shrubby stood up, also throwing money on the table, and asked if he could jump in my taxi. We both walked down to the front, passing a couple having a row at a table by the door.

'Good here isn't it?' I said.

'Someone will end up in the fish tank over there, they usually do.'

'Let's hope it's Shenaya then,' I said it without thinking how awful I sounded. 'I didn't mean that, only joking.' I hurriedly followed up when I realised. Lawrence passed us and went upstairs to the toilets.

Shrubby smiled at me, 'No need to apologise, I think she should be put in there to cool her down a bit, and give us a rest.'

'Maybe we should all jump in and leave her outside.'

'It's a good idea, I like it,' he nodded.

'You first.'

'Would you believe it a lamb chop's beaten me to it,' he said, our eyes following a flying chop's progress into the fish tank.

Lawrence came back down from the loos and stood with us at the door.

'I think I'll jump in your taxi too if you don't mind.'

'Where's Shenaya?' Shrubby asked.

'Erm, at the table I should think, I don't know,' he shrugged.

'Jesus Wildo, you can't just leave her with the lads.' Shrubby was walking back down the restaurant as he said this.

'I wonder what his problem is,' Lawrence said. 'I think he's in a nark.'

'Seems to be the thing in here,' I replied as more food was thrown in anger at the table nearest us. We stood and watched a large splat of green curry hit the window.

Shrubby returned with Shenaya in tow, her youthful face unable to hide the misery she was feeling at being left behind, and we quickly left. It looked like she was about to cry. Outside the night air dampened us while the atmosphere in the taxi, when it arrived, positively clouded with gloom when we piled in.

I could feel Shenaya's resentment and see the back of Shrubby's head pulsing with contained anger while Lawrence kept up a steady torrent of conversation.

'I'll have to hear you play your clarinet at some stage. Maybe when you play in concert next?'

'Please don't, if you value your musical ear you shouldn't. I'd rather you remained in ignorance.'

'Is that a challenge?'

'On the contrary, it's a health warning.'

'Shrub, your place in the band sounds like its safe.'

This comment was greeted with silence.

'I think I've pissed him off, what do you think Grace?'

I didn't want to get involved in their disagreement. 'The weather is very inclement for this time of year,' I said, trying to remain light-hearted.

'Are you sure your dad's not Michael Fish? The weather is a popular topic of conversation for you. I can feel that there are some isobars heading in this direction but warm fronts from here should eventually push through to bring bright sunshine for us all.' As Lawrence said this, his hands moved like a weather forecasters from Shrubby being an isobar to himself then on to me on warm fronts, lightly brushing the part of my jacket my left breast hid beneath.

Shrubby stopped the taxi driver. 'Just here, mate thanks. Nice meeting you, Grace, you're a very nice person.' He took hold of my hand and placed a fiver in it for the taxi. He departed without saying goodbye.

Shenaya was very quiet. There was no sexy talk now. She had her arms folded, her head facing the window, her long legs crossed away from me. Lawrence on the other side of me was relaxed with his right arm along the back of the seat. My head wanted to settle into his shoulder, my brain denied me the pleasure.

'I think I'm next, just up here on the right,' he said. He slowly moved his arm away before placing another fiver in my hand.

'Thanks for coming to see us tonight,' he said, and lightly kissed my cheek.

'I'll get out here too,' Shenaya said, clearly not wishing to prolong her time in my company and, forgoing any kind of monetary obligation for the taxi, she swiftly closed the door behind her with a thump.

I was relieved she'd gone but I couldn't help wondering if she was now going to follow Lawrence and do all the things she'd said she was capable of earlier. I was so perturbed by the thought I wanted to ask the taxi to wait so I could find out if she did trail after him, but my dignity gave my home address so I would never know.

Chapter 10

I was going nowhere the next day or the day after that. The dizziness from the previous night flowered into the flu. Groaning helped, groaning was good. Mum groaned too. Dad felt too ill to groan. The house reeked of illness. Rebecca did her best as nursemaid, phoning my work, banking my large cheque, serving lemon drinks with paracetamol until Natalie came to her rescue and took her away. Left to our own devices, we managed to pop pills to bring down our temperatures with an occasional shudder to the bathroom and back.

Thoughts of James and the pay-off, Anna's marital problems, Lawrence's behaviour, Shenaya's bum, my jealousy and Shrubby's kindness all produced a seething, chaotic mass behind a fevered brow; flashed arses supplanted by pornographic images, kindness by unrequited love and jealousy by bitter rivalry. I temporarily shoved it all to one side to concentrate on being ill properly, which in my case lasted four days. Mum was hovering between bouts of tiredness but Dad remained exclusively to his bed.

As I started to feel better, my concern focused on Anna and whether she had forgiven Peter or not. I'd last seen her wading her way through his clothing in the garden. I vaguely remembered that Rebecca had said someone called Anna had phoned but, as that had been at the height my fever and I had been convinced that giant turkeys were taking over the world, I was possibly making that one up. I phoned her Saturday morning. There was no answer so I tried calling Diane on her mobile number.

'Hello, babe, you all right?' Diane answered, cheerfully.

'I've had that awful flu that's going round, but I'm getting better. I was just wondering if Anna was okay. The last time I saw her she was having a few problems. Have you seen her at all?'

'Absolutely, I saw her at choir practice Wednesday and spoke to her yesterday. She's okay. There's been a bit of trouble, you know, weird phone calls, man with a grudge, police.'

'*Police*?'

'Nothing to worry about, just a drive by really, no-one arrested. Tell you what, I'm calling round to see her later today, I think she's getting her hair done this morning. Fancy meeting up? If you're up to it that is?'

It was agreed to meet up at three that afternoon at Anna's.

After imagining all kinds of scenario's from the police waving as they drove past Anna's house to an all-out raid, shouting, gun shots, body armour, thoughts then turned to the late-night curry a week ago at which tensions had been thrown about as forcibly as the food had. Recollection was a little less messy now that the fever had gone. Lawrence was out of order wandering off, leaving Shenaya at the table without even saying goodbye. Shrubby did the right thing in going to get her, even if I thought she was a horror. But then, Lawrence was so easy going and couldn't help it if his fans threw themselves at him; he was the leading man, the artist, the musical driving force, the inspiration, the sex appeal of the band, and he needed someone mature like Shrubby to smooth over disagreements, to act as his better judgement.

The song dedication – that was unexpected. It made me smile until I remembered that Shenaya's departure had coincided with Lawrence's and doubt crept in. She was so young and, it had to be grudgingly admitted, a bit of a stunner. I wondered if I was reading too much into the choice of song played for my benefit, too eager to find a bit of romance.

I dragged myself into the shower and shoved on the first items of clothing that came to hand. I honestly have no idea who the offensive puke-yellow jumper belonged to, oh yeah it was mine, bought because it was a bargain. Honestly, like mother like daughter. What with chequered brown and pink pants, I resembled an Andy Warhol print.

Dad was looking a bit perkier but couldn't shift the chesty cough debilitating him to a huddled wreck with each onset. I reassured him that half the country seemed to be suffering in the same way, which comforted him not in the least.

Rebecca called round with Natalie and we all had soup for lunch. I digested this along with the news that James was now driving a Porsche 911 and had his house up for sale for more than we'd settled on. Even hearing his name hurt me. I'd thought stupidly, or had hoped, that when he'd walked away from me last week that it was over and done with. Not so. All of a sudden he had a new girlfriend, car, money to pay me off and what looked like a new home soon. Natalie not surprisingly gave vent to her outrage.

'I think you should ask for more off him.'

'I can't do that, Nat, that's the amount we agreed on,' I replied.

'Yes, but he's the one who delayed payment.'

'You were the one, not too long ago, who told me to cut my losses and run.'

'That was before I saw him today. He should be on his knees devastated he's lost you, not running round looking like he's won the lottery.'

Mum remained silent, not wanting to embroil herself into a taxing conversation she wasn't up to.

'It seems to me, he's been playing games with you. I don't know why, but something doesn't add up. Your name's still on the mortgage but he's managed to re-mortgage without your signature?' Rebecca sided with Natalie.

'All it probably means is that he's taken out a loan to sort things out. He did try to explain but, to be honest, I don't want to know. I got the money he owed me and now he's out of my life, apart from the divorce papers and they will be signed shortly. He's not the only one trying to start afresh.'

'Yes but from the look of things he's the one financially able to move on by whatever means. He's the one calling the shots.' Natalie was still fuming but kept any further opinions to herself; opinions I could see were sailing about her head in a highly decorative regatta.

'Look, at the moment I've got a friend whose husband has just been caught cheating and who's been doing so behind her back for years and who has two children who I assume are going to be devastated, so at the moment I count my blessings that I've got no children and I left, when I did, with a little bit of pride still in place.' My voice hadn't stopped for breath and had climbed throughout to top G by the time I'd finished.

'I didn't mean to upset you, I'm sorry. It just seems so unfair that's all,' Natalie soothed. 'I'm going to see Dad, won't be long.' With that, she escaped from the sitting room.

'She's really upset for you; you know what she's like. She takes after Dad. All is either black or white,' Rebecca said, picking up the bowls and plates from lunch, vanishing into the kitchen to return with fresh cups of tea.

'What sort of sister are you, anyway? Leaving me outside the Indian and buggering off,' I said.

'I think a very good one. I wanted to make sure you went. Just earlier that evening you'd been going on about finding it difficult getting out there, so I helped you on your way.'

'You could have stayed.'

'I'd have cramped your style.'

'Cramped my style? What style? We just talked about football, the band, finding clarinet players and … clarinet. SHIT! Beryl. What time is it?'

'Are you calling me Beryl?'

'No, what's the time?'

'Twenty past one, why?'

'Shit. Audition. I've gotta go.' I raced upstairs as fast as my jelly legs allowed me and grabbed my clarinet. I'd not even sorted out any music. How could I have forgotten? I'd left it far too late to cancel and re-arrange without looking like I was unreliable before I'd even got to meet the woman. Without further thought I wobbled at pace downstairs, shouted bye and ran out of the house.

Twenty minutes later and nearly half an hour late I was ushered in to Beryl's cool, beautifully appointed pastel 'Rose Cottage' like a psychedelic antonym, sweaty, exhausted and very apologetic.

Beryl was nothing like I'd expected which further increased my awkwardness. From the sound of her on the phone I'd pictured a rotund, sweet fifty-five year old with glasses and a penchant for chocolate digestives and maybe some dirt in her finger nails from gardening. The elegant woman with long blonde floating tresses and trailing silk scarves who led me into her flowery sitting room defied aging, she introduced me to her fellow musician, a frowning man whose name I've long since forgotten. Under normal circumstances she would have been a lovely ethereal visage of musical delight but as her smile suggested accusation for being late rather than approval for turning up at last, she frightened me.

Is it really necessary to detail quite how awful the audition went? Well, if it is, I'm not going to; even thinking about it makes me cringe. My head throbbed throughout and my nose watered like a melting ice cap, making concentration impossible. Instead of getting better, the sound I managed to produce steadily got worse with growing tension. Should I blame the flu or was I just incapable of getting to grips with nerves when it came to auditioning, one of those could-have-been's ready to blame everyone else for my shortcomings?

It wasn't a long audition, it couldn't finish fast enough. I was told they'd let me know as soon as possible, they still had a few more people to see but I couldn't help notice disappointment in Beryl's face. Suffice to say my embarrassment was so great I couldn't wait to leave; I almost sprinted out of the door and to the car. After hitting my forehead against the steering wheel a couple of times I made for the beach, holding back tears of frustration and watched the tide retreat from the shore.

The last hour had had madness written all over it, all of my own making. I'd panicked and not thought it through properly before hurling myself out of the house. How had I forgotten the audition in the first place and what had possessed me to try and impress while still under the influence of flu? I should have explained I'd been poorly, given her the option of re-arranging if necessary.

I sighed. Sometimes, after an audition or interview, you can try and convince yourself that you weren't that bad and use that optimism to tell yourself there were some good moments, allowing you to step up and imagine more good moments than bad, moving without much argument to no bad moments and being a winner. But not today. Unless every other bugger who'd auditioned totally failed to deliver, I'd not be playing in Beryl's quintet.

It was after three and time to call in on Anna. Did I really want to go? Part of me wanted to stay and freeze to death in the car, but it was only a teeny weeny part because the sane side of me had automatically reached to turn the engine on.

Life looked perfectly normal outside Anna's house, no strewn clothing, no police tape, just a fine, grey drizzle to decorate everything with a damp gossamer sheen.

Anna was boiling a kettle for some tea and trying to locate where the cat poo smell was coming from. We both wandered round the kitchen sniffing and found it behind a loose kick board, nowhere near where the litter tray lay undisturbed.

'Bloody cat,' she said, putting a pair of marigolds on.

I left her to it and joined Diane who was reading a magazine by the fire in the sitting room. The children were all playing upstairs evidenced by the loud bangs and occasional screeches of high-jinks that would no doubt end in tears.

We got down to discussing what had gone on in the last week, we had a good moan about how ill we'd all felt in one way or another from aching limbs, headaches and period pains, that was me, to backache and sciatica, Diane, and piles, Anna. There is no getting away from the fact that age can, in some respects, be defined by ailments suffered and then corroborated by a need to air them.

Peter had come back to find his belongings in the garden and rather than cause trouble had rounded it all up and thrown every last bit into his car with Donald openly watching on from next-door. Discourse had taken place between Anna and Peter, looking at each other through the front room window on mobiles.

'It was the most surreal conversation I've ever had. A stereo confession. He ended up in tears, apologising for lying and for upsetting me. I'm not upset. I don't think Jonny boy took it that well but he needed to know that his wife was cheating on him. It's probably the reason I ended up having to call the police to get him off the front doorstep shouting threats through the letterbox. Donald, next door, nearly had his whole body out of the window to watch what was going on. I think the silent phone calls since then are linked. Anyway, Peter has been extremely magnanimous and has agreed to pay the mortgage until we find somewhere else to live while he stays at his mother's. Nina was kicked out but, apparently, she's been taken back. I know Jonathon Reese-Cracken well, if he wasn't standing for election for council leader he'd have made sure she never stepped foot through the door again. So, now Peter's on his own.'

'If he asked, would you have him back?' I wanted to know.

Anna thought for a second before replying. 'No. If I was the one caught having an affair, I wouldn't expect him to take me back. I think I'd lose all respect for him if he did. It's over, that's it. No point crying about it.'

'Have you cried at all?' I asked. I had Rachmaninov's Second Piano Concerto in C minor (or 'Miss You Nights' by Cliff if time was of the essence) as my weeping companion. There was no point in holding back. Get it all out on a good crying sesh.

'Are you kidding?' Anna's face contorted to that of a rebellious sixteen-year-old in front of a querulous headmistress.

'The only reason I could find to cry if I really tried would be that I found out about his affair long after it had been going on.'

'Absolutely. Good for you,' Diane agreed.

'Crying is good,' I said. 'Without crying I'd have probably tried to do away with myself.'

They both looked shocked.

'Sometimes I cry so hard I have no energy for anything else. What I mean is ... I'll never forget feeling so low I just wanted to end it all and desperately crying my heart out like I was emptying everything out of my body and after that, for some reason, I looked at life from a different perspective. From wishing I was dead I was glad I was alive and found a new starting point to carry on from. I haven't explained that very well, but, I think, sometimes you have to hit the bottom before you can find what it is you want. Listen to me, Grace Freud. Seriously Anna? You've not shed shit-loads of tears or even a poopa-scoopa of one?'

I was a little worried that my friend didn't know what had hit her yet. I wasn't a professional divorcee, or anything, but her lack of emotion made me feel that, for the last nine months, either I'd been wearing the largest drama drawers ever known to mankind or she was in for a shock.

'No.'

'I'm sorry, but that's not normal.'

'Not everyone's like you, Grace. It doesn't mean I'm heartless because I'm not crying. I feel free for the first time in years so why should I cry? Yes, I loved Peter once but we've changed and the moment I found out about the affair, well that was it, I knew I didn't love him anymore. Anyway, I'm not forgetting him and the past, I'm just looking forward.'

'Bloody hell, missus,' Diane admired. 'You're one strong lady. What can you see ahead of you?'

'Well for a start, any job, passing the last of my exams then maybe trying to get into politics in some way. What else can I see, hmm, lots of sex, meeting Jeremy Clarkson, having his love child. I can't wait. I'm going to join the choir committee and cause chaos because I can, and I'll get Fergal to join the choir for entertainment value. Talking of which, how did your date with Lawrence go?'

'I'm sorry, Jeremy Clarkson? What's that all about?' I asked, to which Anna just shrugged her shoulders sheepishly. I rolled my eyes in disbelief and continued. 'That was no date I went on. It was shared with the pub, Shenaya, a full moon and fellatio.' I went on to give a brief outline of what had happened. 'Another thing that worries me is the conversation about condoms. I was serious when I asked what sex was like with a condom. I've never seen a love scene in a film were the man plops one on before getting down to business. I know it doesn't but, does it hurt? Is it really off-putting waiting, and do people lose interest by the time it's been fitted?' The condom issue wouldn't go away in my head.

'Dear God, you make it sound like it involves pins and a tailor,' Anna said and left the room.

'You did have sex with your husband, didn't you?' Diane was looking at me curiously.

'Not you as well. Of course I did. We were at it like rabbits to begin with. I was on the pill, by the time I came off it hoping to start a family the rabbit habit had all but gone.'

'You look too virginal to have sex.'

'Thanks.'

'Don't get huffy. I'm just saying you don't look the get down and dirty type. I can't imagine you screaming your head off in front of a mirror on your hands and knees while being ridden

148

from behind, for instance. You're more the do-it-in-the-dark type.'

'I'll have you know, when we were rabbits we tried ... everything.' I sounded about ten.

'Okay. You disguise your dirty side well.' Diane said. 'I used to scream loud and proud before we had Heather. It's a good job we're detached. Tom's thrown himself off the wardrobe dressed as Tarzan, me handcuffed to the bed. That was a great night.' Her eyes followed her thoughts. 'Yes, before Heather we had fun in the bedroom.'

I tried not to think of it.

Diane started to sing something from Brigadoon, '"I used to be a rovin' lad, A rovin' and wanderin' life I had"...'

Anna came back into the room putting paid to any further rovin' Diane may have wanted to sing about. 'Here we go. One banana, one condom. Show me what you've got.'

I did.

'Not like that. Bloody hell, Grace, you'll wake up in A&E if you try that. Come here.'

'I said you didn't do dirty.'

So followed an intense condom training course lasting three minutes at which point I got fed up and ate the banana. Even if I never went to the extreme of carrying condoms in my handbag, I had enough confidence in my nature to know I would be able to resist Lawren..., any man unless they could provide safety, at least the matter had been considered and I could now put a condom on a banana, which was something. I moved on and wondered if Lawrence fancied me in the slightest.

'I'd like Grace's life at the moment.' Diane said.

'Oh God, no you wouldn't. I've just made a total show of myself in an audition. And before anyone says anything, I don't want to talk about it.'

'It can't have been that bad, I've heard you play don't forget,' Anna said.

'I can't talk about it, it was horrific. Seriously,' I added at Anna's look of disbelief.

'Come on, I know you're messing.'

'I'm not and I want to forget it ever happened, so can we move on?'

'Okay, audition aside I'd like to think that the option of decent sex, with or without a condom, was an expectation of mine rather than a distant memory, you know? Before Heather was born we'd often video ourselves having sex and end up having more sex watching it. How can things change so much? One day you suddenly realise you've not been near each other in months and it's all too much effort. Watching porn on my own is about the nearest I'm getting to sex at the moment. No-one's ever sung a song to me, not even just mucking about. He asked me where you were,' Diane said, as if reading my thoughts.

'Who? Tom? Oh, Lawrence.' I hoped I was convincing in my tone and look of surprise.

'Next time, I'm coming with you and we'll get our own back by pouring chutney into Shenaya's handbag when she's not looking,' Anna said. The cat made an entrance slinking gracefully onto Anna's knee with no sign of apology.

Diane looked sad. 'Absolutely. I wish I could come too, but Tom was really awful with me the next day after we'd gone out. I went upstairs and he was fully dressed and wide awake on the bed waiting for me so I showed him my stockings, thinking he'd be impressed, you know, but instead he just got up and walked out of the house. He didn't come back till Sunday night. It was like I'd committed a crime or something. He doesn't speak often at the best of times but honestly, the atmosphere has been hostile ever since. It's been quiet, quiet and quiet. That's not the sort of thing I do. I don't do quiet. In order to save my marriage I don't think I'll be going out very often.'

'That's hardly fair. How can you let him do that to you?' Anna said. 'He can't stop you enjoying yourself. If he doesn't like it then that's his problem, he never takes you out, never says how nice you look or encourages you in your job or your singing. When was the last time you went on holiday together? Maybe he needs a bit of encouragement from you. If you're always offhand with him he'll be the same back. You could always work the reverse psychology tactic on him by being as nice as pie, paying compliments, massaging his ego to make life easier for you.'

Diane looked doubtful. I sympathised. Massaging an ego was all well and good if the relationship was even and fair but, from my own experience, if it was only being done manipulatively to receive likewise back for a booster it wouldn't work. The egoer would end up depleted and worthless while the egoee would end up basking in an unrealistic assurance furthering the disparity between the two.

'Try it and see, you've got nothing to lose,' Anna pursued.

'He'll think I've gone mad and have me locked up, he's only waiting for the opportunity. God, I've forgotten how to initiate it, but maybe you're right, I'll give it a go, it might even do us both good.'

'Good, because I'd like you both to come to my cousin's hen party in Blackpool in three weeks' time.' Anna was already planning her nights out, organising her own life and others around her as easily as organising a shopping list.

'I've got no chance of getting away; Tom would definitely change the locks if I was to go off for a weekend.'

'Then all the more reason to use your charms on him straight away. Oh please come with me, I need to get away for a short while and it will do both of you the world of good too. Just think we'll have such a good laugh,' Anna cajoled.

An almighty crash above caused the ceiling to shudder, making us all look up then wait expectantly for the wailing of one or more child to follow in its wake.

I remained at the kerbside in the gloomy, damp afternoon as Anna trundled off in the car to the local hospital, one child stretched out on the back seat with a suspected broken ankle followed by Diane promising a MacDonald's to the other two children in her car.

For someone who cleverly marshalled everyone and everything around her, Anna lived in constant chaos. I got the impression that she was only truly happy when mad things were happening to keep her entertained, an ordered life was not for her, not when it came too easy.

Diane, on the other hand, was like a mother hen, taking charge of the children and me so that within seconds jumpers, coats, shoes were sorted and being worn, all electrical items checked, alarm set and the front door shut.

I watched them drive away and felt I'd found my strength through these two women. How? There were no sides to either of them. Any manipulation was done above board and with humour and a genuine ease and happiness took place in their company. The audition debacle, although upsetting and something that might try to mentally obstruct any further music auditions, was for the time being relegated to manageable proportions and it was with a flu-indulged giggling and happy heart, that I got in my car and drove home.

Chapter 11

The day I signed the divorce papers was one that seemed as though it should contain more than it actually did. I forget now whether it was a Wednesday or Thursday and whether the sun was shining or not, there was certainly no thunder and lightning, that I do remember. Divorce had been such a big part of my life, when the moment arrived I felt nothing, not relief, not anger, not anything. The revised insinuations of my behaviour had been toned down and, although I still sounded like a really cold cow-bag, I'd drawn a deep breath and signed. I should have petitioned ages ago, been the instigator. I should really change my surname to *mañana*.

Yes, my old house was up for sale, strangers would soon be walking through rooms I'd once graced and I only hoped they'd be happier than I had been there. The sale seemed to be the only way to get my name off the mortgage.

To add insult to injury Sandra Howard told me at orchestral rehearsal that she had been specifically asked to audition, playing the clarinet, for Beryl's quintet and had subsequently been given the position. I felt sick with jealousy.

'It will be nice to play my main instrument with professionals,' she said, confidingly to me while putting her second instrument, the flute, together. 'Mike was saying before that the standard of auditions was fairly poor.'

If she wasn't having a dig at me then her comment didn't say much for her own talent.

'Actually I was specifically asked to audition as well but I was recovering from the flu so my heart wasn't truly in it.' You bloody old bitch was what I wanted to add but didn't.

'Oh, I didn't know.' Then. 'Oh, I'm so sorry; you must think I'm dreadful.'

Yes. 'Not at all. Like I say, I wasn't well.'

'Poor you.' She tooted her flute without sympathy.

What with that, the whole signing of divorce papers and the sale of the house I wobbled occasionally off my happy path, straying into dark places suddenly, but the trip to Blackpool loomed and all around the golden autumn colours arrived to distract the eye with butterfly leaves carelessly flying about in autumn gusts of wind, only to remind me that Christmas without a partner was around the corner. See what I mean.

In a shock move to capitalise on her freedom, Anna had her hair dyed black much to her children's dismay, both of whom had recovered from falling off the wardrobe with minor twists instead of broken bones and who started to cry thinking that their mum had been usurped by an alien.

Diane kept us updated blow by blow on her moves to find Tom's kinder side. All three of us sniggered during rehearsal and were told off when she mentioned that, whilst lying in bed early on Saturday morning with Tom reading the papers before he escaped to go fishing for the day, she'd slowly undone her brushed cotton pyjama top, , and had jiggled her fine breasts at him. Tom's look of horror wasn't a reflection on her breasts it was the sight of the window cleaner, frozen into a statue, that stopped her in her tracks.

Lawrence gave me a hug in the rehearsal break and asked how I was. He showed positive signs of preference towards me but preserved a friendship level that barely hinted at sexual attraction. The song he'd sung was a distant memory, although Diane hummed it at every possible moment in his presence. He was eager to find out if I'd really enjoyed the band's

155

performance and what I thought of the choice of music played and if I thought the balance of instruments was right. Shenaya wasn't mentioned, neither was Shrubby.

Then Blackpool. It was just a typical hen party really but it changed all three of us but in different ways.

Diane had managed to get leave for Blackpool by taking her daughter to her brother's house sixty miles away on the Friday night. Her brother kindly offered to bring her back Sunday evening. This gave Tom a free weekend making it easier to gain a pass out. Anna, allowed the children to stay with their dad who had found a flat nearby to rent.

We were to meet the other hens on Saturday morning and drive up in 3 cars, seated in a four, four, three formation, eight blondes, two browns and a blackhead. There was a lot of screeching and dirty laughing with excitement as introductions were made, Marilyn, the hen, a page three pin-up and someone I wanted to hate because she was so gorgeous but couldn't because she was so nice, embraced everyone before we swooped *en masse* into the cars and made our way to the motorway. It became apparent within a short space of time that the two cars in front were causing heads to turn. We were at the rear creating nothing but wind turbulence which was not only restricted to outside.

'Anna, that bloody stinks.'

'I'm sorry.'

'What the hell have you eaten?'

'A vegetable curry pie and baked beans.'

'For breakfast?'

'I got up late. The only thing I could find to eat was last night's left over's. Did you just see that man crick his neck to get a good look at Marilyn and mates in front?'

'And that one,' I said, as another male driver and his male passenger waved their appreciation to Marilyn and her friends who responded in kind by flashing their bras.

'Bloody marvellous. Why did I dye my hair? No-one is paying us the slightest bit of notice. Grace, Diane, start flirting.'

'What do you mean flirt?' I looked at Anna then wound down the window and shouted loudly to the hard shoulder. 'Hi my name's Grace what's yours handsome?'

'Christ, if I get my knockers out I'll cause an accident.' Diane tried a valiant smile at the next car only to be rewarded by a child pulling tongues back at her. 'It's not that easy, the cars are going too fast and I can't see who I'm waving at until they're nearly in the car with us. It's a disaster.'

'You two are the pits, or a pair of tits, I can't decide,' Anna grumbled and plopped a 70s CD in the stereo for us to sing along to.

'Beach baby, beach baby give me your hand la la la la la la to September. Me and you and a dog named Boo tra la la la la la on the land. I'm just a load of sheep and I won't work for nobody but you.' Our harmonies were a disgrace and the words defeated us in the end so we just turned the volume up to drown our voices out. It was a jolly girls outing, full of the promise of laughter.

We made it deafened to Blackpool, got lost then found our little B&B tucked away in the backstreets. As one, the bags left, make-up having been applied, liberally in some cases, in cars on the way up, and we all headed for a pub that billed female strippers. The hen predicted that plenty of horny men would be there and was correct in her assumption.

In amongst the football on the big screen and pumping music, roars from over-excited men and women when the

157

dancers made an appearance and removed clothing, in-depth discussion was obsolete, unless you were called Diane and a financial advisor. She was chunnering on to the hen's blonde mum about pensions while Anna, the hen and several others were getting to know the nearest stag party who were doing most of the roaring. I leaned on the bar and twittered a bit to anyone who cared to listen before Anna came over with a tall, dark Yorkshireman whose black eyebrows met in the middle, which made him look cross even though he was smiling.

'Grace this is Colin, and oh, where's Toby gone?' Anna said. 'Oh here he is, Toby this is Grace.'

Toby was a full-lipped, pale-skinned bruiser who carried a huge cuddly elephant on his shoulders.

'Say hello to Nelly as well.' He told us.

We dutifully did and drank to her health. It was obvious that Anna and Colin were starting to gel, fondling each other with familiarity well advanced for an initial meeting. I ignored their ever-increasing closeness so as not to demonstrate any encouragement to Toby. Diane came over to chat but was soon off again, this time giving advice on mortgages with what looked to be the stag's father, which left me plundering my shallow small-talk reservoir to keep a steady flow of rubbish leaking out.

At some point, it was thought a good idea to go out and get some fresh air. All four of us, Anna, Colin, Toby and me, squinted into the sunny but nippy afternoon, and headed for the prom, catching a tram for one stop and catching another back just for the sake of it. Odd what you find funny after a couple of beers.

Down on the beach Anna and Colin were soon walking ahead arm in arm. Toby was still carrying his cuddly toy but seemed at variance with it, he was too bulky, too mature, to make it a cute and loveable attribute. He suddenly sat down on the sand and directed I should do the same. I did so but with a face almost tripping me up with the effort. Anna and Colin had disappeared onto the pier a short distance away.

'Do you like my Nelly then?' Toby was speaking like a four-year-old.

'Hmmm.'

'She likes you.'

'Oh good.'

'It's a lovely day. I think you should lie back here with me and enjoy it.'

'I like the view here,' I said, my eyes staring into the distance, trying to find the sea. I was being barely civil and wanted to tell him to get lost but, because I'm a spineless chicken and because I'd been brought up not to be rude, I didn't. When he placed his hand on my leg though, I jumped as startled as if he'd just punched it. I removed it quickly and turned to face him.

'That's a bit forward isn't it?' I said.

'Er, I don't think so.'

'Well I do, I hardly know you.'

'I'm Toby from Doncaster, twenty-nine, Virgo not virgin. I like pasta. I'm a postman and like weight training, travel and I want to help all the little children of the world.' It was said in the manner of Miss World. I had to smile but was still uncomfortable about being alone with him, like we'd known each other for ages, when actually we'd barely known each other half an hour. I didn't want to be in this situation. I didn't want this man trying to get into my knickers. All he'd tried to do was place his hand on my knee but already I felt that horrible dread encompass me. I didn't fancy him, so why should I lead him on? Poor, or lucky, Toby didn't stand a chance.

'Toby from Doncaster, I'm glad you like pasta but that still doesn't mean you can put your hand on my leg. If you like though we could walk up onto the pier and find the other two or if you'd prefer you can go back into the pub and find your other friends.'

He'd obviously also been brought up to be polite because to his credit, although I'm sure by now he wanted to bolt, he declared he would prefer to be outside with me and we immediately set off in pursuit of Anna and Colin in an air of polite relief.

At first I didn't see Anna; her head was hidden by Colin's in a clinch behind Gypsy Rose Lee's den (or something like it). It was only when she started to laugh as we wandered past that drew our attention to the fact that they were there at all, Colin had been trying to keep his hands warm inside her shirt, discerned mainly by her shifty shenanigans in turning away before greeting us.

Things seemed to deteriorate pretty quickly after that. As the two of them pawed at each other we pretended to be on a higher plain where great minds wandered unadulterated by such wanton activity. We won a large giraffe to add to the elephant, ate candy floss and crisps, drank beer, then some more beer. Oh no, the indigestion and the double vision, both started to attack at the same time.

Whilst the two lads got more ale in, Anna confessed that she was desperate to get to grips with Colin properly and wanted to find somewhere to have sex. The landlady of his boarding house was on the lookout for furtive forays upstairs so his place was out of the question, so she was going to try and sneak him in to ours. I didn't want to sound like her mum but I asked her would she be okay and didn't she find it a bit worrying that he'd discovered his landlady had morals? All of which she waved aside with her usual assured manner. This would now leave me alone with Toby again who must have been wishing he'd picked any other girl in the pub, until I found out from Anna that he had, I was his second choice, he'd been pointed in my direction by the hen he'd rashly chosen to chat up. It could, therefore, be argued that I wasn't his choice at all. This did nothing to improve my ambivalence towards him.

Anna and Colin departed leaving me wondering whether they would make it back to our B&B or whether I'd be bailing them out later for indecent exposure.

I borrowed Nelly the elephant to drape around my shoulders in an effort to keep me warm and we wandered back to the pub. A few of the girls had gone to the fair, some had found tambourines and were dancing on the mini stage to a small crowd of appreciative men and others were swaying, gabbing drunkenly, this included Diane, who by now was slurring full sentences together.

'Eryeravenanisheshime...nen?'

'Lovely. You?'

'Mpished.'

'Maybe drink a bit of water,' I shouted above the noise, downing a whisky to help get to her level of pishedness.

Diane was talked into having a go at pole dancing; her sexy moves included licking the pole up and down, hugging it, before wrapping her legs about it, trying to climb it and landing in a heap on the floor. I decided it was time to go before she did any more damage or I ended up following suit.

Basically, by now, the hen party had splintered and scattered into fragments all over Blackpool front. My aim was to get to the B&B room so that I could burp in peace, possibly slip a light snooze into the bargain before hitting the town again. Toby had gone to the toilet earlier and not returned so he'd either got stuck down it or had escaped through any available window.

Diane was laughing at whatever I said and in return I laughed at whatever she said, we were so funny. We tittered, twittered and wittered like really crap comedians until we realised we couldn't remember the name of the B&B and couldn't remember where the hell it was. All was lost until, through what appeared to be a mist, Anna approached us like a guardian angel and led us back to our room. She'd heard us from the B&B and seen us pass by roughly twelve times before realising that our behaviour was bizarre.

The next hour was a haze of trying to sober up, slapping on more make-up, changing into sparkly night attire for a boogie, Anna bouncing with excitement charged by sex.

'We didn't make it to the B&B. Al fresco sex is the way forward. His hands were everywhere. Once we'd finished we went for a walk then decided to go back for more to the same spot then came back here and had more sex with some whipped cream, a banana and white wine. I sat on his head; I've never had an orgasm like it. I know, I'm naughty,' she smirked. 'How did you get on with Toby?'

'Not as well as you did with his friend, let's just say the only thing sitting on his head was a stuffed elephant.'

Highlights of the evening were dancing without reserve on a packed dance floor to 80s tunes and having a laugh with a bunch of girls from Cleethorpes dressed in Andy Pandy outfits. Colin and Toby turned up towards the end of the evening. Toby must have decided to cut his losses which I decided to reward with a kiss. After twenty minutes of being glued impartially together at the mouth I decided I'd had enough, it was leading nowhere and

I don't know who was more bored. No thunder, no lightning. At least this time it was legal.

We ended up going back to their B&B and playing pool with other residents under the watchful eye of the proprietor. Eventually, totally knackered at four in the morning, Diane and I decided to head for our own lodgings. I kissed Toby goodbye.

'Nice knowing you.'

'Yeah, you too.'

Colin and Anna were still playing pool.

'I'll walk her home,' Colin offered.

I don't know where Diane found the energy but she hadn't stopped talking all night and was still waffling on about something, both of us clacking unsteadily on stilettos away from the B&B, when there was a screech behind us, 'Grace, Diane, run for your lives,' followed by running footsteps.

Without thinking we both legged it down the road overtaking a travelling milk-float. Diane couldn't sustain a fast tempo for long and slowed down as Anna caught us up, wildly looking back to see if she was being followed. There didn't appear to be any sign of life other than the milkman chinking bottles on his dawn deliveries.

'What the hell?' Diane gasped slowing to a walk.

'Bloody hell, I don't believe what I've just done. Toby came back in after you'd left and called you a prick teaser so I hit him on the head with my pool cue and ran out.'

I started to giggle until I was crying with laughter. Anna joined in.

'Come on you two, I'm knackered.' Diane managed to get her breath back.

I giggled a pissed giggle and couldn't stop, especially when I finally bounced into bed and directly bounced out the other side onto the floor.

'Oh my God, look at the size of this on my arse.' Diane stuck her bum out enlarging a blossoming bruise covering most of one cheek. More giggling. 'For God's sake somebody gag her before I kill her,' Diane groaned.

'I know I'll sing the 'The Brave Tin Soldier' that'll work,' Anna said. 'It did when the children were two.'

I bounced back into bed and started to snigger again as she started off in a deep chocolate voice telling the sad story of the toy soldier who fell in love with a dancer made of paper only to come to a gruesome end in a hot stove and melting into a heart, my heart melted with him and laughter turned to sorrow and I cried myself to sleep.

At breakfast the accounts coming back from the evening showed that everyone in their own way had had a good time. The hen and two of her friends had ended up going on to a private party which included a number of showbiz personalities and footballers and had been given a lift back to the B&B in a white limousine containing champagne and caviar.

One of the other girls had ended up having sex in the back of a car in the multi-storey and woke up next morning finding two pensioners staring in at her bare bum through the window. She had clutched at the jacket that should have been covering her to expose her lover's buttocks instead, giving the pensioners a good laugh before they walked off.

Two others spent most of the night trying to find where everyone else had gone by doing a pub-crawl and forgetting who they were looking for.

The hen's mum had ended up fast asleep by twelve o'clock next to a gigantic speaker and was struggling to hear anything anyone said next morning.

We were all tired apart from the girl who had passed out on her bed at seven o'clock and didn't wake up till next morning. The three of us drove home was a quiet affair with sunglasses hiding puffy eyes.

I hadn't exactly proved to myself that I was over James completely but I knew that I had found a life without him. I no longer thought that if he couldn't see what I was doing then I was wasting my time. The ease with which Anna had gone from wife and mother to single and lover didn't so much shock as give me a wake-up call.

As we neared home, Diane started to worry about her reception from Tom. She was convinced he'd know she'd had a go at pole-dancing in public. I told her that she had lacked a certain agility normally associated with pole-dancing so, strictly speaking, pole and dancing shouldn't be used in the same sentence when describing her performance. In fact, there were no words to describe her performance.

'Cack, it wasn't that bad, surely?' Diane pouted.

'D'you want the honest truth? Come on, show us your bum again.'

Anna looked at me quizzically then laughed. Diane sighed, 'It's bloody killing me, I can't sit on it. I think I'd feel a bit better if I'd managed at least one provocative move. Can't believe I licked the pole. I'm just worried that's all. What's Tom going to say if he sees it? I don't do lying but it looks like I'll have to come up with a good one for this, he was bad enough with the hold-ups you gave me.'

Anna suggested that we should have something to eat in a decent pub before getting back. Diane agreed and I was in no hurry so it wasn't until after six o'clock that evening when we finally made it back home.

Dad was wandering round the house covered in a rash. Mum and Natalie had taken to calling him Spotty Muldoon. Mum blamed the salmon she'd cooked the previous day, insisting that he went to the doctor's the next morning. As with most men, though, he resisted her attempts to get him there because, all of a sudden, he felt fine.

I received a phone call from Diane an hour after our return.

'Oh my God, you'll never guess what?' She sounded shaken and, without waiting for me to guess, she said. 'Tom's kicked me out.'

'Holly crap. Where are you at the moment?'

'I'm at Anna's, I've got nowhere else to go.'

'What about Heather?'

'He wouldn't let me see her. I don't even know if she's home yet. Oh, Grace it was awful. He wouldn't let me in the house. He'd packed all my clothes in bags and was waiting for me in the driveway when I got home. He said that I'd been acting strange to hide the fact I was having an affair and that I was an unfit mother. I knew this would happen.'

I felt sick for her. She'd had reservations about going away for the weekend and had been dreading going home and now she sounded lost and frightened.

'He didn't hurt you did he?'

'No he didn't need to, just one look at his face was like he'd hit me.'

'I'm on my way. Get the kettle on.'

Chapter 12

Anna answered the door, a mug of tea in her hand, her hair tousled, her expression troubled and distressed.

'What are we going to do? I feel terrible. It was me that made her come to Blackpool,' she whispered at me in the hallway, handing me the tea and bobbing her head in the direction of the living room where Diane could be heard quietly sobbing.

'It isn't Blackpool that's done this,' I whispered back.

'What if you stay here with her and I go round to her house and demand he lets her see Heather.'

'You can't do that,' I muttered earnestly, certain Anna would do exactly that given any encouragement.

'Why not?' she asked.

'Sounds a bit like poking our noses in and making things ten times worse.'

'Grace, it's better than doing nothing.' Anna turned up the volume.

'Is it?' So did I.

'I'm in here.' Diane reminded us.

She looked terrible; her face was red and sore, her body crumpled in to the defeated shape I knew only too well.

'Come on, Diane, don't cry,' I said, giving her a hug.

'It's all shit and I haven't done anything.' Her voice seemed to come from a tiny escape route in her swollen throat. 'If he didn't want me to go to Blackpool why didn't he say? I'll happily leave him, but I can't leave Heather.'

'He's a bastard and we're going to rescue your daughter.' If Anna had been wearing long sleeves she'd have rolled them up.

'How? I can't get in touch with her, you know?'

'When did your brother drop her off?' I asked.

'I don't know. I've tried ringing his land-line but there's no answer.'

'Try him again,' I said.

'There's no point.'

'What if all three of us turn up at the house and demand to see Heather? Threaten Tom with the police.' Anna was determined to find a solution.

'Threats don't work with Tom. If anything it would only make matters worse and I don't want to cause a scene in front of my daughter.'

'Okay, what if we ask him nicely?'

'We're dealing with Tom here, Anna. Unless you're ... I don't know ... female angler of the year asking for an up-to-date river report, he won't even open the door.'

'Right, that does it. Who does Tom go fishing with?' Anna asked.

'Er, Andy Young and Jason Burke.' Diane answered, violently pulling at a loose strand of cotton on her blouse, ripping a hole in the seam.

'Andy Young? Isn't he married to whiney Jo from the butchers?' Anna queried.

'Yes. Why?'

'Oh, nothing.' Anna thought for a moment. 'I've got a dodgy plan.' She thought a bit more, while we waited uneasily for what was coming next. 'We can't use a rod licence to get him out of the house, don't ask how I know but I think they're due in March. But we can use something else,' she said to herself, and then to us. 'We need to change into dark clothing and we need some shoe polish. Upstairs quickly.'

Half an hour later I shifted from one buttock to the other in the driver's seat of my car, nerves making me want to laugh while Anna, looking like a paratrooper, performed an impersonation of 'whiney, nasal Jo' to the best of her ability on the phone. Diane looked like she wanted to be sick on the back seat. Heather's bedroom light was on, a good indication that she was back.

'Oh, Tom – u hum, u hum, oh I know, no really? Oh, how awful, I know I've got two of my own, u hum, u hum. You know, I've never liked her,' Diane's blood-shot eyes fair popped out of her luminous blotchy face at this, Anna gave a shake of her head in Diane's direction and carried on regardless. 'It's just that Andy forgot to give you his bait...' she scrunched her eyes closed at this, the moment of truth, waiting to see if her gambit paid off. The gobsmacked expression that followed showed how optimistic she'd been for its success. 'Well, I've got the children with me and I'm passing the bottom of your road in about ten, so to save me coming up that bendy road of yours with no street lights, he, he, I'll meet you there, yeah ? Ciao.'

Anna broke the line before Tom could argue. 'Keep your head down Diane. Now all we have to do is wait.'

The absence of reality made me feel like I was in a police stake-out, we were just missing ripping into donut's and slopping coffee into the foot-well to bring the full movie scenario into being. Anna's dodgy plan had received serious reservations from the collective team to its viability. With Diane disclosing the fact that fisherman Andy and wife Jo were going on holiday the following Tuesday, Anna had argued that we at least had a reason for getting rid of stinky bait, her familiarity with fishing starting and finishing with permits. Diane finally agreed that it was worth a try but point-blank refused to use boot polish on her face. I don't know what we were thinking. Anna was filled with guilt and trying her hardest to make it up to Diane. Diane was desperate to see her daughter and I was, well, easily coerced, once I realised they would go ahead with or without me.

My car, an unknown quantity to Tom, was parked facing in the right direction for a quick getaway up the 'bendy' road just past Diane's house. Heather's bedroom light was on and all we had to do was wait for Tom to come out of the house, run down the road to meet Andy's wife, which would give Diane the green light to sprint out of the car, coax Heather out and off we would roar/bunny hop, me as 'the driver', all of us playing our part.

Minutes dragged waiting for Tom's appearance. The stilled car engine ticked as only old crappy cars have the ability to tick.

'He must be leaving it to the last minute before leaving Heather on her own, that's good,' Diane whispered, her head down and poking in between the front seats.

'You don't think he knows it's a trap do you?' I said even more quietly.

'I withheld the number and he sounded convinced. Believe me, if I didn't have my heart set on politics I could have a successful act going as an impersonator,' Anna hissed.

'Absolutely. You *did* sound like her. What was with the "I hate her" bit?' Diane continued the hushed theme.

'I'm not sure but I may have overheard her say it in the pub once.' Anna was now talking out of the side of her mouth.

'What!' Diane split the air in the car with her indignation, her body shot upright. 'I mean, what?' she repeated hoarsely, quickly recovering her crouched position.

'Shush, what's that noise?' I said, grabbing Anna's arm. My head swivelled in all directions to catch the sound of what I thought had been a heavy footstep. All was quiet.

'Grace, you bloody terrified the life out of me.' Anna put her free hand to her heart.

'Sorry.' I let go of her arm.

A knock on the passenger-side window made us all scream in unison. A face appeared almost simultaneously. Anna screamed again. None of us were able to speak.

'What are you doing here?' The face on the outside of the car asked loudly and slowly as if speaking to foreigners.

'Fucking hell, Tom.' Diane was the first to find her voice.

'Well?' Tom looked directly at Diane. Even though his amused expression diffused a certain amount of anxiety, my heart was still hammering at my ribs from fright and my scalp felt as though my hair had fallen out and left me bald. Our plan in tatters, Anna and I well and truly caught poking our noses into their domestic affairs, embarrassment started to take fear's place.

'Hi, Tom,' Anna said breezily, after a momentary scuffle when Diane to get out of the two-door car first.

'Anna. Hello, whoever you are in there.' Tom's palm briefly flicked in my direction still seated behind the wheel. 'Explain?' He turned his attention back to Diane, who'd followed Anna out onto the narrow pavement.

'I just want to see Heather.'

'She's okay, it's you that isn't. Are you totally insane? What do you take me for? What the hell were you thinking?'

'Like I said, I just wanted to see Heather.'

Anna put a hesitant hand up and, unheard by the two protagonists, said. 'I'll get back in the car then, should I?'

'And, like I said before, you're an unfit mother so you don't deserve to see her.'

'How the hell am I an unfit mother? You're an unfit father if you try to deny your daughter seeing her mother.'

'You run off for the weekend, leaving her with strangers and expect to come back as if nothing's happened.'

'Strangers! He's my brother and her uncle, and as far as I can remember I didn't hear you saying you'd care for her while I was away. Double standards.' Diane was starting to shout.

'Yes, but I wasn't off shagging was I,' Tom shouted back.

'Steady on, Tom,' Anna said, again unheard.

'Neither was I,' Diane yelled at him.

'I don't believe you. You're a bloody whore.'

'You're a bastard.'

'Selfish bitch.'

'Arrogant tosser.'

'Slapper.'

'Shitbag.'

'Slag.'

'Areshole.'

'Mum, Dad. Stop it, it's embarrassing.' Heather's small voice broke into their abuse like a sweet piccolo between two angry kettle drums. Having seen her parents batter each other with insults she stood, white-faced in the dark, slim and erect. There was more dignity within that one little body than there was in the sum total of her parents at that moment. I wanted to cry for her.

'Heather.' Diane reached out to her daughter, hugging her and sobbing with relief. Tom looked utterly ashamed and was now noticing for the first time that curious neighbours were showing an interest in what was going on.

Anna stepped into the car and sat on the back seat.

There was silence. Eventually Heather pulled away from her mum and again showed maturity far beyond her eight or nine years by calmly saying, 'Mum, I'll stay with Dad tonight.'

Diane stepped back from her daughter and looked at her, devastated, large tears collecting in her eyes on hearing her daughter say she wasn't going to go with her. To my surprise, I glimpsed sadness, not triumph, on Tom's face.

'Dad and I have been discussing it. I'll come and be with you tomorrow, Mum.' Heather hugged her mum tightly again then she abruptly let go and with a big sob ran into the house, all eyes following her.

'I think we could both learn from her,' Tom said, turning his attention back to his wife.

'I can't believe she doesn't want to be with me.' Diane sounded almost hollow.

'Look, she'll be with you tomorrow and the rest of the week and if it's ok with you I'll have her most, or alternate, weekends. It's what she wants.'

I was pretty sure that Heather's preference would be that this wasn't happening and that her parents weren't on the brink of separating but it wasn't for me to point this out. I'd done enough damage.

'So you've both been having cosy chats while I've been left out in the cold?'

'Grow up, Diane,' Tom said.

'I'll be at Anna's.' Diane turned and got into the car.

I drove away almost slinking down the road in disgrace.

'I'm so sorry.' From the back seat Anna put a gentle hand on Diane's shoulder, her voice low and sympathetic. 'I just wanted to try and help. I may have made things worse.'

'I'm sorry too.' I wasn't proud of what we'd done. We'd created the scene Diane had most wanted to avoid and we'd forced Heather to choose sides. I looked across at Diane. She couldn't bring herself to speak, hatred towards Tom was swallowing her up and she was almost disappearing in its poison, but she nodded her head to acknowledge us. It wasn't until we pulled up outside Anna's house that she turned to us both.

'I know things went badly back there, I completely lost it for a moment and that's not like me. I just want to thank you for caring enough to try and help...' she couldn't carry on. Anna looked at me, I looked at Anna; we both looked at Diane. She was so desperately trying to hold tears back it broke my heart and I shed them for her. We group hugged as best we could in the confines of the car and remained huddled together for comfort.

So there we were, all three of us at different stages of splitting up. Our bond of friendship augmented further by our shared evening of madness. Maybe what drew us all together in the first place was marital unhappiness. Not an ideal theory; so perhaps instead we were searching for strengths that we lacked but found in each other.

Chapter 13

We saw a lot of each other after Blackpool. This was not a time of quiet chats over a meal while sipping delicately at a glass of wine. Our occasions out, when the children were with their dads, started early in the pub and finished when I puked perfect pavement pizzas after closing time, Diane tried to seduce anyone within two paces and Anna screwed anyone who resembled Jeremy Clarkson, which with beer goggles on was a man with legs, arms and a head. As the weeks went by, heading for Christmas, the evenings got steadily worse with truly hormonal teenage behaviour.

Heather had revealed to her mum what had happened once she'd left her uncle's on the evening of our abortive rescue attempt. When she'd asked where her mum was, Tom had informed her that her parents were splitting. She'd cried a lot. He'd been discussing the breakdown of the marriage with her and was trying to find a way of working things out to ease her unhappiness when a phone call had prompted some very strange behaviour from him. He'd suddenly looked very tricky – Heather's word – and had peered furtively out of the drawn living room curtains. After telling her not to leave the house he'd crept across the lawn and out of her view. She had been about to phone her mum when she'd decided to creep out after the shitbag instead, to see what he was up to. Heather liked the word 'shitbag', felt her mother owed it to her to let her to use it and out of guilt Diane allowed her to say it once a day, but not during school time and only if it was referring to Tom.

Since then Diane had found the tiniest flat in the land to live in. She'd started weight watchers and with the aid of stress she was losing pounds. Tom remained convinced that she was having an affair so she decided to go for it without much success. She referred to him as Tom the Tosspot abbreviating it to T Tosser then just Tosser, within a matter of days. I think she terrified the male population with her desperate aggression, her anger at Tom often the source of her chat-up line.

I don't think any of us had been rebels as youths. Anna had dabbled early on with sex; her first conquest when she was fourteen had been to impress her friends. She was certainly making up for her good behaviour over the last twenty years now by taking us with her on her journey of self-discovery. There was no way of telling her she was on the route to possible self-destruction. There was no way of stopping her. She'd met Peter when she was nineteen years' old. An older man by ten years, he represented worldliness, maturity, stability to her at a time when she was tiring of boys who presented only their backsides as they left after getting what they wanted; he had her married and trying for babies before she could say 'Romper suit'. Numerous miscarriages, endless IVF treatment and his hold over her kept her out of a workplace and a world she was now struggling to find a niche in. For short-term employment, until something more suitable came along, she was working shift-hours in telesales.

Diane had been engaged twice before meeting Tom, running off to Gretna Green with him to essentially save on wedding expenses and maybe ensuring that he didn't get cold feet like the other two had. It was her little bit of rebellion which backfired when her mother, denied the joy of seeing her daughter get married, chose not to speak to her, only relenting after Heather was born. The reconciliation occurred only months before she passed away. Did Diane ever regret her decision? She never said.

Me, well let's face it, drinking too much and swearing was as outrageous as I got, I tried to forget my near holiday rape and apart from that only a severe love-bite episode in my teens stood out in my memory, oh and a time when I threw sand in to a post box at the school bus stop to put out the fire that another girl started. Guess who got caught?

All in all, I knew things were getting out of hand the moment I saw a pair of men's shoes outside the ladies toilet door of a Chinese restaurant whilst having a pee.

To explain properly it was a saloon bar door with slats so you could see out but not in and didn't reach the floor so the shoes appearance stopped me mid-tinkle.

I dithered over what to do before flushing and opening the door to be faced by George, a burly rugby player who, along with his two friends, had joined us at our table earlier that evening. I won't go into detail as to how and why other than to point the finger firmly in Anna's direction with her Clarkson radar blipping and her audacious charm working wonders on a smitten waiter.

We all chatted and laughed like old mates, no-one does drunk as well as a rugby player does. There is a deep, secret pit inside them where all alcohol goes *en masse* to ferment slowly over the next number of years, not hours, so when others have passed out or are careering into walls or fighting, the rugby player is able to hold conversations from party politics to having it up the arse with a carrot as a dare.

George, the most vocal and the 'married one' of the three lads, kept getting up from the table and disappearing. He had done so when Diane had slipped off to the loo, I'd not thought anything of it but maybe I shouldn't have been so surprised to see him there when I went.

'It's all yours,' I said, referring to the cubicle I'd just vacated rather than myself.

'That's what I'm here for, you little sex kitten.' His hands were round my waist before he'd finished the sentence.

'I haven't washed my hands, do you mind?' I tried to push him off.

'No. You are a beautiful woman and I want you.'

'No you don't, you want any woman and I don't want you, so get off. Anyway you're married.'

'So? Kiss me.'

'Bloody hell you don't give up, do you.' I puckered up, had a brief meeting of lips before shoving hard at him and legging it. It hadn't been such a bad kiss. Pity really, for his wife in particular.

I wasn't going to make a scene but I sat down and kept kicking Anna under the table until we left at which point the lads came after us and asked if we were up for it. Anna waivered, Diane seemed game until I told them to 'Get lost,' and marched off with two protesting women, one either side of me. I was becoming a seasoned pro at this end-of-night malarkey.

'What the hell were you both thinking?' I sounded like a frustrated mother.

'Well it doesn't matter tonight, George has my number I'll see him some other time.' Anna pouted.

'He's got my number too.' Diane piped up.

They both waited a second before saying in unison. 'Bastard.'

'He bloody well accosted me in the toilets.' I was outraged.

'He told me I was beautiful and he wanted to see me naked on his bed,' Diane sighed. 'Cack and pants. I thought I'd struck it lucky.'

'I was planning a dirty weekend with him.' Anna ripped up a small piece of paper with his number on. 'Now I'll have to call the carpet man in to measure the floor in the bedroom again if I want sex. He had such a small appendage I thought it was his finger.' She said things for effect, embroidering the truth on occasion to get a reaction. I doubted she'd had someone round to measure her floors so I carried on as if I'd not heard her, too scandalised with the present to worry unduly about the alleged carpet man's physique.

'Well, George certainly hedged his bets. I mean, were they thinking of a gang bang or were we three women to shag George while his mates looked on?' I said. Thinking back to how naive I was less than a year before, this was indeed a different person speaking now.

'Is that you, Grace?' A voice said from behind us.

I hadn't seen the stocky man pass us in the street, being so engrossed in the conversation, and I turned to see Shrubby standing uncertainly with his hands in his pockets.

'Oh hi, what are you doing here?' I hoped that he hadn't heard my outburst but considering its content I'm pretty certain he must have.

'I live just down there. I'm on my way back from a gig.'

'This is Shrubby who plays in Lawrence's band.' I introduced him to Diane and Anna.

'Oh, I remember your face now. And where's the rest of the band?' Anna asked, her eyes lighting up as if she'd just been plugged in at the mains.

'They're at the gig still.'

'Oh pity, I would have loved to have heard you play. Grace has told us how good you are, she thinks you're marvellous, don't you, Grace?' Anna said, smiling directly at him.

'I've got a recording back at mine if you'd like to hear us, and I'm literally round the corner.' Shrubby suggested.

'Won't we wake your wife and children?' I asked.

'If I had either then maybe,' he smiled.

'Oh.'

'Do you have any red wine?' Diane asked.

'Plenty.'

'That's that then,' she said, happier than she had been minutes before. 'Lead on MacDuff.'

'Actually, Lawrence may well call round in a bit. I've got some old smoky whisky for him and I think he wants to pick it up before going home. That's if he remembers.' Shrubby told us as we started back on ourselves then turned down a side road. I was still trying to figure out why I thought he was married with kids. Perhaps he just looked like he *was* married with kids.

Anna had her psychology head on. 'We are not coming back to yours in the hope that your friend may turn up, we'd already made the decision before you mentioned this.'

I wanted to push her into the nearest bush and leave her there. I opened my mouth to try and explain what she meant then closed it. There was no getting away from it; she'd made it clear to him that his extremely good-looking mate had just added to the incentive to get us there.

Shrubby took her forthrightness in his stride. 'Lucky me then.'

'Now I've offended you, are you always on the defensive?' Anna said to Shrubby as we walked up his front garden path.

'Are you always so blunt?' he replied, and opened the front door to let us in.

It was a very clean and precise house, white walls, dark mahogany floorboards, deep velvet rugs, tasteful pictures and everything exactly where it should be. I was surprised. James had had a tendency to leave cups hidden in unlikely places, fungal organisms encrusting the dregs of tea at the bottom to really

180

piss me off. He never put towels back on the towel rail but left them in a heap for me to pick up and fold, and would never, ever, ever make the bed, even though the job consisted of pulling the duvet over and popping two lovely little silk pillows at a jaunty angle on top. One minute if that. The more I nagged, or pleaded in the end, the more determined he became to ignore me and to make more mess. That's respect for you. Anyway it wasn't an issue any longer. I quickly tried to push the sudden rush of venom back and instead wondered if Shrubby was normal.

He sorted drinks and put on some chilled music, which wasn't the music he'd promised but I didn't say anything. Even his music stand in one corner of the room was part of the decor and looked more like a showpiece than, one assumed anyway, a well-used part of his life.

We all sat around listening to the music with no conversation. It was a little embarrassing and I felt it my responsibility to act on this and start one, seeing I knew him a tad better.

'So where have you been playing tonight?' I asked.

'I'm not blunt, am I blunt?' Anna suddenly said as if I'd sparked her into life once more, I may as well have just farted instead of racking my brains to come up with such a sparkling opener.

'Sometimes you are.' Diane answered her.

'In a bad way? I just like to get straight to the point and not lie or cheat people,' Anna said.

'Does that mean that those who hold back are liars and cheats or does it mean that they think of others so as not to offend them?' Shrubby asked, and they were off on a full-scale debate as to the moral responsibility of speaking one's mind and the virtues of holding back. Anna thrived on sparring discussion. I let their argument wash over me and sauntered over to his CD collection, happily delving in to compile a playlist.

We had more drink and ended up cranking the music up, playing our favourites in rotation. We didn't hear the doorbell and we only realised someone was trying to get in when a face appeared at the window. Lawrence grinned at us from outside; he hadn't forgotten his smoky whisky after all. I was in a state of complete euphoria. Here I was drinking lovely whisky with friends and playing great music with a good-looking male to bring out our best girly qualities. All three of us became giggling comedians trying to be funny and make Lawrence laugh.

'I know,' Anna said, 'Grace should play the clarinet for you. Shrubby do you have yours here?'

'I've got one upstairs sure,' he replied

'I don't think so somehow, I'm pissed and I'll slobber down it,' I said and tapped her on the head with a CD box.

'Come with me and have a look at it.' Shrubby stood up and I followed; ribald comments such as him showing me his bell end, his big pipe, and blowjobs pursuing us up the stairs.

Upstairs was in exactly the same pristine condition until he opened the back bedroom door to expose his Achilles heel. Yes indeed, all of his rubbish was stacked onto the bed, around the bed, under the bed, on top of two wardrobes and hanging out of a set of drawers.

'I was beginning to wonder if you were human,' I said, startled at the mess.

'I never let my mum see this room. She'd have a fit,' he said, disarmingly.

'I think I can see why.'

'I love it though. I sometimes just open the door and chuck stuff I need in for the sake of it, then go and reclaim it later.'

'Hmmm.' I looked at him cautiously.

'She's a very strong woman my mother, if I didn't keep this place clean she'd be moving in to look after me. It's my little piece of delinquency.'

'We never grow up do we? It doesn't matter how old we are we still behave like children.' I sympathised with him as he went to burrow into a large box to bring out a clarinet. He started putting it together.

'Please don't do this to me, don't make them make me play it,' I begged.

'What's it worth?'

'I'll keep your untidy room fetish a secret.'

'Sorry, but it's well known. All the lads come here every now and then to trash the place. Half the stuff in there is theirs.' He led the way downstairs.

'I won't tell your mum.'

'She's not really that bad.'

'What about your neighbours?'

'They're deaf.'

'Right that does it; I'm going to set Shenaya on you.'

'No, no not Shenaya, anything but that. Grace, I'd like to hear you play, even if you are slightly pissed.'

'Oh, God.'

We entered the room to cheers.

'Now that's a fine-looking instrument.' Diane admired.

'Thank you,' said Shrubby, checking the reed.

The embarrassment I felt in front of video man was nothing compared to the shame I felt now, stood like 'one of Lewis's' in the middle of the living room, a flaming red rash on my chest and cheeks. Shady recollections of my last audition battered at my brain asking to be let in and have a say on what was going on. I refused them entry and tried to warm the instrument up.

'Go on then, what are you going to play for us?' Diane asked, as curious as the others as to whether I really could play.

'Bill Bailey won't you please come home.'

It has to be said that initially, what with nerves and the fact that it was a strange clarinet and the fact that my brain was awash with whisky, the song lacked a tune. I could see everyone's faces set in polite pity. I stopped and started again. This time I shut them out. I didn't want to see that look on their faces, the one that suggested I put the instrument down and left the room quietly. Instead I played my heart out, remembering everything Mr Gerrard was teaching me and imagining that this was a concert hall with Monty Sunshine alongside me. I was nowhere near the maestro's genius but I gave it my best shot.

I only opened my eyes when I'd finished, hearing Lawrence cheering. The girls were clapping.

'I told you so,' Anna said, like a proud parent.

'Not bad,' said Shrubby.

'What do you mean not bad? That, my friend, was bloody brilliant.' Lawrence stood up and gave me a huge hug.

'I need a drink,' I said after Lawrence released me from his warm, strong grasp.

'Now you, Shrubby,' Anna said, on a roll. 'Come on, don't be shy.'

He stood up and took up the clarinet with ease then, starting with confidence that left me standing in his wake, he played 'Sleepy shores' running cleverly into 'It had to be you.'

We all started to sing along towards the end, cheering when he finished on a final flourish.

'Like the juxtaposition, nicely done, mate,' Lawrence said, a far off look on his face. I assumed his mind was away in gigland, imagining his own piano arrangement. Maybe, amongst those thoughts, I was stroking his hair, massaging his shoulders, kissing his neck. The room was getting very warm.

'It's my fall-back signature tune,' Shrubby explained, sitting down and taking a slug of beer.

'Not bad.' I smiled at him.

'Lawrence, you should sing us a song now.' Anna was keen to carry on doing turns so without much encouragement needed he asked Shrubby to accompany him and sang 'Summertime'. It was, and always will be, my all-time favourite song, what a choice. It gave us a good excuse to stare at him, and I could feel the old fire and fur rug dream coming back to me with no Shenaya to destroy the moment. His gorgeous voice turned my insides to mush.

As I watched him I realised that he wasn't as handsome as I'd built him up in my mind. He wasn't as tall either but for some reason his confidence conferred on him greater height and beauty than he really possessed, which made him more attractive.

Anna and Diane were in raptures when he finished.

'How are we going to follow that?' Anna asked Diane.

'Brigadoon?'

'I'm not singing anything from bloody Brigadoon. I know, 'The Boxer'.' Anna stood up and pulled Diane with her.

With one false start and a fit of the giggles when it all went wrong, they proceeded to harmonise throughout the song with the rest of us joining in for the chorus.

'I've had a lovely evening,' Diane said, languishing back on the settee. 'But I'm going to have to go to sleep.'

Lawrence smiled. 'I'm tired too. I'll make a coffee and then ladies I think we should all make a move and let old Shrub get his beauty sleep.'

'I'll come with you, you don't know where the coffee is.' Shrubby followed Lawrence out of the room.

'I thought you said that Lawrence didn't really get on with his band,' Anna said to me.

'I didn't say that at all. I said there was a bit of conflict but didn't say they didn't get on.' I wondered how what I'd said in the past and what I'd thought was going to remain there was now being misrepresented and maybe even overheard by the people I'd been talking about. 'Anyway I'm ready to go home now.' I swiftly changed the direction she was going in.

'Same thing.' She wouldn't let it drop.

'No it's not. One implies that they never speak unless they have to, the other says there was a disagreement. Pretty much like the one we're having now, which doesn't mean we don't get on.'

'I say to the honourable gentleman that I disagree with your disagreement about being disagreeable and disagreeably disagree to a degree that disagrees with everything you have just disagreed to.' Anna baaed like a sheep. 'Just practising for prime minister's question time.'

We baaed at each other.

The coffee Shrubby and Lawrence came back with was strong enough to put hairs on our chests. Lawrence asked for evidence.

There was a moment as we were getting ready to leave and waiting for Anna to put her boots on and Diane to come down from the bathroom when my eyes caught Lawrence's and for what seemed an age they remained locked. I felt the heat mount in my face. Lawrence looked away first. I started to breathe again and tried to regain a bit of composure, nearly losing it completely when Shrubby, holding the front door open, said directly to me, 'Penny for them.' He'd seen us, he knew.

'Hnya,' was what came out. Oh God.

'Sorry?' He raised his eyebrows.

By now Diane and Anna had congregated at the door and were looking at me oddly.

'Hi there, I mean, meant, sorry. Frog, throat, thing.' I blustered, pointing at my neck. 'I've had a lovely time thanks.' What I wanted to say was, 'Hey, tidy house freak, go and play with your household cleaners and leave me alone.' Oh how I wanted to take his place and be in Lawrence's band.

We left in a flurry of thanks and your welcomes.

That night, or what was left of it, Diane and I stayed at Anna's tiredly dissecting the evening and the meaning of every word uttered by Lawrence.

'What would you do if Shrubby left the band and Lawrence asked you to fill in,' Anna asked as she delicately patted moisturiser around her eyes.

'Oh, as if,' I said, having thought of nothing else for the last hour. 'He wouldn't ask me anyway so no point in mulling it over really and Shrubby is so lovely and way more accomplished than I am.' I felt sick with benevolence I didn't feel, and lay awake picturing myself performing at Lawrence's side, receiving accolades for my brilliant, yet understated, talent. When I *did* fall asleep I dreamt the clarinet refused to play for me then walked off stage in a huff.

Chapter 14

I received my *decree absolute* on the 15th December, my 39th birthday. I hadn't even considered turning up to the local courts and it was read out whilst I was either counting money that didn't belong to me or I was in mid-spiel trying to sell a new account to an unsuspecting pensioner who just wanted ten pounds out of the bank.

The magistrate must have been talking to an empty room, the walls echoing to the sound of another faceless marriage being dissolved.

That evening I cried. I closed the papers back into the envelope and threw it into a box under the bed that held the *decree nisi* and my old diaries containing entries as riveting as 'had cottage pie for tea' and 'bought new CD.' I went downstairs and heard Dad talking on the phone, proudly saying how lucky he was to have five successful kids.

'And our Grace is a genius on the clarinet, nearly as good as my Swannie River on the harmonica.' He winked as I walked past. 'She's semi-professional, playing all over the place; she's got a great future ahead of her.'

Anybody would have thought I was playing clarinet at The Royal Albert Hall not the village hall, in my prime and not in decline. He deserved a large scotch, I poured him one.

The orchestra prepared to play Christmas Carols with a school choir on the Sunday before Christmas Day. The choir prepared to sing Christmas Carols on the Monday before Christmas Day. Even in my sleep my head sang a confused mix of Oh Royal Night, Once in Holy Herald's City and Hark the David's Angels sing.

Joan Sarney organised a Christmas get-together meal, which comprised vegetarian turkey, no gravy, a bottle of wine between ten people with a sharp exit for dessert.

A grander affair was organised by the choir. We were booked in, the Saturday before Christmas Day, to a black tie do. The Nota Gains were part of the entertainment followed by a disco. I had been shopping with Anna, Diane and the kids the week before and bought a long evening gown, Diane had bought a lovely dark velvet suit and a camisole top and Anna had bought a pink winceyette nightie for herself. People are full of surprises. She only needed a big electrical slipper to completely shock.

I had my hair done on the morning of the event then I went Christmas shopping that afternoon with Dad. He wanted to get Mum a special present. This was a novelty because generally he gave money out to one of his good daughters to get something she'd like. We went to an art shop in town where he found what he was after. It was a picture of a woman barefoot on a beach, her arm shading her face from the sun, a lively wind blowing at her hair and moulding her dress to her shapely legs. It looked like Mum. It was lovely.

As we left, Dad looked behind then put his arm out. I stopped.

'What?' I thought we were trying to hide from someone.

'What?' Dad answered.

'You just put your arm out.'

'Bloody hell, I was indicating.' We fell about laughing, even the man behind us smiled when seconds before he'd been scowling as he nearly went into the back of me.

'I sat down the other week at my desk and went to put my seat belt on,' I said, pushing our way through frantic shoppers to get back to the car.

'Your mum walked off with someone else's shopping trolley yesterday, and only realised when she was at the till and packing a top-shelf dirty magazine in with aftershave and razors. Away with the fairies. Sorry.' He apologised to a harassed looking woman after accidentally hitting her child on the head with a wayward tube of wrapping paper.

The drive home was one of hanging on for grim death, his mission to insult every other driver on the road when they got in his way. I'd forgotten how dangerous it was in the car with him when combined with shopping in any form. We scattered pedestrians in our wake as we approached the village until we were forced to stop at pelican lights and a brave man ventured out in front of us.

Glancing further ahead I observed none other than James coming out of the jewellers shop next to the chemist and the bookies, deep in conversation with an older looking man. He didn't see me and I was glad; my orange fake tan would have seriously offended him. They stepped into a silver Porsche, James in the driver's seat, and drove off. Although I wanted him to move on, my generosity didn't extend to him prospering better than I did and I was quickly consumed with jealousy. He *did* have a Porsche. Where did he get the money for that from? Where was he going? What had he been buying?

The lights changed and we were off, like Dick Dastardly and Mutley, following James just two cars ahead. I wished we were right behind him. I wished Dad was up his bumper.

'Anything funny?' Dad asked. I must have snorted.

'I've just seen James with his posh car and thought I'd like to set you loose behind him.'

'What d'ya mean?' He was a tad affronted. No one likes to have their driving criticised.

'Well, only because you're faster than I am.' I scurried for cover.

He was kind enough not to mention my abysmal record in reversing cars, especially an event that had taken place only weeks after I'd moved back home. Things were at an all-time low and I'd reversed his car out of the drive, flustered by someone allowing me into the road, and promptly hit my sister's car parked opposite, damaging both whilst my own stood unscathed on the path. I still hadn't got round to recompensing either of them, I kept forgetting only to remember every now and then when faced with the dodgy repair work on the bumper of Dad's car. He never mentioned it; I may have taken advantage. What with that, the chip incident and another minor skirmish, reversing into a lamppost that refused to get out of the way, I had no room to criticise anyone's driving.

I went back to wondering what James had been buying for Simone. A necklace, a bangle? What if it was an engagement ring? It wasn't any of my business but why was he getting married so soon after a divorce? It was absolutely ridiculous. It could be that she was pregnant. Well, if that was the case, she'd look fat in a wedding dress. Ha! What if the baby wasn't his? Hang on, what if I was going mad?

I looked across at Dad behind the steering wheel in his sheepskin jacket and smiled. Indicating in the shopping precinct? If I was going mad I was going to be in good company.

I got ready that evening singing to Christmas number ones'. 'All I want for Christmas is you, Lawrence.' I lowered my voice at his name and, with a last flourish of mascara, snapped the stereo off and teetered down the stairs in my high heels and long frock.

'By 'eck love, you little smasher.' Dad beamed with pride. Mum loved my dress, said she'd seen one similar in the Charity shop the other day for £4.99 but it was a size 18 so it would have been too big. It was good to know. They were also going out to a party, both dressed smartly, Dad suited with his RAF tie, Mum in her skirt that all the fuss had been about earlier that year. One thing was certain, Dad's tie would not be so beautifully placed about his collar when they returned from their evening out later. When they left I fidgeted until it was time for me to go. I must have looked in the mirror a dozen times checking eye-shadow, hair, lipstick. I was thoroughly sick of my face by the time I left the house.

I picked Diane up first. She resembled a 1950s screen siren, her curves shown off to the full, her hair dyed dark brown and curled onto her face, her eyes darkly accentuated and her lips red and full. We arrived in a state of glamour at Anna's who, low and behold, was in a state of undress, a towel wrapped round her peachy skin. Resigned to this by now we sat down having helped ourselves to a glass of wine each. Half of the items in the living room were missing, gone to another home; it wasn't just the children who were to be split down the middle.

'I've made a Christmas hat, look,' Diane said, and pulled out of a plastic bag a coat hanger shaped to fit the top of her head covered in silver tinsel with mistletoe drooping from one end. It was something reminiscent of the old Doctor Who series where cyber men were made of tinfoil and the scenery of cardboard.

'You're not seriously going to wear that are you?'

'Absolutely, but not seriously, more ... jokingly.'

'Okay.'

'You may borrow it if you wish, after I've had a go,' Diane said, putting it carefully back in the bag.

'I'll look forward to it.'

'No you won't. I'm not offended that you think the wheels have finally fallen off, you'll be pleading for a go later.'

I wasn't convinced.

'Just wait and see. That'll teach you, Tom Tosser,' she said under her breath.

With Anna ready at long last, blonde hair like an angelic halo, red satin dress devilishly clinging, we headed off to the party.

Fergal was the first face we saw as we entered. His beard neatly trimmed, his grey hair flowing freely but tidily, a contained Grizzly Adams. He immediately offered to buy a round, pulling Anna with him to the bar. Diane and I followed the sound of 'Merry Christmas' by Slade into the next room. Starched white cloths covering large circular tables were festooned with crackers, streamers and candles, and glinting light from a glitter-ball in the centre of the room bounced off tinsel bunting draped from the ceiling, furnishing the entire display with shimmering sparkle.

Diane seated herself at one of our society's tables placing her hat under it and the room quickly filled up with people milling about, trying to sort out who was sitting next to whom, attempting to arrange seating to their advantage.

'Paula, Glen, we're sitting here, come and join us!' Diane shouted. Anna and Fergal came from the bar carrying the drinks, followed by Paula and Glen. There was a general air of anticipation that made us all tipsy, our voices lifting a semi-quaver or two on the first sip of alcohol. I idly wondered where Fergal's wife was, I'd never met her and as he'd always fondly referred to her as 'the ram' I'd expected him to have a woman with curly horns in tow.

There was no room at our table when Lawrence arrived. Paula was, after all, the society musical director and as such drew people to share in her esteem. Our new piano player, Kenneth, sat like a frightened rabbit next to me, murmuring what sounded like strange incantations under his breath then whistling. Knowing from experience what it's like to be a shy outsider, I tried to engage him in conversation but he merely looked at me startled, told me basically to back off because his wife was into martial arts and returned to his muttering. I was, therefore, more than a little miffed when I observed Lawrence and Shrubby sit at another table. I blew into a party blower that shot downwards into my drink, taking orders directly from my bad humour. This was going to be a really shit do. Why did that make me smile? Don't know. To the right of me Diane was shouting rude remarks over to Lawrence's table and receiving even ruder comments back, which was making her laugh very loudly. I was about to join in when Irene, sitting next to Kenneth, asked me a question. It must have been about five minutes later, although it felt longer, when Lawrence came over to our table. He stood by Paula's chair and looked directly at me.

'Everyone okay here?' he enquired, interrupting Irene who was enthralling our half of the table with the time she wore a sequined off-the-shoulder dress and shook hands with someone famous I'd never heard of.

'Oh, Lawrence how lovely you made it.' Phil Simpson's wife, Kristina, who was wearing the lowest cut, verging on indecent, dress I'd ever seen, spoke breathily, sounding like Marilyn Munroe wishing the President happy birthday.

'Looking forward to hearing you play later,' Phil said.

'Then I won't get too drunk now then. Or should I?'

'Entirely up to you, dear boy, whichever makes you play better,' Phil said expansively, waving his empty wine glass about before diving in for more from the bottle.

'How are you, Grace? You look lovely tonight,' Lawrence said to me.

All faces turned and looked. I wanted to slide under the table in embarrassment, but instead I beamed and did the one thing you should never do with a compliment. I threw it away.

'Does that mean I don't normally?' I should really have just hit myself on the head with a plank of wood and been done with it.

'Women! You all look lovely tonight ladies. I'll enjoy having your knickers thrown at me later.'

'Really, Lawrence, what are you like?' Phil Simpson's wife breathed and I had the impression she was wriggling out of her knickers under the table as she spoke.

'I won't be; I'm not wearing any.' Anna smirked at the surprise on the faces round the table; Irene's in particular demonstrating distaste, giving rise to a loss of wine from Diane's nose before she laughed and choked at the same time.

'I'm joking; it would take me half an hour to get out of the bloody holdy-in things I'm wearing. If I did throw them they'd cover the stage and take me with them.'

Everyone laughed.

'Enjoy your meal.' Lawrence left.

I felt sick. Why hadn't I just thanked him for the compliment? Anna smiled at me encouragingly.

The food started appearing and before long none of us could move, weighed down by turkey and wine, fair sinking beneath silent, gaseous belches of fulfilment. I felt gross, my support pants working hard to manage the additional stone it now felt I was carrying.

'Paula's not drinking, have you noticed?' Anna whispered.

I hadn't, being too consumed with what was going on elsewhere to consider this bombshell, however I gave Anna a knowing look, jumping to the same conclusion immediately.

'More wine anyone?' Phil was already slurring, trying too hard to get more wine out of an empty bottle.

'Darling, I think the bottle may be empty.' His long-suffering wife reached up to take it from him.

'Ah, shut up,' Phil said to her then stood up and wandered away to the bar. She leapt up and followed him

'What a prat,' Fergal said loudly to the rest of us.

'I hope you're not referring to me there,' Shrubby said, rounding the table to sit in one of the now vacant seats. The last time I'd seen him I'd wanted to take his place in the band so badly I'd wished him ill. I still did. I dreamt of nothing else these days. The first time I'd met him he'd called me a nice person. I wasn't.

'Nota Gain, hello.' I tried to be funny. No one laughed.

'Is there something in the food we've just eaten to make everyone so rude?' Fergal asked.

'I was just ... never mind. It was a really crap joke.' I got a fleeting impression that Shrubby was offended. 'Sorry.' I looked straight at him to apologise. Penetrating brown eyes looked back at me, all seeing eyes that seemed to say, I know you want me out of the way; I know you want my place in the band. I bluffed a smile to hide away from him.

'Shrubby here is a Nota Gain with Lawrence, everyone,' Anna explained.

'Oh, you're with Lawrence.' There was a buzz of excitement round the table. 'Where's the rest of the band? How long have you been with them? What instruments do you play? Do you sing? Are you single?' He parried the rush of questions capably.

'You may be the first person then to try out my new hat,' Diane said, reaching below the table to wrestle with the plastic bag her hat was contained in.

'What does she look like?' Anna said.

Diane, undeterred, fitted the tinsel coat hanger on her head with the message loud and clear, the sorry looking piece of mistletoe hanging over her forehead.

'Hey up, I'm in.' Shrubby rubbed his hands as Diane left her seat and marched over to him, by now gaining looks from those nearby who thought they were seeing things. Sniggers started around the table as she bowed her head over Shrubby to get her reward.

'What a great idea,' Fergal said. 'Can I have a go next? Anna you can borrow the hat too, and you Irene and Paula. In fact, just line up ladies,' he said to the whole table.

Shrubby by now was flapping his arms, indicating he needed air. Diane let him go eventually and beamed at the table.

'Who'd like to try my hat next?'

'Go on, Anna,' Fergal urged.

'I like this table,' Shrubby said. 'Oh, have to go, have been given my orders.' He put his hand up, acknowledging the call from Lawrence the other side of the room, then stood up. Everyone by now was watching the hat, fascinated as it changed heads, comments flying from eager mouths. I felt something at the back of my chair and looked one way to see an arm, the other to see a body then upwards to see a face.

'Maybe you'd like to try the hat on later,' Shrubby said, so quietly I thought I'd misheard him. He was gone before I could reply, my heart pounding blood to all corners of my body.

Diane, pink with excitement, came and sat down next to me. Anna was now wearing the hat, somehow managing to look good with it on.

'Come on you, let's go and get some drinks, look what you've started,' I said to Diane.

'What?' She was all innocence.

We went to the bar. Phil had his arm round his wife, more to steady himself by the looks of things than out of any affection. A good-looking man who dwarfed everyone around him with his height and body mass came and stood by us at the bar. He was, quite simply, the most gorgeous male in the place, square jaw, dark hair, melting chocolate-brown eyes with a smile of perfect white teeth. I know this because he smiled at me and started chatting.

'Who are you here with?' he asked.

'Deanhead Choir. You?'

'Thursby Rugby Club. We're here because of Trev Shrubb.'

'Oh Shrubby, I've just had to give his tonsils a good seeing to,' Diane said.

'Why is he ill?'

'He wasn't when I left him.' She gave him a look of pure satisfaction.

'Are you the one he keeps going on about?' he asked her.

'I wouldn't know; I could be though because I have these, hey, hey.' Diane looked surprised then pushed her breasts closer together and pouted her lovely red lips. I had a sudden inkling that I knew to whom he was referring. No, it couldn't be, I was being far too presumptive, he must know loads of women. But, what if it was? I could feel my blood zoom in all directions again. Diane really needed to learn how to be less like a ladette when she'd had a few, all decorum losing itself in excitement. I slapped

198

her hands which were still pushing her boobs together and made her laugh.

'Sorry about my friend, she's never met ... people before.'

Dave, our newfound gorgeous friend, was very impressed all the same with her attributes and followed us back to our table. Sounds of a strumming bass guitar and a pip or two on the trumpet overrode 'Stop the Cavalry' currently audible from the speakers. I heard a clarinet go up and down the scales and felt vulnerable all of a sudden. I hated the feeling, I didn't want it to be true that Shrubby had the hots for me, I hadn't encouraged him in any way. I chided myself for being so big-headed and had to ask myself how old I was. Any further thoughts were disrupted by the DJ.

'One two, one two. Good evening ladies and gentlemen, Merry Christmas and welcome to a night of partying, the lads are ready so without further ado let's have a warm welcome for Lawrence and the Nota Gains.'

We all whooped and screamed as the piano did a solo intro. The hat was now on the head of an old lady with flossy, white hair who must have been eighty if she was a day. She leant over and kissed what looked to be her husband full on the lips receiving cheers from her fellow comrades round the table. Who were these people? I felt envious of the old couple, my mind conjuring up in a few seconds a rose cottage in the sunshine, lemonade on the patio, straw hats, watering cans, old wellington boots, apple trees and grandchildren running in flowing white clothing across a lawn the old couple had devoted their lives to.

This was how Lawrence and I would be in old age, how lovely. There he was on stage now, looking so distant and untouchable, totally involved in a world consisting of nothing but music. Already people were up throwing shapes, dancing, eager to work off their dinner, aiding and abetting indigestion. And it wasn't long before I was there with them, along with Fergal, Anna, Diane, Paula now wearing the hat, Glen and our gorgeous friend Dave with a few other rugby mates, all dancing like crazy, trailing tinsel, singing along, every now and then posing with new moves.

At one point, when I thought a heart attack imminent, I sat down at our table and watched, drinking a large glass of water then more wine. I noticed that Fergal kept grabbing Anna at any given opportunity and Anna responded in kind. Diane drifted over and sat down with me.

'Where's Fergal's wife?' I asked.

'Oh, didn't you know, they've split up. She threw him out just over a week ago. I'm not quite sure why. It could be that their children have grown up and are independent or she was just fed up with him, I don't know, but he's living in a flat not far from me at the moment, I thought I'd told you.'

'Is she having an affair?'

'What, the ram? I don't think so, but maybe she is.'

I said nothing to allude to the relationship that seemed to be blossoming between Fergal and Anna, Diane was quite capable of seeing it for herself. I loved both of them and it seemed fitting that they were together. I wondered who Diane would find and hoped it would be someone nice, someone like Shrubby. No, he was my conquest. But what if Shrubby really was referring to Diane and not me? That wasn't such a great thought after all and I looked over at him on the stage, feeling a sense of ownership. I didn't want him as a partner but then I didn't want him to be anyone else's either. I was a contrary cow-bag.

'You're being called.' Diane shoved me.

'Grace Scott, calling Grace Scott.' Lawrence was speaking into the microphone, 'We want you up here to play 'Bill Bailey'.'

Diane sprang up shouting, 'She's here, she's here,' dragging me up. This was the second time he'd done this to me, putting me in a spotlight I shied from but relished at the same time. I had no option but to saunter as nonchalantly as I could over the dance floor, up the little staircase to one side of the stage then onto it.

Lawrence bowed as I approached, increasing my embarrassment and Shrubby grinned at me sheepishly. The other lads looked a bit wary but seemed game to give me a chance. I mouthed 'Pig,' to Lawrence before taking up the proffered clarinet from Shrubby and tooting loudly down it to pretend I didn't have a clue how to play it. My, how people laughed ... not at all.

Chapter 15

I remember standing there for what seemed like five minutes watching the audience from the stage before playing a single note but I didn't, apparently I just went for it or so I was told by Anna later. It was strange to see people turn and watch then start to jig as the rhythm started with Rich joining in with the drums and Percy strumming on the bass. From somewhere I thought I heard a banjo. Maybe not. I started to perspire from the heat on stage, a fine haze misting about me from the warmth I was generating. Fortunately, I had danced some of the turkey off so it was neither trying to regurgitate down the clarinet nor burst out of my knickers with the deep breaths I was taking.

When I came to the end I heard people clapping. That was it, I wanted to do more but the clarinet was taken from me and I did a small curtsey before trundling back off the stage to stand with the great unwashed again. It was all a blur but I knew I hadn't shamed myself by a poor performance, that possibly people, who were expecting a Les Dawson type of effort, were mildly surprised when I played in tune.

My long dress hid the legs that shook beneath it, legs that carried me to a chair and treated my bum to a hearty thwack by completely giving way on descent. As my drink found my mouth, my eyes caught sight of gorgeous Dave wearing the hat and snogging Phil Simpson's wife, little and large. It bought a perspective to what had just happened. While I concerned myself with the enormities of my performance, expecting every person in the room to have an opinion on it, on me, they didn't. I was already forgotten. It was easy to see how stars managed to get so carried away with their own importance when I'd only played one tune, had applause and suddenly thought I was the queen of the party.

I received congratulations from Anna and Diane who said they were going to be my agents, a wink from Fergal and a kiss from gorgeous Dave who refused to let go of the hat now he had it, then all of a sudden we were all up dancing again as though my brief performance hadn't happened. Paula was called onto the stage to sing 'Think' from The Blues Brothers. We all went bananas.

Lawrence and the boys finished with 'Hold on I'm coming' with everyone up dancing, Lawrence now away from his piano and relishing his front-man status, Sangster and Shrubby dancing in time throwing their instruments up and down, Percy playing bass guitar with the ease he strummed his double bass. I was so proud and in love with them all.

The disco went into full swing, Phil, the chairman, body popping on the dance floor to the surprise of the older members of the society. I managed to hold a serious conversation on keeping tomatoes with a keen gardener and one of the few sober people in the building until gorgeous Dave came to my rescue and pulled me onto the dance floor. It was there that Lawrence, Shrubby and Percy all joined in and pranced around with us.

The evening was drawing on; my feet were tired and my glass was empty when I sat down at last, joining Anna and Fergal for a quiet moment. I spied Diane on the far side of the dance-floor running away from a tall fair-haired man wearing her tinsel hat. I removed my shoes and stretched my toes relaxing my body back onto the chair, a small smile of happiness lifting my mouth contentedly.

From lowered eyelids, I watched Fergal hold up a piece of mistletoe above Anna's head and her respond with intoxicated abandon. They moved apart and Anna smiled naughtily over at me.

'I think it's your turn,' she said to me across the table. 'Here Shrubby, I dare you to use this.' Shrubby had just come over to the table to drink from his pint. She gave him the mistletoe. 'I think you should kiss Grace.'

My heart almost stopped beating with shame. I remained where I was, portraying a woman at ease, feeling anything but. Shrubby kept hold of the mistletoe but didn't hold it aloft and move in for the kill, he just stood looking down on me. I had a sudden feeling that he was going to decline and I held my breath, not knowing what to anticipate and unsure which outcome would bring relief. The mistletoe remained at his side as he bent and came to within an inch of my lips. I couldn't help but smile with nerves because, even then, I was uncertain he would complete his task. Our lips met, I felt my heart drop down to my stomach, which in turn seemed to be in a state of collapse. His mouth was firm and persuasive, soft and gentle, I didn't stand a chance. He moved away too soon and I had to keep my eyes lowered, looking to one side so he didn't see the desire that betrayed my reposed attitude.

I couldn't believe it. How the hell had that happened? I'd never felt so stunned, my head told me one thing and my body just decided to ignore it, reacting against it as though my insides had just been touched individually by his mouth. I sat up wondering if he felt the same but he was downing the remainder of his pint in one, the mistletoe discarded on the table.

'Now your turn,' Anna said to Fergal, grabbing hold of the mistletoe and shoving it above our heads. I desperately wanted the same response to Fergal's kiss to assure me that what had just happened wasn't out of the ordinary but his was a variation on a plunger sucking soggy vegetables from a sink. His beard, not nearly as soft and fluffy as it looked from a distance, scoured my chin unfavourably. I was acutely aware that Shrubby was still at the table.

'Come on you lot, New York, New York,' Diane shouted, running over to the table, her tinsel hat back on her head and wearily bobbing to one side.

We were dragged into a circle and put our arms round the people either side of us to sway in time to the classic end-of-night song. Although I, like everyone else, tunelessly yelled along to Frank Sinatra, all around kicking legs flew higher and higher with exuberance; I was still in a state of unreality over Shrubby. He was two bodies away laughing with his neighbour over getting a pointed stiletto shoe rammed into his leg. To my dismay, my eyes kept straying in his direction, even when the song was over and the lights came up. I watched him wander out to the bar area until hidden from view.

'What's up?' Lawrence came and sat down beside me.

'Nothing,' I replied.

'When a woman says that it means 'something'. Come and sit here with me and tell all.' He led me to a table.

'Okay, I'm pooped.'

'That was some performance before, I'm glad we got you up. I've just been approached by someone asking for your telephone number,' Lawrence said.

'Oh? Who?'

'Some woman with very strong perfume and a beautiful pair of boobs. I don't know who she is. She was over there a minute ago talking to Shrubby. As I don't know your number I asked her for hers instead, unfortunately she gave me the finger, you know the one with a wedding ring on it. Theory blown for girl on girl action at the same time. Oh God, Phil Simpson's wife is on the rampage again.' Lawrence disappeared under the table, both of his lean hands placed on my knees. I could feel him laughing more than I could hear him.

'Oh, wasn't Lawrence sitting with you just then?' Katrina asked. Tit tape, having lost its battle to keep her dress in place, gave her the appearance of a post-op patient.

'No not with me, you must have been seeing things. I'll let him know you're looking for him though if I see him.' I thought for one hideous moment that she was going to sit down next to me. 'Oh, I think I've just seen him leaving out of the bar.' I pointed to emphasise my statement.

'Thanks.' She hurried off.

'You can come out now,' I said to the table.

'I like it here.'

I lifted the tablecloth and looked under it. Lawrence was gazing at my mid-section. 'Earth calling Lawrence,' I said softly. He let go of my knees and bumped his head.

'What are you two up to?' Paula asked as she passed us on her way to retrieving her handbag.

Lawrence started knocking on the floor and on the chairs as he climbed out of hiding, doing a spoof on Basil Fawlty.

'Jean Webster was looking for you before, I thought you'd gone,' Paula laughed.

'Who's Jean Webster?' I asked.

'She's something to do with the North Western Symphony Orchestra. I'd say she was pretty impressed with your performance,' Paula said.

'Symphony orchestra? But I was playing jazz, or was I?'

'You have lessons with Sam Gerrard don't you? It's his, doobree doo, you know, daughter. She'll no doubt be there at your concert tomorrow evening, not to put you off or anything.'

I was non-the-wiser other than to the fact that she was not a lesbian and had great tits. It suddenly hit me that Lawrence had had his hands on my knees for a good couple of minutes and I'd not even given it a second thought. Bugger, I'd not made the most of the situation and now the moment had passed because, with Lawrence in full view again, we were attracting the attention of the others who migrated over to us, all wanting to know if anything was planned now the party was over. Anna sidled up to me and told me she was going to go home with Fergal, who was waiting for her down the road, otherwise everyone could have piled back to hers.

The staff expertly shepherded us out of the hotel and left us standing in the cold December night. All the while, I had been looking for Shrubby but there was no sign of him and with Diane conspicuous by her absence, it lead to a calculation of devastating proportions. I didn't know whether it was because I'd misjudged who he kept on going on about to his friend or whether my friend was kissing someone who, less than an hour ago, had made my whole being escape from the known world. My phone lit up with a text. 'Gone home, have company, tell all 2moro.' It was Diane. My heart retreated to a dark corner to console itself.

Paula was the last to come out, looking very pale. Glen was at her side with his arm round her shoulders keeping her warm. She offered me a lift home as they passed it on the way home, explaining that she'd stopped drinking hours ago. Straggling partygoers were keen on trying to get into a bar that was open until fall-over-o'clock. I was torn between the sensible thing, go home, or the ludicrous freeze-your-arse off ending up going home anyway thing to do. Despite the fact that Lawrence was walking off in the direction of the nearest bar I didn't follow, even when a number of others moved off in his wake.

I was cold. Without giving it anymore thought I got into Paula's car, which had pulled up beside me. The opportunity had been there to stay in Lawrence's company and I hadn't taken it. Maybe I'd have liked him to invite me specifically; maybe I wanted Shrubby there too to look after us all.

Glen nodded at Paula then turned to me and said, 'Just to let you know that Paula's expecting, she's had the scan, everything is fine. We've not told many people yet but Anna guessed and we thought you might be wondering why she wasn't drinking.'

'Oh Paula, I'm so pleased for you both. You shouldn't have stayed out so long, you must be knackered.'

'Apart from having just been sick and my doobree doos, you know, boobs feeling like ton weights I'm okay actually, two weeks back I'd have struggled past ten o'clock.'

I was glad of the distraction, wholeheartedly partaking in their excitement over names and preference of sex, not how they did it but rather boy or girl preference. Without warning I felt Shrubby's lips on mine and the rest of the conversation went unheard.

'See you for the concert Monday night. Take it easy the pair of you,' I said getting out of the car and waving them off before I headed up the path and in through the front door.

The hallway was in darkness. I stumbled over Roger, stretched like a draught excluder across the entrance to the living room, and switched the main light on, its stark illumination hurting my eyes. I preferred the dark. I turned the fire on, turned the light off and sat in the warm, glowing gas flames. I gazed into them, letting the increasing orange brightness diffuse my vision, and let my thoughts fancifully wander where they wanted, not curtailing them in any way.

Reality returned with the sound of keys in the front door. The next minute, like a tornado, Mum and Dad entered, bathing everything in the ghastly overhead light again, discussing how much the taxi home had cost and whether or not to have a cup of tea and some toast before going to bed. As I'd suspected earlier, Dad's tie was being worn like a medallion halfway down his chest, his footsteps unbalanced, his eyes crinkled with humour.

'Put the kettle on, Ted,' Mum said.

'I can't, it won't fit me,' Dad said with the hint of a slur. He parked himself on the arm of the chair. Mum went to sort the tea out. She opened the back door to let Roger out, filled the kettle and popped some toast in the toaster.

'Nice time, love? Good ... we did. I was told off tonight. I took my jacket off before Mr Captain had removed his.' Dad said, slipping off the arm of the chair and into it.

'Who's Mr Captain when he's around?' I asked.

'The golf club's captain. Bum on him. Bloody stupid game anyway.' Dad sniffed and pulled a face to make me laugh.

'Toast, Grace?' Mum shouted from the kitchen.

'Go on then.'

Dad's eyes were drooping until he coughed and woke himself up.

'Bloody cough,' he muttered. 'Any whisky, Bren?' he called.

'No,' Mum lied.

I got off my backside and went to help with the tea.

'Your dad's had too much to drink. He was doing his usual best buddy thing, acting the fool, telling everyone they were great, even Mr Captain who, I've found out on the way home, has a chandelier light fitting he's wanting to get rid of.' She raised her eyes heavenward resigning herself to its portent.

'Here, give me the mugs.' I took the tea in while Mum carried the toast, the smell of which brought Dad round. By the time he'd finished he was surrounded in crumbs. They both wanted to know how the evening had gone. I told them about playing on stage and had a laugh about the mistletoe hat.

I'll clear up, Mum, you get to bed,' I said. She looked tired and Dad, now fed, was snoring. 'See you in the morning.'

With a lot of persuasion, Mum eventually got Dad up the stairs. I brushed the crumbs that silhouetted where he'd been sitting off the chair and onto the carpet ready for the vacuum tomorrow then carted the mugs and plate out and threw the last unwanted piece of toast to Roger. With the house now drifting off to sleep, I went and sat near the fire's warmth again and back to dreaming into the flickering firelight.

Chapter 16

I received a call from Diane next day while I was practising, half-heartedly, for that night's orchestra performance.

'I'm so sorry about leaving you last night Grace, but everything happened so suddenly. One minute I was wearing my hat snogging away in the bar, then the next minute I was being shoved in a taxi home. I just got carried away with the moment. I don't normally do getting carried away. It was only when I got to the front door that I thought you might worry, you know?'

I steeled myself to hear that Shrubby was good in bed and that he'd taken her to a place she'd never been before, you know the usual crap. I couldn't blame her, I'd not exactly claimed him as my own, I didn't even know that was what I wanted, I just knew it would hurt when I heard her say it.

I postponed the moment by saying, 'It was all a bit mad last night at the end. I got a lift home with Paula and Glen and was eating toast and drinking tea at one in the morning,'

'Fantastic. I've had sex, I've had sex, I can't believe it; it was amazing.' Diane was beside herself with excitement.

'So I take it that he's left the building.'

'He's gone to get some bacon, but he's coming back and we're going to eat late breakfast in bed.'

'Say hello to Shrubby for me when he gets back.'

'Say hello to who? Shrubby? Why, is he going to join us for a threesome?'

'Oh so ... sorry, who was amazing last night?'

'Rich, you know, the drummer, he's got the most amazing arms.' She was in raptures and so was I. 'Got to go, he's at the door, really sorry about last night again but I thought you'd be pleased.'

My clarinet practice took on a completely new dimension after that. It was uplifting, and, even if I say so myself, dynamic.

Mum and Dad went to buy some bits and pieces to hang on the Christmas tree, which didn't need any more to adorn it as it was busting out all over, but Mum liked her baubles. While they were out I put the stereo on and played 'The more I see you' by Chris Montez, dancing like a ballerina, a very bad one, in the living room until I was spotted by the next-door neighbour, whereupon I pretended to be cleaning the windows. It was a joyous morning.

I called round to Anna's for a cup of tea. We sat in her kitchen, dunking biscuits, laughing at the previous night's shenanigans. Outside the weather had taken a turn for the worse and warning gusts of hard-hitting rain spat noisily on the window. I had my back to the radiator and my hands round a mug to keep me warm. The plates on the rail were not to be part of Peter's future and remained looking down on us. I eventually plucked up the courage to grab a chair, stand on it and turn the demented Cairn terrier to face the wall. Anna didn't bat an eye.

'Phil Simpson was sick in the taxi. He was with Kristina, Irene and her husband. They all had to get out and order another one and pay twenty pounds to the taxi driver. They were left waiting an hour in the middle of nowhere until another taxi turned up. Kristina got her tits out to try and get the taxi driver to change his mind. Irene's going ballistic, says she's got the flu and it's all Phil's fault. Phil is apparently blaming Irene for saying to the taxi driver, "Do you know who I am?" which got them kicked out.'

We snorted.

'Diane has finally had sex,' I said.

'I know, about time. Maybe now she'll calm down and decide what she wants in life.'

'How's that?'

'She's been determined to get back at Tom for what he's done. He's been the one calling the tune and, in her own mind, having sex with someone else was how she was going to separate herself from him, now she's her own person. On top of which she's had a bloody good seeing to.'

'Now that would really confuse me.'

'We're all different. Anyway, talking of sexy, Lawrence said you looked lovely last night. You did look fantastic.' I knew why she was my friend!

'I think you looked stunning,' I replied. Without a word of a lie, Anna would look good in a plastic bin liner, curlers and slippers.

'Well, there we go, we both looked fabulous. Why didn't you go to the bar with him and the others?' she asked.

'I don't know now, I just get the impression that he's used to people running after him and I don't know how much effort he would put into someone who didn't. D'you know what I mean? Don't know if I can be bothered at my age. I've learnt three lessons from James. Number one, never get involved with a man again. Number two, never allow anyone near enough to cause damage, and number three, keep a lid on expectations.'

Anna looked thoughtful. 'One and two are a bit extreme and, if you don't mind me saying, really boring. What sort of life is that? Maybe you should just go out with someone else then, it's about time you did. How about Shrubby? He won't wreck your head and you could try to get into the swing of things with him. He likes you.'

My heart swooped like a kite in a keen wind. 'Oh yeah. Oh shit.' A dunked piece of biscuit plopped back into the mug as I raised it ready for munching.

'I saw the way he looked at you, he wasn't thinking your frock was pretty, I doubt you were even wearing one in his eyes.'

'Bloody hell, what a waste of a hundred and twenty quid.'

'Give me that.' Anna took the mug away from me as I looked distractedly at the biscuit breaking up and ruining a good cuppa, and boiled the kettle again.

'What about you and Fergal?' I asked her.

'If I'm totally honest I'm a bit fed-up, actually. I think I'm ready for a bit of romance. Fergal's never going to sweep me off my feet. He only likes sex in bed. When I mentioned trying sex in the garden, he freaked and said he'd catch pneumonia. The other night he did a massive fart after we'd made love and then he laughed saying he needed to go for a shit before he followed through. I'm all for speaking your mind but it really turned my stomach.'

'Eeyuck. So another one bites the dust,' I said, sorrowfully.

'No, he's coming back later, after the concert.'

'Oh...' I was taken aback with what she'd said, not a first where Anna was concerned. A man had talked of poo and farting whilst in bed and she was still keen to do it all again. If it had been me, I would have probably been in tears and felt so unclean it would have taken me a year to get over it. I was looking for the perfect setting, the perfect man, the perfect sex. As she'd recently pointed out, how boring.

'I want to be more like you and have a few men on the go at once. I don't know where to start though and the consequences frighten me. I'm just a frigid old cowbag.'

'No you're not. I wish I was more like you. It's ironic, where sex is concerned the more a girl puts out the less a girl gets put back in, apart from the obvious. I know this but still... All I want is someone to exchange an intelligent conversation with, someone who is interested in me and what I say and think. Peter wanted the young girl he married to remain as she was, the one who did anything he said and kept him on a pedestal. Fergal's a bigger gossip than a celeb magazine. And all he wants is sex. Where are all the decent men, Grace?'

She sighed and came back to the table looking a bit cagey with fresh cups of tea.

'I'm not sure if I should tell you this or not,' she said after a minute.

'What? You can't do that, you have to tell me.'

'Well, Fergal knows your James.'

'He's not my James anymore, but tell me what you know.'

The weather outside was turning nastier by the minute with darkening clouds draining the natural light out of the kitchen. I could hear more persistent rain striking the gutters above the window and racing along to the downspout, gurgling loudly on reaching the drains.

'James owed him some money, well over a year ago now. You know that Fergal is a car dealer and it was all over a car he'd bought from him. I don't suppose you remember James buying a Mini by any chance?'

I shook my head, dreading what was going to come next.

'Oh.' She looked strained. 'I don't know the full ins and outs but Fergal is a bit of a gambling man and so, it appears, is your ex-husband. Fergal got his money from him when James had had a big win on the horses. I don't know any more and I wasn't going to say anything but I thought you should know. I feel awful now.'

'A Mini?' I tried to understand what she was saying but to me, at that moment, it was like trying to work out a giant logarithm without paper or calculator.

Anna didn't say anything.

'A Mini? I've always wanted a Mini. Why would he buy a Mini and not tell me? You're not thinking that it was for someone else, are you?'

Anna shrugged.

'I know we didn't share things but ... gambling?' His duplicity was dawning on me. No wonder he didn't put up a fight when I told him I was leaving. It must have been a relief to see me go. The cheque he'd handed over, was that from gambling? I'm afraid I couldn't let myself believe it, I thought I knew him and now it seemed I hadn't the foggiest idea who I'd been married to.

'What the hell else was he up to?' I started to get upset. 'Am I going to find out he's got people buried under the patio, or that he's really a woman?'

'I know how you feel there.' Anna spoke at last. 'I don't want to pontificate but the fact remains you are better off without him and I told you because it was wrong that I knew and you didn't. He's out of your life now so, no matter what you hear, it's not going to alter things. I've watched you over the last couple of months change from someone who was scared of her own shadow to someone who stands up and gets counted. Don't let this knock you back down, please, or I may have to smack you with a wet kipper.'

'You're right; I don't care what he did, I'm just glad to be out of it. I just wish I'd done it a lot sooner.'

'You might be jumping to conclusions with the Mini, I mean, maybe he was buying it to sell it on, a bit of wheeling and dealing, ducking and diving.'

I sat quietly contemplating what I'd found out and see-sawed between anger and resentment. I didn't know what to think. If it was a business venture why hadn't he told me? I was his wife. If it had been bought for another woman why hadn't he left me? If it had been for him to enjoy then why had I never seen him drive it? If I went to James now and confronted him, told him exactly what I thought of him, what would that do? Nothing, we were divorced. It was over. If I did nothing what did that make me? Stupid? I'd lived in denial for too long, coping in my own way to retain my strongest asset, my dignity. I relied heavily on it now to help me put all I'd been told into perspective.

'I'm glad you told me, Anna.'

'What are you going to do?'

'What can I do? It would destroy me completely if I found out he'd been seeing another woman while married to me. I don't want to go there. I'd rather not know. Gambling and cars I can cope with, it possibly even helps me understand why it all went wrong.'

Anna got up and gave me a hug. The rain was now throwing itself down in despair outside.

'Here, have another biscuit. Just be thankful you don't have to cope with Fergal's bodily functions.'

'I'm glad I'm single.' I truly meant it.

It was a nightmare journey home. It was dark, the weather was foul, the roads full of puddles, traffic, pedestrians, shoppers and mental Christmas lights. My mind was churning like a newspaper press, headlining 'woman arrested for trying to run ex-husband over in clapped out old banger,' or 'clapped out old banger arrested for trying to run ex-husband over with another woman.' I was being daft as a way of dealing with what I'd found out. My revenge was that I had found a better life without him. Whether he knew it or not, I knew it and that was all that mattered.

Back at home, I put my stereo on quietly in the bedroom and played Rachmaninov's second piano concerto, sobbing into my pillow until I fell asleep, and I was cold and grumpy when I woke up in the dark an hour later. The smell of Sunday roast dinner invaded every corner of the house and the sound of classical Christmas Carols heralded from the living room below, Mum must be ironing.

It was a scene of domestic bliss downstairs, Dad painting with oils in the front room; Mum indeed ironing, illuminated brightly by a monstrous chandelier hanging heavily from the ceiling. Roger was chewing on a dinosaur-sized bone in the kitchen. I asked permission for a bath and sank into it for half an hour.

I would never know what had gone on behind my back during the course of my marriage, but certain discrepancies now seemed to make sense.

He'd always been vague over his business finances, giving the impression that money had no hold over him, which I'd attributed to his affably cute nature. It had made sense for me to pay the mortgage, electricity, gas and the council tax from my regular income, which alleviated the pressure of earnings from the shop. He'd suddenly come home with an expensive new gadget, essential for modern day living then sell it on a couple of months later, telling me it wasn't so essential after all. Money had occasionally disappeared from my purse. Money had strangely been found in my jacket pockets. Grandma's antique gold arm bangle... Once, he'd given me two hundred pounds to go clothes shopping and when I'd asked why, he'd replied, with a cheeky wink, that he'd had a win on the gee gees. I'd taken it as a huge joke. I'd never even queried it. How long would I go on thinking about the anomalies in our relationship? When did I draw a line and say "enough"?

Balancing perfectly between losing all rationale when I thought of James was a sense of optimism when I thought of Shrubby and Lawrence, I forced myself to think of the latter. It was hard but I had to live in the here and now. I could use Shrubby in the way I'd been used, and at the same time enjoy myself. Why not? Every other bugger seemed to please themselves, therefore so would I. That was if I ever saw him again. I could then move on to Lawrence with the experience I'd gained from Shrubby. It was a plan but not one I was 100% certain about.

Mum, Dad and Natalie were coming to see me play in the orchestra that evening so there was a sudden rush of activity to get ready. I was late and was still trying to park somewhere near the hall ten minutes later, ending up shoving the car under a bush more or less a mile away. I say this with some exaggeration because the weather, having spewed its rainy contents earlier, was now in respite but a freezing wind made any small distance feel like a mile.

I arrived just as pandemonium seemed very close to becoming mayhem in the hall corridor. Joan Sarney took control and ushered the musicians and the choir into a large room set off stage where chaos resumed on a smaller scale. She was going to be conducting us all and took matters very seriously.

'The order will be strings, woodwind, brass, percussion, choir. Look at the seating plan on the wall, here,' she pointed to the wall, 'and file yourselves, in order, at the side of the stage, here.' Joan pointed to a sign over a door clearly marked 'Stage Entry'. There was every chance we had suddenly been transported back to World War II on a mission to blow up a dam, her disposition being that of Captain Mainwaring.

'Spit that gum out, girl,' she shouted at a pretty girl who was blatantly pulling chewy from her mouth and wrapping it round her finger.

'I think she needs another cucumber job, don't you?' Fergal said at my side.

'She needs a tranquilliser, what's got into her?'

'A cucumber?'

'Fergal you really are vile sometimes.'

'I know.'

'Remember don't slouch, smile and watch me at all times.' Joan was in teacher mode, prepared to take prisoners if necessary and shoot them. I was in awe; I'd only ever seen the fluffy side of her.

The orchestra went to take its places, in order, warming up immediately. I saw Natalie, Mum and Dad and smiled back at them as they waved. With everyone seated at last, the choir marched in, followed lastly and importantly by Joan. She bowed to the applause and we were off.

It always made me think of the Tom & Jerry Die Fledermaus cartoon, when she tapped her baton on the stand in front of her to begin. She bore Tom's slightly lofty demeanour, eyes closed, nose skyward. She would suddenly disappear down a hole cut out by a naughty mouse then, one by one, we'd all fall with her. The orchestra was to play a Christmas medley intro. 'The First Noel' was my clarinet solo, coming in after the oboe. I loved every bit of it; this was where I was most confident. Goosebumps ran down my back at the end of my solo with Fergal adding a frosty air to my performance with Christmas bells just audible above the orchestra. There was a moment towards the end when, playing 'Troika' faster than a sleigh could slide downhill through the snow, the strings were at variance with everyone else but we managed to bring it all together by the end.

Any bitter feelings I had earlier in the day melted away with sheer joy, almost brought to tears when by girl with the voice of an angel as she sang 'Oh Holy Night' with the choir backing her. We ended the evening with 'Hark the Herald Angels Sing' with everyone in the hall singing, by which time we could have played any duff note and not been heard above the enthusiastic audience.

The choir filed out after much applause and we all started to put our instruments away. A few people were dashing off to the pub but most, with it being Sunday, were heading off home.

'Grace that was marvellous, I want you to do it all again.' Mum was overflowing with glad tidings.

'I thought you were the best,' Dad said kindly, proudly standing by me.

'Aah, I wanted to cry when that girl sang 'O Holy Night'.' Natalie gave me one of Dad's hugs, arm around the neck with a sharp squish into the body.

There was a woman hovering not far away when Natalie finally let go of my head. Dad had already spotted her and was still standing at my side, letting everyone know he was my dad. She looked enquiringly at me.

'Grace Scott?' she asked, coming forward with her arm out to shake my hand. Her voice was deep and husky and maybe on an equivalent level to the Queen for poshness.

With all that had gone on earlier I'd forgotten Mr Gerrard's daughter, Jean Webster.

'Grace, I'm Jean Webster, my father teaches you? That was a lovely performance.'

I thanked her. Mum and Dad said they would see me back at the house and Natalie followed them out of the hall, waving back at me as she went. Jean Webster asked if she could have a quiet word and while Fergal packed his instruments away and a large group of stragglers gathered in one corner of the hall, their clamour and enthusiasm echoing as the room emptied, we sat down in the front row seats.

'Grace, I don't know if you know but I'm heavily involved in The North Western Symphony Orchestra, a trial educational model subsidised by the government, funded by large business, to bring music to disadvantaged youths, which has recently been given further subsidy, and there is a position going to be vacant shortly for a clarinet player. I think you should audition, I'd like you to.'

'Oh my God, really?' I sounded about nine, my pitch far too high for an adult of thirty-nine. I lowered my voice down to her level. 'Gosh, how lovely.' Now I sounded like the Queen.

'There's plenty of time, auditions aren't until April. There will be many people auditioning, so choose your music carefully and just to let you know you could also be asked to sight read a piece of music as part of the audition process. May I give you one of our audition forms? I rather presumptively brought a few in my bag, along with details on the orchestra, salary etc. Our policy is to play the more well-known and popular classical and operatic pieces, it is, after all, how we get bums on seats and appeal to a more youthful audience and we travel a lot throughout the year around the country. We don't really go in for inflated egos, I like to think we're more like a big happy family.' She handed over five A4 sheets of paper and a brochure.

'Oh, Jean, there you are.' Joan Sarney came in from the back of the hall, having been chatting with her relations in the lobby by the front doors.

Jean ignored her. 'All the details are there as to where to send it when completed, but you can pass it to my father if you like, he'll make sure I get it. He's a big fan of yours.'

I blushed. Joan was now virtually on top of us, ending our exchange. I said goodnight to both of them, mixing my Jeans and Joan's and leaving in a whirl of confusion.

Fergal was still packing up. He winked at me mouthing 'congratulations.' I helped him cart the remaining instruments into his van. It was starting to spit as I made my way to the car, not that I cared in the slightest. My days were becoming more bizarre. One minute I was cowed by my past, the next I was being inspired by what the future could hold. The North Western Symphony Orchestra. It felt unreal. Was I being given a second chance? I saw a dog with only three legs hobbling down the road, its owner, a little old lady, hunched against the cold and I broke down crying in the car.

Chapter 17

Christmas came and went. Christmas Eve had been a case of drinking whisky with Mum and Dad at Natalie and Mick's then singing Everton songs with Dad on the wonky way home - Everton songs, I must have been drunk.

One family Christmas tradition, which may seem a trifle odd or even twee, is that as many family members as possible participated in performing something, anything from music and poetry to telling jokes, on Christmas night. This might seem like a good waste of drinking time but this was precisely why it had been brought into being, because there's nothing like the fear of performance to keep a sober head. To quickly dispel visions of a hearty fire in the parlour, ladies in pretty gowns and men in top hats playing charades, when I say music and poetry we're not talking Mozart or Milton. For our delights we had a few keyboard Christmas carols, The Two Ronnie's mastermind sketch, a song all about a badly fitted kitchen to 'All I Want for Christmas Is You', and Mum and Dad miming to 'My old man's a Dustman.' Dad had secretly been at the scotch, contrary to performance regulations, and other than being dressed like an old fashioned bin man he could have been miming 'The Hallelujah Chorus'. Mum was taking her cockney Lambeth walk seriously, stalwartly ignoring his incompetence while he tried to keep up, failing to remember any of the really crap old jokes in the song. What a pair of glorious idiots.

That was it, on Boxing Day everyone went home and festivities were reduced to lounging on the settee, eating chocolates and watching film repeats. I'd been through a Christmas I'd built up to be the test of my spirit, seeing others sharing everything, their laughter, their love, and had actually really enjoyed it. I thought of Anna and Diane and wondering how they were coping. They had children which made a big difference. Great if the kids were around, absolutely unbearable if they weren't. Oddly, in my case, this year was less painful than the last. I could try all I liked to make my relationship with James look normal on the outside but the strain of it had been paralysing on the inside. The past had happened to someone else, I don't know what I was doing at the time but it wasn't me in the hazy memories of desperate longing for love, of withering slowly into a lonely shell of self-pity. I wanted to tell that person, the old me, to get a grip and to stop being a soppy old tart.

I'd managed to get the whole Christmas week off from work. I think Max, my boss, had had enough of me. I knew I was lucky to have a job but my work ethic was in trouble, my attitude stank and I was becoming a truculent upstart in the bank environment, finding it harder and harder to accept new guidelines and rules being introduced. If I was to be treated like a teenage new girl I'd bloody well behave like one, it wouldn't get me far but, hey, I'd only reached the dizzy heights of general dogsbody by being co-operative.

A couple of days later I met up with Anna and Diane for lunch. We were in a pub which wasn't too far from Anna's, which meant it wasn't too far from where Shrubby lived. It wasn't my decision to eat there but I was on for-my-eyes-only standby in case he should turn up with Lawrence. Anna had spent Christmas Day with Peter and the children to maintain a semblance of continuity while Diane had spent it down at her brother's, Heather having the day with her dad.

'She said Tosser's very lonely. She said he's told her he's sorry he sent me away. Sent me away, I don't do sent away, if I'd wanted to stay I would have, bags packed or not. She certainly

225

takes after her mother for perseverance and I know she's only saying it to try and get us back to together, God bless her. If she's not, I'm glad he's lonely, it serves him right.'

Diane was without remorse. I don't think I was a hundred percent certain that her last comments were strictly true either. I could see lesson two quite blatantly through her demeanour, her barriers were up and no one was going to be allowed to cause further harm. Rich, the drummer had filled his boots, and hers, and hadn't been seen since. She didn't mind at all, it kept damage to a minimum.

Anna had spent Christmas Eve with Fergal after the children had gone to bed and he then had spent Christmas Day with 'the ram' and his three grown-up children. He'd not been seen since either. Anna wasn't taking this so well. Peter was taking the children to Devon for the New Year and they were at this moment somewhere on the M5. She wasn't taking this well either, looking tired, her anxiety palpable as we sat at the bar, browsing the lunchtime menu. Our conversation was stilted while finding a table to plonk ourselves at, all three of us mulling over the Christmas we'd had, failure to raise any humour an indication as to how well it had gone.

I longingly looked at the bangers and mash picture on the cover and plumped for a tuna salad while Diane was content with a baked potato, her diet still going strong. Anna ordered curly chips for a starter with dips and garlic bread then added her main course of vegetarian lasagne, chips and garlic bread.

'Where do you put it all?' Diane asked.

Anna shrugged and glugged her gin and tonic. She'd had an elderly couple round that morning to view her house just after the children had left. They hadn't gone through the estate agents, had instead turned up unexpectedly, asking if they might have a look round. She'd ended up making them a cup of tea and having a chat while, by the sounds of things, they'd tried to escape.

'That'll teach them, turning up out of the blue. I'm more pissed off with Peter for taking the children away. I couldn't say no, they desperately wanted to go with their dad. I know, do you think I should call Fergal and ask him if he wants to come for a drink?' she asked.

'I wouldn't if I were you. Let him do a bit of the running, wait for him to call you,' I said, you know, being the expert at relationships.

'I'll text him then,' she said, positively ignoring my call for restraint, her thumbs working quickly over her phone keypad. 'I knew this would happen. Now I'm on my own and I'm missing the children and all Fergal can think about is keeping his wife happy, not one thought for me.'

'You don't think the Ram's, you know, phew, phew him?' Diane whistled, indicating bonking, a bit tactlessly.

That was exactly what Anna was thinking and her mood gathered after she'd sent the text to him and got no reply. When her starter arrived she churned the same curly chip for five minutes in one of the dips, brooding menacingly at it. I almost felt sorry for the chip.

'Eat the chip,' I said eventually, pulling it out of the dip and putting it to her mouth. Diane and I mopped up the rest before it was all taken away and the main meal presented.

'Well, we are a happy bunch; it's not surprising nobody wants to be with us with faces like ours. I think we should get another drink before one of us starts crying,' I said. I glanced out of the window; it had been a clear, frosty morning, which was now turning into a bright, freezing day with people hurrying past, in the main wearing enormous Christmas jumpers and jackets. Even though he was surrounded by a giant blue scarf, swamped beneath a leather jacket which was way too big for him and half hidden by gorgeous Dave and two other friends, I recognised Shrubby; so I was at least in a position to be prepared for his appearance, he was not prepared for mine, which was quite apparent from the startled look I received when he saw me on entering the pub. I received a nod of recognition. I couldn't help the small frisson of disappointment that Lawrence wasn't out with him.

'Isn't that Dave who was at the Christmas party? You know, the really handsome rugby man?' Diane asked.

We all had a good look.

'I'll go and get some more drinks,' Diane said, quickly moving out of her chair to the bar, her baked potato left to go cold.

I surreptitiously ran my tongue over my teeth to make sure they weren't being decorated by any lettuce.

'Your teeth are fine,' Anna said, looking at me thoughtfully. She was such a slow eater, her lasagne looked untouched and tepid. Her phone beeped. She looked slightly happier when she'd read its message. 'Fergal,' was all she said.

Diane was still at the bar and I'd started doing my I'm such an exciting person routine by looking so animated I could have been mistaken for Minnie Mouse.

'Fergal, what does he know about anything?'

'He's coming out later for a drink, hope you don't mind, it's just that I need some male company tonight, with the children not being here I may as well make the most of it.'

'Mind? Me? Of course not, Fergal is a good laugh and you know I like his company, even if he, you know, doesn't completely float your boat.'

'Are you alright?'

'Me? Fine. I think the drink's gone to my head. Diane is taking her time.'

I could hear her laughing at that moment on her way back to the table with more drink.

'I've just told Shrubby he's safe today, the hat fell apart on the way home from the party. We get on so well, you know?'

'Really? Then why is he pulling faces behind your back?' Anna asked then started laughing when Diane turned to look behind her at the bar. 'Fooled you.'

The afternoon had taken on new aspect now that Shrubby and gorgeous Dave had turned up. They came and joined us and Dave, outrageous with 'Carry On' quips sprouting from him at any opportunity, had us cheered up in no time. He was spoken for but it didn't stop Anna flashing sultry eyes and flirting in a way only she could. Fergal arrived and joined our happy throng, adding nothing but sarcastic, under the breath comments, trying his best to upset those around him, his face like tripe, his easygoing, affable nature a ghost of its usual self. He actually looked angry. Shrubby sat opposite me, carelessly joining in, unaware that my head was desperately trying not to think of his mouth on mine the last time we'd met.

I was sat chatting to an old school friend, who I hadn't seen in years, when Shrubby came and sat beside me. My friend returned to her family and I turned to Shrubby.

'Nice Christmas?' I stammered.

'Very, thank you. You?'

Preliminaries over, we both sat at a loss as to what to say next. My conversation may not be the most scintillating but I usually mustered something up in dire situations.

'You'll be glad to know I'm not after your job,' I said suddenly.

'That's good news. Can I ask why you don't want to be in construction?'

'Good question. I didn't know that was what you did. What do you do?'

'Construction,' he said unhelpfully, then expanded. 'I train kids of sixteen to twenty-one in specialist engineering.'

'Ah, your kids.' That's why I'd thought he was married. 'Sounds better than banking.'

'Why don't you want my job then?'

'I've been asked to audition for an orchestra, and I thought it would interest you, you being musical and all that.'

'If I can help in any way then I will.'

'Would you audition for me?'

'Only if I can borrow those high heel boots you're wearing. Any suggestions on how to hide stubble?'

'Balaclava?'

He smiled. 'I don't suit them. You'll sail through.'

We discussed when the audition was and what would be expected and then discussed the gig he was playing later, then music in general, and chatted away like old mates. We'd moved on to where we would go if we had the money to travel anywhere in the world, when he suddenly stopped mid-sentence and looked at me earnestly, his eyes fully locking onto mine. All sound around us seemed to fade, taking a leaf from our conversation.

'Would you go out with me for a meal one evening?'

It would be over fifteen years since I'd last gone on a date. My nerves failed, I decided to ignore the question rather than answer it, to put the moment off where decision would be inevitable.

'The Amazon, now that would be amazing.'

'Is that where you want to go for a meal? I was thinking of somewhere a bit nearer.' He looked disappointed at my response; I was disappointed at my response and was plucking up the courage to say I'd love to go when gorgeous Dave parked himself down next to us with his pint.

'Not intruding between you two am I? Can I just say that your friend Anna is barking mad. She says that Liverpool Football Club is the only team to support, but they're not even challenging for the title. Man U are top of the league so in my book that makes them the best. There's no argument.'

'Yes there is, Liverpool are the best, they've won more league titles than anyone, the supporters are the best, and, and so's the anthem,' I said. It was all a bit flirty to be honest.

We had a full-scale, pointless discussion on who was the best team. If Lawrence had been with us he'd have been arguing Arsenal's case. But he wasn't so it was two to one in favour of Liverpool until Anna joined us and then it was three to one. As we were of the fairer sex we had to prove we knew our football by explaining the off-side rule. Poor Anna was caught out when she said it meant the man who normally scores goals for his team feels ill and changes sides in confusion.

'As opposed to the backside rule which means the player scores with his bum,' she concluded.

'You know your football,' Dave said.

'Yes, I don't know what Grace was talking about, all that nonsense about the last attacker being behind the last defender, or whatever, when the ball's played forward. I mean, come on, what sort of stupid game's that?'

Is there any way of explaining how the mind works, or is it just mine that's so contrary with its mistress? Now I wanted everyone to go away so Shrubby could ask me out again. I hadn't forgotten Lawrence; it was just with Shrubby's close proximity it was difficult to consider him. I may kiss Lawrence at some stage and feel nothing in which case he would diminish further. It was really that simple, or was it? An image of James fleetingly passed through my head, one of him smiling a cunning smile behind the wheel of a Mini Cooper. Just because almost a year had passed and Christmas had spelt a new dawn, didn't mean that he wouldn't arrive unbidden every now and then into my head. It was in dealing with it that signified a change. He disintegrated in seconds without causing havoc.

'Are you coming, Anna?' Fergal asked, approaching the table.

'Maybe,' Anna replied. 'Depends on what you have in mind.'

'A football game on Sky.'

'Then no.'

'Right, okay then, I'll see you over the New Year, bye everyone.'

Anna flashed her best come-to-bed eyes at gorgeous Dave, got up even though she'd indicated she wasn't prepared to leave, grabbed her coat, said a quick goodbye, looked at me for forgiveness and followed after Fergal.

'Looks like Anna will be learning the off-side rule tonight after all,' Dave commented.

I didn't like what I'd just seen. Anna was not a woman who subsided so easily to others' wishes. She was the one who normally controlled what went on around her, and there she was running after Fergal like a servant. Fergal, who I knew a little too much about to fully appreciate his sex appeal. Fergal, who laughed and joked constantly but who today looked like one cross word would send him into orbit. I got up to go after her but when I got to the door she'd already gone and wasn't anywhere to be seen.

I sent her a quick text to let her know if she wanted me to call me she could, went back inside and approached Diane who was talking to one of Shrubby's friends and asked if I could have a quiet word with her.

'What's up, my love?' she asked once the friend, who I think was called Rex, had gone to join the others.

'I'm a bit worried about Anna. She's not herself and neither is Fergal. What should we do?'

'What can we do? She's a grown woman and won't listen to a word that we say. You may as well blow raspberries for half an hour than have a talk to her about what she's doing to herself. Fergal would be the first person she's actually been with more than once since she and Peter split. It may just be that they've had a lovers' tiff and hopefully will sort it out, you know? I'll send her a text and make sure she's okay. I'll have to get back soon; Heather's been at her dad's all day. I don't know, one day on, one day off, the poor child's running between the Tosser and me trying to make sure we're both kept happy. I can't make her understand that her happiness is the main thing and that we come second.'

'Is there no chance of you getting back together?' I remembered the sadness on his face the night of our failed rescue mission. 'If he really is missing you it's a starting point. I've never asked you this before but is it all his fault that the marriage failed?' Diane looked slightly mutinous at this so I hastily carried on. 'I'm only going by my own experience and I can say that, up until the car business came to light, I always wondered if I'd done everything I could to save my marriage.

Tom's not gone out and found someone else has he? As far as you know he's not gambling, jacking-up, pimping or murdering people behind your back. He really could be ready to change for you. I mean, I'm not suggesting that you have to go back, or even that you should, just, you know, don't be too harsh. Perhaps it makes Heather feel better splitting herself between you in the hope that somehow a miracle will happen.'

'Absolutely,' she sighed. 'But I can't and won't go back to how it was. I'll never forget what he said to me that night after Blackpool or forgive him for the way he treated me. As long as I've got a beer and nice underwear I'm happy now.' Since her pop sock incident, Diane had taken more pride in what she sported in undergarments. 'Seriously though, I've had long chats with Heather over the reason for her dad and me splitting up, and keep telling her it wasn't anything she'd done. But she wants us to get back together again, even though we never did anything together as a family. Do you want to get a taxi home? If so, can I jump in it? It's freezing out there and I don't do cold.'

'Now?'

'Soon.'

I had an unfinished conversation to consider before leaving and it felt that it would remain as such if my option to stay a bit longer was removed. It was only six o'clock.

'I'll phone for one now then, where's the bloody phone?' I must have been a bit frantic; considering I'd not long sent a text to Anna it took a while to locate it amongst the other rubbish being harboured within my rather stupidly over-sized bag. I felt my heart sink as I dialled the number. I glanced in Shrubby's direction and caught him looking at me. I couldn't look back. My eyes slithered over him with unresponsive blankness. I'd blown it as I always did. I stood waiting for someone to answer the phone the other end with the knowledge that I needed a lobotomy to make any kind of indent into my behaviour. He was making definite signs of leaving, standing up throwing back his head and downing the last of his pint.

It was after the third hello I realised I was through to the taxi rank.

'Ten minutes, okay, thanks.'

I looked up and he'd gone. I wanted to weep; instead I gave the thumbs up to Diane. 'Ten minutes.'

My mobile starting ringing in my hand, for a second its potty ringtone frightening the life out of me, my thoughts so engrossed elsewhere. The number was unrecognised.

'Hello?'

'Who's that?'

'Trev.'

'I think you have the wrong number. Are you the taxi firm?'

'No, what taxi firm? It's Shrubby.'

'Oh.' As the penny dropped, I did the most unattractive laugh ever down the phone and stopped it abruptly.

'Are you still there, Grace?'

'Er, yeah.'

'You're not making this easy are you.'

Nerves made me laugh.

'You didn't answer my question before. Would you like to go out for a meal with me?'

Here was the moment I thought I'd blown just minutes earlier.

'Oh, okay.' It was said with a smile but that's as committed as I got.

'Are you doing anything New Year's Day?'

'Er, no I don't think so.'

'I'll pick you up one o'clock. Wear something warm.'

I did another moronic laugh down the phone.

One o'clock; that was an early meal. I automatically thought an evening meal with candlelight as a romantic date. With us going out to eat at one I'd be back home for three. Especially with the speed I ate.

I was going on a date be it breakfast, lunch or dinner, I was going on a date. Now all I had to consider was how to chuck him after it. Or consider being chucked. Bloody hell, what had I done?

Wear something warm. Oh well, I supposed it was better than saying, wear nothing. At that point, my insides dissolved.

'I think that's our taxi,' Diane said, coming over to me and putting my coat over my shoulders, at the same time handing me my bag. 'See you, Dave. Have a good New Year. See you, guys.' She turned to me. 'Put your coat on properly, you'll freeze out there if you don't.' With that she fussed out of the pub and into the waiting taxi.

'I think Dave likes me, we get on so well, and Rex told me I looked like Elizabeth Taylor. Come to think of it, I hope he was referring to her younger days. Was Shrubby embarrassed by my snogging him with my hat on, at the party? You seemed to be chatting ages.'

I told Diane about my impending date. 'I think it's just a mate thing really though, I mean one o'clock isn't a romantic date is it? Probably be in a greasy cafe, somewhere local.'

'You sly thing. I'm really pleased and I'm sure you'll have a fab time. He's a nice kisser too.' She nudged me in the arm.

Chapter 18

Next morning Mum and Dad were getting ready to drive up to Rebecca's for New Year. Scotland, possibly the best place to celebrate New Year anywhere and if I hadn't already made plans with Anna and Diane I'd have been packing my bag to travel up with them. I'd been woken to the sound of 'Matchstalk Men and Matchstalk Cats and Dogs' and the smell of burnt bacon. Pandemonium followed as the car was loaded and three attempts were made to leave, both Mum and Dad forgetting their reading glasses, Mum's toothbrush, Dad's bryl cream. The phone rang as I waved them off for the fourth time from the front door in my pyjamas and huge, new Christmas reindeer slippers that Roger had taken offence to.

I shoved him away as I answered the phone. I didn't recognise the voice on the other end.

'Help me.'

'Who is that?'

There was a loud wet sniff for a reply.

'Hello?'

'It's Anna. Oh, Grace, help me.'

'Where are you?'

'Home, I've done something stupid.'

'I'll be there in ten minutes.' I ran upstairs, threw some clothes on and hurtled out of the door within two minutes of the call.

There was no answer from the front door when I got to Carpenters Road so I cautiously went round the back. The backdoor was slightly ajar with bits of broken china hazardously breaking out onto the small step outside. My heart started to beat faster as I called Anna's name, dreading silence, needing a response, anything that would confirm she hadn't taken drastic action since her phone call. There was nothing but a sinister hush to precipitate my entrance. Visions were in my head by this time of blood-spattered walls, a body, limp and grey in death.

I gingerly pushed the backdoor further ajar, crunching and cracking aside the fiesta of crockery that greeted me, lying in great quantities on the kitchen floor. I was shocked at the mess; nothing had been left unscathed. The toaster was in bits in the corner by the fridge along with the pitiful sight of the kettle, which was shedding water in its final death throes. Glass bottles containing oil, sugar, teabags, coffee, spaghetti and herbs lay in state, their contents of which now spewed forth to congealing together on the counter top and slowly dripping heavily down the cupboard door.

'Anna?' There was no answer.

I jumped melodramatically as the boiler flared up, causing the hairs on the back of my neck to react similarly. It was like being in the middle of a bad dream, and I hesitated; fear of what I might find momentarily overriding urgency, then I took another step into the kitchen, splintering crockery further underfoot.

It was at that moment I caught sight of a hand behind the far kitchen door, a moving hand attached to an arm. I slithered across the kitchen, grinding broken plates into the floor tiles with legs flailing in all directions, and got to the rest of the body.

Anna faced upwards towards me from the floor where she sat in her frilly, winceyette nightie and dressing gown. Her eyes showed exhaustion and something heading towards shame. I noticed angry, red marks that looked like small pinpricks on the inside of her quivering wrists, evidence of some form of bungled self-harm.

'What are we going to do with you?' I asked, kneeling down and looking more closely at the marks.

'I'm so ashamed, I just lost it. I flipped and went on the rampage.' Her voice was steady, her frustrations expended. 'I just want to sit here forever and not have to think ever again.'

I took her hands. 'If anything should happen to you I would seriously have to come after you and kill you again and I'm not the only one, there'd be a queue. Bloody hell, Anna, you frightened the life out of me.'

'I'm sorry.' She really looked it, her face full of remorse.

'Can you tell me why you've done this?' I gently pried into the cause, not wanting to upset her again but needing to gain some insight into her loss of control, wondering if a call should be made to her GP for further help.

She started to quietly cry. 'I'm tired, really tired.'

I sat down on the floor opposite her. I didn't know what to say so I just sat and waited. Comfort can be given in many ways, it doesn't have to be vocal or physical, it can sometimes just help knowing someone's there, someone to share the pain in some small measure. After a short spell of quiet reflection she removed her hands from her face, her eyes pink and watery, and sniffed.

'I miss my children. I've not slept for over a week. I feel like I've lost everything. Even the cat's run away.'

She sniffed between nearly every word but we were making progress.

'The cat's always running away and the children will be back before you know it; they're only away for a week.'

'I know. But I've not slept for over a week worrying for them, for me. I think my head's going to explode.' She paused. 'I can't be alone, I hate it.'

'Why?'

'It's shit.'

'I like being on my own sometimes, I appreciate having company once I've been by myself.'

'But you're nice; I'm not nice company, I'm horrible so why would I want to spend time with me? Most people run away from me.'

'If you don't mind me saying, that's total bollocks. Everyone I know thinks you're marvellous. You've become my best friend. You inspire people, you've inspired me.' She looked at me with a doubting face so I backed my statement with a vigorous nod and a stern look. 'It's true; if it wasn't for you, I'd probably now be pushing biscuits up the bell end of a clarinet and spitting them out at people.' I'm sure there was a smile lurking in her eyes.

'Do you think you could manage a cup of tea?' Without waiting for a reply I tripped back over the broken plates and found a broom propped up by the back door. After brushing a pathway to save further accidents, I found a pan to boil some water, the kettle now being defunct. I rounded up a plastic duck cup and a stainless-steel beer tankard, these being better options to drink out of than the cat tray or milk pan. Managing to salvage two teabags and some sugar that had missed coagulation, I made my way back to her and proffered her the duck mug.

'Exactly how much sleep have you had?' I asked.

'None last night, precious little the night before or the night before that.'

'I don't think you'll feel any better until you get some sleep. I know it's a vicious circle, the anxiety's keeping you awake, but you're not able to think straight without it. I know if I don't get my sleep, I'm hopeless. What if I get you some herbal sleeping tablets? Would you take them? Do you think it would help?'

She nodded as if the same thought had occurred to her. She looked around at her surroundings for the first time, taking in the consequences of her anger then glanced down at the duck mug. 'Is this to make sure I don't do any more harm?'

I laughed.

'Oh my God, look at the mess I've made. Look at the waste. I was so angry, I just started smashing things. I hated those stupid, fucking plates anyway.' She was referring to the unattractive plates I'd had problems with in the past.

'I think the plates had it coming actually, especially the spooky Cairn terrier one. This tea is disgusting.' I put it down to one side and noticed that her hands had stopped shaking. The marks on her wrists had already started to fade and I couldn't fathom out what she'd used to make them, until I noticed a rubber T-Rex dinosaur head poking out from under a corner of her dressing gown. It wasn't looking very happy, its roaring mouth ripped and drooping at the jaw.

'Not exactly a killer dinosaur is it?' Anna said as she followed my gaze and picked the toy out from its hiding place. 'I was going to use a cracked piece of plate but it looked too sharp. He seemed a better option.'

I couldn't hide the smile. 'Did Fergal stop over last night?' I asked.

She shook her head. 'We had a massive fight. He called me a slapper and stormed off about eleven o'clock.' She sighed. 'I haven't been quite honest with you, or anybody for that matter.' She stopped again as if forming a sentence in her head before going any further. 'I've been having an affair with Fergal, on and off, for nearly a year.'

I looked at her in disbelief.

'I know, Peter and his affair and everything,' she said bluntly. 'I think subconsciously I knew he was having an affair way before I found out.'

The front doorbell rang and a voice shouted 'Hello' through the letterbox. Diane.

I got up and turned out of the small dining area, up the hall and opened the door.

'What's happened?' she asked, stridently.

I led her to the kitchen. Anna had managed to get up off the floor and was sat at the round kitchen table, her hands cradling her plastic mug of lukewarm tea. Diane took in the mess. She looked at me then put her arm round Anna and kissed the top of her head. Diane had received a garbled message on her answering service along the lines of, 'Help mer, meh ha, meh hee mmmm huh.'

'I've been shopping in the sales, loads of bargains now I've lost weight and can fit into them. I've only just got back and heard the message or I'd have been here sooner,' she explained. We all sat round the table. A woodpigeon cooed soothingly outside from the flat garage roof outside the kitchen window, before noisily flapping away to join a friend further down the garden.

'I tried to kill myself with a rubber dinosaur,' Anna said to Diane.

'Where the hell where you putting it?'

Anna turned her wrists upwards but already the marks had all but gone.

'Why?' Diane asked.

'I'm so unhappy, my children have left me, my husband's taken them from me, I've got to move out of my home soon, my so-called lover pushed me away last night and walked out after calling me a slapper. The cat's moved out. I've been for countless interviews and nobody wants me and I'm working somewhere so demoralising I can't talk about it and I can't sleep, I'm going crazy.'

'What do you mean? Did Fergal hurt you?' Diane asked.

'He pushed me. I've got a bruise on my arm where I went into the banister rail.'

'Bastard,' Diane said.

'He's not really, I've got something to tell you and you're going to hate me.' Anna looked at me then said a second time. 'I've been having an affair with Fergal on and off for about a year. We had a terrible row last night, I got incredibly drunk and tried to stop him going back to his wife by standing in front of the door and pushing him back, he had no option if he wanted to get away from me, I fell into the banister post.'

'That's what they all say,' Diane said, angrily.

'It's true. I was the one that hit him and punched him, I was really angry. Did you hear me when I said I've deceived everyone with this affair?'

'I knew,' Diane said.

I sat back and watched as the drama unfolded.

'How? How did you know? You couldn't possibly. Why didn't you say anything?' Anna asked in an accusing tone.

'Well, it was quite by chance that I had to go back to the hall one evening after rehearsal, about six months ago, because I'd left my mobile in the ladies. I thought the caretaker might still be there but it was all locked up, you know? Fergal hadn't joined then so I didn't recognise the car, which was the only one in the car park in the far corner rocking like Status Quo. I suppose it would do with his bulk banging in it. It was the shout, 'Harder, Anna,' that kinda gave me the idea it was you.'

Anna was silenced. It was a strange sight; I'd never seen her so lost for words.

'That clears that up then,' I said.

It was decided that I would go to the chemist and get some sleeping pills, Diane would start to tidy up the mess, Anna would have a shower and would phone her GP and get some advice. We would stay and have a takeaway dinner and when Anna was fast asleep we'd go.

'I'm not going to tell my doctor that I tried to do away with myself though.'

'Theoretically you didn't,' I said, finding my purse and putting my coat on to go to the chemist.

Anna said, 'Thank you,' and squeezed my hand before going upstairs to shower.

It was nice to get some fresh air, even if a gloomy overcast sky kept the light of day locked out. I managed to find a kettle and some mugs from a hardware shop, some essential milk, teabags, sugar, bread, butter and biscuits from the supermarket and was coming out of the local chemist with the sleeping tablets when I bumped into Lawrence. He wasn't looking where he was going and nearly knocked me back inside.

I'm so sorry,' he apologised and then realised it was me. 'Grace, Happy Christmas.' He gave me a kiss on the cheek. He looked terrible.

'Happy Christmas, is everything alright?' I asked him, immediately jumping to the conclusion that he'd heard of my forthcoming date with his friend and he was sorry now that he hadn't asked me first.

'It's Gnasher, I think he's on his way out.'

'Oh no.' If he'd chosen to look, embarrassment at my inclination to suppose he cared who I went out with would have been clearly written on my face.

'I can't stop. I've left my brother with Gnasher while I try and find something that might entice my poor four-legged friend to eat.' He held up a plastic bag full of doggy items as evidence. 'The vet says that if he hasn't managed to eat by tomorrow I should take him back to the surgery and may have to consider having him put down.'

'I hope he gets better, Lawrence, if there's anything I can do let me know.'

I don't think he heard me; he looked like he was about to weep and, saying a hurried goodbye, he was quickly swallowed up in shoppers. I turned in the opposite direction and headed back to Anna's.

Over and over again I saw Lawrence's face as he'd turned away; a look that was reminiscent of James' when we'd initially tried to sort out our affairs, Diane's on being thrown out of her house, Tom's on seeing his daughter's unhappiness and of Anna's that morning on her kitchen diner floor. Vulnerability. I wanted to put my arms round everyone, even James, and surround them with love to protect them and keep sadness away so that I would never have to see that look again.

The kitchen, empty but tidy when I got back, looked a little more homely once the new kettle was boiling, and with the mugs set out in a row and biscuits displayed on a tray it could almost pass as normal, apart from Diane singing 'Waitin' for My Dearie' from Brigadoon with a shocker of a Scottish accent.

'Fucking hell, where's the dinosaur, I'm going to finish off what I started,' Anna said.

'Och, wee lassie, don't be like that.' Diane fluttered a dishcloth at us and sang. '*Foolish ye may say, foolish I will stee.*'

'Stee? What's stee? Anna, can I have the dinosaur after you?' I poured the tea out.

'Och aye the noo to you. *Many a lassie as ev'ryone knows...*' At this point I pushed her out of the kitchen.

Anna's doctor's appointment was for three o'clock and she felt capable of driving herself there with the promise she would let us know later how she'd got on. A few weeks earlier she'd traded her car in at a garage that was in direct competition with Fergal's and, with her flirting skills, she'd managed to get £300 more for her old car than offered initially. Fergal had been angry she hadn't gone to him first but she liked to think she was now independent. She wanted to do things her way.

Diane said she would be round later with Heather and I promised the same so we all trundled off on our separate ways.

Anna's car had given me an idea so I stopped at Fergal's used-car sales place and wandered round looking at improbably priced cars. It was about time I spent some of the money I'd received from the house equity. The more I had for a property the better, but really in the last year my crappy car had just got crappier to the point where bits were falling off as I was driving along, giving me the unhappy impression that the impending MOT would be more shocking than buying a new car. I had no flirting skills and, with Fergal nowhere to be seen, I came away bamboozled with nought per cent finance deals and a sneaking suspicion that I'd agreed to buy a four by four monster fit for driving up Snowdon. My idea was a good one though and within a week or two I would seriously look at buying a replacement for my battered, but faithful Fiesta.

On an impulse, I drove down to the beach and sat in the car chewing on an innocuous sandwich, watching the tide turn. As the dulled daylight started to fail, it gave the illusion that the distant wind-turbines were floating away on the horizon. I noisily crushed the plastic sandwich container, stuffing it into the glove compartment, and realised I hadn't touched my clarinet for four days and, considering that soon I would be auditioning for a life changing experience, this was bad. I hoped I wasn't going to use this excuse when I failed and would then have to remain in the bank forever.

Diane came to the door when I got back to Anna's.

'She's in bed,' she said quietly in the hallway. 'The doctor prescribed her some really strong knock-out pills and she's out like a light. He's also recommending a course of tranquillisers or something to help get her back on track. Heather love, don't walk through there without any shoes on.' Heather backed into the living room again, having thought to see if any biscuits lurked in the kitchen, she changed her mind.

'I'll get her some.' I found the biscuits I'd bought earlier and passed them to her. She and Diane were sat arms around each other watching a 'Christmas Special' film.

Diane reached over for a biscuit. 'She's going to be out till tomorrow. We'll stop here, may as well. Are you stopping too?'

'Nah, I'll get off home and see to the dog. Talking of which, Lawrence's dog is very poorly.' I told her about meeting him that morning.

'I hope he doesn't take you up on your offer of help. I don't think Shrubby would approve somehow of you holding Lawrence's hand when you're going out with him in two days' time.'

'I hadn't thought of that. Bugger, does that mean I can't see other people just because I've promised to meet someone for lunch? I hate this dating lark. We're just going to be friends, I can see other people if I want.'

'I don't think Shrubby's that kind of man really, you know? I may be wrong but I don't think he gives his affections away easily, he's more of a one woman man as opposed to Lawrence, who I get the impression likes the ladies and likes them to do all the running. Anyway what am I talking about, all men are bastards so, yes, you can have your cake and eat it.'

'Mum, shut up, this is the best bit.' Heather rebuked her mum for talking over the film and looked hurt by her mum's last words.

I took my leave, safe in the knowledge that Anna was now getting some much needed rest. I played the clarinet long into the evening, a clicking metronome ticking the passing of time.

Chapter 19

Anna looked and felt better on New Year's Eve. We'd had a long debate on how and why her relationship with Fergal had started and why it had come to such a sticky end. He had been unhappy at home with his girls flying the nest; his wife had been working longer and longer hours was not interested in his interests. In all the time I'd been involved with the orchestra I'd not seen his wife once. He spent most of his time in the garage which he'd had converted to a sound-proofed studio. It had been here that Anna and Fergal's bodies had first touched and clothes had been torn off in fifteen minutes of frenzied lust. How she'd ended up in there was subject to his wife being away, Peter being away on business, and a classical performance that evening that had been dedicated to 'lovers' ending in Ravel's Bolero, getting most of the orchestra hot under the collar. There's no accounting for taste, much as I loved playing it, there is no song more conducive to making me keep my clothes on.

Anyway, the relationship may have fizzled out and been a one-off experience but for the fact that 'the ram' and Peter were both away again at the same time the next week after rehearsal, and this time Anna and Fergal made it to the bedroom fully aware of what they were doing. To my mind, people cope with unhappiness in very different ways. I'd never turned to another man to fight that awful feeling of loneliness, I'd become more introverted, allowing the hurt to slowly and insidiously seep inside without an outlet. Diane had denied there was a real problem in her marriage, ready to plod on forever at odds with her partner behind a barrier so thick nothing could get to her. Anna, on the other hand, kept telling herself it was only because Peter was never at home. If he was, she would finish the affair because she loved her husband, wanted his love back not just his money, and this wasn't hurting anyone, it was saving her marriage in a warped sense.

With this philosophy, clinging to the idea that her husband would never stray because of his ex-wife's infidelity, it had swiped her sideways on finding out he'd not only been having an affair but was paying for long weekends away under the pretext of work. As she saw it, at least she'd kept hers cheap and local and had had the decency to call it off after she'd revealed to Peter she'd been doing voluntary work. Honestly.

Fergal started sniffing round again when she'd turned up at the orchestra rehearsal urging me to join the choir. He made it clear he would never leave his wife but if, from time to time, she wanted sex he would be happy to oblige.

She had used him then, as she had used other men, in my opinion, to gain some form of self-confidence, misinterpreting one-off sex as a form of love. It gave her a buzz to know she was attractive and men found her exciting, she was in control, the challenge was on. The excitement continued for a number of months until repetition and a dose of thrush in the mouth reduced it to its sordid reality.

It was when 'the ram' showed Fergal the door that Anna got herself in more of a mess, becoming increasingly unhappy. She wanted him but, it seems, because she didn't want to be on her own any longer rather than through any great feeling of love. Fergal, perhaps disillusioned with being single or perhaps finding the excitement had been in the affair not the relationship, was trying to worm his way back to his wife, and Anna played every trick in the book to keep him with her, further rebuke not an option.

So there we have it. Anna's self-respect, which had been failing anyway, plunged dramatically dragging her with it. Her anger against Peter, who had been the cause of her misery and who had walked away without any sort of fight for her, bubbled upwards. Her kids had gone away, leaving her at the mercy of her own mind. She was going to have to find a place to live; sell her home and hold down a really shitty job in telesales until something better came along. Her lover was backtracking away from her, her bank ominously approaching her, her future presenting a bleak outlook, she was on her own and she couldn't handle it. The past year had finally caught up with her and the outcome had been the demise of the painted plates and a cruel end to the rubber dinosaur.

Once she started crying there was no stopping her. Diane and I refused to let her spend New Year's Eve in bed as per her demands. Some members of the choir, including the three of us and Fergal, had organised to get together New Year's Eve and we'd spent seventy pounds each on tickets to a restaurant which was throwing a party with a bagpiper to bring in the New Year. Earlier that morning Fergal's ticket had plopped through Anna's letterbox bringing more tears. There was no message.

'I fucking well paid for that ticket,' she cried. 'Out of money I don't have.'

'We could try and sell it.' I consoled.

'I'll ring the restaurant,' Diane said, more sensibly. 'After we've decided what we're doing tonight. Are we going or not?'

We spent a subdued evening at the restaurant. Anna, once denied her night of self- indulgent sorrow, allowed a modicum of gaiety to counteract it, by waltzing to 'Mr Bojangles' with the restaurant owner. Diane drank red wine till it poured, quite literally, back out of her. I cried when the bagpipes saw 2002 out

251

and 2003 in. A New Year with lots of changes in prospect, commencing later in the week with my first date in over fifteen years and who knew what after that. The three of us sang Auld Lang Syne and group hugged, it was good to know that when all else had gone pear-shaped our friendship had pulled us through. I rang Natalie, got through on the third attempt and shouted Happy New Year to her as party poppers exploded around us. I rang Mum and Dad at Rebecca's and managed to speak to someone called Dougal who had taken Dad under his wing and was teaching him the Highland Fling. I wished him luck and drank to their health when the line went dead.

Chapter 20

I was ready by twelve o'clock the following day which meant I only had an hour to wait for Shrubby to turn up. I felt so sick I'd skipped breakfast and watched *The Railway Children* while waiting, fiddling with a tassel on the cushion I'd plonked on my lap to stop my legs from bouncing with nervous energy. Would I need any money? Should I offer to pay halves with everything? Should I be offended if he took my money from me? Should I be insulted if he didn't? At ten to one I decided I didn't like what I had on and threw the cushion aside, tearing upstairs to change. At one o'clock I was back downstairs in what I was originally dressed in, jeans, T-shirt, woolly jumper, fleece, coat, woolly hat. At ten past one I thought I'd been stood up. At quarter past one the doorbell rang.

With an air of cool I didn't feel, I walked straight out of the house, hat and coat already donned, shouting bye to Roger. If Shrubby saw this as too eager then that was his problem. He was wearing a woolly hat, the same horrible leather jacket he'd worn the previous day, a pair of jeans and walking boots. We said our hellos and wished each other Happy New Year across the top of his shiny clean, black car before getting in.

'Have you heard how Lawrence's dog is?' I asked as we set off up the road.

Shrubby hesitated before speaking. 'Gnasher had to be put down.'

'Oh no, poor Gnasher, poor Lawrence.'

'He's alright, well, a bit devastated but the poor dog hadn't been well for some time so in a way it's a relief for him. Lawrence has turned to his own form of Buddhism and is leaving gifts for the God of Dogs in Gnasher's basket every day.'

I sat quietly. I'd never met Gnasher. Why did I feel so awful?

'Any ideas as to where we're going?' Shrubby asked me when he realised I had no conversation.

'Have you?' I answered with a sinking feeling that maybe I was going to have to decide.

'Yes of course I do,' Shrubby said. I felt at sea in the car. It wasn't James driving and it wasn't my Dad, it was a man I'd met a couple of times, usually after alcohol, and now he was taking charge and I was going to have to pretend that this was okay by me, something that I was at perfect ease with.

'Are we going to Russia?' I asked, covering my discomfort with absurdity.

'No.' He lengthened the no to signify the attempt was good but not the right answer.

'Your house? The pub? The M56?'

'There's a clue in the front pocket.' He reached over and pulled it open. A red and white scarf fell out.

'The football? No?' I hesitated until I saw his smile of assent.

'Yep, Liverpool, Bolton.'

I became Mrs Chatty with excitement. Football, we were going to be friends, there was no real romance; I offered him the money for the ticket. He declined my offer. Maybe it was a bit of a romance then after all. I was in a state of confusion as to how to act, should I link his arm as we got out of the car to stroll along with others to the ground? It didn't feel right; I put my gloved hands in my pockets and decided that 'friends' felt better.

It wasn't that cold, there wasn't much of a breeze; the afternoon sky wasn't too dull. We had a quick drink in a pub heaving with football fans and then walked next to each other, the crowds becoming thicker the nearer we got to the stadium. Giant police horses stood their ground, disinterested parties to the result, while merchandisers did a brisk trade outside the ground selling hats, scarves, posters, adding to the general melee. I bumped into at least three people, all of who were eating meat pies.

'Best leave the pies to those whose constitutions are used to them,' Shrubby advised when he saw my gaze follow the good-looking man I'd had the fortune to run into. Why, all of a sudden, was I ogling nearly every man I passed? I never normally looked up above shoulder level. Now, suddenly, I was smiling away at anyone whose eyes met with mine. I wondered if it had anything to do with the company I was keeping; Shrubby was a nice bloke, he was funny, smart, talented, easy-going, but he wasn't blessed with a great deal of hair, he wasn't six foot, he wasn't drop-dead gorgeous. I found that I was comparing him unfavourably to the male totty all around me.

The roar of the crowds in the stadium cascaded down through the turnstiles, bringing about an attack of goose-bumps that helped me momentarily forget my misgivings. The ground was full, banners and scarves unfurled and held aloft, and 'You'll Never Walk Alone' was being sung by the Kop as we found our seats. I was sitting next to an Irish man in his sixties called Eddie, lifelong Liverpool fan who constantly berated the team like they were his children and said 'Fecking' at least twice in every sentence. The first half itself was a tense nerve-wracking forty-five minutes followed by a tense nerve-wracking wait in the ladies queue for a toilet.

In the second minute of the second half Liverpool won a penalty. When Stephen Gerrard, Liverpool's captain, scored I leapt off my seat, turned to my neighbour Eddie and gave him a hug, a second after that I turned to Shrubby and, facing each other, we both jumped up and down, one arm in the air in tribal jubilation.

The game ended one, nil. The night had already discreetly descended above the stadium lights as we were shoved and pushed out onto the streets.

We had a slow drive back amongst the traffic; our conversation was fragmented listening to the radio and the comments after the game. I thought our date was over and it was with some regret that I searched in my pocket for the front door key.

'I had a lovely time thank you, the score helped,' I said when the car came to a halt.

'I've changed my mind.' He started the car and headed off down the road, me still in it. 'I'm starving, you must be too; I'll buy you dinner.'

We ended up in a small French restaurant with tables' inches apart from each other, conspiring towards familiarity with other diners. I gave the menu a cursory glance and stuck to tried and tested paté for starter and steak and chips for main course, while Shrubby on the other hand sat back and looked like he was reading a newspaper rather than a menu, glasses perched on his nose. He finally decided on something called 'smelp' for a starter and 'poisson a la soupcon petit choux fleur', or something like that, for main. I was impressed.

The wine and lemonade was loosening my tongue and I was gibbering away about my job and how I didn't want to be back there tomorrow, when our starters arrived. Shrubby had my glass replenished and we tucked in. No sooner had I broached my starter when I sent my knife clanging to the floor. I bent down to pick it up and took a good look at Shrubby's starter and, I have to say that, from a bystander's point of view, the smelp looked like a bowl of sick, bright yellow in colour with purple and orange things bobbing about to assist the comparison. It smelt like a cheesy horse's arse and I could see that Shrubby thought pretty much the same, although he was trying hard not to show his revulsion. I tried hard not to show I'd noticed.

I saved him a piece of toast and some paté just in case he didn't make it through his 'smelp'. It was a wasted act of generosity because before I could offer my uneaten bit of starter, I obliterated the table with my drink as the long glass, full of wine and lemonade, slipped through my fingers at a frightening speed and saturated everything.

I felt the date was going well by this time!

My first date with James, if I remembered rightly, was one of lingering looks, fingers touching briefly while reaching for a bottle of wine, the candlelight playing in his dark eyes across the table. It had been perfect. This was my first good memory of James.

Getting back to the meal in the French restaurant, Shrubby looked relieved, his barely touched 'smelp' ruined with a centimetre of wine floating over its surface, to me, improving its overall aspect. The waiter flapped, the people next to us pitying our misfortune, their meals still intact, their tablecloth not.

'No really, honestly, don't worry about replacing the starter, seriously it was lovely but don't worry.' Shrubby was insistent and insincere. We didn't have long to wait for the main course. They must have seen us coming and were doing their best to get us, me, out as quickly as possible.

Our conversation had started to get a little more personal with Shrubby wanting to know why I hadn't taken playing the clarinet further when I was younger.

'I played in a youth orchestra, went to college, you know the usual, started auditions and fell for James, my ex-husband, who had his pine shop here, and I wanted to be with him rather than in Cardiff where my audition was. Was I mad? Said like that it doesn't make any sense. Maybe I used him as an excuse not to take the final audition; scared I wouldn't pass and be a failure.' I sliced through my steak angrily. 'After that I got lost in self-doubt and told myself I was crap. If you say it often enough it becomes true.'

'No it doesn't, you just start to believe it.' Shrubby preferred not to comment on the chip, which fell off my fork and onto the floor, leaving my teeth biting on thin air. He attacked his own dinner.

I was past caring although hot cheeks belied this. I wouldn't be seeing him again after tonight so may as well stand up, drop my trousers and shout 'kiss my arse' to the restaurant.

'That chip had been planning an escape from the moment it got to this table. Did you see that?' I said, kicking it out of view.

'I did indeed; it just leapt off your fork and ran for it. Chips are like that.' He had kind eyes, helping to smooth over my little indiscretion. 'I think you've every chance of getting the clarinettist job with the Orchestra, and if you don't, I'll start to worry that you may take my place in the band. I think Lawrence would prefer a bit of beauty to my ugly mug.'

At the mention of his name my heart bumped against my ribs. 'He said that he was hopeful that you were going on tour this year. What'll you do about your day job if you do?'

'I'm the only one working full time now and that won't be for much longer if I intend to go. It's all there; the contract, the tour dates, everything. Now Gnasher has gone there's nothing to stop Lawrence carrying out his plan. If I go I'll just help with lyrics and play the music. The others are trying to come up with new stuff all the time. At one point on our tour we're supporting 'Crestwave', you know, that song 'Love in my Lunchbox?'

'Bloody hell they're famous. Aren't they?'

'Not quite, you and I have heard of them but I can safely say that over three-quarters of the population here haven't and no-one in the U.S. has.'

'America?'

'That's where we're off to in March, supposedly.' Shrubby pushed his plate away decisively, marking indecision towards his statement.

'You don't seem keen.'

Shrubby looked at me and smiled. 'It's a long way to go when you're not even anywhere near being established in your own country. But, we think our type of music will be more appreciated over there. Who knows? If we don't try it we'll never know.'

'Everysink alrise wis yer meal?' A cute, Scouse accented, French waiter enquired, hovering over us.

'Perfect, thank you.' Shrubby didn't look away when he said it. 'Do you want a coffee? Two coffees please.'

I shifted in my seat. 'Have you been married before?'

'Yes, for a year, straight out of Uni when I was twenty three. She decided that she preferred someone else and that was it. It was not a nice time in my life.' He didn't seem to want to expand on this, his fingers playing with the top of his fork, the tablecloth becoming etched with the prongs.

'Let's drink to never again then,' I said cheerfully. We chinked glasses. 'What made you take up the clarinet in the first place?'

'My music teacher at school was beautiful, we all fancied her. As simple and basic as that. I think half the class took up an

259

instrument of some sort. Ignore the pun. I'll help you all I can with rehearsing any pieces for your audition; you could come round to mine if you like to practise. You know, I don't think you could have chosen a better music instructor than Mr Gerrard, apart from him being one of the best, his daughter Jean's really nice. I've known her since university; she frightened the pants off me in those days but she's good at her job and really well connected, so if she likes you it's a gift horse and you've got to get the job, even if I have to tell you how wonderful you are every hour on the hour to get you to believe it.'

I think the people next to us were intrigued with our conversation; theirs seemed to have dried up with hands doing the talking instead, harmoniously joined across the table. I wondered how long they'd been together to get to such a level of bliss, or boredom.

Our coffees arrived. 'I don't think you need go to such extremes, I'm a fatalist, what will happen, will happen. No point fighting it,' I said, plopping four brown sugar cubes into my coffee and grinding them down with a teaspoon.

'If you sit back and wait for things to happen then they never do,' he said. 'You have to get out there and make it happen, if you don't, life passes you by.'

'I haven't even completed the application form yet and I don't think I made my possible audition happen, it just did.'

'Yes you did make it happen. I'll admit I got you up to play on stage and because of that Jean Webster heard you play, but you'd already joined the amateur orchestra that led you to Mr Gerrard, that was you that, not someone else deciding for you.'

'Hmm, I suppose, but what if that was supposed to happen anyway. My brain hurts.'

My brain hurt because it had picked up on the '*I* got you up on stage' bit. I wanted to think about this and had time to when Shrubby sauntered off to the gents. The couple holding hands left, still holding hands. He could have meant *I* because he was here and just said I rather than we or Lawrence. He could have meant *I* because he wanted me to think he was instrumental in my destiny. He could have meant *I* because he was.

It was a chip moment, chips being present at significant times of my life. Anna forcing her chip into submission the day Shrubby asked me out, me dropping the runaway chip during my first date, chips on the bonnet of Sandra's car the night I joined the orchestra. I was becoming as anal as she was, 'I could mean I as in I.'

I wanted to believe it was Lawrence's idea that I'd been asked up on stage at the Christmas party, to make him my destiny, the one who cared about me. It was what I had assumed and what he'd been quite happy letting me believe.

On Shrubby's return, I offered again to pay my half of the bill to which he refused telling me it was his good luck gift for my auditions but if I wanted to I could leave the tip, then he asked if I wanted to go for a drink before heading home but with having work next day, I declined.

Initially I was quiet in the car on the way home listening to an Animals CD. I didn't know how to get the subject onto who was responsible for getting me up on stage and I don't quite know why it mattered to me so much, but it did. I skirted round the issue waiting for the killer moment to strike.

'So did you enjoy the Christmas party then?'

'Yes.'

'You enjoyed playing for us?'

'Yes.'

Open questions, open questions, I told myself. 'Why did you enjoy playing for us? What do you get out of it?'

'Enjoyment?'

'Ah. Is it worse when you know people in the audience?'

'No not really, I'm used to it.'

It was hopeless, it seemed to me he knew what I was angling at and was being deliberately obtuse to stop me from finding out.

'I could have killed you for getting me up like that with no warning.' I said.

'I'm not sorry. I even got my banjo out on stage for the occasion, and wasn't arrested.'

'D'you know, I remember now, I thought I heard a banjo. You play the banjo as well?'

'Very badly, but yes.'

I looked at him at the steering wheel driving me home from a really lovely day out. The unlit motorway gave little in the way of disclosing his face but the jazzy dashboard glowed over his features and showed he was smiling.

I put my head back on the head-rest. I think I could take it as read that Shrubby was the instigator behind me ending up on stage; he was the one responsible for more than I was willing to accept. We were nearing home by now and my thoughts were running into whether to lean over when he stopped and kiss him briefly, or just leg it instead.

We pulled up at the house, with no curtains drawn its black windows gazed at us unblinking probably thinking, seen all this before, the end of night snog, the wave at the gates, the sigh on opening the front door.

Shrubby remained looking out of the windscreen and I looked down at my hands. 'Worried Life Blues' seemed louder now the car engine was static, so when Shrubby said, 'I chose the song our band dedicated to you, I saw you come into the pub then disappear.' I only just heard him.

'Thank you.' My own voice was barely louder than his.

'I want you brown eyes, I want you till my day's end, but I want you as a lover, you're no good to me as ...' The Animals were turned down. 'I don't want to wake your neighbours,' Shrubby said by way of explanation.

'I've had a lovely time, thank you.' My eyes were darting everywhere except in his direction. 'I must go, but thanks again.' I dithered with the leaning over business and must have looked like I was trying to dance. Shrubby looked faintly amused then bemused as I got out of the car, apology oozing out of my every movement when I poked my head in the car prior to shutting the door and said, 'Thanks. Goodnight.'

His car drove off but I didn't see it, I only heard it, because by then I'd made it to the front door, crippled with self-loathing.

Chapter 21

Despite my objectionable behaviour and the fact that I wasn't a hundred per cent certain I wanted to see Shrubby again, as a number of days went by I was disturbed to find myself looking at the phone expectantly every time it rang.

It was a quiet Thursday evening two weeks later and I was getting to the point of planning a journey to his neighbourhood and conjuring up a reason to accidentally bump into him when Dad answered the phone. The call received was one of abusive language with someone ringing from a phone box and apparently, while having problems getting money into the slot, shouted, 'Fucking well get in, what the fuck? This bastard machine isn't working. Hello, Grace...' beep.

'I think that may have been a call for you,' Dad said, replacing the receiver and returning his concentration to *Where Eagles Dare*, a film he could recite verbatim.

The phone rang again and this time I picked it up and walked into the kitchen to allow the film to continue undisturbed.

'Has your dad just answered the phone?' It was Shrubby.

'Yes, why?'

'Think I've just sworn at him.'

'I know. He's fuming and said you're never to enter this house.'

'No.' He sounded horrified.

'I'm afraid so. Oh well, it was lovely knowing you ... only kidding.'

'Bloody pay phones. Is he really angry?'

'No. But he really does hate bad language.' I started laughing.

'Would you like to come to mine on Sunday for dinner?'

'Should I bring my dad? You could make amends.'

'I'll buy him a pint some time and apologise properly.'

'What are you going to cook?'

'It's a secret. Bring your clarinet with you.'

'It's not that tasty.' Was I really flirting? Even though I'd run away from him he still wanted to pursue some form of relationship, he must be out of his mind. Once I'd said goodbye I slid across the tiled kitchen floor in my socks to the kettle and did a bit of 'the twist' before switching it on.

Anna and Diane called for me on Saturday and we had a great day house-hunting. Anna had had an offer on her house for the asking price from the couple she'd made tea for and, with the thought of a new start in a new house now becoming something of substance, she leapt into action and offered for the third property we viewed. 'Plate day', as it became referred to, was a dim and distant memory already. She was back in control, all the stronger for her lapse. A job she'd interviewed for, courtesy of a friend of a friend, before Christmas came good. She'd soon be working in the housing department of local government. Her vision as a future local councillor was firmly in her sights. She decided that from now on she would flirt as outrageously as she could but the days of reckless shagging were over, no more Jeremy Clarkson goggles. From one extreme to the other, the excessive drinking was dramatically reduced, chips banned from the house and great quantities of strawberry yoghurt shipped in to spur on her health kick.

'I want to change the world, and you can't do that if you haven't lived life a little. I think Grace is right, you sometimes need to hit rock bottom before you know where you're going. I feel alive for the first time in years. I'm going to get fit by running every day. I'm going to take up proper singing lessons and I'm going to sound like Maria Callas in six months.'

Diane and I went back to hers in the evening and had a few drinks. Diane didn't stay long, saying she had to meet someone and wouldn't tell us who, which left us at liberty to examine Rich and the relationship's chances at length, once she'd gone.

I turned up at Shrubby's house on the Sunday with my clarinet and a ton of sheet music ready to be pushed, criticized and told 'could do better'. I'd seen Mr Gerrard at the beginning of the New Year and his first remark about my meeting his daughter was that she was too well paid if she could afford boobs like that. I told him how grateful I was for recommending me to her at which he flapped his hand, the one without the beer bottle, and said if I didn't get the job he'd force me to drink his beer down the clarinet. He recorded me playing Stravinsky's 'Three Pieces' to enclose with the application form and told me to keep studying and rehearsing Mendelssohn's scherzo from 'Midsummer Night's Dream', Brahms 'Symphony number three andante', Rimsky Korsakov's 'Capriccio Espangnol' and Mozart's 'Clarinet concerto'. He suggested I try and get someone to play piano for accompaniment and gave me some sheet music for the lucky person. A thought glanced off Lawrence and ricocheted towards Daphne Pearson, the excellent but garlic-stinking piano player for the orchestra, to be my accompanist. I'm afraid I didn't even consider Kenneth, piano player for the choir with the martial arts wife.

So there I was on Shrubby's doorstep with impossible dreams running through my head when he opened the door to let me in. Smooth laid-back rhythms flowed from his kitchen where it was obvious some hot, creative, culinary masterpiece was in progress, judging by the colour of his face. He tidied the counter top, a tea towel draped over his shoulder while I watched, chatting about Mr Gerrard.

We left the kitchen and spent two and a half hours going through some of the pieces of music I'd been set as revision. He stopped me occasionally with the odd comment here and there, occasionally trying to help with his own clarinet to hand. At one point he removed the pencil lodged behind my ear and wrote something on the music sheet, sending a little shiver down my back when he gently returned it, hardly evident but noticeable all the same. I was exhausted when I finally laid the clarinet down and the pencil to rest on his music stand, and flopped onto his settee. He left me there while he went to sort out dinner, Mozart, his chosen accompaniment sending me off to sleep.

'Are you making smelp? Or do you need it?' I asked, walking into the kitchen half an hour later. He turned from the sizzling open oven, his eyes invisible behind steamed glasses.

'No and no. Smelp, shmelp.' His eyes magically reappeared as the oven door closed.

'Shame really, I was looking forward to a bowl.'

'I'll just go and be sick then.'

We sat in his dining room eating roast chicken with orange sauce by candlelight. He was the nicest man I'd ever met, advancing bad behaviour from me. I rattled on about how I never wanted a steady relationship and that I'd never get married again, no reasons given, just warnings. At least this time I didn't end up dropping food on the floor although I'm surprised that I didn't end up wearing it after my comments. Shrubby's past verged on, for the want of a better word, mysterious. He may have had fifty million girlfriends or two, may have lived in a commune or alone all his life because the only item I extracted from him was that he was an only child and his mum and dad were divorced. I say this with some exaggeration because thinking about it he did tell me he had a passion for Cadbury's crème eggs and that he didn't like brown shoes. I preferred people to offer information and wasn't comfortable in delving too deeply into someone's past if not imparted easily. It was Shrubby's idea that he ask Lawrence to accompany me with the piano, said Lawrence wouldn't mind, he had too much time on his hands anyway.

'How does he have too much time on his hands if he's working?' I asked.

'He and his brother have got property all over the place but, to be honest, I think his brother prefers Lawrence away from the business and more of a kind of sleeping partner. Lawrence is one of life's dreamers and, let's face it, there's only one thing he wants to be doing. And he will succeed; if he lands in a bath of fermenting crap he comes out smelling of aftershave. He's one of those.'

'Do you really like him?'

'Of course I do. He may be good-looking, rich and talented but he hasn't got what I've got.'

'What's that?' I realised how bad that sounded as soon as it was out but it was too late and not worth digging a hole for.

'You round for dinner.'

The light was dim enough to disguise any discoloration of skin-tone from either of us.

'Or my crap coffee making, fancy one?' I asked, light-heartedly.

While I made a cup of coffee, Shrubby called Lawrence and came into the kitchen chatting very loudly down the phone.

'Tomorrow night, six thirty?' He raised his eyebrows at me in question. I nodded back. It was orchestra night but who cared, I'd either be late or not there at all. I found it slightly disconcerting that Shrubby didn't seem to have any problem with me going round to another man's house, especially when that man happened to be as enigmatic at Lawrence.

'This coffee's nice,' Shrubby lied humorously when he came off the phone and took a slurp.

'I told you.'

'It just needs coffee in it really.'

'I know it looks like a mug of milk, but that's the only way I make it, and I'm not changing for anyone.' I was at it again.

'You have to be careful. Once you've changed the way you make coffee that's it, there's no way back, let me tell you it's verging on insanity. I knew a girl who changed the way she made coffee and within a week she'd turned into a foul-mouthed, caber-tossing leprechaun.'

His cheerful rebuff at my puerile behaviour shut me up. We let the coffee go cold and chatted about what he would do with the house while he was away and how long that would be. He didn't like to talk about this either so with my reporter head on I managed to divulge that it all depended on how successful they were on tour. I'd been defensive almost to the point of aggressive all evening while he'd been discreet and ambiguous about his past and his future. Not a match made in heaven. I looked at my watch.

'I should go, its ten o'clock and I've got work tomorrow and this coffee is starting to look like semolina.'

'Let me get your coat. Doing anything next Saturday?'

I pulled a non-committal face, gathering my music and clarinet from his living room and, once he'd helped me into my coat, made for leaving, James Brown singing about a man's world in the background.

'I don't think I'm doing anything next Saturday apart from playing this thing. Thank you for a lovely meal, and for giving me your time this afternoon,' I said.

We'd reached the front door.

'Do I get a reward then?' His voice was low.

I hesitated, my arms full. The next second I found his lips and felt the same intensity sweep through me as it had before. Music papers fluttered onto the path unnoticed. As his hand gently caressed my neck I jumped back and hurriedly picked the scattered papers up, nearly falling off the step. He watched as I drove off. I know this because I had to go down the road, turn and come back up it passing his silhouette at his front door. Sleep was an elusive component in bed that night.

I was just as restless all the next day in work and not due to lack of sleep. Every time I thought of Shrubby my insides seemed to have a party and every time I thought of calling round to Lawrence's later, my insides became anxious. They were positively beside themselves when I rang his doorbell six-thirty prompt that evening.

What did one man want with a house this size I wondered as I waited; two impressive-looking garages to one side, one with a red sports car parked in front of it. There must be at least five bedrooms going to waste and God knows how many bathrooms. I half expected a butler to answer.

Lawrence came to the door dishevelled and groggy; it looked like I'd just woken him up. His face lit up though when he recognised who it was at the door, which made me feel welcome immediately.

'Grace, come in.'

The hallway was huge with an enormous staircase beckoning me upstairs straight away on entry. Warm cherry woodblock flooring made our footsteps echo as we crossed the hall into a room full of music. It was like a bookworm walking into a library full of favourite novels.

A grand piano held pride of place in a huge bow-window recess, two gigantic keyboards took up one corner of the room with a third keyboard in another. Two guitars leant against the wall by a carved wood fireplace and CDs, vinyl albums and singles shared space with piles and piles of sheet music stacked in bookcases against the length of the room. On the floor next to the guitars was a furry dog basket.

'I'm so sorry to hear about Gnasher.'

'Thanks. It's a bit cold in here, I'll light the fire, won't take me a minute.' He sauntered out of the room leaving me to wander along a music collection as unique as its owner. He came back in with two bottled beers, a piece of chicken which he gently laid in the dog basket, and a box of matches and within seconds a fire was smoking in the hearth; quickly giving the impression of heat with baby flames of pale orange tentatively flickering through entwined logs.

'You can take your coat off if you like,' he said, taking it from me. I didn't feel the cold. I could hardly swallow, being stood before the very fire I'd pictured myself in front of with him, it simply caused my throat to dry up completely. I gave him the accompaniment music for two of the audition pieces, keeping Mozart's 'Clarinet concerto' in the bag as I didn't feel up to it.

He suggested that we play them right the way through and he would give any hints at the end rather than stopping and starting as Mr Gerrard normally would and Shrubby had. Lawrence had to stop me almost immediately. We started again after I'd taken a gulp of beer. I couldn't quite fathom if Lawrence was listening to me or getting carried away with the music, his long fingers stroking the piano keys, his eyes glazed and unfocused in the parts when I wasn't required. It was rather off-putting. I didn't play at my best.

Once we'd finished he gave me his verdict.

'We need another beer.' He left me to go in search of two more chilled beers, my own hardly touched bottle was too hot to handle at present, placed as it had been in front of the inferno now fiercely devouring what little wood was left in the grate. Did I really want to know what he made of my performance? Had he honestly been listening anyway? When he returned he threw another log on the fire. Grasping onto the freezing bottle of beer I was handed, I waited for his opinion.

'Your technique's really excellent.'

I waited for more, the bit where the 'but' came. It didn't. I finished off my beer very quickly, it was the only thing cooling me down. Lawrence did the same before he went and sat at his piano again, absently plinking the notes to 'Arthur's theme'.

'We could do it again another day if you like. I'm free early Thursday evening if you want to run through something else.'

I had my usual lesson with Mr Gerrard at seven-thirty Thursday. I put my clarinet away. All the care I'd taken with make-up, hair and what I was wearing, a waste of time. I wanted him to drag me over to the piano and confess undying love, that I drove him insane with passion prior to creating havoc with my clothing. This wasn't going to happen although the setting was perfect.

I heard myself say, 'That would be great. Six-thirty again?'

'Can you make it six? Have you heard the new song we're going to release? I've got a copy here for you if you want one.' He was smiling broadly at me.

I left with a CD recording of 'Dixie Blues'.

I was back at Lawrence's again six o'clock Thursday. This time I could faintly hear the piano from outside, standing as I did at the front door before making it known I was there. Beethoven's 'Piano Concerto Number 5'. It was totally lovely and I felt guilty for disrupting it, my hand hovering over the doorbell a couple of minutes before quickly pressing it.

He was full of smiles when he let me in, leading me directly to the same room we'd practised previously, the fire already lit and warm, a beer ready waiting in a bucket of ice. He was wearing a white shirt with jeans, smelling fresh and clean, his light-brown hair still damp from a recent shower or bath.

'I'm a bit more prepared this evening,' he said, sitting down at his piano.

'So am I.' I fought my way through sheets of music to find Mozart's masterpiece.

'I thought I'd get myself ready now, I've got friends coming round later, so if the doorbell goes don't be surprised.'

There was me thinking he'd spruced up for my appearance. I dropped the music all over the floor, one landing in the dog basket covering a curly slice of beef. I sprang down to gather it all up and facing me was a sheet with the word 'lovely' over the top bar. I remembered Shrubby taking the pencil from behind my ear. It was madness to think that I'd not noticed what he'd written, simply because he'd touched my skin.

I placed it in order and handed the music sheets to Lawrence, taking the clarinet and holding onto it tightly. It gave great comfort. I lost myself in Mozart's music.

'Well, I don't think we need to say too much on that, need we?' Lawrence pulled his hands above his head and stretched. His eyes glowed with what almost looked like pride as he looked at me. I blushed, God dam blushes gave me away all the time.

'You don't think...'

'No, I don't think anything. That was cleaner than Domestos, you're a natural.' He put his arms down and reached for his beer. 'Do that for your audition and the job's yours, if not, fancy a trip to America?'

I laughed. 'Mozart's got the Blues.'

'What do you think of our recording?'

'I've been humming it all day.'

The doorbell rang.

'Is that the time? No, they're early. Bloody hell.' He stood up, brushing past me.

I breathed the scented air he left behind and packed away, gathering music and shoving into the plastic bag from whence it came.

From outside I heard loud voices.

'Lawrence mate, how are you?' A man, I was relieved.

'Hi gorgeous.' A woman, I wasn't.

'Lawrie!' Another woman, it was getting worse.

I waited by the fire not wishing to introduce myself as I left, a bit like an unwanted salesperson.

'Sorry, Grace.' Lawrence entered the room.

'I've got to go anyway, so don't worry.'

He walked with me to my car.

'Thanks Lawrence.'

'Don't mention it, anytime. I've enjoyed having you round, free Sunday early evening, six again?'

I nodded, hopefully not too enthusiastically, and he gave me a full on the lips kiss, but for only a second. It was so quick I felt nothing. A curtain twitched, Lawrence winked at me mischievously and headed back inside.

Mr Gerrard's lesson was incredibly hard to concentrate on and more than once he suggested I go out of the room and come back as the person from last week.

I traded my car in the next day and drove away in a shiny, red Punto. Fergal personally saw to it that it was a bargain. There were tears when I said goodbye to my trusty, crappy Fiesta, transferring all the rubbish from one car to another. Fergal walked away in disbelief when I threw my arms over the bonnet in a fond farewell.

Shrubby picked me up lunchtime on the Saturday. I was ready for him when the doorbell rang, allowing me to slip out quickly without painfully embarrassing introductions. Dad was smirking at me as I closed the door, I glowered back at him.

Shrubby gave no indication to where we were going other than north, following the motorway past Warrington, Preston, Blackpool, and it was only when we were stood outside a hall in Lancaster with a huge poster of the North Western Symphony Orchestra, billed as that night's entertainment, that I understood. I wanted to go and find a wig and a pair of glasses to hide behind, and told Shrubby so, who looked at me and pointed his finger to his head and whistled. We wandered round the part of Lancaster Castle that wasn't a prison, the afternoon getting progressively colder until the first signs of snow softly floated about us. After a MacDonald's drive-thru meal to warm us up we headed for the concert hall.

The orchestra were performing some of the works of Grieg and Sibelius, an appropriate choice for the wintry weather outside. I devoured every bit of the magic. I fell in love with the conductor who seemed to be able to get more out of a tiny flick of the wrist than any of Joan Sarney's confused arm aerobics ever would, and it started to hit home that I could possibly be a part of all this, which became nearly too much to take in. Tears welled and had nowhere else to go but downwards, forcing me to let them face-dry so Shrubby didn't notice. It wasn't until I'd managed to get past this that I could properly appreciate the music.

We remained in our seats and ate ice cream in the interval going over our favourite pieces, both of us attuned to the clarinet in particular, and it was only when we headed for a drink at the end of the performance that we saw the blizzard conditions outside the hall's revolving doors.

Chapter 22

'That's not good,' Shrubby said. We were waiting in the lobby along with many others, trying to decide what to do.

'We could find a wine bar and wait for a brief period to see if it abates.' It was ever thus after I'd been to an orchestral evening; my turn of phrase always lent towards a character out of an Enid Blyton book. 'I mean, if it bloody well stops chucking it down long enough.' I shrugged off the attitude. The wind whistled through the rattling revolving doors.

'We can't stay here. Follow me,' Shrubby said.

Once outside we could see how deeply the snow was drifting, parts of the street barely coated in snow, other parts two to three foot deep in the stuff. A couple of coaches, engines shuddering in the cold, windscreen wipers flinging snow from side to side, waited for passengers. The wind fairly blew us down the road, shooing us on our way and we clung to each other to remain upright.

'Quick, in here.' He dragged me into a hotel, its entry having recently been brushed clear of snow. We sat in a miserable bar with no music and one other couple who were obviously having an on-going disagreement, loud whispered recriminations reaching us where we sat watching the snow swirl outside the window.

'We have to make a decision here, and I'm going to leave it up to you,' Shrubby said.

'Why me?'

'Because the decision is to either hope that the motorway is safe to drive on if we can get to it, or stay over and wait to see what the weather's like in the morning.'

'I vote for a snowball fight,' I said flippantly. Staying would most likely mean sharing a room. I couldn't be such a prissy as to insist on a room to myself, on the other hand sharing would mean having to consider the inevitable. If I said I wanted to try getting home, the signal to Shrubby would be that I was insufferably frigid. He was watching me think all this through. I thought of Anna and what her reaction would have been, and of Diane, and of how both would have been delighted to be in such a predicament, how they would have made the most of it. Why was I so scared?

'I think we should stay anyway.' I heard myself say it and couldn't believe I had.

Shrubby looked a bit taken aback too, the rest of his pint vanished in seconds. We looked at each other.

Without a word we both stood up and left the bar. I can't say I remember much about the room we managed to find ourselves in, other than it had two single beds with a bedside table between them and hideous dark blue and pink curtains at the window.

Fumbling, I took my coat off and sat on one of the beds. I was shaking inside and all my head could think of was condoms and of how lumpy I was. My stomach wasn't flat, my legs too short, my boobs without cleavage, my bum with cellulite. What would he make of them, would he be disappointed? James had been.

Shrubby came and sat next to me and turned my face toward him.

'I've waited a long time for this moment.' His voice was low and so close to my ear the hairs on the back of my neck shivered.

I was shivering all over two hours later, naked underneath a sheet I'd wrapped myself in, standing in the bathroom in front of the mirror, looking at my reflection but not seeing it. Conflicting

278

emotions swept through me from elation to feeling positively sick. Having only ever slept with one other man, one who'd never explored the female anatomy's erogenous zones with any real interest, added shock value to what we'd just been capable of and my face was burning even though the rest of me was beginning to freeze in the cold bathroom. The voyage of discovery hadn't included the great condom issue (or a mirror and a wardrobe), improvisation with hands and mouths creating an intimacy deeper and more intense than I'd ever experienced. The hotel didn't provide breakfast nor did it run to providing protection. Returning to the bedroom I curled up into Shrubby's warmth and, with his arm reaching out to pull me closer, fell into an exhausted sleep.

Very early next morning I awoke and showered, Shrubby was still fast asleep. The dimly lit room looked like a family of four had been sleeping in it, both beds used, a sheet draped over a chair, clothing littering the floor. None of it felt wrong but then none of it felt quite right either and I wanted to disassociate myself from what had happened to keep a safe distance between us. Shrubby had made it clear how he felt for me and I didn't want to deal with it. I crept out and went to see if I could find a newsagent. The snow was turning to slush.

Shrubby was awake and freshly showered, a towel wrapped round his midriff, when I returned to the hotel room.

'It's raining now so the roads should be fine, and I need to get home pretty handy this morning,' I said, without giving a reason.

'Okay.' He started to dress. I discreetly watched, while giving a great show of tidying the room.

Fifteen minutes later we were sat in a motorway cafe having breakfast. Conversation was light, keeping to the news in the papers I'd bought, until I suddenly said. 'I've never said your name; I don't know what to call you.'

'Whatever you like, as long as it's got 'beefcake' preceding it.' He looked up from his paper.

'Should I call you beefcake Shrubby then?'

'You called me Trevor last night.'

I pinged into colour. 'Trevor it is then. Can you pass me the sugar, Trevor?'

He handed me four packets of sugar, his fingers lightly touching mine.

'I've been thinking,' he said.

I looked in askance for the rest of the sentence.

'Well, I've been thinking that ... I know that you'll pass the auditions and I'm not suggesting for one minute that you won't, it's just that...'

I ripped open the sugar with my teeth, waiting for him to continue.

'Well, if for some reason it should fall through, which it won't, but if it should then you could always come to America with me, with the band, instead.'

The sugar in my hand sailed out of the packet onto the table, missing the cup.

I gazed at him, trying to work out if he was serious. There was no mistaking his sincerity.

'I ... I'm flattered that you would consider me tagging along with you.'

'You wouldn't be tagging along.' He looked away. 'Maybe I shouldn't have asked, it was just an idea, in fact, forget it. Anyway, I suppose we ought to get going.'

He was embarrassed and regretting the sudden rush of blood to the head in asking me to travel with him. I understood perfectly and left the tea untouched, the sugar left scattered on the table.

The rest of the journey was spent listening to music and, as I hadn't put my contact lenses in, watching fuzzy scenery sail by while every now and then my temperature rose uncomfortably when I drifted to the previous night. I sharply veered away from his recent and sudden suggestion. It helped that the music was loud, The Who, Skunk Anansie, Red Hot Chilli Peppers, and prevented any deep train of thought. Really I should be thinking of another performance, but the one from the orchestra had been overshadowed somewhat. We arrived back home, no sign of any snow around, making last night more surreal, and said goodbye.

'Look I'm sorry about asking you to drop everything to go to America instead. I don't know what I was thinking, I mean I'd love you to come with me, us, but you've got your audition and a promising career ahead of you.'

'What, more promising than spending time with a bit of 'beefcake'? Beefcake Trevor.' His eyes crinkled, humour playing at their corners. 'I like, Trevor,' I continued, getting used to saying his name.

'I like Grace.'

I noticed a faint stretched pale colouring down the length of his nose; it only appeared when the rest of his face changed hue. Impulsively, I reached out and gently put my hand to his cheek, feeling his stubble prickle my palm.

'Sorry to hurry home but, amongst other things, seeing that orchestra last night's just made me want to play the clarinet until my fingers fall off.'

'You can practise at mine if you like,' Shrubby offered, leaning his cheek into my hand.

'Oh, I'm going to Lawrence's later to practise.'

He moved his face away from my hand.

'Okay.' He paused. 'Oh, I can't anyway, I'm meeting the lads soon, and later I'm out. In fact I'm a bit late as it is, I'd better get going.'

I felt the air in the car change as if the door had already been opened.

'I had a wonderful night.' I tried to close the metaphorical door.

'It was good.' He turned the engine on. Not only was the door open, I was being pushed out of it. 'I'll call you,' he said, putting the car into gear with his foot remaining on the clutch.

'That would be lovely.' I pulled on the handle to open the door proper, totally bewildered. Was it the Lawrence comment that had caused this sudden disenchantment? If so I was at a loss to see why, it had been Trevor's idea in the first place. I leant over and kissed his cheek then climbed out. No sooner had I done so than the car moved off leaving me stood on the pavement, arm outstretched in surprised farewell.

Feeling foolish, I turned and walked into the house, anger cracking the fixed, dried cement smile worn since getting out of the car.

I should be thinking orchestra not bloody men. I angrily stomped upstairs. How dare he, how dare anyone treat me like that, how dare he cause confusion with his dithering, how dare he be like me? Come with me to America, no don't bother, come to mine, oh, sorry you can't I had something planned already. It felt like he was playing games and wondered why I was allowing it to get to me. Remember lesson two? Never allow anyone close enough to cause damage? I'd bloody well go to Lawrence's and practise and I'd bloody well do what I wanted, not what I thought was right by others. By doing what I thought was right by James I'd ended up divorced; I wasn't starting that crap again. Shrubby, Trevor, whatever he wished to be known by, could quite literally bugger off. I threw my boots into the corner of the room. From the window I could see Mum and Dad in the garden, twice their normal size with the amount of clothing they had on, slowly digging over the vegetable plot behind the shed. I got changed, made them a cup of tea and then practised on the clarinet.

I heard Mum and Dad come in from the garden, Dad swearing at Roger for getting in his way, Mum huffing at Dad for shouting at Roger. Dad came into the front room and sat down heavily on the small two-seater settee set against the wall.

'Play 'Vilja', none of that Stravinsky stuff,' he said, while I pulled a face. 'Go on, 'Vilja', don't be rotten,' he encouraged; 'Vilja' from the *Merry Widow* was one of his favourites.

I played it for him, while he closed his eyes, his fingers tapping to a beat only he could find on the arm of the chair. I thought he looked shattered, overdoing it in the garden probably.

'That was great,' he said, opening his eyes. 'We're both going to miss you if you move away with your new job, who's going to play the clarinet then?'

I smiled at him. 'Wanna hear 'Bill Bailey'?' For the next three minutes his fingers battered hell out of the arm of the chair.

With Trevor's manner being far from agreeable to my turning up at his friend's for a further clarinet session, it was with some trepidation that I rang on Lawrence's doorbell later that day.

He came to the door and beamed happily when he saw who it was. He certainly always made me feel welcome. I wondered if he knew I'd been asked, however bizarrely, to travel to America with him and the band. I said nothing and handed him a box of bottled beers as a thank you. We followed the same routine; I went into the music room and sorted the sheet music out while he went to get a beer for us both and a piece of meat for the dog bed. I played the clarinet, he played the piano. How dare Trevor question my integrity. All I was doing was playing the audition pieces, pieces that I loved and hoped would get to be performed in front of an audition panel. What was so wrong about that? I started to tidy my things away. I didn't want to outstay my welcome, especially when the phone rang and he went to answer it, his popularity such that every time I called he had friends phoning or calling round. I could hear his voice get louder as he made his way back to the room still on the phone.

'Yeah, yeah, I know, yeah, right okay, yeah, see you tomorrow, right yeah, bye.' He popped the phone onto the mantelpiece and picked up the plastic bag carrying my music. 'It's sounding good,' he said. 'I believe you saw the North Western Symphony Orchestra play last night.'

'They were fabulous. Just amazing, I can't believe I've even been considered good enough to audition, they must feel sorry for me, or maybe I'll get a letter saying ha-ha fooled you.' I sounded like I was rooting for a compliment but I wasn't, I really meant it. There were better clarinet players than me out there and we all wanted the same thing. I walked into the hall, he followed me out.

'You're good enough. Would you like to stay a bit longer? Have a few more beers and you could even stay the night if you want.' He looked at me expectantly. I looked at him as if he'd just said show me your tits.

'Best get home, Mum and Dad will be wondering where I am.' I can't believe I said that, but I did. I can't believe I didn't then apologise and march up to his bedroom, but I didn't. I opened the front door and took the plastic bag from him when it became apparent that he wasn't going to walk me to the car as he had last time.

'I've invited friends round for a small party tonight but never mind, maybe another time.' He put his hand up in farewell.

'Maybe, and thanks,' I said cheerfully. His front door was already closing.

'Well, I think today's gone fabulously well, not,' I said to myself as I drove home. 'Certainly know how to wrap men round your little finger don't you? Got them eating out of your hand, haven't you? There's nothing I don't know about men.' What the hell had I done to upset both Trevor and Lawrence within a day? Why had Lawrence suddenly decided now to make a move? Had I misconstrued the whole situation? Had he really meant, you could stay in the spare room if you have too much to drink but you won't catch me coming at you, love? There'd been no mention of friends coming round initially. Or had there? Had I just assumed he was trying to get me into bed? Shame! On reaching home my phone bleeped. Message received from unknown number, I really must update my contacts. 'Had great time in Lancaster, thanx for sharing, will ring you, Trevor x.'

I walked into the house to find Mum and Dad in hysterics in the kitchen. Dad was laughing so hard he had tears in his eyes. There was nothing for it but to join in.

Chapter 23

Next day, Monday, and there was no sign of Mum and Dad when I got home from work and there was no note to say when they would be back. It had to happen eventually, I'd fallen into the selfish trap of relying on tea being delivered to me more or less as I walked in from work. I found a pizza and some chips in the freezer and threw them in the oven. Grumbling about how hungry I was I went upstairs to change, opening a letter addressed to me on the way. I hurled myself onto the bed ecstatically, grumbles turning to shrieks. My application had been accepted, the audition date set for 29th April.

I'd spent most of that day dreaming of walking away from the bank to a new life in America, having a man like Trevor to look after me. In all of those thoughts I was laughing, everyone laughing with me, light-hearted, without a care in the world, jamming in the sunshine under palm trees. With the letter now held in my hand the sunshine and palm trees rearranged themselves into rain clouds and huge oak trees, the laughter shared with sheep and strangers instead.

The phone rang as I pulled my jeans on and pushed my feet into my giant slippers simultaneously.

'Hi Grace, it's your mum here. Listen, I don't want you to panic, it's nothing serious so don't panic, but your dad's in hospital and he's going to have to stay overnight. It's this cough and it seems that there's a lot of protein, or something, in his blood which they want to check up on, so don't panic. Can you bring his hair cream from the side of the bed, oh, and a tin of pears if you're coming to visit him? Ward 14.'

The don't panics made me panic. I raced upstairs, found the lavender hair cream, hared back downstairs, grabbed my bag and a tin of pears, and made it to the car before I realised I was still wearing my gigantic slippers and had left the oven on. A quick adjustment to footwear and oven and I was at the hospital within fifteen minutes. Parking took another fifteen minutes, increasing my chances of being put in the bed next to my dad.

My worries were laid to rest though when I saw him sat up in his bed, in his pyjamas, surrounded by family, laughing and joking as if holding court in his own living room. It was a busy ward, the nurses cheerful, already on first name terms. His cough was no better but no worse. Natalie had baby Matty with her, held firmly within her grasp; nearly a year old, he was now big enough to hurt if smacked in the face by him and tottered everywhere if put down. Her daughter, Katie, sat on the end of the bed eating a large bunch of purple grapes, each one held preciously up to the light before being devoured, occasionally offering one to her granddad. Mum looked worn-out.

Earlier that day the GP, after a number of previous visits, had finally decided to take a urine sample and immediately told Dad he would be making arrangements for a hospital bed. Dad could either make his own way there or the GP could organise an ambulance, but to hospital he must go. Mum and Dad had packed an overnight bag and he had driven to the hospital. Dad was his own master; no ambulance was going to be required. The high amount of protein in the sample necessitated urgent attention, which was worrying but trying to get answers was nigh-on impossible. Dad's arm was bruised from the number of blood samples he'd had to give.

'Good girl, you've got my pears,' Dad said when I produced them from my bag.

'What's the food like?' I asked him.

'We've had chicken, it was fowl.' We all groaned.

I had an orchestra rehearsal that night but decided to leave it until Dad insisted on my going.

'No point in hanging around here. I'll be fine. Go on, I'll see you tomorrow, probably at home.'

I leaned over and gave him a hug and a kiss. 'See you in the morning, Dad.'

I looked back at him in the bed as I left and was overwhelmed with love and affection. I'd have swapped places if I could. He was heedless of this; side-tracked by a nurse who'd just arrived to take his temperature.

Rehearsal was shambolic. Sandra had found out about my audition and wasn't happy, although her smiling face didn't let up while she flung nasty comments about my ability throughout the break. She was beginning to realise the mistake she'd made in encouraging lessons.

'Don't you think the clarinets were a bit too loud? Well I heard Grace, definitely too loud. Grace, you were too loud. Maybe it was just your phrasing; I've told you before that you need to watch your end phrases.' Then seconds later, 'Grace, you need to tweak your reeds. I'll do it for you, if you don't know how, before we start after break.'

I ignored her and stalked outside with my cup of tea. Fergal came after me.

'I'm going to punch the bitch if you don't,' he said.

'She's the least of my worries at the moment.' I told Fergal about my dad. He was very supportive and gave all the right encouragement to make me believe Dad would be fine, everything would be fine. I asked him how Sandra had managed to find out about my audition. Fergal's colour deepened in his face, I left the matter alone. He asked me how Anna was.

'As mad as ever. She's moving house, got a new job.'

'I'll always be fond of her you know but I'd never be able to control her, she's too independent,' he said.

'That's something I don't think she is,' I replied. 'She gives a good impression though.'

We walked back into the scout hut to empty our cups and run them under the tap.

'There you are, Grace, do you want me to have a look at your reed? Maybe I could run through that last piece, to put you right before we start again.' Sandra was relentless and I had had enough. I slammed the cup onto the draining board.

'Fuck off, Sandra, touch my clarinet and I'll kill you. Just who the hell do you think you are?'

She opened her mouth then closed it, turned bright red and walked away without saying a word. I thought Fergal was going to explode with joy. Anna would have been proud of me. However, I was shocked at my response, it didn't make me feel any better but at least the constant harassment from her was temporarily halted. I made sure of this by picking up my stuff and leaving, Joan Sarney was oblivious to the anarchy unleashed in her rehearsal, her flowers not working their usual magic. I called in on Anna and had a good bitch, and a carton of strawberry yoghurt. It wasn't a happy drive home; I missed the crappiness of my old car.

Dad wasn't home the next day or the day after that. He was having every test done under the sun and somehow was starting to look more ill than he ever had at home. Rebecca had come to visit and was staying with us, as was Harry. Mary drove up but didn't need to stay; she could make it home if she did the afternoon visit.

I would come away from a hospital visit and secretly challenge the world around me to prove he'd get better quickly. I couldn't stop it; it was as if I was looking for signs from God.

'If this set of traffic lights stay on green, he'll be okay.' They stayed on green. I felt a brief sense of relief until the next challenge. 'If the sun comes out before I reach home, he'll be okay.' It didn't, I felt nothing but dread until the next challenge. 'If there's a piece of toilet paper in my left pocket he'll be okay.' There was; relief. 'If I don't play the clarinet, he'll be okay.' And so it went on.

On the Sunday after being admitted into hospital, Dad coughed blood. It frightened us to the point that Natalie searched out a nurse and demanded that a doctor come at once to check up on him. With it being a weekend though and only a skeleton staff, a junior doctor turned up and did the usual checking of pulse, heart, blood pressure, giving little in the way of reassurance. Dad said that his fingers were hard to move which was upsetting him because he couldn't drum but had his CD player and headphones at the ready when we left.

'If I play 'Vilja' on the clarinet, he'll be okay.' I played 'Vilja' on the clarinet. The next visit he was feeling worse and it became apparent how seriously ill he really was. He was transferred to a renal ward where the doctors had tried to take a biopsy from his kidneys and he'd collapsed. Before any of us knew it they were mentioning the possibility of intensive care.

It was difficult to keep a finger on what was going on outside the hospital walls. The bank was the place I least wanted to be but even so I was there every day, in body if not in spirit. Diane and Anna offered support by getting me drunk on the

Wednesday evening after choir rehearsal and allowing me to slam Diane's kitchen door five times to vent some anger.

We held a lively inquiry into who Diane was seeing and after mentioning anyone we'd ever met and some we hadn't, she told us it was Tom. We were so shocked we had another drink to find out more. Heather's perseverance had finally paid off. Diane had been going to Relate with Tom, working through their issues. At first they had hated, accused and sulked. He hated the way she made him feel inadequate, she rarely wanted sex, she was too fussy, too bossy, always doing stuff, nagging him to change into something he wasn't, it did his head in. She hated his lethargy towards his family, his bombastic manner to almost everything, his dismissive attitude to her work, he never wanted sex, it made her feel worthless. Neither of them had adapted well after the birth of their child. He conceded that he'd become a creature of habit, his jealousy hard to contain when challenged by anything that threatened change. She allowed that she constantly needled him, any type of reaction being better than going unnoticed. He admitted that he'd not wanted her to leave, that he'd over-reacted and had felt unable to stop what he'd started. She admitted she hadn't wanted to leave.

It took a separation to realise they missed each other. With both accepting a portion of blame, it was becoming easier to see their differences and deal with the ones that caused the most grief. They were starting to like each other again, finding that time and age hadn't dulled the marriage, complacency had. It made me think that to have the capacity for so much hate there must have been too much love to lose.

'I know it sounds mad, but if I hadn't spent the night with Rich I'd have never considered trying to make things work with

Tom. I needed to make sure I wasn't missing out on anything and although it was great sex with Rich, I really missed Tom.'

'Does Tom know about Rich?' I asked.

'No, and I hope he never does. I'm not going to tell him. It meant nothing and was a means to an end. It's not going to help our relationship is it? And I don't do remorse.'

Anna looked shocked. 'You have to tell him. There has to be honesty or your relationship is built on a lie and won't last.'

'It will last. You may disapprove but like I said, it meant nothing. I don't want to ever see Rich as anything but a kind of 'guardian angel' who pointed me in the right direction. It meant nothing and nobody gains anything by me telling Tom. Oh, apart from righteous honesty. Great.'

'Some guardian angel! I want one. I still think...' Anna started.

'Anna, don't even go there. I hate to say it but you're in no position to lecture about deceit in marriage.'

'I'm not lecturing, Diane. It's exactly because of what I did that I feel I can offer you some advice.'

'It's because of what you and Grace have been through that makes me want to do anything I can to save my marriage, and confessing to a one night stand that meant nothing isn't going to help. I'm thinking of my daughter. You've said in the past that we all handle things differently and none of us are the same. This is the way I have to deal with what's happened, you know? Grace has cried a lot, you've flipped a bit and I've been angry.'

Anna shrugged. 'What if Tom finds out?'

'I'll deny it.'

'I wish you all the luck and happiness in the world then.'

'More wine anyone?' I flashed the bottle. Two glasses leapt forward.

We discussed Trevor and Lawrence, I wasn't going to tell them but I squealed under the influence of drink and confessed to having slept with Trevor, and told them about Lawrence's offer to stay the night. They were highly amused at me blaming Mum and Dad for not accepting. This only took the emphasis back to my dad.

I spoke to Trevor the next day and arranged to see him after visiting hours; this was prior to finding out that Dad had been moved from the renal ward to coronary care.

Dad had a mask on to help him breathe but was still managing to laugh about an episode he'd had earlier on trying to eat ice-cream. The nurses were lovely with him and kept telling him to put the mask on because he kept taking it off to chat. We told him to listen to us instead of trying to get his two pennies worth in. I watched him on the bed and knew that my lovely Dad was trying to hide how badly he really suffering. His body didn't so much shake as wobble and every tiny thing he did was being monitored by what looked like a panel of screens across the room, blipping and beeping, making sense to someone but frightening the rest of us.

Rebecca broke down and cried in the corridor, unable to understand what was going on. Dad was immortal; this sort of thing didn't happen in her world of loveliness. Harry looked stunned, unbelieving, he looked like a child. Mum, for the first time since he'd been admitted, seemed lost. Natalie kept a grip on herself although I could see she was deeply worried. Mary wasn't present she was due up at the weekend. I was frightened. I tried not to show it by saying every now and then, 'It's the best place, look at the care he's getting, it's the best place,' sounding anything but convincing.

'Aren't you supposed to be seeing that man with the name of a tree?' Mum asked as we arrived home, en masse, to raid the drink cupboard that evening.

'Shrubby? I'll ring him and tell him I'm not going round. In fact, I just won't turn up it won't be a problem.' I didn't want to see Trevor; I wanted to drink myself stupid with the family around me.

'Oh no you don't, you don't just not turn up.' Natalie was adamant. 'Mum, tell her.'

'Grace, it's up to you but I think you should go. I would like you to go, it will do you good.' Mum sat back on the settee with a mug of tea in one hand and a whisky in the other. Harry and Natalie pushed me out of the house. I found myself outside looking up at the clear night sky with stars bleakly shimmering and shivering in the cold. I still couldn't believe that, while I was looking up at something so eternal, Dad was fighting for his life.

'If the engine starts first time, he'll be okay.' It didn't. It started at a second, frantic attempt and I reversed suddenly without checking properly, eyes bleary.

'You stupid bitch, you nearly hit me.' A woman walking past the path as I was reversing shouted and looked like she wanted to smack me. For a second I wanted to scream back at her, tell her that I wished I had hit her before remorse seeped through me and I apologised, keeping the window up.

Trevor was full of life and smiles when I arrived at his. We'd only spoken on the phone once since Lancaster, affording both of us time to evaluate what we wanted from our relationship. I stood on the doorstep wishing I wasn't stood on the doorstep when he let me in. I could have tried to explain what was going on but I kept him at arm's length, knowing I was being totally unfair to him and that he deserved better of me. He had music blaring and was sorting his bookshelves out alphabetically in genre, getting ready to pack it all away come the time to move out. I sat in the tiniest corner of his settee and sipped at the glass of red wine he offered. After an effort at small talk, which quickly became no-talk due to a lump growing in my throat, he came and sat down next to me.

'Is your Dad okay?'

'Not really.'

'Is there anything I can do?' he asked.

'No,' I whispered back.

'You're freezing.'

'I'm fine.'

He left the room and came back with a small fur throw and put it over my legs. His gentleness only distressed me more. He turned the telly on, made a cup of tea and came back into the room, sitting next to me again.

'You're not up for going for a drink? He asked.

'I'm so sorry, I shouldn't have come. My dad's seriously ill. I don't want to think about how we left him tonight...'

'In that case I'll put a film on, and, if you still feel bad, I'll understand if you want to go home.'

We sat and watched 'Trading Places' which I drifted in and out of, heavy thoughts never far from the coronary care unit. At some point Trevor put his arm out to me and I moved into his shoulder. I could feel his heartbeat, steady and strong. There was a dreamlike quality to the evening, no speech required throughout the duration, both of us now covered with the fur throw. He kissed me lightly on the cheek and gave my hand a squeeze before I left, not long after the end credits.

'If you need anything, you know where I am.'

It was Saturday morning that we were told that Dad was going into ITU. Although we all knew he was very ill it still came as a total shock. Mary made it up the motorway and was with us when we were told to come to the hospital.

A nurse was there to greet us at the doors of the corridor leading to intensive care. Everything should have been hushed, muffled within its boundaries due to the very nature of the ward. I shouldn't have been able to hear people passing outside, laughing, the squeaky wheels of a trolley and thuds of laundry being piled close by, or the siren of an ambulance in the distance.

'Ted is being settled right now, it'll only be a minute before you can go and see him. We have two at the bed at one time policy, so if you can take it in turns that would be lovely.'

We were told that they were going to put him completely out, find out what the problem was, give his body a rest and within a day or two we would know more.

Mum remained at his side as one by one we walked down the corridor into the ward. Mary went first, followed by Rebecca, Natalie then Harry. I went last.

It was a lovely, bright room with nine beds in it, the sun gleaming off the white floor and walls from the many windows set to one side. Although there was plenty of noise with monitors pinging, nurses and doctors chatting, phones ringing, radio playing, it was surprisingly restful.

Dad was in the first bed on the left and was sat up with an oxygen mask over his nose. There were two nurses sorting out trays and equipment at the side of his bed. He looked exhausted but he was grinning behind his mask; an early kick-off with the Liverpool-Everton game had bought a one goal lead to Everton.

He coughed as I approached and he grimaced when he took the mask off to find it wet inside.

'Weargh! Look at that, no don't.' His voice was hoarse.

One of the nurses smiled and cleaned it out for him, popping it back onto his nose, the hissing sound of oxygen instantly stifled as she did so. Mum had her hand resting over his. I didn't know what to say. None of this felt like it was really happening.

'How are you, Dad?' I asked, stupidly.

He raised his eyes at me. It made me laugh. I was determined, as we all had been, not to show any fear.

'How's the auditioning going?' he asked, muffled by the mask and distracted by a nurse fiddling with something at the side of the bed.

'Oh great, but I need you back to drum the beat, so hurry up and get better. Anyway, think your team are good enough to win do you?' I answered, referring to Everton's goal.

He gave me a breathless yes. The nurses were making it obvious that visiting time was coming to its conclusion, that there was work to be done that couldn't be done while we were hanging around.

'Short but sweet visit. I think I'd better go.' I took hold of his hand and desperately held back tears that were pushing hard to get out. I leant over and gave him a kiss.

'See you in the morning, Dad.' He looked back at me with the brightest blue eyes, a faint smile behind the mask.

I left Mum to say goodbye and walked down a corridor that seemed to have no end, finally reaching the others. There are no words to describe how we all felt; the missing adjectives were worn on the faces looking back at me. Our hopes were based on the fact that whatever the problem was, it could be fixed now he was receiving the ultimate in care. That night Dad went to sleep blissfully unaware that his team had lost.

Chapter 24

Dad never made it out of intensive care. A month of hope shattered with the dreaded words, 'There's nothing more we can do;' a month where life carried on but was barely noticed, like eating food while watching telly. Life would never be the same again for any of us. There at his bedside, as he slipped away, it seemed the most peaceful of all things. If it's true that once you die you look down upon yourself before heading for the bright light, he would have seen his wife and children at his side below and known he was loved, he would be smiling.

Everything in his body had slowly shut down. The spots, months previously, had been the first indication that there was some form of blood disorder. The cough had been as a result of his lungs allowing fluid in. Vasculitis. Never heard of it, wished I'd never had to be introduced to it. In my mind, I thought he'd never fully recovered from the flu we'd all caught. Wracked with guilt I blamed myself for not pushing Dad to go to the doctor's earlier. I'd been living under the same roof; surely I could have done more. I'd been so wrapped up in my own concerns, the clarinet, Trevor, Lawrence, James, I'd not bothered to interfere with those of my dad's. I'd never given him the money to repair his car after I'd put a dent in it. I'd never told him I loved him. Why? Why hadn't I been at his side in intensive care more often? Why hadn't I been able to say something while he was sleeping to make him better? Why couldn't I have taken his place?

Scotch was liberally poured the morning of his funeral, to help get us through it. Dad hadn't been religious, his belief that there was something out there for us all when we breathe our last, more hopeful than ardent. I knew he was well respected and liked but it was overwhelming to see how many people turned up to say goodbye to him, from old work colleagues and friends, to a little old lady, eternally grateful for her hundred year old washing machine which, thanks to Dad's diligence, was still working and capable of getting her smalls clean.

After the funeral, the marquee in the garden, and mourners alike, sank beneath an onslaught of heavy rain and booze. If he had anything to do with the weather on the day of his funeral, he certainly made sure we were aware of his presence the morning we buried his ashes next to his brother in his family burial plot. As the urn was put into the ground there was a flash of lightening followed immediately by a crack of thunder that shook the earth. That was it, no rain followed in its wake. It was the thunder I always expected but that never occurred at important moments, and it couldn't have picked a more auspicious time, even the man from the funeral parlour looked sufficiently impressed. In my head I heard Dad's voice, 'See that? Like a coiled spring.' I stumbled away from the graveside, getting to the car just before the ache of despair threatening to rip me apart, broke my heart with convulsive, gut-wrenching sobs. Our hero, my hero, the one man who'd always been there to get us, me, out of trouble and to offer advice, able to make things better, was lost forever.

Travelling home, we drove up the road that, a year ago, I'd been towed by Dad with near disastrous consequences and Mum, on the backseat, said, 'Oh, here's where we nearly ended up in the bushes, last year.' She put her head in the crook of Harry's shoulder and soaked it.

Chapter 25

It seemed almost callous to continue, but life did, even though, once in a while there were moments when the reality of never seeing Dad again swiped me sideways almost physically. Moments like opening the personal CD player he'd taken into hospital and finding Frank Sinatra inside.

I had an audition looming, one that had had no preparation at all.

I'd not played the clarinet for well over a month; I didn't want to. I hadn't been to see Mr Gerrard. I hadn't seen much of Trevor and nothing of Lawrence. They were busy preparing for their tour and, besides which, I had been too distraught to give them much thought. I'd seen Anna and Diane a couple of times but can't say that my company enhanced the evenings in any way but it did me good to get out and forget for a short time.

Trevor had taken me to the pub a couple of times but it had been on a friendly basis, there had been no amorous overtures. He'd listened and allowed me to get drunk as I'd twittered about anything but what was happening in the hospital, escaping its weighing dread for a short time. He'd told me that the band was due to fly out to America at the end of March, would be landing in New York and carrying on from there for six to nine months touring. He asked me if I wanted to practise at his again but I declined. I hated the clarinet. I saw Dad's pride, heard him drumming on the sideboard, whistling tunelessly along.

Trevor remained silent and seemed to understand. He hadn't come to the funeral, he'd never met my dad and had only ever spoken to him once, the brief, swearing encounter on the telephone being the unfortunate incident.

Anna and Diane paid their respects, they'd met him a couple of times at various concerts we'd done, and they helped sort drinks out and serve chilli from slow cookers dotted around the kitchen.

Even James came back to the house to raise a glass to his ex-father-in-law. He revealed that he'd finally sold the house and was moving to Chester with Simone. He had a sale on if I was interested. I shouldn't have done it, the occasion not appropriate for airing grievances, but I'd asked him if he'd bought any Minis lately.

'Minis? What d'you mean?' He looked genuinely surprised.

I hesitated, was almost about to leave it there and say 'Forget it,' when I recalled this look from the past, but with refreshed eyes I now saw a trace of guilt and fear there too. 'It's a car, with four wheels and an engine? Bought with cash from Watson's Cars? Ringing any bells?'

His face turned a dusky shade of terracotta beneath hollowed cheeks of perfect stubble I'd once ached to plant kisses on.

'I ... it was ... the thing was ... I don't ... Mini?' After floundering, he warily reverted to innocence.

'D'you know what, James, I don't care. Life's too short.' The eyes that looked back at me were now totally devoid of any expression. My own remained coolly detached. 'I really hope you find happiness with Simone. It means a lot you came today. Thank-you. Take care of yourself.' I smiled and turned to walk away.

'Grace, I never meant to hurt you.'

'I know. And I never meant to hurt you either. Now, where the hell's my drink?'

He left shortly after, Natalie pulling faces behind his back. I put my arm round her and we both wandered down the garden to the marquee in search of some scotch.

I was proud of how I'd dealt with James. I'd been every inch the woman he'd never seen in me. I hadn't poured a pint over his head as I'd so desired in the past, I hadn't been kindness and light in an effort to please. I'd been his equal.

Aunty Kath, a quite eccentric relative who had lost her husband a few years previously and who said, 'Darling' a lot, stayed on after the funeral for the next week, with the aim to help Mum readjust. I don't know who needed looking after more.

The weekend after the funeral was Anna's moving date. Organised as she was, she couldn't get the removal van there any earlier than twelve o'clock due to favours being called in via a friend of a friend to keep costs down, which meant that packed boxes were piling up inside and outside the house when I arrived that morning to help out. Doors and windows were wide open, a lovely spring air zipping through the house, cleansing it of its winter of discontent. Children were getting under people's feet and orders were being shouted by Anna from upstairs, 'No, that goes in bric-a-brac and that's electrical ... that's battery operated, give that here!'

I was given a job to do as soon as I walked through the front door, the cutlery drawer. Diane, wearing Marigolds covered in black grime from the cooker, cheered when I put the kettle on and stood up to give me a hug without arms, more of a shove really.

'Don't know when this was last cleaned, 1942 by the looks of things.' She returned to cleaning out the oven.

'She's more boudoir babe than kitchen queen, we both know that,' I said, tipping a mish-mash of cutlery onto the counter top.

'Who?' Anna came into the kitchen, wearing the epitome of moving-house gear, faded dungarees, CAT boots and a cotton scarf over her head.

'You, you daft cow,' I said.

She hit me over the head with a cookery book. The mature woman that I now considered myself, didn't stop me from childishly throwing a soaking dishcloth at her which landed with a slap on her surprised face. Diane took her gloves off and, before we knew it, water was everywhere and we were soaked, slipping dangerously, laughing hysterically. Anna's mum came in and told us all to grow up and look at the mess we were making, and stopped the children from joining in by barring the way into the kitchen.

'This bloody kitchen,' Anna said when she'd caught her breath back, a yellow and green sponge jutting out of her dungaree bib. 'Even empty it's a shithole.'

For the first time in over a month, I'd completely let go and felt no guilt attached in doing so. I pulled a dishcloth out of my bra and sighed, slopping through an inch of water to pop the kettle back on.

After clearing up the aftermath of the water fight, we sat outside in the garden in the early spring sunshine, surrounded by pink cherry blossom and daffodils, and drank tea, trying to dry ourselves off a bit.

Anna's family were lending a hand, her mum and her dad, her two brothers, one of her sister-in-laws, three teenage nephews and one ten year old niece, plus few of us not adding much in the way of help other than offering counsel on how best to pack. There was something being sat in the sunshine chewing the cud over house-moving manoeuvres, while all around us bushes, trees and buds fluttered their eyes open with fresh, green brilliance.

The next door neighbour, Donald, stopped mowing his pristine lawn and handed a bottle of wine with a card over the back garden fence.

'It's a Good Riddance card,' Anna said, once he'd started up his lawn mower again. 'He's just being nosey, look at him now, pretending the grass needs cutting.'

Diane said she fancied him, Anna felt her temperature. I lay back and let the sun dry my jeans which were soaked in the crotch area, giving the appearance that I'd wet myself.

'Hello, hello, hello, any work going on here, thought you were moving today?' Lawrence's voice came from the back gate. I put my hand to my eyes to see him approaching us, quite content to remain were I was until I saw Trevor coming up behind him. I shot up like a deckchair. Anna hadn't mentioned they would be turning up to help out.

She got up and greeted them. 'Thanks for coming, I know it looks bad but we've been at it since eight this morning so we needed a break. It's all Grace's fault, coming here making tea.'

'Have you had a water leak or something?' Lawrence asked, taking in the wet clothing.

'No, that again I'm afraid is Grace's fault.'

I stood up and collected cups, our peaceful time now over, and took them inside. I'd given both Lawrence and Shrubby a smile of welcome and then a cheeky grin at the mention of wet clothing.

For the next two hours, which flew by, we all cleared, packed, boxed, taped, marked, shouted, thumped, bumped and heaved anything that stood still long enough. At one point Lawrence popped a box on Anna's head and twizzled her around and at another point he locked her in the wardrobe that he and her brother had spent ten minutes trying to get down the stairs.

The van, when it arrived an hour late, was half the size expected, demanding those good at logistical thinking to come up with a plan. The men huddled, debating for fifteen minutes on how to best get round this problem with man talk and scratching, the women discussed the subject for two minutes before moving on to how the curtains would fit in the new house, the children jumped on and off the van.

It all got sorted and after many trips backwards and forwards with cars bursting with boxes, Anna finally shut the door for the last time on Carpenters Road and walked away without an ounce of regret.

Occasionally during the day I'd had moments where I'd been carting a box with Shrubby or handing things over to Lawrence but the whole process had been more conducive to grunts than in-depth conversation. Later, early evening, Anna ordered Chinese to be delivered which arrived at the same time as Tom did to help. Diane, who'd gone to fetch him, issued a general introduction to everyone then, holding his hand, led him over to me.

'Tom, this is Grace. She was the getaway driver, remember?' And she laughed.

No word of a lie, my jaw dropped three foot.

Stood with a crispy duck pancake in one hand and a beer in the other in Anna's new kitchen, we waited till everyone helped themselves to food and found corners in various rooms in which to sit back and take a well-earned rest before we asked questions.

I whispered to Diane, who was looking very smug, her eyes following Tom out of the kitchen. 'How's it going?'

'Fabulous. I think I've rediscovered my soul mate, we both want the same things, you know? If it carries on like this I'll be moving back in with him.'

'Are you sure?' Anna whispered, nearly choking on a sesame seed.

'Absolutely, we want to be together, he's only half a person without me, he says I complete him, you know? And he sang to me down the phone the other day, he sang 'Baby come Back', including the talky bits like Shaggy.'

'How revolting, I'm going to be sick,' Anna said, loudly and rudely. I giggled. I loved it when Anna was rude; she got away with it where others didn't.

She lowered her voice again. 'It wasn't long ago he was a fat bastard and would rather go fishing than have sex with you. Even you called him Tom the Tosser ... Tom, thanks for helping out,' she said quickly as he came back into the kitchen and put his plate next to Diane's.

One thing about Diane was her ability to hear only what she wanted. She took no offence at Anna's comments; her skin was thicker than a hippo's when it came to negative forces, protecting her big heart. It was a great trait and one I longed for. As long as she was happy, she was big enough and daft enough, like the rest of us, to make her own choices for better, for worse.

Trevor bought his plate out. My stomach performed a gymnastic routine when I looked at him. He was going away shortly and I most likely wouldn't see him again, or if I did it would be a chance meeting, ten years from now, shopping in Asda with his groupie wife. Once he arrived in America, I figured he wouldn't be coming back in a hurry. It was strange but the night we'd spent together had been put away in my head behind a door, seeming indecent to consider it when my world was again being ransacked and torn to shreds. Now that I was in the aftermath and he was leaving soon, I was able to take stock and realise how incredibly wonderful it had been and, as usual, how it was too late to do anything about it, his overture to travel with him a distant memory. He took hold of my hand and led me out into the garden. Anna caught my eye and smiled.

'I haven't spoken to you since before the funeral, how are you?' We sat on a garden chair; the bright, spring day had turned into a beautiful cool evening.

'I'm alright.'

He looked at me closely so I looked closely back at him. I was not about to break down and cry, I was in full control of my emotions.

'I'm so sorry about your dad. I was thinking of you all the time, you know that don't you?'

I nodded, not aware this was the case but accepting it from the honesty in his eyes.

'It was a good funeral; we all got pissed and played his favourite music. He would have been chuffed. Anyway, how are your plans for the 'Not Agains world domination tour' going?'

'We had our final gig last night. That's it now. We fly out next week. One of our songs is being used in a small independent movie being made in New York and our manager has organised a few promotional gigs to coincide with its release, so, it's all been brought forward. How's the practising going?'

'Great, yeah. Bit cold out here isn't it?' I made to stand up and was held back by Trevor's arm.

'Grace, don't let this slip. Promise me you'll audition.'

'Of course I will.' I was too blithe, too blasé. I stood back up. 'Come on, it really is cold.'

I walked slowly back to the house, turning as I reached the back door to see Trevor still sat on the chair.

'Come back to mine.' His voice floated to me on the evening air.

I hesitated. I wanted to, very badly. I wanted to give him everything I had. I knew how strong his arms were, remembered where his fingers had touched, where his mouth had kissed. My throat went dry. A voice inside me interrupted and said, *Anna, must make sure she's alright.*

I walked back over to him. 'Would you wait for me?' I said in his ear.

'Yes.'

Without another word I walked back into the house, my insides like trifle.

With Anna's encouragement, people had started to leave. She looked exhausted, her eyelids heavy in a pale face. After all the excitement of the day came the low to follow.

'Want me to stay with you?' I asked.

'With the van being late and a total disaster, everything's a mess upstairs. Mum's taking the children home with her tonight so I can sort their bedrooms out tomorrow properly for them.' She yawned. 'You're more than welcome to stay, if you really want to. I've got whisky, somewhere.'

Trevor came in from the garden and smiled, walking past us to find the others. Anna gave me a look in suspiciously. I shrugged. A burst of laughter erupted from the lounge.

'I know I said I was going to clean up my act, but a certain person has been flirting with me all day,' Anna said quietly, she didn't need to say anymore.

Funny, knowing she was referring to Lawrence, the man I'd painted pretty pictures about in daydreams, meant only that she wasn't going to be on her own that evening. I'm not sure if she was telling me this to allow me to go or if she was uncertain about hurting my feelings.

I gave her a hug. 'Are you sure?'

'I could quite happily go to bed to sleep but, come on, I'm not going to turn down the alternative.'

So it was that I phoned Mum to tell her I wouldn't be home that night and gave a lift to Trevor, Diane and Tom. Diane and Tom who, between them, had managed to polish off the last of Anna's vodka. Looking in the rear view mirror at the 'newly acquainted' couple in the back, I realised how well they suited each other and wondered how they'd ever managed to get themselves so beleaguered in their relationship. I dropped them off outside the smallest flat in the land, Diane drunkenly and loudly proclaiming a disturbing amount of inside information as to what real love was. Trevor put his hand briefly over mine, resting on the gear stick and took hold of my hand as we walked up his pathway, the small gestures of affection chipping away at barriers I'd built to save myself.

He poured a large glass of wine for each of us. I led him upstairs.

Chapter 26

Hands touched me to wakefulness next morning. A warm sun, shining through closed orange and gold curtains, gave the room a dulled ochre glow.

Much later we lay looking at each other.

'Why didn't I meet you years ago?' Trevor murmured.

'I wasn't up for selection years ago.'

'I didn't want this to happen. I knew I'd be in trouble if it did.' He looked away.

'I know hardly anything about you but I'm glad it did.' I brought his face back to look at me. His hand stroked my shoulder.

'What do you want to know?'

'I don't know. Maybe, would you have been up for selection years ago?'

'On and off. A number of girlfriends, some a bit more serious than others, but nothing I couldn't have walked away from. Divorce hey? For a long time it taints all relationships after it doesn't it.'

'But it can also give you back your life,' I said.

'Are you going to pick the clarinet up today?'

The quick turn in conversation threw me. The warmth I felt from his gaze vanished, a freezing grip quickly closing over the inside of my throat at the thought of playing the clarinet. How did he know I hadn't played for a while?

'Grace, I'm not stupid. You have to at some stage.' He sat up. There was an incredible ache tearing at my insides. I rolled over, turning away from him, the pain in my eyes hurt too much to allow him to see it.

'You have to, not for your dad, or anyone else, but for yourself.'

'What do you know?' I was angry at him for him mentioning my dad.

'Nothing. But I do know that whatever's going on in that head of yours has to be faced, not ignored.'

'You didn't know my dad. You weren't even at the funeral.'

He was silent for a moment; his voice was soft when he spoke again. 'I wasn't, I wish I could have been, he sounded like a really great man, and being your dad makes me certain he was. But, I didn't turn up to the funeral because I was thinking of you and only you, and that's what I'm doing now.' He paused. 'I didn't mean to upset you. I'll go for a shower and leave you alone.' He slipped away from me and out of the bedroom, his bare bum creating a momentary diversion and receiving an appreciative following from the bed prior to its exit. I flopped back on the pillow and stared at the ceiling.

He came back in minutes later, showered and dressed and planted a kiss on my forehead.

'I'll say this once and won't ever say it again – don't give up. I'm going to make some breakfast.'

Before I could answer he'd gone.

I got out of bed, clutched at some clothing and went into the bathroom, passing half-empty suitcases on the landing, a reminder of Trevor's imminent departure. The face that looked back at me from the mirror was one I hardly recognised, partly because I'd slept with make-up on and it now resembled an artist's pallet and partly because anxiety was drawing the features in to a screwed up ball. Trevor had touched a nerve as he crept under my skin and into my heart.

Tentatively I was feeling my way in the field of love, something that I thought had been broken by my divorce was slowly being fixed. Lesson two disregarded as I allowed someone near enough now to cause damage. The clarinet issue was too disturbing to prod; I really didn't want to go anywhere near there.

There was movement downstairs; I quickly jumped into the shower. Trevor was poaching eggs when I entered the kitchen ten minutes later.

'Just in time,' he said, laying a perfectly cooked egg on a piece of toast.

I sat at the small breakfast bar in his kitchen, he sat opposite me. Harold Melvin and the Blue Notes were bemoaning the love they'd lost, on the radio.

There was no feeling of disquiet now. I didn't want to leave. I wanted his company, wanted him around me; I wanted his approval.

'I didn't mean to upset you before, Grace.'

'I know. It's just going to take time.' I gave a little stab at the egg before me and watched the bright, yellow yolk spill out. 'I don't wish to talk about it, you'll be leaving soon and you've got enough on your plate without worrying about anything else.'

'You know that the offer is still there to come with us to America.'

I made no reply, the yellow of the egg started to drip from the toast onto the plate. America, the palm trees and sunshine were back again, I could go there and stay with Trevor and he would take care of me.

'If you really can't go through with the audition then come with us.'

'It's a nice idea.' I had money in the bank that could be used to be with him, it didn't have to be spent on a house. The egg now had a skin developing over it. I cut into its softness and managed a mouthful.

'What would the rest of the band say?'

'They all like you, so why not? Besides, if they want to ask anyone along they can.'

'This is Lawrence's band, what would he say to you if you asked him?'

'Rather Grace came and you played in the band than not.'

'Are you serious?'

Trevor paused. 'That's what he said when I told him I'd asked you; that would have been just after Lancaster though, he may need reminding.'

'I meant are you serious about me travelling with you.'

'How serious an answer would get you to consider it?'

'That's good enough.'

'Honestly?'

'I need to think about it. I mean, do I need a visa and all that paraphernalia? Even if I came out for just a month or two, I could always maybe prolong it if things went, you know, if I was or you were, you know ...' I spoke my ideas aloud, grinding to a halt. 'In the meantime, I'll have to get home to make sure my mum's okay, and Anna may need some help and you've got packing to do.' I stood up. I had no belongings to take with me apart from my knickers which I'd shoved in my jacket pocket and which decided to attach themselves to my car keys as I pulled them out. I looked at them in dismay, all dignity fleeing as it had done previously with James when my sex goddess act went tits-up, willy-down.

'Are you going commando?' Trevor asked. My departure was delayed by an hour. What sort of daughter and friend was I? What sort of a husband had James been?

When I finally got home I said hello to Aunty (at my age?!) Kath and Mum, who were sat amongst a tableau of black and white photos of long-gone relly's. Roger had been banished to the garden and was looking mournfully through the patio window, his nose leaving wet trails through his misty panting breath that fogged the glass. I showered, changed and drove round to Natalie's. She was starting to think that she was having premonitions. Earlier, she'd felt rather than heard a voice telling her that one of the children was in danger. She ran into the house from the garden where she was hanging the washing, and there was Matty with his fingers in the electric cupboard, she was convinced it was Dad who'd told her. She plonked a tiny kitten on my knee, a new acquisition to the family, and we had a cup of tea while I told her about Trevor and how I'd fallen for him, in between bouts of both children pulling at our clothing and them being told to go and draw daddy, Matty following Katie around like a loyal subject. I needed to tell someone before I burst about the offer of going to America. I could tell Natalie anything, she didn't know him.

'Have you thought of bereavement counselling? Yes, go and draw daddy. I mean, any decision of that size should be made of sound mind really. If you bugger off to America then realise what a bad decision it was, you're left with nothing. Besides, from a selfish point of view, I don't want you to move to the other side of the world. And you've turned your back on music once before remember? You're thinking too much again, aren't you?'

'If I go to counselling that's going to make me think even more.'

'Maybe Dad will come to you too, and help. More tea?'

I put my head round the living-room door as I left, to wave goodbye to the kids and left without saying goodbye at all as both were taken upstairs in disgrace after drawing a big daddy on the wall with crayons, lipstick and a red felt tip pen. Life goes on, my dad and his brother were probably sent to bed for something similar when they were young and I knew for a fact that Natalie and I had been; sporting pink hand-marks on our backsides for our efforts.

Anna was in her dungarees making beds when I arrived. We immediately sat down to a cup of tea. After talking to Natalie the urge to discuss what had passed between Shrubby and I had gone, freeing up space to give Anna my full attention.

'He,' she said of Lawrence, 'is insatiable. My God, there's not much of him but what there is, is all muscle; he's as lean as the 'eat yourself healthy' chicken I've got defrosting. It must be all that energy on stage. His performance in bed … We went through four condoms and I don't mind telling you but I'm struggling to sit down today. He likes it a bit rough.'

'Is he the one?'

'Good God, no! Apart from the fact he's leaving for London tomorrow, high maintenance isn't my thing. If I had to tell him once I told him a hundred times how good he was in bed, and then I had to listen to a recording of their new single and had to tell him twenty times how good that was. I even lent him my hairdryer and mousse, he used my eye-drops and I'm fairly certain two wax strips have gone missing. No, I'm content at the moment to let things happen rather than trying to get things to happen where men are concerned. Speaking of which, how did you get on?'

'Great, I dropped Diane off with Tom at hers. It was like having two teenagers on the backseat.' We both nodded at each other.

'And Shrubby?'

'Lovely.'

'Oh dear, I'm not going to get any details am I?'

'He's asked me to go to America with him, twice now.'

Anna smiled at this piece of information. 'He's a hell of a nice man. He was so worried about you when your dad became ill. He wanted to help you but didn't know how. I think he felt that he would just be there if you needed him but, personally, I think he wanted you to need him a bit more than you did. He even asked my advice on whether to go to the funeral or not. He said that if he did turn up it wouldn't allow you to properly grieve and he didn't want to put you in a position of feeling that you had to be with him or that he should meet the rest of your family for the first time under such sad circumstances.'

'Why has this happened now?' I put my head in my hands.

'How do you mean?'

I couldn't speak. Tears slipped through my fingers.

'Oh, Grace.' She put her hand on my shoulder. 'I know, let's phone Diane and tell her that Andrew Lloyd Webber wants her as a lead in a new production of Brigadoon.'

I couldn't help but giggle. Not that it was that funny, it was just unexpected.

'He's already called.' Diane entered through the open kitchen door carrying cream cakes. 'I said no, darling, I'm too busy, got friends to find partners for.'

'Grace has found her own, and the one I had last night turned out to be a bigger insecure girl than me, and has put me right off.'

While Diane listened with amusement to the amount of sex Anna had waded through and her initial envy turned to disappointment, I thought of Trevor. My destiny was with him. The audition wasn't going to happen, especially when the man I'd fallen in love with was not going to be with me. Dad had always said that Mr Right would come along, that he was out there just waiting to make an appearance. Well he was right. I was now totally convinced that Trevor had come to me when Dad had started to fall ill. God works in mysterious ways. The sorrow of bereavement and loss, side-tracked by love. What if, right, what if I did audition and didn't get the job, what happened then? I'd be left with nothing...

'...absolutely. Hey Grace, think how shocked Phil Jackson's wife would be to find out Lawrence waxes his chest hair, he'd be able to wear a frock like hers.' Diane punched me in the arm with amusement. 'Oh, come here.' She looked at my face and gave me a bear hug. 'Go to America with him, love.'

'It's not my place to give advice but I think you have to audition,' Anna said, giving advice. 'If you don't, you could end up hating Trevor and be left with nothing.' Her words mirrored my thoughts from a different angle. 'Are you just going to be left watching the band every night when you have the talent to be up there performing yourself? If you'd been going out together for longer maybe there would be more reason to consider the choices. You hardly know him, you've only seen him a few of times and been to bed with him twice but that's not what long-term relationships are made of. Bloody hell, you of all people should know how hard it is to make it work; you need to be on an equal footing at least to have a chance. Is he prepared to sacrifice anything for you?'

I shrugged. My face betrayed me.

318

'I think he would, I've seen the way he looks at her.' Diane stood up for romance.

'If you feel so deeply about him, maybe you should go and have some fun. You deserve it, but I think you have so much to lose if you do. Here, have a bun.' Anna handed me a cream cake. 'Chin up, love, whatever you choose you'll be happy.'

I left knowing that my happiness was in Trevor's hands.

Trevor called round later, having been with the band all day, and Mum and Aunty Kath met him for the first time. The three of us had devoured two bottles of white wine with dinner and he was very cheerfully greeted and received two Darlings in the space of two minutes before I bustled him out of the front door. I left them tucking into a third bottle.

We went for a drink in a trendy wine bar, playing salsa and chilled music where I told him I wanted to meet up in the USA, if the offer was still there. He ordered a bottle of champagne and we toasted the decision, clinking glasses and crossing over arms to drink it.

'I've spoken to Lawrence again, and he's not got a problem with it. He's looking forward to having you along. Our manager's a woman anyway so you'll be company for her.'

I had no idea that their manager was a woman. I felt weird. I had another glass of champagne and felt a bit better once we'd had a laugh writing my resignation to the bank on the back of a serviette. We ordered more champagne and I told him I was travelling to see the world and had enough money to support myself; I wasn't going to be a financial burden on him or the band. He asked if I could go on a coffee making course before joining them. I asked him to go on a courtesy course to get some manners. He said he would if I did. At this point I started to see two Trevors.

'You're not going to believe this but my Rubbish room has been cleared. Totally. I found a few dead bodies, a new species of life and a rock-hard banana skin.' Suddenly he became serious. 'Grace, I need to ask you if you're certain that you're doing the right thing.'

'Are you regretting asking me?' I tried to plink the end of his nose, missed and poked him in the eye instead.

'I'm concerned that's all. I want you near me, but you've got the opportunity to play in an orchestra and you're passing it up to travel to America with me. I seem to recall you telling me recently that you passed up final auditions years ago to be with James and now I can't stop thinking that history is repeating itself.'

'I hate the clarinet. It's let me down, big time. I wish I'd never played the sodding, buggering thing. Maybe in time I'll be able to just pick it up and play, there'll be other opportunities, but right now ... no.'

'I almost feel guilty asking you to drop everything to be with me.'

'Okay. What if I *did* audition and got the job? Would you stay behind to be with me?' I joked; trying to focus on Trevor's concerned face.

There was silence. We stared at each other. Flashbacks, like photos on a projector, rapidly sequenced in front of me. Sharp, very vivid, snippets of James on one knee, producing a ring and me throwing myself at him in joy, not wishing to be parted. James unable to move his business but wanting me with him. Had I expected more from James all those years ago because of what I'd thought I'd given up for him? Had I secretly blamed him for my lack of guts? I felt sick at myself and drained the champagne in the glass down in one.

Trevor didn't speak. He took hold of my hand and I knew the answer.

'Don't feel too bad, I shouldn't have asked.' I smiled one of those awful smiles that turns down ruefully at the corners. 'It's not going to happen anyway so...'

Still Trevor said nothing.

'Please don't look like that,' I said.

'I'm convinced that if you audition you'll pass.'

'I'm convinced, I'm convinced ... I'm going to be sick.' I got up quickly and, within the confines of the toilet cubicle, heaved much of the celebratory champagne back up. There was a message here somewhere; either champagne or stress got me losing weight faster than any diet.

I returned to the table and, after chasing my hand around in my bag for a minute or two, produced a scabby old chewy.

'I thought you were joking,' Trevor said, looking at the ghostly apparition that returned to him.

'No, I think I'd better get home.' I chewed rapidly on the gum, like a football manager at the side-lines of a game. I wanted to flop my head on the table and go to sleep.

'Come on, you.' Trevor stood and came to help me up.

Recollection of the journey in a taxi home is jumbled. Did I really ask the taxi driver if he wanted to buy a clarinet and ask him if Rachmaninov's Second Piano Concerto in C minor made him cry? Did I then proceed to ask why not and then lecture him on the scales from major and chromatic to diminished sevenths? I think I may have done, with Trevor trying to steer the conversation onto the more normal lines of where the taxi driver was going next.

I do remember shouting 'Bed' before collapsing on it.

Chapter 27

I woke suddenly in the middle of the night. I looked at the source of the dim green light in the darkness to my left and saw the radio alarm clock's time display winking at me, four o'clock in the morning.

I lay motionless for a moment until compelled to move and break the oppressive silence. I stepped out of bed and stood, shivering, exposed to the chill night air. It was so still outside, even the trees were fast asleep; I was the only living thing awake. I went to get back into bed but found myself in the corner of the room where I kept the clarinet, all tucked up in the velvet interior of its case. I opened it up and gently touched the note pads, which soothingly depressed on contact. On automatic pilot I put the clarinet together and held it, feeling the warm wood almost breathe beneath my fingertips.

The mouthpiece came to me of its own volition, my fingers moving with familiarity over the notes to 'Vilja'. It sounded almost eerie in the darkness. Sad and prolonged tears fell throughout, the notes unsteady, barely audible in parts. When I came to the end, I was almost concave from the unbearable longing in my heart. It was then, as the last note faded into silence, that I felt a puff of wind, like a breath, on my cheek.

I quickly turned, there was nothing there.

'I really miss you, Dad,' I whispered and dropped the clarinet, stifling further tears with a violent collision of face into pillow.

I woke up next morning, sprawled face down on the bed with a horrible taste in my mouth. After a few minutes savouring a headache, that I remembered playing 'Vilja' in the dark hours before dawn. With my head still muffled in pillows I wondered why Mum or Aunty Kath hadn't walked into the room and asked what the hell I thought I was doing, playing a clarinet at such an ungodly time.

I'd done it, I may have had to resort to a virtual champagne-induced coma but, I'd done it. I'd faced my dread and confronted the blame I'd laid on myself for Dad dying, the guilt I carried for not seeing how poorly he was and for not correcting all my faults before he passed away. Playing the clarinet hadn't killed him and not playing the clarinet hadn't made him better. The stupid traffic lights, which were on green when they should have been on red, hadn't killed him and Liverpool losing to Birmingham hadn't made him better. I knew that now. It was all irrelevant and, quite frankly, I must have been unhinged to think that any of this had made one bit of difference to the outcome.

I remembered the breath of wind on my face and knew Dad had been here with me. I touched my cheek, certain that everything would turn out for the best. I started to hum 'Vilja' into the pillows.

There was a knock on the bedroom door. 'Can I come in?' It was Mum.

I shouted yes into the pillows and raised a heavy head to watch her enter. She sat on the bed.

'How are you feeling?' she asked, placing a cup of tea on the bedside table.

'Shite.'

'Grace, what would your father say?'

'I think he'd laugh.' Mum raised an eyebrow. 'Okay, maybe not.'

'Trevor's very nice; he cares for you a great deal. He stayed a bit after we'd got you upstairs to bed. He wasn't fazed by two drunk old birds firing questions at him. I like him.'

'So do I.' I felt sick. 'I'm so sorry; I don't know what happened last night. The wheels well and truly fell off. And I'm sorry if I woke you this morning.'

'You didn't, why were you sick again?' Mum asked.

'No, for playing the clarinet.'

'Didn't hear you, love. Kath hasn't mentioned anything. Mind you, I'm not surprised; we've both got terrible heads this morning.'

I looked at the side of the bed where I knew I'd laid the clarinet to rest before dropping off to sleep. It wasn't there.

I did a double take. Did I leave it there? I jumped out of bed and went to the case from where I'd taken it earlier that morning and there it was, looking at me from its velvet bedding. I knew, or thought I knew, I'd not put it back. I remembered letting my hand fall over the side of the bed and dropping the clarinet less than an inch onto the carpet.

'What's the matter?' Mum asked.

I closed the lid slowly and drifted back to bed, deep in thought. I must have dreamt it. It was as I sat up and reached over for the tea Mum had kindly bought me that I knocked a reed off the pillow.

'I think I'm going mad,' I said, picking it up.

'Well, it would have been nice to hear you play a song. I've not heard you practise in a long time. We've all been so wrapped up in what's gone on, I've not really thought about it till now. Why don't you play Kath a tune today, let her hear you, seeing as your Dad was always banging on to her about how good you are?'

'He always did build us up, he was so proud of us all.'

'He was also a pain in the arse sometimes,' Mum said affectionately, which made us both cry and laugh at the same time.

Mum went downstairs and I sat slurping tepid tea, thinking. I hated what was going on in my head. I needed to phone Trevor and apologise for puking and being such a drunken old soak. No, I needed to see him face to face. I was off work; the one thing the bank allowed was a period of fourteen days bereavement leave. I was now into my second week.

Two hours later, dressed in the most feminine clothing I possessed, make-up working hard to hide the ugly grey tinge to the skin beneath, I pulled up outside Trevor's. Removing sunglasses to reveal dark patches below my eyes in the rear view mirror, I gave up on subterfuge, threw the glasses back into the car, cleared my throat and made my way to his front door.

He didn't say anything when he opened it but took my chin in his warm hands and brought his lovely lips to mine. I put my head on his shoulder and let it rest there, breathing him in, wanting to stay there forever, safe.

Eventually I pulled away and he led me into his living room. As I suspected he was very organised, two chairs and the telly the only furniture left, the sofa, pictures, books, CDs all packed away in storage. He was ready for the off.

I'd thought and thought all morning and had a nice, considered little sentence going which explained that my state of mind was not what it should be, that I longed with all my heart to be with him in the USA, but he was right about auditioning and I'd hate myself and resent him for not giving it a go.

'I'm not coming with you.'

He turned away and sat down in a chair furthest away from me. 'I'm glad.'

'Oh.' I sat heavily on the other chair.

'I hope this means you're going to audition then?' he asked.

I nodded.

'I should never have asked you. I was just being selfish.'

'I played the clarinet last night. At least I think I did. Not quite sure, could have dreamt it.'

'And were you brilliant?'

'Actually I was, so it must have been a dream.'

'That's not even worth commenting on.' He looked like he'd just swallowed a tub of acid.

'To be truthful I think it may have been so weak and out of tune, my clarinet decided to run and hide back in its case while I was asleep.'

'You were all over the place by the time I got you home last night.'

'I'm very sorry.'

'I'm not, I got to undress you while you sang some Cliff Richard song or other, and I got to kiss you just after we'd cleaned your teeth and just before you chundered again.'

My blushes were out of control, I closed my eyes with sheer embarrassment.

'Oh my God, please don't.'

'Do you remember telling me you loved my naked bum?'

In front of my mum? I could feel the blushes extending to my neck and chest. Eyes still closed I shook my head.

'Or me saying, "I love you?"'

I kept my eyes closed although they were fighting to open up with surprise and look at him. 'You must have been pretty drunk yourself.' I was melting on the spot.

'I love you.' He said it slowly.

326

Now I opened my eyes and looked at him across the room. I didn't know what to say. Repeating it back to him seemed tacky: saying nothing, ignorant. He was looking at me without expectancy but with a genuine need to know my feelings, possibly aware that what he'd get back wouldn't be normal.

'You make me twice as mushy as peas inside.' What the f..., where did the Lancashire accent come from?

'Is that good?'

'Oh, it's the best.'

He had to think about this one. I could almost see him trying to move then alphabetise mushy peas from the food column in his head to the column marked under romance.

I tried to help him. 'I'm going to miss you very much when you go. I wish you could stay here but then that would make me selfish, wouldn't it.'

He smiled at me with relief. 'Cup of tea?'

'Love one.'

'Come and have a look at the Rubbish room, you won't recognise it.'

Over the cup of tea, we talked about the bands itinerary and my audition. They were planning to stay in New Orleans for the largest part of the trip, but I lost track of the countless other destinations planned and was beginning to regret not going with them, it sounded more like the holiday of a lifetime. It was just as well Lawrence had deep pockets to finance it because if it all went to plan they could be away for up to a year. My audition was less set in stone.

'I'm determined to be a jobbing musician. If I don't get to play in this orchestra I'll just have to keep trying elsewhere.'

'You shouldn't think like that, you won't get the job with the orchestra.'

'I have to, I have to be realistic.'

'Have some faith in yourself.'

'I'm not a natural show-off.'

'You don't have to be.' He paused. 'If, and I only mean if, you don't get through the audition then maybe you could come out to meet us?'

'Trevor, much as I'd love to, I can't. In fact I don't think it will help me to know I've got that option.'

'How d'you mean?'

We hadn't broached how our relationship was to be handled in the time apart. It had suddenly become rather serious. All I knew was that it wasn't a good idea to promise chastity for up to a year. Not that I thought for one minute that once we'd parted we'd go around shagging all and sundry, highly improbable on my behalf going by past form, but a year was a long time to keep faith in someone travelling abroad in a band full of testosterone. Call me a cynic but the rose coloured glasses worn in younger days were getting mottled with age.

'I don't want to rely on you. No, let me finish,' I said as he tried to butt in. 'I've decided that the only way for us is to remain friends, feel free to see other people and see what happens.' I smiled with what I thought was understanding. 'I'm not prepared to be the one that stops you from turning down opportunities and having the best time of your life. I don't believe you'd return to your hotel alone every night and I wouldn't want you to either. I don't want to live in the hope you'll come home in a year's time and want to take up what you left behind.'

'Then come with me.' He sounded rather petulant. Did he want me to fail? I could feel my insides bristling preparing for flight. The coy sweetness earlier was rapidly turning sour.

'You're not listening to me and I'm trying to be sensible. What happens if you meet someone and I'm sat here waiting for you?'

'I won't.' He was adamant.

'That's the most ridiculous thing I've ever heard you say. How long will it take before insecurity, distrust or jealousy starts invading the distance between us?' I was turning red again but this time with exasperation. 'What if you've turned down every offer of a good time to come home and find me shacked up with someone?'

'Saying I love you means nothing then?' he asked, looking like a wounded soldier. 'Surely *that* would class as the most ridiculous thing I've ever said in that case.'

'Don't try making it sound like I'm a cold-hearted bitch. If you're not prepared to see reason then there's no hope for us.'

'You may as well go then.'

I felt like I'd been slapped. 'I didn't mean...you know what? Forget it.' I stood up, shaking with pent up resentment. 'You don't want to be friends, that's fine. You want to have your cake and eat it, well, sorry, but this time round I'm going to achieve what I should have achieved years ago and no one's going to stop me. Not you, or, or anyone.' I was standing now ready to run for it.

'I don't want to stop you so get that idea right out of your head now, but it's a pity it's taken all this time to suddenly find your true calling.' He was getting angry. 'I've told you how I feel and what I get in return is that I remind you of a tin of mushy peas. I want to come back to you but if you're determined to find someone else in the meantime then there's not a lot I can do is there?'

I wanted to cry. I was about to lose him. 'No there isn't, not if you see it like that. You know, for some reason, I honestly thought this conversation would be the other way round.' I paused, 'I'm sorry.'

'You'd better go.'

'Have a wonderful time in America.'

He remained seated and silent. A blurred, hasty departure preceded a fight with the car door and a crunch as I sat on my sunglasses. I grappled with the broken pieces and lashed them onto the back seat then drove to the beach and wandered aimlessly for miles and hours along the shore. A light breeze shifted the sand, stinging eyes and causing tears, well that's my excuse. The tide was out; small, long-legged birds pecked and trilled along damp, wavy sand, a dog chased seagulls on a sandbank in the distance. White and grey clouds gathered for a meeting to discuss the probability of rain.

Had I just ruined everything or had I saved us both from the sapping heartache caused by the slow decline of a relationship? How could I have said he was twice as mushy as peas? Even by my standards, it was eye-wateringly bad. I'd felt he was playing games and I was being manipulated at the time but now, sitting in a sheltered cooey between two large rocks, I came to the conclusion that he wasn't. After such a short time of knowing one another, and from what he'd seen of me during our relationship, I couldn't quite understand why he really believed we had a future. I didn't deserve such devotion. I squinted at the Welsh coast on the horizon, regretting leaving him the way I had, regretting my inability to trust, regretting our timing, regretting sitting on my sunglasses. Flippancy didn't help. I was aching so badly inside it made me feel weak. I pulled my knees up to my chest then wrapped my arms protectively around them like a barricade and remained huddled against the world. Amongst the carnage of all that regret the words from 'That's Life' started running through my head. I wasn't going to roll up in a big ball and die. I had to go and repair the damage I'd caused.

I scrambled up and ran back along the shore like an Olympic sprinter. The grey clouds had prevailed at the meeting and large, wet raindrops were splashing in glorious abundance from the outcome by the time I reached the car.

Trevor wasn't in and looking through the living room window I noticed that the television was no longer there. I stood on his doorstep in the rain, hoping that he would suddenly appear round the corner saying, 'Surprise.' My phone needed charging, I had no paper and no pen. I walked away, head bowed, soaked to the bone and sat in the car for a few more minutes before driving home.

I plugged the mobile in and tried phoning him but there was no answer. I sent a text, there was no reply. He was simply too hurt or not bothered. I drove back to his house later that day and still there was no answer. I was starting to panic. I couldn't let him go without telling him that I would wait, that I really did love him. Better prepared than earlier, phone charged and in view for activity, I sat in the car and spent half an hour bent over a pad of paper getting more and more reckless with flowery sentiments. "Dear Trevor, I don't want to live without your love", rip, crunch and plop, it hit the back seat. "My love, you are my one and only", rip, crunch, plop. "Please come back to me", rip, crunch, plop. Way too soppy. Irritated beyond belief, I sat back and closed my eyes, humming the small part of a melody over and over again and suddenly I knew what to write.

Dear Trevor,

I need to see you before you go. In the immortal words of The Animals, 'I want you brown eyes, I want you till my day's end, but I want you as a lover, you're no good to me as a friend.' I will wait, however long, till you return.

Call me,

Grace xx

I found and discarded an old wage slip out of an envelope in my handbag, crossed out my name on the front, scrawled a shaky Trevor Shrubb above it and put the letter through his door. There was nothing else I could do. I was too proud to keep calling.

I played the clarinet for Aunty Kath, drove everyone mad with repeated scales and waited for a call. It didn't come. It's hard to concentrate on the dynamics of a piece of music when your mind is full of other things - Trevor's declaration of love, his apparent about turn, my dad's death, my mum's heartache at losing him. The one thing I did find though was that the provoked emotions seemed to improve the sound I made from the clarinet; it wasn't consciously done and didn't descend to melancholic but it reached a maturity and sensitivity that I now appreciated had been lacking previously. Mr Gerrard remarked on the change the very next day, saying my colour spectrum just got bigger. He patted my shoulder and left his hand there when I broke down and wept.

At every moment I had my mobile on display, waiting for Trevor, willing it to light up with his name. With every hour that passed my determination to do something positive increased to compensate for the havoc caused by his failure to react to the call, text and letter. Odd, as he'd pointed out, that it took a failed affair to inspire ambition. Something told me that if I didn't do this now I never would. I had a few other audition options, one for a quartet intending to tour Ireland for three months later in the year, another via someone who knew someone's brother's, ex-girlfriend's, uncle's son who was looking for a session musician for a local band called Folk'L Jazz, and I bought the Loot and the Stage circling totally impractical jobs.

Friday was on the wane and I'd lost all hope of seeing Trevor again when I received a text with no name to trumpet the sender's origin. 'At Heathrow. U were right I was being selfish but is hard when u find love and lose it. Don't want to stop u fulfilling dream, really go for it and I'm congratulating you now 4 getting the job. When return will find u and buy u a v large whisky and then u can buy me one back, all my love, eva your friend, Trevor x.

He'd gone. That was it. He'd gone. What had I done? My letter? It must still be sat on his doormat. God, what a mess. My future now utterly relied on me. This wasn't a Cliff moment. I found Rachmaninov and disappeared for an hour.

Over the next four weeks the audition took over. Mr Gerrard had friends in all musical places. His professionalism and talent extended to those he recommended and I found that one word from him in the right ear opened doors wide enough to get a foot in. The rest was up to me. To find the true meaning of performance he told me to go busking. He didn't care where but I needed to report back to him when I had. I chose Chester. Busking isn't for the faint-hearted, I found out how it felt to be invisibly visible. People passed and, without any eye contact, money was thrown into the straw hat doubling up as a collection tin. A middle-aged foreign couple started dancing to 'Bill Bailey' and a small group of people gathered to watch but soon wandered off once the dancing finished. With my two euro's, a shiny button and my seven pounds twenty five pence wage for the morning I found a 'Big Issue' seller and handed it over.

The more committed I became to changing career the more opportunities came my way and the audition for The North Western Symphony Orchestra became a challenge of manageable proportions.

I felt fine the morning of the audition; I had a new, pixie-short, dyed auburn hair cut and was wearing the comfiest clothing I could find, outside of pyjamas.

In the luminous first-light, I detoured to Dad's grave with some red roses and stood silently for a minute. 'Wish me luck.' I touched the cold marble stone, not finding any encouragement from the act but finding a certain amount of solace instead. There wasn't a breath of air and only a frenzied dawn chorus disturbed the graveyard's tranquillity.

I wished I'd taken Anna up on her suggestion of coming with me as I travelled up the M6 feeling more and more anxious. I'd declined her offer on the grounds that I couldn't bear crashing the car with her in it when I failed.

My allotted time was 10 o'clock and I had an hour before that to practise in one of the rooms set aside for those auditioning. A number of the applicants were already there when I arrived. Did I give off the same air of confidence they did? I doubted it. I started to feel ill. What the hell was I doing here? I must be mad. Whispering words in my head sneakily told me I was too old for all this. Here we go again. Was this what had stopped me last time? Had I thought myself too young then? I'd forgotten how frightening and daunting rejection could be.

A friendly, elongated young lad with the lightest of bum fluff feathering his chin and upper lip led me to a room to practise. It smelt of school, the parquet flooring polished to a shine. I took

Trevor out of his case and put him together. Yes, I'm afraid I'd resorted to giving my clarinet a name. The car was called Ted. The three octave scales I tried initially sounded like I'd never played the clarinet in my life. As for a slurred chromatic descending scale, I hoped the walls were soundproofed. I looked down and noticed my chest was physically moving to the beat of a frantic, terrified heart.

Whether madness played a part in my head I don't know, but my fists clenched in anger and I actually wanted to punch my boob to stop it from bouncing. I can't say if it was this thought, the thought of Dad's laughing face, or the thought of kissing Trevor, that calmed me down but whatever it was I started to breathe and relax. I hugged Trevor to me. I could do this, I knew I could, every inch of me wanted it; I deserved to be here. I wanted to laugh out loud, but I didn't because that truly would have been mad. With a lighter heart, the scales became familiar friends, Gershwin's Rhapsody in Blue, moodily exhilarating, Stravinsky's Firebird, the start of a new beginning. By the time I was called I was in a zone where nothing could touch me.

The first audition was a blind audition, requiring me, the auditionee to be behind a screen for the first round, I'm not sure whether this was a good thing or not, but it helped to imagine no one was on the other side. I'd just finished playing the cat theme from Prokofiev's 'Peter and the Wolf' when a voice from beyond the screen asked me to leave the room immediately. Less than thirty seconds. My first reaction was 'bloody hell that must be a world record for rejection'; my second was 'I'm going to be forced to drink Mr Gerrard's beer out of the clarinet', and my third was to creep out and try to become invisible.

It was as I was collecting my things together that the lad with the bum fluff met me and asked me to follow him, leading me to

335

an office which looked more like a library (actually it probably was a library) kindly telling me I'd been recalled and to wait. I was numb, sat in a room on my own intently watching dust float in a sharply defined band of sunshine that beamed down from a lofty window and painted the floor with a bright oblong of light. God's eye looking down on me. All the while I could hear clarinet scales clashing from different quarters of the building.

After a length of time the door opened and a woman wearing something similar to a Chanel suit smiled at me and went to sit in the shadows opposite. She was followed quite soon after by an attractive man in his mid-twenties and before long there were twelve of us. One by one we were recalled, this time to play with a piano accompanist and the screen was removed. Jean Webster gave me a welcoming smile and I successfully blocked out the rest of the panel, going straight for the nothing can touch me zone.

I was still there late afternoon with four others, two of whom I'd become quite friendly with; Boris from Germany, studying music, in his last year at Leeds University, and a beautiful coloured girl, Lolia, in her early twenties from Edinburgh, who'd studied at the Birmingham Conservatoire. She was as nervous as I was which was encouraging. Chanel suit was still with us and apart from telling us all that she had played in a number of professional orchestras in her time, she kept herself to herself. I was not going to be intimidated, I bigged up the local orchestra so much that Joan Sarney was on a level to Sir Simon Rattle by the time I'd finished. The other person who'd made it to the final five spent most of his time on the toilet.

The waiting was getting to all of us. What would I do if I failed now having gone so far? Down to the last five was good, but it wasn't life-changing. I'd been here before. I tried to keep a lid on my expectations, but I wanted to play in this orchestra so badly I found it difficult to sit still and not run off down the corridors shouting, 'Gizza job.'

The five of us were called back into the audition room and one by one we had to play in front of each other and then with each other. Some of the wind section from the orchestra had taken seats at the back of the room and looked on from their privileged aspect of employed members. It was horrific. No other word. Horrific.

Boris and the man who'd spent most of his time in the toilet were told they could go and thanked for their efforts and, after the three of us left had played a short piece with the flute, oboe and bassoon players from the orchestra, we were told to wait.

Back in the darkened library someone had switched a light on. None of us spoke. Through the high window I could see an early evening pale blue sky. A distant door banged, echoing though the largely empty building. Someone in the corridor outside the library started whistling 'Matchstalk Men and Matchstalk Cats and Dogs'. Every muscle in my neck and chest tightened then swelled and my heart seemed to stop.

The sound of clicking footsteps approached and a silhouette materialised in the frosted glass panel of the door and paused. This was it. We looked expectantly at it as the handle turned.

Chapter 28

I was in turmoil travelling home. I really should have had someone with me. The tendency to veer into the hard shoulder made it a dangerous journey full of tears. It was dusk, a golden sky slowly fading with glinting, lemon highlights tipping clouds preparing for bed.

I would be handing in my notice at the bank on Monday. I was still in a state of shock but in two weeks' time I'd be a member of the North Western Symphony Orchestra. It sounded so good said slowly. To give it its full title, I would be rehearsing with the North Western (UK) Symphony Orchestra.

I thought Natalie was going to explode with pride, Rebecca was ecstatic because I would be moving a bit nearer to her. Mary started practising harder than ever on her piano. Harry sent me a bottle of champagne - o-oh! Mum rejoiced with the practical view that while she was losing the company she was gaining on wardrobe space. When I handed him my letter of resignation and once he got over the shock, Max Bergin at the bank gave me a big, tearful hug. 'I thought you were here forever, or at least until you got the sack,' he said. 'What colour do we use on the time sheets for time served?' No more time sheets. I couldn't believe it. I didn't even try to hide the smile of joy.

Diane threw a double celebration party for my leaving and her moving back in with Tom. I stood for a moment on my own, people milling around me and quietly observed, as if from outside looking in, those who'd come to mean so much to me. A chance advert in a paper had lead me to Anna and as a consequence to Diane who had both given me confidence by offering unconditional friendship, it was like I'd known them all my life and I loved them both dearly. They'd led me to meeting all the people there at the party, many of them odder than my sock drawer, but all of whom were kind and generous to a fault.

Is it me or does any form of success make people look at you differently from when you were floundering in misery, or is it because, all of a sudden, you feel different and you don't make people anxious around you? Shy, retiring, bordering on boring Grace had legged it and a new more-confident Grace had become visible. Phil Simpson animatedly discussed his barn conversion project with me, a bottle of wine in one hand, a full glass in the other. I was even introduced by Kenneth to his martial arts wife who, I'm afraid to say, looked more capable of eating a pork chop than executing one of the karate variety. Irene cornered me at one point and told me about the time she met Princess Anne until Anna rudely, but appreciatively, pulled me to one side.

'You realise you're leaving me just as the 'couple of the year', she nodded towards Diane and Tom, embark on a programme of finding a partner for me. I don't know whether to laugh or be afraid. I've already been introduced to someone called Sven who's a mountain climber. That tall, blonde man, by the door next to Fergal, see him?' She waved across the room. The mountaineer gave a hesitant wave back. 'Where do they find them? I have to say he's the best looking one yet. I think I'm being set up with all of Tom's cronies; I'll slowly go through them all one by one. Last week it was someone called John who dropped the words 'twat' and 'fucker' as often as the words 'the' and 'and' into every sentence. I had to pretend that one of the children had a migraine and I was needed at home to get away. Never give up trying is my new motto, because like your dad said, Mr Right's out there. Maybe I need to travel abroad to find him. I'm really worried that he's possibly living in Italy and I'll never meet him. Oh, I believe Sandra's auditioning for the Liverpool Phil, or so she says.'

'There's no vacancy at the Liverpool Phil, what's she talking about. She really should take up playing the trumpet; she blows her own often enough. Good luck to her.' I blew a raspberry, dismissing she who had blanked me ever since I'd told her where to go. 'You will come up and stay won't you?'

'Wild horses wouldn't stop me.'

Diane came over to us and slapped a big, sloppy red wine kiss on my cheek.

'Okay?'

'Just commenting on Tom's friends. Sven looks nice for Anna,' I said, looking over again at the mountaineer.

'Absolutely.' Diane stopped then looked about. 'Sven? Who's Sven?'

'The mountaineer, over there. Don't make it obvious,' I said. Diane rubbernecked without discretion.

'You mean, Derek the barrister?'

'Derek?' Anna looked crestfallen.

'You call him Sven if you like, love, but he may look at you like you're a bit soft.'

'Too late. Why didn't he say something? I've been talking about Chris Bonnington and crampons for the last half hour.'

'I'm sure he found it very interesting but you could talk about candle wax for half an hour and he'd listen to you, I think he's that smitten,' Diane said. 'Heard anything from Trevor?' She turned her attention to me. Her matchmaking knew no bounds.

'No.'

Paula joined us, her stomach stretching a maternity top. We all had a feel, as you do, and were all convinced we felt what was inside kick.

'I've heard from Lawrence. The boys are doing really well; they've even been on a couple of doobree doos, local TV programmes, playing live and being interviewed. They're having a great time partying and gigging. Lawrence is like a pig in muck, says the chicks out there are amazingly gorgeous. You know what he's like, doesn't like to make much effort.'

Mixed emotions greeted this comment. Although I was happy for Trevor, I wasn't so saintly to hope that he was enjoying the parties to the extent it appeared Lawrence was.

Paula was still talking but I'd drifted away with illicit thoughts of a cute, naked bum and a kiss that had had the power of turning me inside out, and was only bought back to the present when she repeated my name. 'Grace, I said there's a minibus full of people coming up to see your first performance. Joan Sarney's going round now organising it. I think she's more excited about driving the bus, to be honest. Is she a bit mad?'

'Hmm, have to think about that one ... yep, totally barking.' I took a sip of wine and smiled; I only needed a pot-pourri.

'I can't wait...'

Epilogue

My first concert and the last bars of Rimsky Korsakov's 'Capriccio Espagnol' are coming to a climax. There is a split second of hush before cheers rush at us from the audience. I have finally found where I belong, and happiness, infused by adrenaline, is making me lightheaded. I know that my family and friends are out there and I am assured, as only the recently bereaved can be, that Dad is there with them too, I can feel it.

My confidence isn't as strong when it comes to Trevor. I've had no contact with him but I like to imagine that on his return home the first thing he will see is my letter. It will tremble in his hand as he opens it, it will swirl and drift to the ground in the draft of a slamming door, it will bring him straight to me. I can't say that occasionally I look out of the window of my tiny flat in Lancaster to see if he is strolling down the road carrying a bottle of scotch because, if I'm honest, I look every day. I hope one day he'll be out there in the audience – I'm unable to keep a lid on my expectations – I know one day he'll be out there in the audience, and I sit quite still, optimistically in awe of life, on a natural high, to the sound of applause.

THE END

About the author

Andrea Kim Otter was born on 2 December 1962. The third of five children, Andrea grew up in a very close family, one that gave her the love and support she would need in later life.

Throughout her working life Andrea had a wide range of jobs but always her enjoyment of work came from the strong and long-lasting friendships she made with her colleagues.

One evening, while working part-time in a local pub, she met the man who would become her first husband. The two married in 1988 and, although they separated after ten years, Andrea remained close to his family and the two stayed in contact until 2013.

When she wasn't at work Andrea spent many hours learning to play the keyboard and composing her own songs, at the heart of which was her passionate love of music. Her eclectic list of Top 40 favourite songs, which typically for Andrea actually contained 53 songs, was under constant review.

From a very young age Andrea showed talent in the Arts, painting and drawing to a very good standard and excelling at ballet dancing. In later years she developed her love of the stage, joining two light operatic societies, and was in the cast of many successful musicals including *Chess*, *Return to the Forbidden Planet* and her favourite of all, *Titanic*, which was performed at the Liverpool Empire Theatre to rave reviews.

In 1999 she met her second husband-to-be at an after-show party and the two were married three years later in 2002. It is fair to say that the two shared a sense of adventure; together they bought a farmhouse in France, spending many warm summers renovating the house, drinking wine and playing music

343

as loud as possible. In 2006 the couple embarked on a 'round the world trip' touring South America, New Zealand, Australia and Thailand. Whilst visiting Ecuador Andrea fulfilled a lifelong ambition, visiting the Galapagos Islands, but rather than the wildlife it was the people that left her with the longest-lasting memories and she committed to finding a way to help the country's children.

In 2011 Andrea and her husband moved to the Lake District and enjoyed the best of what the area could offer, walking and climbing in the hills and welcoming a new addition to the family, Indie the black Labrador. It was during this time that Andrea finally completed writing this, her first novel.

In 2012 Andrea was diagnosed with cancer and typically battled the disease head-on, as always, with a smile on her face. Determined to prove the doctors wrong, Andrea fought bravely for 18 months before passing away on 19 December 2013.

This book has been published for many reasons. Firstly, it's a good read and we want you to enjoy Andrea's slightly cheeky outlook on life. Secondly, it is published in her memory as an epitaph for the love, light and music she brought to those who had the privilege to know her. Thirdly, profits from its sale will be donated to The Book Bus Foundation which works to improve children's lives in Africa, Asia and South America. You can find out more about the great work this charity does at www.thebookbus.org.

Acknowledgements

There are many people without whom this book would not have been published and, if you will forgive me, I will attempt to name them as best I can: Andy (for your encouragement to Andrea, editorial skills and support for me), Stu and Tally, Martyn and Nats (I hope the four of you know why), Cath, Laura, Ste, Neil and Dot (and Casper), George (that's not his real name), Hilda, Lorraine, Mel, Iain and Carolyn, Charmian and Peter, Derek and Rose (merci beaucoup) and everyone else who was there for Andrea when she needed you and there for me when I needed picking up out of the gutter (which has been often) but at the end of the day this is for Andrea who made me the person I am, who brought love, laughter, adventure and light into my life.

Dave - July 2014